The Complete Pirc

John Nunn

COLLIER BOOKS
Macmillan Publishing Company
New York

Copyright © 1989 by John Nunn

All rights reserved. No part of this book may be reproduced or transmitted in any form or by any means, electronic or mechanical, including photocopying, recording or by any information storage and retrieval system, without permission in writing from the Publisher.

Collier Books
Macmillan Publishing Company
866 Third Avenue, New York, NY 10022
Collier Macmillan Canada, Inc.

Library of Congress Cataloging-in-Publication Data
Nunn, John.
    The complete Pirc / John Nunn.
    p. cm.
    Includes index.
    ISBN 0-02-029491-3
    1. Chess—Openings. 2. Chess—Collection of games. I. Title.
GV1450.2.N86   1989   89-697   CIP
794.1'22—dc19

Macmillan books are available at special discounts for bulk purchases for sales promotions, premiums, fund-raising, or educational use. For details contact:

                Special Sales Director
           Macmillan Publishing Company
               866 Third Avenue
               New York, NY 10022

First Collier Books Edition 1989
10 9 8 7 6 5 4 3 2 1

Printed in Great Britain

CONTENTS

Symbols		iv
Preface		v
Introduction		vii
1	Austrian Attack: Introduction and 5 ♘f3 0-0 6 ♗d3 ♘c6	1
2	Austrian Attack: 5 ♘f3 0-0 6 ♗d3 ♘a6 and 6 ... others	12
3	Austrian Attack: 5 ♘f3 0-0 6 others	23
4	Austrian Attack: 5 ♘f3 c5 6 dc	38
5	Austrian Attack: 5 ♘f3 c5 6 ♗b5+ (and 6 e5)	45
6	Austrian Attack: Miscellaneous	58
7	Classical: Introduction and 6 0-0 ♗g4 7 ♗e3 ♘c6 8 ♕d2 e5	68
8	Classical: 6 0-0 ♗g4 7 others	78
9	Classical: 6 0-0 c6 with h3	83
10	Classical: 6 0-0 c6 without h3	93
11	Classical: 6 0-0 others	99
12	Classical: 4 ♘f3 others	107
13	The system with ♘c3, ♘f3, h3 and ♗e3	113
14	White plays ♗e3 and ♕d2	122
15	White plays ♗c4	135
16	White plays ♗g5	146
17	White plays g3	153
18	White plays c3	165
19	White plays c4	174
20	Unusual White systems	193
21	Black plays an early ... c6	198
22	Odds and Ends	208
Index of Variations		212

SYMBOLS

=	chances are balanced
±	slight advantage for White
∓	slight advantage for Black
±	clear advantage for White
∓	clear advantage for Black
± ±	White has a won position
∓ ∓	Black has a won position
∞	the position is unclear
+	check
Ch.	Championship
corr.	postal game

A number in brackets after a move in the text refers to the diagram of that number.

PREFACE

The purpose of this book is to cover the Pirc and Modern Defences in sufficient detail to enable players of all standards to employ them when Black, or to meet them with White. In my earlier book on the Pirc*, I made a special effort to keep the length of the book down by eliminating irrelevant information. I adopted the same approach this time, but the increased size reflects the many new ideas which have arisen over the past eight years. Every chapter has been completely rewritten, but the reader will notice the most significant differences in those lines which have become popular in the 1980s.

In some chapters I have reorganized the material to clarify the layout, but the numbering of the chapters remains the same. In one case I transferred a line from one chapter to another, but otherwise the division of material is unchanged. I have made a special effort to include all variations of relevance to the Pirc/Modern, rather than adopt the 'see another Batsford book' approach. Thus the chapter on lines with c4 contains some variations which might well belong in a book on queen's pawn openings. Transpositions are the author's bane in a book such as this, but I hope I have noticed most of them!

Once again readers will find that those variations which are currently in common use receive the most detailed treatment, but enough information is given on less fashionable lines to enable the reader to get by. In contrast to an opening such as the Najdorf, where tactics abound, most variations of the Pirc depend more on strategy and often both players have a wide choice of reasonable moves. It follows that general principles play a greater role than in many openings, so where I have had to restrict the choice of material I have chosen examples which demonstrate typical strategic plans.

Some readers may be disappointed to find that there are fewer complete games this time, but to compensate there are more diagrams.

Finally, I would like to thank all those people who commented on the earlier book, pointed out errors and made suggestions. I have not invariably adopted these, but it is always useful for an author to hear his readers' opinions.

* *The Pirc for the Tournament Player* (1980)

INTRODUCTION

What are the ideas behind the Pirc and the Modern? These openings bear some relationship with the Benoni and King's Indian in that White is allowed to form a big centre and Black develops his bishop on g7 at an early stage. Clearly Black plans pressure against d4, but it is not usually enough to attack with pieces. So Black must employ his pawns, playing ... e5, or less frequently ... c5, to disrupt White's centre. It is important to emphasize that Black must not delay in organizing his counterplay, or he will find his pieces too passively placed to allow any opening up of the position and will be forever prevented from playing any central thrust.

The Austrian Attack, a popular and aggressive system characterized by the moves 1 e4 d6 2 d4 ♘f6 3 ♘c3 g6 4 f4 ♗g7, is dealt with first, in Chapters 1–6. Play is unusually tactical and so there is more detailed analysis in this section than in the rest of the book. It is unfortunate, but there are some opening lines which are so sharp that one cannot afford a wrong move, so there is greater emphasis on memory.

While the Austrian Attack leads to tactical battles, the Classical System, considered in Chapters 7–12, strives to maintain a slight advantage for White without the risk of allowing Black any initiative. Although Black has good equalizing chances, it is clearly frustrating to play for at most half a point, so special emphasis is placed on ways Black can try to stir up trouble. Chapter 13 considers a related system based on crossing the Classical with an early h3 and ♗e3. The idea is to delay the development of the f1 bishop in the hope of saving a tempo by playing ♗c4 directly. This line has become very popular in the past few years, but despite its good practical results the theoretical verdict is not so clear.

The next five chapters cover less common, but nevertheless important, lines for White. In Chapter 14 we deal with ♗e3 and ♕d2 by White. In the last few years many players have turned to this as a means of avoiding the heavily analysed Austrian and Classical systems. It leads to complex positions with no early liquidation, so decisive results are common. Special mention should also be made of Chapter 17, which covers g3 by White. Although this was almost unknown ten years ago, it became the height of chess fashion in the early eighties. Then new and effective ideas emerged for Black and the g3 system has suffered an almost equally rapid decline.

Chapter 19 deals with the sequence 1 e4 g6 2 d4 ♗g7 3 c4, which can transpose to the King's Indian if Black wishes. We deal only with lines by Black which do not lead to this transposition, that is lines in which an early ... ♘f6 does not occur.

The last three chapters cover very unusual systems for both colours, but perhaps a few words about Chapter 21 would be useful. This features the plan of ... c6 and ... d5 by Black, whereby he initiates play on the white squares rather than the dark squares. This has seen a recent revival, so the coverage has been considerably expanded in the current edition.

1 Austrian Attack: Introduction and 5 ♘f3 0-0 6 ♗d3 ♘c6

1	e4	d6
2	d4	♘f6
3	♘c3	g6
4	f4 *(1)*	

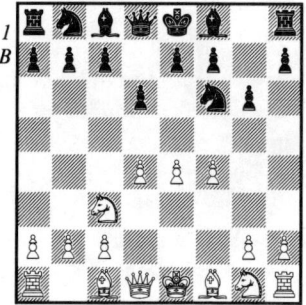

Initially the Austrian Attack was the most popular system against the Pirc Defence, and this trend has persisted until very recently. In the last decade more positional lines have diminished its importance, but the Austrian Attack remains one of the most crucial lines in the Pirc, especially as the sharp play does not allow second-best moves by Black.

White's aim is to develop rapidly behind his broad pawn centre, possibly with ♘f3, ♗d3 and 0-0, and then launch an attack by e5, gaining time by expelling the Black knight from f6. This plan is so strong that Black must react against the White centre by either ... c5 or ... e5. After 4 ... ♗g7 5 ♘f3 it is possible for Black to attack the centre at once by 5 ... c5, based on the tactical point 5 ... c5 6 dc ♕a5 attacking the e-pawn and thus regaining the pawn on c5. This forms the basis of Chapters 4 and 5. However the fact that Black has not yet castled leads to certain complications (see Chapter 5), so many players prefer to play 5 ... 0-0, postponing the decision about whether to continue ... c5 or ... e5. White's most popular reply is 6 ♗d3 although other moves are possible (see chapter 3). In this chapter we examine 6 ... ♘c6 aiming for ... e5, while 6 ... ♘a6 intending ... c5 is the subject of the next chapter.

4	...	♗g7
5	♘f3	0-0
6	♗d3	♘c6 *(2)*

2 | Austrian Attack: Introduction and 5 ♘f3 0–0 6 ♗d3 ♘c6

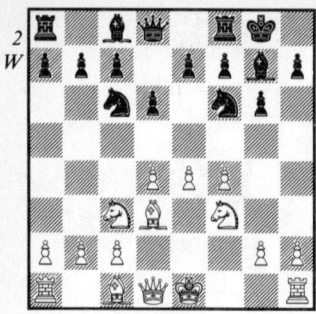

At this point there are two main alternatives. White can either regard ... e5 as a threat and prevent it, or he can continue with his development.

A: 7 e5
B: 7 0-0

Other, more passive, moves are of course possible but these generally allow Black to equalize without difficulty. Here is a short selection:
(a) **7 f5** (letting the c1 bishop into play, but losing time) ♘b4 8 0-0 (8 fg hg 9 ♗g5 c5 is also quite happy for Black) ♘xd3 9 ♕xd3 c5 10 d5 a6 11 a4 ♗d7 12 a5 b5 13 ab ♕xb6 14 ♔h1 ♗b5 15 ♘xb5 ab 16 ♖xa8 ♖xa8 17 fg hg (the exchanges have greatly reduced White's attacking chances while Black has some prospects on the queenside) 18 ♘g5 ♖a1 19 ♕f3 ♕a7 20 g3 ♕a2 21 ♕e2 ♕c4 22 ♕xc4 bc 23 ♔g2 ♗h6 (23 ... ♘d7 would have made it more difficult for White to bring his QB into play) 24 ♗f4 ♖xf1 25 ♔xf1 ♗xg5 26 ♗xg5 ♘xe4 27 ♗xe7 f5 with equality, Suetin–Ftacnik, Sochi 1977.
(b) **7 ♗e3** (this was quite a popular move at one time, but is very rare now) e5 8 fe de 9 d5 ♘e7 10 h3 (10 0-0 ♘g4 is fine for Black since after 11 ♗d2 c6 White has problems along the b6–g1 diagonal; 10 ♕d2 c6 11 dc ♘xc6 12 0-0 ♗e6 is similar to the main line, while 10 ♕d2 ♘g4!? is also possible) c6 11 dc ♘xc6 (so often in the Pirc Black's outpost on d4 proves more important than White's corresponding square on d5 since the former is supported by the bishop on g7) 12 0-0 ♗e6 13 ♘g5 ♕e7 (it is important not to allow White to activate his bishop by ♗c4) 14 ♕e2 ♘d4 15 ♕f2 ♘d7 16 ♘xe6 fe! (after 16 ... ♕xe6 White would be able to use d5) 17 ♕d2 ♕b4! with a fine position for Black, Martin–Adorjan, Las Palmas 1977.
(c) **7 d5** (when played voluntarily this is hardly ever a good move since White's centre can be broken up by ... c6) ♘b4 8 0-0 c6 9 dc bc 10 h3 ♕b6+ 11 ♔h2 and Black is even slightly better since the exchange on d3 gives him the advantage of the two bishops.

A

7 e5 de

We now consider:

Austrian Attack: Introduction and 5 ♘f3 0–0 6 ♗d3 ♘c6

A1: 8 fe
A2: 8 de

A1

8 fe (3)

For over a decade this was thought completely satisfactory for Black, but the recent idea of 12 ♕d2!? may swing the balance back in White's favour.

8 ... ♘h5

Assorted other moves have been tried:
(a) **8 ... ♘d5** (this move is somewhat doubtful because it allows White to support his centre by c3 without loss of time) 9 ♘xd5 ♕xd5 10 c3 ♗e6 (after 10 ... ♗g4 11 h3 ♗xf3 12 ♕xf3 ♕xf3 13 gf White has a promising ending) 11 ♕e2 (11 0-0 f6 12 c4 ♕d7 13 d5 ♘b4 14 ♗e2 ♗g4 15 e6 ♕d6 16 ♗e3 c6 17 ♕b3 a5 18 a3 was also slightly better for White in van der Sterren–Marangunic, Brussels 1984, since White's pawn chain is not easily broken up) ♖ad8 12 ♗f4! (not 12 ♘g5? ♘xd4! 13 cd ♕xd4 14 ♘xe6 fe 15 ♗c4 ♗xe5 16 g3 ♖f2! 17 ♕xf2? ♕d1 mate, Suetin–Zhidkov, USSR 1972; White was already losing on move 17, e.g. 17 ♗xe6+ ♔h8 18 ♕e3 ♖xh2 19 ♖xh2 ♕d1+ 20 ♔f2 ♖f8+ 21 ♔g2 ♕f1 mate) ♕d7 (preparing ... f6 by defending the c-pawn) 13 0-0 f6 (this leads to a bad position tactically but it's hard to see another move) 14 ef ef 15 ♗xc7 ♖de8 16 ♗f4 ♗xa2 17 ♗c4+ ♔h8 18 ♕d3 ♗xc4 19 ♕xc4 (the d-pawn is very strong) a6 20 ♖fe1 ♖xe1+ 21 ♖xe1 ♖e8 22 ♖xe8+ ♕xe8 23 d5 ♘e5 24 ♗xe5 fe 25 ♘g5 ♗h6 26 ♘e6 ♗e3+ 27 ♔h1 ♕d7 28 ♕e4 ♗f4 29 g3 ♗c1 30 ♕xe5+ ♔g8 31 ♕b8+ 1–0 Petronic–Polihroniade, Wijk aan Zee 1977.

(b) **8 ... ♘g4** (originally thought playable, this move has also been abandoned) 9 ♗e4 (defending the d-pawn and preparing ♗xc6 in some positions) f6 10 h3 ♘h6 11 ♗d5+ (now White can maintain his pawn on e5) ♔h8 12 0-0 ♘f5 (the analysis of Botterill and Keene giving 12 ... fe 13 de ♘b4 14 ♗b3 ♕xd1 15 ♖xd1 ♗f5 16 ♗g5! ♖ae8 17 a3 ♘c6 18 ♘d5 ♘f7 19 ♘xc7 ♖c8 20 ♘e6 ♘cxe5 21 ♗xe7! with a clear plus for White has never been challenged) 13 ♖e1 ♘fxd4 14 ♘xd4 ♗xd4 15 ♕xd4 c6 (15 ... e6 16 ef ♗xf6 17 ♕c5 ed 18 ♗h6 ♖f7 19 ♘xd5 b6 20 ♕e3 ♗b7 21 ♘xf6 ♕xf6 22 ♖f1 is also very good for White,

Gligoric–Quinteros, Vinkovci 1970) 16 ♗f4 cd 17 e6! ♕a5 18 ♘xd5 (the pawn on e6 prevents Black developing his queenside pieces) ♖d8 19 c4 b5 20 ♕c5 (winning material) ♗b7 21 ♗c7 ♖dc8 22 ♕xe7 ♕d2 23 ♖ad1 ♕xb2 24 ♕d7 bc 25 e7 ♖e8 26 ♗d8 1–0 Hofmann–Muller, East Germany 1978.

(c) **8 ... ♘d7** 9 0-0 ♘b6 10 ♗e3 f6 (10 ... ♗g4 may be better, but the whole idea looks dubious) 11 ef ef 12 d5! ♘e7 (12 ... ♘xd5 13 ♗c4 ♘e7 14 ♗c5) 13 ♗c5 ♖e8 14 ♖e1 ♗f8 15 ♘e4 ♗g7 16 d6 and Black is in a bad way, Skrobek–Ftacnik, Poland – Czechoslovakia 1978.

9 ♗e3 ♗g4 *(4)*

10 ♗e2

10 ♗c4 is well met by 10 ... ♘a5 11 ♗e2 c5 12 dc ♘c6 (or 12 ... ♕b8), while 10 ♗e4 f6 11 ef ♘xf6 12 ♗xc6 bc gives Black active piece-play.

10 ... f6
11 ef

The correspondence game Gokeskovian–Ozvath 1972–6 continued wildly with 11 e6 f5 12 d5 ♘b4 13 ♗c4 ♗xf3 14 gf ♕d6 15 ♕d2 (15 a3 ♕e5) c6 16 0-0-0 a5 17 ♗b3 ♗xc3 18 bc ♘xd5 19 ♗xd5 ♖fd8! and Black is winning. White's position is not strong enough to justify e6.

11 ... ef

11 ... ♗xf6 12 ♘e4 ♕d5 (12 ... ♗xf3 13 ♘xf6+ ♘xf6 14 ♗xf3 e5 14 de ♘xe5 15 0-0 is bad for Black, Timman–Kuzmin, Bled–Portoroz 1979, since there is no good move after 15 ... ♕xd1 16 ♖axd1 ♘xf3+ 17 ♖xf3; the knight cannot move without allowing White to penetrate to d7, while 17 ... ♖f7 18 ♖af1 is a deadly pin) 13 ♘xf6+ ef 14 0-0, Katalimov–Kuzmin, USSR 1980, and although the position is double-edged, White should be slightly better since Black may miss his black-squared bishop.

12 0-0

The only recent development of any importance in the 7 e5 line is the idea of 12 ♕d2!?, intending 0-0-0. Unfortunately practical experience is very limited: 12 ... ♕e7 (12 ... ♘e7 13 0-0-0 ♘f5 was played in Tyagunov–Paul, corr. 1985, and now 14 h3 would have been good for White according to Tyagunov) 13 0-0-0 ♖fe8 14 ♖he1 ♔h8 15 ♗h6 ♗xh6 16 ♕xh6 ♕g7 17 ♕xg7+ ♔xg7 18 h3 with advantage to White, Timman–Nijboer, Netherlands 1985.

12	...	f5
13	h3	♗xf3
14	♗xf3	

Zuidema–Fuller, Skopje Ol. 1972 went on 14 ... ♘g3? 15 ♗d5+ ♔h8 16 ♖f3 ♘e4 17 ♗xe4 fe 18 ♖xf8+ ♕xf8 19 ♕d2 and White has a good position owing to Black's weak and well blockaded e-pawn. But the position at move 14 must surely be fine for Black, for example 14 ... f4 15 ♗f2 ♘g3 16 ♖e1 (16 ♗xg3 fg leaves White with a weak d-pawn) ♘f5 exerts uncomfortable pressure on d4.

A2

| 8 | de | ♘d5 |
| 9 | ♗d2 *(5)* | |

This variation is harmless.

| 9 | ... | ♘b6 |

Or:

(a) 9 ... ♘cb4 (dubious) 10 ♗e4 ♘b6 11 a3 ♘a6 12 ♕e2 ♘c5 13 0-0-0 ♘xe4 14 ♘xe4 ♕d5 (14 ... c6 15 ♗a5 ♕e8 16 ♕f2 ♘d5 17 ♕h4 f6 18 ef ef 19 ♖he1 was very passive for Black in Ljubojevic–Donner, Wijk aan Zee 1973) 15 ♗b4! (or 15 ♘c3 and now Parma–Keene, Dortmund 1973 continued 15 ... ♕c4 16 ♕xc4 ♘xc4 17 ♘d5 ♗g4 18 ♗b4! with a distinct advantage for White; Parma suggested 17 ... ♘xd2 as an improvement, but Black's position still appears dubious) ♕a2 16 ♘c3 ♕a1+ 17 ♔d2 ♖d8+ 18 ♔e3 ♖xd1 19 ♖xd1 ♕xb2 20 ♘a4! ♕xa4 21 ♖d8+ ♗f8 22 ♗xe7 ♘b6 (22 ... ♕b6+ 23 ♔d2 ♕a5+ 24 ♗b4) 23 ♖xf8+ ♔g7 24 ♖d8 ♗g4 25 ♗f6+ ♔h6 26 ♖xa8 ♕c3+ (26 ... ♘xa8 27 ♕d2) 27 ♔f2 ♗xf3 28 gf ♘xa8 29 ♔g3 c6 30 ♕f1 1–0 Adorjan–Wright, England 1975.

(b) 9 ... ♗f5 (also not to be recommended) 10 ♗xf5 gf 11 ♕e2 ♘xc3 12 ♗xc3 ♕d5 13 ♖g1! (an excellent move, preparing g4 to pinpoint the weakness on g7) f6 14 ♖d1 ♕e6 15 ef ♕xe2+ 16 ♔xe2 ♗xf6 17 ♗xf6 ♖xf6 18 ♖d7 when White has a better pawn structure and more active pieces, Stean–Botterill, British Ch. Play-off 1974.

(c) 9 ... ♗g4 (little tested, but playable) 10 h3 (after 10 ♗e4 e6 11 h3 ♗xf3 12 ♕xf3 ♘d4 13 ♕f2 c5 14 0-0 f6 15 ef ♘xf6 16 ♗d3 ♘h5 Black's control of d4 gave him a good position in Grigorian–Spilker, USSR 1978) ♗xf3 11 ♕xf3 ♘b6?! (I am not sure why Black rejected the obvious 11 ...

♘db4 followed by ... ♘d4) 12 0-0-0 ♘b4 13 ♗e4 c6 and now White is better, Morosov–Hund, corr. 1983.

10 ♕e2

White also gets nothing with 10 0-0 ♘b4 11 ♗e2 ♗f5 12 a3 ♘4d5 (but not 12 ... ♘xc2 13 g4 ♗d3 14 ♖c1 ♗xe2 15 ♘xe2 picking up the knight) 13 ♘xd5 ♕xd5 (an ideal position for Black with this pawn structure – all his pieces have been developed on active squares without incurring any pawn weaknesses) 14 ♗b4 c5! 15 ♗a5 (15 ♕xd5 ♘xd5 16 ♗xc5 ♖fc8) ♕c6 with an edge for Black, Stean–Botterill, Hastings 1974/75.

10 ... ♘b4
11 ♗e4 f5
12 ef ef

A fine position for Black. White's pieces are clustered uncomfortably in the centre and he has no time to castle in view of the threat of ... f5.

13 a3 f5!

14 ab fe and White is in trouble, e.g. 15 ♘xe4 (15 ♘e5 ♗xe5 16 fe ♕h4+ 17 g3 ♕h3 18 ♘xe4 ♗g4 19 ♘g5 ♕h5 20 ♕e3 h6! 0–1 Pinter–Adorjan, Hungary 1975 was even worse) ♗xb2 16 ♖d1 ♗f5 17 ♗c3 ♗xc3+ 18 ♘xc3 ♕f6 19 ♘e5 ♕e7 20 ♖b1 a5 21 ba ♖xa5 22 ♖f1 ♕c5 23 ♕d2 ♖e8 with a crushing attack against White's king, Ljubojevic–Timman, Malta Ol. 1980.

7 0-0

This seems to be more testing than 7 e5. Black has two possible replies:

B1: 7 ... e5
B2: 7 ... ♗g4

There is little to choose between these lines; in either case White should keep a small advantage.

7 ... e5 *(6)*

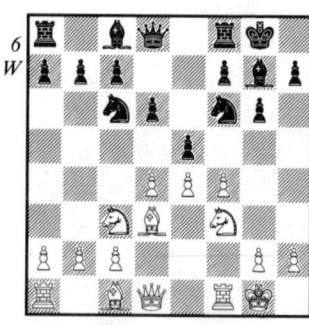

8 fe

No refutation of this move is known, although it can lead to very sharp play. White must take on e5, but even theory is undecided as to whether fe or de is better. After 8 de de 9 f5 ♘b4 (if 9 ... gf 10 ef, then the move 10 ... ♘b4 is well met by 11 ♗g5 when 11 ... ♘xd3 12 ♕xd3 ♕xd3 13 cd leaves Black with development problems; however 10 ... e4! 11 ♘xe4 ♗xf5 12 ♘xf6+ ♕xf6 13 ♗g5 ♕e6, Sax–Hazai, Hungary

Ch. 1977, or 13 ♘e5 ♕xe5 14 ♗xf5 ♘e7, Morgado–Roos, corr. 1982, is a very safe line for Black since the theoretical weakness of Black's kingside pawns is irrelevant) 10 fg (10 ♗g5 ♕d6 11 ♔h1 ♘xd3 12 ♕xd3 ♕xd3 13 cd c6 14 ♖ad1 ♘d7 was played in Sax–Torre, Rio de Janeiro 1979, and now 15 g4! would have given White an edge) hg 11 ♗g5 ♘xd3 12 cd ♕d6 (or 12... ♕d7 13 ♕b3 ♕xd3 14 ♖ad1 ♕a6 15 ♗xf6 ♗xf6 16 ♘d5 ♗d8 17 ♘xe5 ♕e6 18 ♕c3 c6, van der Wiel–Timman, Netherlands 1979, and now 19 ♘f4 ♕e8 20 ♖d6 would have left Black hard pressed to stop a sacrifice on g6) 13 ♔h1 there are three examples:
(1) **13 ... c6** 14 d4 ♘h7 15 d5 ♘xg5 16 ♘xg5 ♕e7 17 ♘f3 ♗d7 18 ♕b3 b6 19 ♖ad1 ♖fd8 20 ♖d2 c5 21 d6 ♕e6 22 ♘d5 ♕xd6 23 ♘g5 ♗e6 24 ♕g3 1–0 in view of the threat of 25 ♕h4, Sax–Donner, Buenos Aires Ol. 1978.
(2) **13 ... ♗e6** 14 ♕d2 a6 15 ♖ad1 c5 16 ♕f2 ♘d7 17 ♕h4 f6 18 ♗e3 ♖fd8 19 ♕g3 ♘f8 20 ♘h4 ♔h7 21 ♖f3 b5 22 ♖df1, Krebs–Rombach, corr. 1982 and now Black played 22 ... ♖ac8? allowing 23 ♖xf6! 22 ... ♕e7 would have made life harder for White.
(3) **13 ... ♘h7** 14 ♗e3 ♖d8 15 ♕e2 c6 16 ♖ad1 ♗g4 17 h3 ♗xf3 18 ♕xf3 ♕e7 19 ♕f2 b6 20 a4 ♘f8 21 ♖d2 ♘e6, Lamford–

Lyall, corr. 1980, with an equal position.

On the basis of these examples White can only hope for a slight advantage after 8 de, and maybe not even that.

8 ... de
9 d5 ♘e7 *(7)*

Or: (1) **9 ... ♘b4** 10 ♗c4 ♘e8 11 ♗g5 (perhaps 11 ♗e3 is better, since Black may well have to play ... f6 later in any case) f6 12 ♗e3 ♘d6 13 ♗b3 a5 and now Balashov–Timman, Moscow 1981 continued 14 a4 ♔h8 15 ♕d2 b6 16 ♖ae1 ♗a6 17 ♖f2 ♕d7 with an unclear position. I don't like 14 a4, which makes it hard to remove the well-posted knight at b4. After 14 ♕d2 Black cannot play 14 ... a4 because of 15 ♘xa4, so White can complete his development while retaining the option of a3.
(2) **9 ... ♘d4** 10 ♘xe5 ♘xd5 11 ♘xd5 ♗xe5 12 ♗f4 with a further branch:
(2a) **12 ... ♘c6** 13 ♕d2 ♗e6 14 ♗xe5 ♘xe5 15 ♘f6+ ♔g7, Mednis–Kaiszauri, Reykjavik 1982, and now 16 ♕c3 ♕d6 17 ♖ad1 ♖ad8 18 ♗e2 ♕b6+ 19 ♔h1 is good for White.
(2b) **12 ... ♗xf4** 13 ♖xf4 ♕g5 14 ♕f1 ♗e6 15 ♕f2 c5 16 ♘f6+ ♔g7 17 e5! with a very strong attack for White, Dolmatov–Kuzmin, USSR 1981.
(2c) **12 ... ♕d6** 13 ♕d2 c6 (13 ... f6? 14 ♗xe5 ♕xe5 15 ♕f4! ♕xf4 16 ♖xf4 ♔g7 17 ♖af1 and f6

dropped off, Ljubojevic–Parma, Yugoslavia Ch. 1982) 14 ♗xe5 ♕xe5 15 ♘f6+ ♔g7 16 ♖f2 c5 17 c3 ♘c6 18 ♗c4 with a small advantage for White, Marjanovic–P. Nikolic, Sarajevo 1982.

In these lines the exposed Black king appears to be more important than his control of e5.

10 ♘xe5 c6

Or 10 ... ♘fxd5 (not 10 ... ♘xe4 11 ♘xg6 ♘xc3 12 ♘xe7+ ♕xe7 13 bc ♕c5+ 14 ♔h1 ♗xc3 15 ♗h6 ♗g7 16 ♗xg7 ♔xg7 17 ♗xh7 with a quick win for White in Drosson–Roshkov, corr. 1986) 11 ♘xf7 ♘xc3 12 bc (12 ♘xd8 ♘xd1 13 ♗c4+ ♔h8 14 ♖xf8+ ♗xf8 15 ♘f7+ leads to perpetual check) ♖xf7 (for a long time it was thought that White had a winning attack, but it turns out that matters are not so clear) 13 ♖xf7 ♔xf7 14 ♗c4+ ♗e6 15 ♕f1+ (15 ♕f3+ ♗f6 16 ♗xe6+ ♔xe6 17 ♗a3 is another possibility, when 17 ... h5? 18 ♖d1 ♕h8 19 ♕f1! and 17 ... ♕h8? 18 ♖f1! ♖e8 19 ♕g4+ ♔f7 20 e5 are very good for White, the latter line being Efimov–Karsin, USSR 1987, but 17 ... ♕d2! 18 ♕h3+ ♔f7 19 ♖f1 ♔g7 20 ♕e6 ♕e3+ 21 ♖f2 ♕e1+ forces a draw according to Efimov) ♗f6 16 ♗xe6+ ♔xe6 17 ♕c4+ ♔d7 18 ♗a3 (18 ♗e3 ♗e8 19 ♖f1 ♕d6!, or 18 ♗g5 ♔h8! with good defensive chances) ♕g8! (18 ... ♔e8 19 ♖f1 ♘c6 20 e5! wins) 19 ♖d1+ ♔e8 (not 19 ... ♔c8? 20 ♗xe7) 20 ♕b5+ ♔f8! 21 ♖f1 ♕e6 22 e5 ♕b6+ 23 ♕c5 ♕xc5+ 24 ♗xc5 b6 25 ♗a3 c5 and Black held the ending in Berecz–den Broeder, corr. 1986.

11 ♗g5

Better than 11 ♗c4 ♕d6 12 ♘d3 cd 13 ed ♘exd5 14 ♘xd5 ♘xd5 15 ♔h1 ♘b6 and Black had slightly more than equalized in Bellin–Botterill, British Ch. 1977.

11 ... cd

11 ... ♘fxd5 12 ♘xf7! ♖xf7 13 ♖xf7 ♔xf7 was played in Moiseev–Labunsky, USSR 1986, and now 14 ♕f1+! ♔g8 (14 ... ♘f6 15 ♗c4+ ♗e6 16 ♗xe6+ ♔xe6 17 ♕c4+ is genuinely good for White) 15 ed ♕b6+ 16 ♔h1 ♘xd5 17 ♖e1 gives White a dangerous initiative without any sacrifice.

12 ♗xf6

12 ed ♘exd5 13 ♕f3 ♕c7! 14 ♖ae1 ♗e6 15 ♔h1 a6 was unclear in Cabrilo–Kuzmin, Kla-

dovo 1980, while 12 ♔h1 ♕d6 13 ♘f3 de 14 ♘xe4 ♘xe4 15 ♗xe4 ♕b4 16 ♕e1 was just very slightly better for White in van der Wiel–Seret, Montpellier 1985.

12 ... ♕b6+
13 ♔h1 ♗xf6 14 ♘xd5 ♘xd5 15 ♘c4 ♕d8 16 ed b5 (16... ♗g7 17 ♕f3 followed by a4 allows White to keep the pawn) 17 ♘a5! (17 ♘d2 ♖b8 was unclear in Dolmatov–Kuzmin, USSR Ch. 1980/1) ♗g5 (17... ♗xb2 18 ♘c6 ♕d6 19 ♖b1 just leaves White a pawn up) 18 ♕e1 ♖e8 19 ♕f2 (19 ♕b4!? leaves Black trying to justify his pawn sacrifice) ♖f8! (19... ♕xd5 20 c4! is strong) and in Roos–Messere, corr. 1986 White unsoundly sacrificed a piece by 20 ♖ae1 ♕xa5 21 ♖e8 ♗f5! 20 ♕g3 looks better, to meet 20... ♗h4 by 21 ♘c6.

The conclusion is that 7... e5, although playable, often leaves Black on the worse side of a drawish position. For this reason 7... ♗g4 has been preferred in over-the-board play, although this too fails to equalize.

B2

7 ... ♗g4
8 e5

8 ♗e3 e5 9 de de 10 h3 ef 11 ♗c5 (11 ♗xf4 is more sensible, but after 11... ♗e6 Black has no problems) ♗xf3 12 ♕xf3 ♘h5! 13 ♗xf8 ♗d4+ 14 ♔h2 ♘e5 15 ♕d1 ♕h4 16 ♗e2 f3 17 ♕e1 ♘g4+ 0–1, De Peaza–Edelman, New York Open 1984.

8 ... de

8... ♘h5 9 ♗e3 de 10 de f6 11 ef ♗xf6 12 h3 ♗xf3 13 ♕xf3 ♗d4 (it looks unnatural to exchange this bishop but White was already threatening f5) 14 ♘e2 e5 15 ♘xd4 ♘xd4? (15... ed 16 ♗d2 ♘e5 17 ♕xb7 ♖b8 18 ♕e4 ♘xd3 19 ♕xd3 ♖xb2 is better, but White maintains a large advantage) 16 ♕e4 ♘xf4 17 ♗c4+ 1–0 as Black must lose a piece after 17 ... ♘fe6 18 ♕xe5, Mednis–Vadasz, Budapest 1978.

9 de ♘d5
10 h3 *(8)*

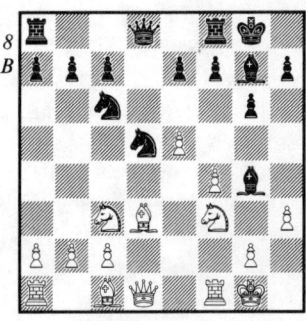

This has emerged as the most promising move for White. Other lines tend to peter out to a draw, e.g. 10 ♘xd5 ♕xd5 11 h3 ♗xf3 12 ♕xf3 ♕xf3 13 ♖xf3 ♖ad8, or 10 ♕e1 ♘db4! 11 ♗e4 f5 12 ♗xc6 ♘xc6 13 ♗e3 ♗xf3 14 ♖xf3 e6 15 ♗c5 ♖f7, Ljubojevic–Timman, match 1987.

10 ... ♘xc3

Or: (1) **10 ... ♗f5** (dubious) 11 ♗xf5 (11 ♘xd5 ♕xd5 12 ♗xf5 was slightly better for White after 12 ... ♕c5+ 13 ♔h2 gf 14 ♕d3! ♘b4 15 ♕xf5 ♕xc2 16 ♘d4!, Thipsay–Bell, London 1986, or 12 ... ♕xd1 13 ♖xd1 gxf5 14 ♗e3, Portisch–Vasiukov, Amsterdam 1969) ♘xc3 12 ♕xd8 ♘e2+ (12 ... ♖fxd8 leads to the same thing since 13 ♗xg6 hg 14 bc leaves Black without compensation for the pawn) 13 ♔f2 ♖fxd8 14 ♗xg6 ♘xc1 15 ♗e4 ♘xa2 16 ♗xc6 (16 ♖xa2 also gives White a slight advantage) ♘b4 17 ♗xb7 ♘xc2 18 ♖a4 ♖ab8 19 ♖xa7 and the extra pawn gives White reasonable winning chances.

(2) **10 ... ♗xf3** 11 ♕xf3 ♘cb4 (11 ... ♘xc3 12 bc ♘a5 13 ♖d1 ♕c8 14 c4 ♖fd8 15 ♗d2 was good for White in Pokojowczyk–Clausen, Copenhagen 1984) 12 ♘xd5 ♘xd5 13 c4 ♘b4 14 ♗e4 c6 15 ♗e3 f5 16 ef ef 17 f5 with a clear advantage for White, Tobor–Habedank, corr. 1986.   ℬe6

11 bc ♗f5

11 ... ♗d7 12 ♕e1 ♕c8 13 ♗a3 ♗f5 14 ♕h4 f6 15 ♖ae1 ♗xd3 16 cd ♕d7 17 ♖e3 was somewhat better for White in Marjanovic–Marangunic, Yugoslavia 1983.

12 ♗e3 *(9)*

Better than 12 ♗xf5 and now:
(1) **12 ... ♕xd1** 13 ♖xd1 gf 14 ♘d4 ♖fd8 15 ♗e3 ♘xd4 16 cd e6 17 g4 fg 18 hg f6 19 ♔f2 c5 20 c3 and now Parma–Gu. Garcia, Camaguey 1974 continued 20 ... cd 21 cd ♖d5 22 ♖ab1 b6 23 ♖dc1 ♖f8 24 ♔e2 ♖a5, while van der Tak–Kristinsson, corr. 1980 went 20 ... ♖ac8 21 ef ♗xf6 22 dc ♗xc3 23 ♖xd8+ ♖xd8. In both cases White has a very slight advantage, but by far the most likely result is a draw.

(2) **12 ... gf** 13 ♗e3 e6 (it is probably better to swap queens and transpose into line 1) 14 ♕e2 ♕d5 15 ♗f2 (Chandler–Torre, Jakarta 1978 continued 15 ♖fd1 ♕a5 16 ♕c4 ♖fd8 17 ♖xd8 ♖xd8 18 ♖b1 ♖b8 19 ♘d4 ♘xd4 20 cd c6 and Black is not worse) ♘e7 15 c4 ♕a5 17 h4 with an edge for White, Dolmatov–Cummings, Mexico 1980.

12 ... ♕d7

Or 12 ... f6 (12 ... ♗xd3 gives White a free hand and after 13 cd b6 14 ♕e2 ♘a5 15 d4 ♕d7 16 c4 ♖ad8 17 ♖ac1 f6 18 d5! White had a dangerous attack in Weinstein–Lein, New York 1976) 13 ♗xf5 gf 14 ♕e2 (14 e6 ♕c8 15 ♕d5 ♖d8 16 ♕xf5 ♖d6 with equality, Diesen–Matulovic, Odzaci 1978) ♕d5 (14 ... fe 15 ♖ad1 ♕e8 16 fe ♘xe5 17 ♘xe5 ♗xe5 18 ♗h6 ♗g7 19 ♗xg7 ♚xg7 20 ♕e5+ is good for White) 15 ♖fd1 with an edge for White, Trapl–Ftacnik, Trnava 1979.

13 ♕e2   ♖fd8

One may advance arguments in favour of either rook move. **13 ... ♖ad8** leaves a rook on f8 in case Black should want to play ... f6, while **13 ... ♖fd8** anticipates the need to play ... b5, when White's c4 will open lines on the queenside, activating the a8 rook. However the key point in this position does not depend on which rook Black moves to d8. There will soon be an exchange on d3, when White will play cd and try to push c4 and d4. Black must prevent this by ... b5, but this gives White the chance to establish his bishop outside the pawn chain with ♗c5 followed by d4. Of course this is not the end of the world, but it gives White an awkward, nagging advantage. After 13 ... ♖ad8 14 ♖ad1 (the rook on f1 is generally more useful than the one on a1, hence ♖ad1 rather than ♖fd1) ♗xd3 15 cd b5 and now **16 d4** ♕d5 17 c4 bc 18 ♖c1 ♘a5 19 ♗d2 e6 (19 ... ♗h6!?) 20 ♗xa5 ♕xa5 21 ♕xc4 ♗h6 left White with no real advantage in Parma–Eising, Mannheim 1975. However the above discussion shows that **16 ♗c5!** is the critical move, with play similar to the main line. In Balashov–Wedberg, Helsinki 1983 Black tried to do without a rook move by **13 ... ♗xd3** 14 cd b5 15 ♖ad1 f6, but again the thematic 16 ♗c5 ♘a5 17 d4 c6 18 ef ♗xf6 19 ♘e5! was good for White.

14 ♖ad1   ♗xd3
15 cd   b5

In Nunn–Hoi, Buenos Aires Ol. 1978, Black tried to invert moves by 15 ... ♕d5 to prevent the bishop coming to c5, but 16 c4 ♕a5 17 d4 e6 would have been good for White after the correct 18 ♗f2 followed by ♗h4 displacing the rook from d8.

16 ♗c5

Not 16 d4 ♕d5 17 g4 ♘a5 18 f5 ♘c4 19 ♗g5 f6 and White's attempted attack has achieved nothing, Nunn–Chandler, London 1979.

16 ...   ♕d5

17 d4 ♖ab8 18 ♖de1 e6 19 ♘g5 with a plus for White, Balashov–Pfleger, Hannover 1983.

The generally depressing nature of all these variations explains the rise of 6 ... ♘a6, which is covered in the next chapter.

2 | Austrian Attack: 5 ♘f3 0-0 6 ♗d3 ♘a6 and 6 ... others

1	e4	d6
2	d4	♘f6
3	♘c3	g6
4	f4	♗g7
5	♘f3	0-0
6	♗d3	*(10)*

From small beginnings in the seventies the move 6 ... ♘a6 has risen to be one of Black's main lines against the Austrian Attack. In contrast to 6 ... ♘c6, very sharp positions often arise, making this line ideal for Black players aiming to win. An inevitable corollary is that there is a greater risk element, the main danger being that White's kingside attack will break through before Black's counterplay has developed. After 6 ... ♘a6 White has a choice between 7 e5 and 7 0-0. Both moves have been popular, even though they lead to quite different types of position, with 7 e5 being the more positional of the two. At the moment 7 0-0 is causing Black more sleepless nights.

Black occasionally tries other 6th moves, but none of these can be recommended and we only cover them briefly.

6 ... ♘a6 *(11)*

(a) **6 ... ♗g4** 7 h3 ♗xf3 8 ♕xf3 (now White has the option of castling queenside) ♘c6 9 ♗e3 and now:

(a1) **9 ... e5** 10 de de 11 f5 (if White can meet ... e5 by de and f5 without encountering any tactical problems then he usually gets the advantage because he has a straightforward plan of kingside attack by g4–g5) ♘d4 12 ♕f2 b5 (12 ... gf 13 ef b5 14 0-0 c5 15 ♘e4! and the stranded knight on d4 is a weakness) 13 g4 (13 0-0 c5 14 ♘xb5 ♘xb5 15 ♗xb5 ♘xe4 16 ♕f3 ♘d2 17 ♗xd2 ♕xd2 18 ♗d3 ws also good for White in Parma–

Planinc, Ljubljana–Portoroz 1977) c5 (13 ... b4 14 ♘e2 ♘d7 15 ♘g3 ♘c5 16 ♗c4 ♕h4 17 0-0-0 was no better in Reeve–Schleifer, Canada 1986) 14 g5 c4 15 gf ♗xf6 16 0-0-0 with advantage to White, Jansa–Pavlik, Czechoslovakia 1966.

(a2) **9 ... ♘d7** 10 e5 ♘b4 11 0-0-0 c5 (11 ... ♘xd3+ 12 ♖xd3 c6 13 h4) 12 dc! ♕a5 (12 ... de 13 ♗b5) 13 cd ed 14 a3! de (a desperate sacrifice) 15 ab ♕a1+ 16 ♔d2 ♕xb2 (threat: ... ♕xc3+) 17 ♘d5 ef 18 ♕xf4 ♖ad8 19 ♖b1 ♕e5 20 ♕xe5 and White won in R. Byrne–Korchnoi, Moscow 1975.

(b) **6 ... ♘bd7** 7 e5 (7 0-0 e5 8 fe de 9 d5 c6 10 dc bc 11 ♔h1 may keep a small advantage, but 7 e5 is the critical move) ♘e8 and now:

(b1) **8 ♘g5** (very direct) e6 (this looks awful; 8 ... h6 is bad after 9 ♘xf7 ♔xf7 10 e6+, but 8 ... ♘b6 is unclear) 9 h4 c5 9 10 h5 cd 11 hg hg 12 ♕g4 with a crushing attack, Guido–Vavra, corr. 1982.

(b2) **8 h4** appears very dangerous.

(b3) **8 ♘e4** (a safe route to a modest advantage) c5 9 c3 cd (9 ... ♕b6 10 ♘ed2! cd 11 ♘c4 is good for White after 11 ... ♕c6 12 cd ♘c7 13 0-0 ♘b6 14 ♘e3, Gligoric–Rocha, Hastings 1964/5, or 11 ... ♕d8 12 cd de 13 fe ♘b6 14 ♘e3 ♘c7 15 0-0, Hazai–Liptay, Hungary 1975) 10 cd de 11 de ♘c7 with a space advantage for White.

(c) **6 ... c5** (White has no trouble keeping his pawn centre intact after this move) 7 dc dc 8 e5 ♘d5 9 ♘xd5 ♕xd5 10 ♕e2 ♘c6 11 ♗e4 and Black has a miserable position. The outpost on d4 is easily covered by c3 whereupon Black is left with less space and no way to activate the bishop on g7.

(d) **6 ... c6** (it is very risky to meet an aggressive line like the Austrian with such a passive move) 7 0-0 (7 e5 ♘d5 lends point to the move ... c6; in Watson–Nikolic, Graz 1987 the continuation 8 ♘xd5 cd 9 h4 ♗g4 10 h5 gh 11 c3 de 12 fe f5 13 ♗g5 ♕d7 misfired and Black won) and the three examples I found all ended in wins for White in under 25 moves: 7 ... ♗g4 8 ♔h1 e5 9 de de 10 f5 ♘bd7 11 ♔h1 ♗xf3 12 ♖xf3 ♘h5 13 ♗c4 was Kopp–Novak, corr. 1981, 7 ... **b5** 8 a3 a6 9 ♔h1 ♕c7 10 e5 ♘d5 11 ♘g5 ♘xc3 12 bc c5 13 f5 was Maier–B. Andersson, corr. 1982 and 7 ... **♘a6** 8 h3 ♘c7 9 ♕e1 ♘d7 10 ♗e3 c5 11 ♖d1 cd 12 ♘xd4 ♘c5 13 ♗c4 ♕e8 14 f5 was Cvitan–Nikolic, Graz 1987. These games may exaggerate Black's problems after 6 ... c6, but in my view the move is illogical.

After 6 ... ♘a6 the way divides:

A: 7 e5
B: 7 0-0

A

7 ... e5   8 ♘d7

Or 7 ... de (7 ... ♘e8 8 ♗e3 c5 9 dc ♘xc5 10 ♗xc5 dc is similar to 6 ... c5 above in that Black cannot activate his g7 bishop; after 11 ♕e2 ♘c7 12 ♖d1 ♕e8 13 0-0 ♖b8 14 a4 ♗d7 15 ♘g5 ♗c6 16 f5 White had a very dangerous attack in Klovan–Donchenko, USSR 1977) 8 de ♘d5 9 ♘xd5 ♕xd5 10 ♕e2 ♗f5 11 ♗xf5 gf 12 ♗e3 (12 0-0 may be met by 12 ... ♘c5 13 ♖d1 ♕e4 14 ♕xe4 fe 15 ♗e3 ♘a4 16 ♖d4 ef 17 ♖xa4 fg 17 ♖d1 f6 with rough equality, Marjanovic–Zaichik, Kirovakan 1978, or 12 ... f6 13 ef ♗xf6 14 ♗e3 transposing to the next bracket) c5 (or 12 ... f6 13 ef ♗xf6 14 0-0 and now 14 ... ♕e4 15 c3 ♘c5, Ree–Timman, Netherlands 1971 is better than 14 ... ♖ad8 15 ♗xa7 ♕e4 16 ♗e3 ♘b4 17 ♖f2 and Black could not justify his pawn sacrifice, van der Sterren–Haik, Budel 1987) 13 0-0 and White has only a small advantage. After 13 ... ♘c7 14 ♖ad1 (14 ♖fd1 ♕e4 15 ♕d3 ♘e6 16 ♕xe4 fe 17 ♘d2 f5 18 ef ♗xf6 19 c3 ♘d4 is unclear, Klovan–Zaichik, Daugavpils 1978) ♕c6 (not 14 ... ♕e4 15 ♖d7 ♘e6 16 ♘d2 and 16 ... ♘xf4 is impossible) 15 ♕d3 e6 16 c4 ♘a6 17 g4?! Black managed to draw in Kapengut–Zaichik, Daugavpils 1978 but 17 a3 would have left Black in a depressing position without active chances. The positions after 7 ... de 8 de ♘d5 are similar to those arising from 6 ... ♘c6; Black is in no immediate danger but his winning prospects are small. The text move is more combative and has been overwhelmingly popular in practice.

8 ♗e3

This positional continuation has gradually come to replace more direct ideas;

(a) **8 h4** *(12)* (dangerous but objectively White's position is not strong enough to justify this kind of attack) and now:

(a1) **8 ... de** 9 fe (9 de ♘ac5 frees Black's position) c5 10 h5 (10 e6 fe 11 h5 is met by 11 ... ♕c7, threatening an annoying check at g3) cd 11 hg hg 12 e6 dc! 13 ef+ ♖xf7 14 ♗xg6 ♖xf3 15 ♕d5+ e6! 16 ♕xe6+ ♔f8 17 gf ♘e5 with a winning position for Black, Borkowski–Balcerowski, Poland 1979.

(a2) **8 ... c5** 9 h5 cd 10 hg hg (10 ... dc 11 ♘g5! is too dangerous) 11 ♘g5 and now Black has a choice:

(a21) **11 ... ♘dc5** is designed to eliminate the dangerous bishop, and after 12 f5 ♘xd3+ 13 ♕xd3 ♗xf5 14 ♕xd4 ♕a5! 15 ♕h4 ♕xe5+ 16 ♘ce2 ♖fc8 White's attack collapses. However 12 ♔f2! is better, threatening 13 ♖xh8+ ♗xh8 14 ♕h1, and after 12 ... ♘xd3+ 13 cd ♖e8 the position is completely unclear.

(a22) **11 ... de** 12 f5! gf! (Borkowski–Nunn, Groningen 1974/5 went 12 ... ♘f6? 13 fg ♗g4 14 gf+ ♖xf7 15 ♘e2 ♕d5 16 ♗g6 ♖ff8 17 ♕d3 e4 and now 18 ♘c3! would have been good for White) 13 ♕h5 (13 ♘ce4 ♗b6! 14 ♕h5 ♕h6!) ♘f6 14 ♕h4 dc and Black may well defend, although the position is hideously complicated.

(a23) **11 ... ♘xe5!** (probably best) 12 fe dc 13 ♔f2! ♗xe5 (13 ... de 14 ♗e3 ♕d6! 15 ♖h4 cb 16 ♖b1 ♖d8 17 ♕h1 led to a draw in De Firmian–van der Wiel, Wijk aan Zee 1986) 14 ♗e3 (14 ♖h8+ ♗xh8 15 ♕h1 ♔g7 appears to defend) e6 15 ♔e2 and White still has attacking chances, but I doubt if they compensate for the three pawn deficit.

(b) **8 ♘g5** and now:

(b1) **8 ... de** 9 fe (9 de ♘dc5 leaves the knight on g5 poorly placed) ♘b6 (9 ... h6 is worth thinking about; if the knight retreats then ... c5 is possible, while 10 ♘xf7 ♖xf7 11 e6 ♖f6 doesn't look good for White) 10 ♗e4 (10 ♗xa6 ba 11 ♘ge4 f6 ½–½, Timman–Dzindzihashvili, Amsterdam 1978) c5 11 d5 ♗xe5 12 ♘xh7 ♗xc3+ 13 bc ♔xh7 14 ♕h5+ ♔g8 15 ♗xg6 is only good enough for a draw, Sveshnikov–Davies, Moscow 1987.

(b2) **8 ... ♘b6** 9 h4 (9 ♗e3? ♘b4 and Black gains the two bishops since 10 ♗e2 ♗f5 is unpleasant) ♘b4 10 h5 ♘xd3+ 11 ♕xd3 ♗f5 12 ♕e2 ♕d7 and Black's control of the white squares should enable him to fend off White's attack.

(c) **8 ♘e2** (with the same idea as 8 ♘e4, namely supporting the centre with c3, but at the same time defending the d-pawn) c5 9 c3 cd 10 cd de 11 fe f6!? (11 ... ♘b6 12 0-0 ♘b4 followed by 13 ... ♘4d5 and ... f6 is also reasonable) and White's centre crumbles as 12 ♗c4+ ♔h8 13 e6 ♘b6 14 ♗b3 ♘d5 15 ♘f4 ♘ac7 surrounds the pawn on e6.

(d) **8 e6!?** fe 9 ♘g5 ♘f6 10 ♕e2 c5 (10 ... ♘b4 11 ♗c4 d5 12 ♗b3

♕d7 is perhaps more critical – Black's pawn formation is maimed and his c8 bishop is out of play, but the same can be said of both White bishops and at least Black has a pawn more) 11 ♗xa6 ½–½ Bouaziz–Schussler, Dortmund 1979. In the final position 11 ... ba 12 ♘xe6 ♗xe6 13 ♕xe6+ ♔h8 14 dc gives White the advantage while 11 ... cd 12 ♘xe6 ♗xe6 13 ♕xe6+ ♔h8 14 ♗xb7 ♖b8 15 ♗f3 dc 16 b3 is less clear, but again White seems to be better.

(e) **8 ♘e4** c5 (in Mednis–Vadasz, Budapest 1976, Black played more slowly and after 8 ... ♘b4 9 ♗e2 ♘b6 10 c3 ♗f5 11 ♘fg5 d5 12 ♘g3! ♘c2+ 13 ♔f2 ♘xa1 14 ♘xf5 gf 15 ♗d3 White had a very strong attack; 8 ... de was slightly better for White after 9 ♗xa6 ba 10 de ♘b6 11 0-0 f6 12 ♕xd8 ♖xd8 13 b3 ♘d5 14 c4 ♘b4 15 ♗b2, Jansa–Adorjan, Sochi 1976) 9 c3 (9 ♘eg5 h6 10 ♘xf7 ♖xf7 11 e6 ♖f6 12 ed ♗xd7 13 0-0 cd 14 ♘xd4 ♘c5 with advantage to Black, Eslon–Hoi, Can Picafort 1980) cd 10 cd de 11 fe (11 de ♘dc5 is, if anything, a bit better for Black) ♘b4 12 ♗b1 (12 ♗e2 ♘b6 13 0-0 ♗f5 14 ♘g3 ♗e6 15 ♗g5 f6 16 ♕d2!? ♘c6 17 ef ef 18 ♗e3 ♗d5 leaves Black with a slight but persistent advantage owing to the isolated d-pawn, Buchal–Nunn, Ostend 1975) ♘b6 13 0-0 ♗g4 14 ♘eg5 (14 ♗e3 ♘c6 15 a3 ♘d5 16 ♗f2 ♗h6! is fine for Black, Sowray–Nunn, Oxford 1979) ♘c6 15 h3 ♗xf3 16 ♘xf3 ♕d7 with equality, Klovan–Karasev, USSR 1977.

After 8 ♗e3 *(13)* there are three lines, but one is dubious:

(a) **8 ... c5** 9 ♗xa6 cd 10 ♗xd4 de 11 fe ba 12 e6! fe 13 ♗xg7 ♔xg7 14 ♕d4+ ♘f6 15 0-0-0 was slightly better for White in Timman–Nunn, Wijk aan Zee 1981.

(2) **8 ... ♘b6** 9 a3 (9 0-0 ♘b4 10 ♗e2 transposes to the next note) c5 10 ♗xa6 cd 11 ♗xd4 ba 12 ed ♕xd6 13 ♗xg7 ♕xd1+ 14 ♖xd1 ♔xg7 and Black's active pieces compensate for the doubled pawns, van der Wiel–Short, Marbella 1982.

(3) **8 ... ♘b4** 9 ♗e2 (9 ♗c4 c5 10 ♗xf7+?! ♖xf7 11 e6 ♖f8 12 ed ♕xd7 13 ♕e2 ♕e6 14 ♔d2 b6 15 a3 ♗a6 with a plus for Black, Timman–van der Sterren, Netherlands Ch. 1981) ♘b6 10 a3 (10 0-0 ♗h6 11 ♘e1 de 12 de ♗f5 13 ♗c5! was good for White in Hamilton–van der Wiel, Grand

Manan 1984, but 10 ... ♗f5 11 ♖c1 ♘4d5 12 ♘xd5 ♘xd5 13 ♗d2 ♗h6 is better, e.g. 14 ♘e1 de 15 de c6 intending ... ♕b6+) ♘4d5 11 ♘xd5 ♘xd5 12 ♗d2 c5 13 dc dc 14 0-0 f6 with just an edge for White, Timman–Nunn, London 1982.

B

    7 0-0   c5
    8 d5 *(14)*

8 dc ♘xc5 9 ♕e1 b5! 10 a3 ♗b7 11 ♔h1 a5! gave Black a favourable type of Sicilian, Glek–Azmaiparashvili, Tallinn 1986.

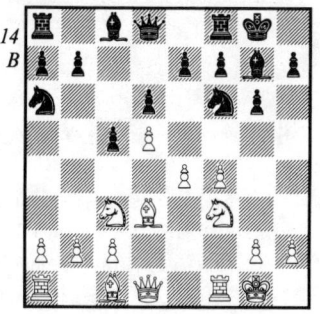

    8 ...   ♖b8 *(15)*

Or:

(1) **8 ... ♘c7** (intending ... e6) 9 a4 (9 ♕e1 e6 10 de fe 11 e5 is also promising, Thipsay–Kantsler, Frunze 1985) e6 (9 ... a6 10 ♕e1 was very good for White after **10 ... b6** 11 ♕h4 ♗d7 12 f5 b5 13 ♗h6 c4 14 ♗e2 gf 15 ♘g5 e6 16 ♖f3, Bellin–Pribyl, Holland 1978 and **10 ... ♗d7** 11 a5 ♗b5 12 f5 gf 13 ♕h4 e5 14 ♗g5 f4 15 g3 c4 16 ♗e2 ♘ce8 17 gf, Adorjan–Bohm, IBM 1977) 10 de fe 11 e5 ♘fd5 12 ed ♕xd6 13 ♘e4 ♕e7 14 ♘e5 and White is better, Nunn–Pfleger, England 1979.

(2) **8 ... ♘b4** and now:

(2a) **9 ♗c4** e6 10 a3 (10 de ♗xe6 11 ♗xe6 fe 12 e5 de 13 ♕e2!? ef 14 ♗xf4 ♕e7 15 ♖ae1 ♘bd5 16 ♘xd5 ♘xd5 17 ♗g5 ♕d6 18 ♕xe6+ ♕xe6 19 ♖xe6 is level, Bellin–Nunn, Hastings 1975/6) ed 11 ab (11 ed ♘a6 12 h3 ♘c7 13 a4 a6 14 a5 ♗d7 15 ♕d3 ♖e8 16 ♖a3 ♘b5 with equality, Lanc–Hoi, Prague 1980) dc 12 bc dc 13 ♕e2 ♗e6 14 ♖d1 with an unclear position, Kuhn–Kauschmann, Bundesliga 1986.

(2b) **9 ♗e2** (this is much more convincing) e6 10 a3 ♘a6 11 de fe (11 ... ♗xe6 12 f5! is dangerous) 12 e5! de 13 ♕xd8 ♖xd8 14 fe ♘g4 15 ♗g5 ♖f8 16 ♘e4 ♘xe5 17 ♘xe5 ♖xf1+ (17 ... ♗xe5 18 ♖xf8+ ♔xf8 19 ♖d1 ♗d4+ 20 ♔h1 is also good for White) 18 ♖xf1 ♗xe5 19 ♗f6 ♗d4+ 20 ♗xd4 cd 12 ♘f6+ ♔g7 22 ♘e8+ ♔g8 23 ♖f4 with an excellent position for White, Skrobek–Sapi, Hradec Kralove 1976/7.

(3) **8 ... ♗g4** (the move ... ♗g4 has recently become popular at various points in this line; see B2 for the closely related variation 8 ... ♖b8 9 ♔h1 ♗g4) and now:

(3a) **9 ♗c4!** (the idea is that once Black has exchanged on f3, the bishop at c4 will make ... e6 an unpleasant prospect) ♘c7 19 h3

♗xf3 11 ♕xf3 ♘d7 12 a4 a6 13 ♕d3 (13 ♖d1 ♖b8 14 a5 was also good for White according to Chernin) ♘b6 14 ♗a2 ♕d7 15 a5 ♘c8 16 ♗d2 b5 17 ab ♘xb6 and White has a positional advantage, Dolmatov–Chernin, USSR Ch. 1987.

(3b) **9 ♔h1** ♗xf3 (Black exchanges voluntarily to make White take with the rook; once the knight has gone to c7 White will be able to take with the queen because ... ♘b4 is impossible) 10 ♖xf3 ♘c7 11 a4 a6 12 a5 ♘b5 13 ♗d2 ♖c8 14 ♖a4 ♕d7 15 b3 ♘e8 16 ♘e2 with a slight plus for White, Ivanchuk–Tabataze, Leningrad 1985.

(3c) **9 h3** ♗xf3 10 ♖xf3 ♘c7 11 a4 a6 12 a5 (12 ♕e2 e6 13 de ♘xe6 14 ♗e3 ♖e8 15 ♖ff1 ♘d4 16 ♕f2 b5 with active counterplay for Black, Bagaturov–Chikovani, USSR 1984) ♘b5 (12 ... ♘d7 was played in Dolmatov–Kuzmin, USSR Ch. 1987 and now 13 ♘e2! would have been better than 13 ♗d2 as played, which allowed 13 ... e6! equalising) 13 ♘e2 c4! 14 ♗xc4 ♘xe4 15 ♗xb5 ab 16 ♕d3 f5! 17 ♕xb5 ♕c7 18 c3 ♕c5 and in Ehlvest–Azmaiparashvili Black had sufficient compensation for the pawn.

The point of 8 ... ♖b8 is that if White continues with 9 ♕e1 the reply ... ♘b4 forces the exchange of the bishop on d3. The alternative is 9 ♔h1, waiting for ... ♘c7 before playing ♕e1, but this involves a slight loss of time. Nevertheless 9 ♔h1 has scored very well and so far Black has not come up with an antidote to White's kingside attack.

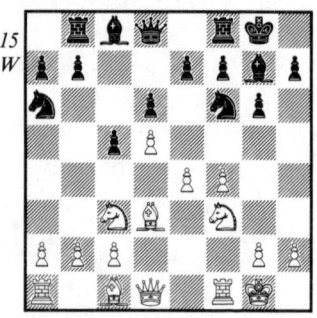

B1: 9 ♕e1
B2: 9 ♔h1

Other moves should not worry Black:

(a) **9 ♕e2** ♘b4 (9 ... ♘c7 looks less consistent, but 10 a4 a6 11 a5 b5 12 ab ♖xb6 13 ♘a4 ♖b8 14 c4 e6 15 e5 ♘fe8 was highly unclear in Dolmatov–Gipslis, USSR 1985) 10 ♗c4 e6 11 de ♗xe6 12 ♗xe6 fe 13 e5 (13 a3?! is bad because it drives the knight nearer d4, and after 13 ... ♘c6 14 f5 gf 15 ef ef 16 ♕e6+ ♔h8 17 ♗f4 ♘h5! Black was slightly better in Kinlay–Nunn, London 1977; 13 ♖d1 is approximately equal) de (13 ... ♘fd5 14 ♘g5!) 14 fe ♘fd5? (14 ... ♘d7 looks about level) 15 ♗g5 ♕c7 16 ♘b5 ♕b6 17 c4 h6 18 cd hg 19 ♘d6 ♘xd5 20 ♘xg5 c4+ 21 ♔h1 ♕e3 22

Austrian Attack: 5 ♘f3 0–0 6 ♗d3 ♘a6 and 6 ... others

♕g4 1–0, Kaidanov–Piket, Lvov 1988.

(b) **9 a4?** ♘b4 10 ♗c4 e6 11 de ♗xe6 12 ♗xe6 fe 13 ♔h1 ♕d7 14 ♗e3 ♕c6 15 ♘d2 d5 with an ideal position for Black who has started his central pawns moving to the embarrassment of White's minor pieces, Suetin–Vadasz, Budapest 1976.

B1

9   ♕e1   ♘b4

9 ... ♘c7 is bad because White gains an important tempo over line B2.

10   ♕h4   b5

By 10 ... c4 11 ♗xc4 ♘xc2 12 ♖b1 ♕b6+ 13 ♔h1 ♘e3 14 ♗xe3 ♕xe3 Black can gain the two bishops, but White's massive lead in development is far more important.

11   a3

11 f5 c4 12 a3 ♘xd3 13 cd cd 14 ♗h6 b4 15 ab ♖xb4 16 fg fg 17 ♘g5 ♗xh6 18 ♕xh6 gave White a very dangerous attack in Sznapik–van der Wiel, Amsterdam 1984. The idea does not seem to have been repeated, perhaps because 12 ... ♘bxd5! 13 ♘xd5 ♘xd5 14 ed cd breaks up White's centre to Black's advantage.

11   ...   ♘xd3
12   cd   ♗g4! *(16)*

Or 12 ... ♗a6 (12 ... e6 is another sensible move; 13 de fe 14 ♗e3 a5 15 ♘g5 h6 16 ♘f3 b4 was good for Black in Wockenfuss–Chandler, Bundesliga 1980, but White's play was very passive) 13 b4 (13 e5?! de 14 fe ♘xd5 15 ♘g5 h6 16 ♘ce4 ♕b6! 17 ♖f3 f5 was very good for Black in Grünfeld–Nunn, Malta 1980) ♘d7 (13 ... cb 14 ab ♕b6+ 15 ♔h1 ♘xe4 16 ♖xa6 ♕xa6 17 ♘xe4 ♖bc8 18 ♖g1 ♕b7 19 f5 f6 20 fg hg 21 ♕g3 g5 22 ♘fxg5 fg 23 ♕xg5 ♖c2 was highly unclear in Lein–Keene, Buenos Aires 1978) 14 ♗d2 e6 15 de fe 16 ♕h3 ♖e8 17 f5 ef 18 ef ♗c8 with an edge for White, Sax–Nunn, Malta 1980. Although either 12 ... ♗a6 or 12 ... e6 might be satisfactory for Black, 12 ... ♗g4! has proved so effective that it must be the preferred move.

13   f5

13 ♘g5 h6 14 ♘f3 b4 15 ab cb 16 ♘d1 ♕b6+ 17 ♗e3 ♕b5 18 f5 g5 19 ♕g3, R. Kuijf–Pein, Lugano 1984, and now 19 ... ♕xd3! would have been slightly better for Black. **13 b4** cb 14 ab ♘xe4 15 ♘xe4 ♗xf3 16 ♖xf3 ♗xa1 17 ♘g5 h5 18 g4 ♕c8 is

also good for Black according to Bohm.

13 ... ♛c8

Black was successful with 13 ... b4 in De Firmian–Wolff, USA Ch. 1985, which continued 14 ab cb 15 ♘e2 ♛b6+ 16 ♔h1 ♖bc8 17 ♘f4 ♗xf3 18 ♖xf3 ♛a6 19 ♗e3 ♛xa1+ 20 ♗g1 ♖c1 21 ♘h3 ♖f1 22 fg hg 0–1. This could be important if Friedstein's suggestion in the next note is good for White. The weakness of White's back rank is a recurrent motif in this variation.

14 ♗h6

Friedstein suggests the fascinating line 14 ♘g5 b4 15 e5 de 16 d6! bc 17 de cb 18 ef(♛)+ ♔xf8 19 ♘xh7+! ♘xh7 20 fg and wins. I think Black should play 14 ... h6 15 ♘f3 b4 as in Kuijf–Pein above, with a double-edged position. In any case Black has the reserve option of 13 ... b4, so the evaluation of this line as satisfactory for Black is not changed.

14 ... ♗xf3

15 ♖xf3 b4 16 ab cb 17 ♘d1 ♛c5+ 18 ♘e3 (18 ♘f2 ♗xh6 19 ♛xh6 ♛d4 20 ♖f1 b3! led to another demonstration of White's back rank problems in Nunn–van der Sterren, Ramsgate 1981 after 21 ♖h3 ♖fc8 22 ♔h1 ♛xb2 23 ♘g4 ♘xg4 24 ♛xh7+ ♔f8 25 fg ♛g7! 26 ♖h4 b2 27 ♖xg4 b1(♛)+ 28 ♛xg7+ ♔xg7 29 gf+ ♔h6 0–1) ♗xh6 19 ♛xh6, Prizant–Sorlie, corr. 1984, and now

instead of 19 ... ♛d4 with an unclear position, Sorlie recommends 19 ... ♘g4 20 ♛g5 ♘e5 21 ♖h3 f6 followed by ... ♖f7 with a slight advantage for Black.

B2

9 ♔h1 *(17)*

This appears to be much the most dangerous choice.

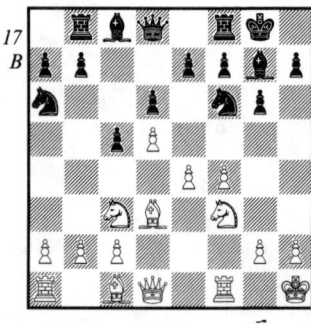

17
B

9 ... ♘c7

There are two reasonable alternatives:

(1) **9 ... b6** 10 a3 (10 ♘b5!? is interesting; if Black defends a7 then White plays c4 supporting the centre, while otherwise Black has to sacrifice a pawn) ♘c7 11 ♛e1 (this is similar to the main line) b5 12 ♛h4 a5 (12 ... c4 13 ♗e2 a5 14 f5 gf 15 ♘d4 ♗d7? 16 ♘xf5 ♗xf5 17 ♖xf5 ♔h8 18 ♗g5 and Black had no compensation for his shattered kingside, Kuzmin–Torre, Bangalore 1981; 15 ... b4 was better) 13 f5 b4 14 ab ab 15 ♘e2 gf 16 ♗h6 ♗xh6 17 ♛xh6 ♘g4 18 ♛h5 ♘e8 19 ef ♘ef6 20 ♛h4 and again White

has a very dangerous attack, Franzen–Richardson, corr. 1986.

(2) **9 ... ♗g4** and now:

(2a) **10 ♕e1** ♗b4 11 a3 (11 ♕h4 ♕c8 12 ♘d2 ♘xd3 13 cd b5 14 ♕f2 ♕a6 15 h3 b4 and Black is better, Stehouwer–van der Wiel, Netherlands Ch. 1984) ♘xd3 12 cd ♕b6 13 ♘d2 ♕a6 14 ♕e3? (14 ♕g3 ♗d7 15 a4 was better, but after 15 ... ♘h5! Black is not worse) ♗d7 15 a4 e6 16 ♖a3 ed 17 ed ♖fe8 with advantage to Black, Velimirovic–van der Wiel, Sarajevo 1984.

(2b) **10 ♗c4!?** ♘c7 11 a4 a6 12 a5 b5 13 ab ♖xb6 14 h3 ♗xf3 15 ♕xf3 ♘b5 16 ♘e2 (the manoeuvre ♘e2 and c3 is characteristic of these ... ♗g4 lines; White prevents the Black knight occupying d4 and reduces the length of the diagonal for the ♗g7) ♕c8 17 c3 and White is slightly better, Stoica–Varasdy, Bajmok 1984 (this is similar to Dolmatov–Chernin in the note to Black's 8th move).

(2c) **10 f5** ♕c8 11 ♗e2 (11 ♗g5 ♗xf3 12 gf c4 13 ♗e2 b5 14 a3 ♘c5 15 ♕d2 ♕d7 16 ♗h6 was unclear in Grünfeld–Wolff, New York 1987) ♘c7 12 a4 a6 13 ♘h4 ♗xe2 14 ♕xe2 b5 15 ab ab 16 g4 ♖a8 17 ♖xa8 ♕xa8 18 g5 ♘h5 19 ♘d1 and the transfer of this knight to the kingside gives White attacking chances, Grünfeld–Kindermann, Biel II 1986.

The conclusion is the same as for 8 ... ♗g4; in both cases the reply ♗c4 offers the best chances for White to gain an advantage.

10 a4   b6

10 ... a6 11 a5 b5 12 ab ♖xb6 makes it harder for Black to develop queenside counterplay. In Marjanovic–Rukavina, Bor 1983, White continued 13 ♕e1 ♖b4 14 ♘d1 e6 15 de ♗xe6 16 ♗d2 ♖b8 17 c4 ♗g4 18 ♕g3 with a good position.

11	♕e1	a6
12	♕h4	b5
13	ab	ab
14	f5	*(18)*

After 14 e5 Black should play 14 ... de 15 fe ♘fxd5 16 ♗h6 f6 when although White has a dangerous attack Black is fairly solid and may well be able to defend. 14 ... b4 is worse, e.g. 15 ♘g5 h6 16 ef ef 17 ♘xf7! ♔xf7 18 f5! bc 19 fg+ ♔g8 20 ♗xh6 ♗xh6 21 ♕xh6 ♕d7 22 bc with advantage for White, Spassky–Kavalek, match 1977.

18
B

14 ...   gf

14 ... c4 15 ♗e2 ♗d7 proved disastrous after **16 ♘g5** b4 17 e5 de 18 ♘ce4 h6 19 fg fg 20 ♗xc4 ♘fxd5 21 ♘f3 e6 22 ♗g5 hg 23 ♘fxg5 ♖f5 24 ♕h7+ ♔f8 25 ♕xg6, Thipsay–Willmoth, London 1987, or **16 ♗h6** ♗xh6 (16 ... b4 was better, but 17 ♘d1 ♗xh6 18 ♕xh6 ♘xe4 19 ♘f2 ♘f6 20 fg fg 21 ♗xc4 is still good for White) 17 ♕xh6 ♘g4 18 ♕h4 ♘f6 19 ♘g5 ♘ce8 20 ♕h6 with an immense attack, Plachetka–Jansa, Trnava 1987.

15 ♗h6 c4

Not 15 ... b4 16 ♘e2 ♗xh6 17 ♕xh6 ♘g4 18 ♕h5 ♘f6 19 ♕h4 e6 20 ♘g5 ed 21 ed ♔g7 (or 21 ... ♘cxd5 22 ♖f3 followed by ♖h3) 22 ♘g3 h6 23 ♖xf5! 1–0, Barczay–Vadasz, Hungary Ch. 1976.

16 ♘d4

Better than 16 ♗e2 b4 17 ♘d4 (17 ♘d1 ♘xe4 18 ♘e3 e6 is bad for White) ♗xh6 (not 17 ... bc 18 ♘c6 and the queen cannot go to e8 because of ♕g5) 18 ♕xh6 bc 19 ♘c6 ♕e8 20 ♘xb8 cb 21 ♖ab1 c3 with a double-edged position, Moore–Nunn, Oxford 1980.

16 ... ♗xh6

After 17 ♕xh6 cd 18 ♘c6 ♕e8 19 ♘xb8 b4 we reach a critical position for the assessment of the whole line. It appears to be good for White, e.g. 20 ♘d1 (20 ♘a4 dc 21 ♘b6! is also very promising) dc 21 ♘e3 ♔h8? (21 ... ♘xe4 was the only move, since after 22 ♖f3 ♔h8 the move ♖h3 is not possible, but 22 ♘c6! is still awkward for Black) 22 ♘c6 ♘xe4 23 ♖a7 ♗a6 24 ♖c1 1–0, Oll–Maxwell, World Junior Ch. 1984.

Since the direct kingside v queenside line is good for White, Black has to fall back on 8 ... ♗g4 or 9 ... ♗g4, but in both cases the reply ♗c4 gives White some positional advantage.

3 | Austrian Attack: 5 ♘f3 0-0 6 others

1	e4	d6
2	d4	♘f6
3	♘c3	g6
4	f4	♗g7
5	♘f3	0-0 *(19)*

Apart from 6 ♗d3, three other White 6th moves have some importance. 6 ♗e2 is infrequently played, mainly because it allows Black to attack White's centre by 6...c5. However it is much better than its reputation and Black's hopes rest mainly on D. Gurevich's idea mentioned in the note to Black's 10th move. 6 e5 is the start of a direct attempt to mate Black by h4–h5. Black can duck the challenge by 6...de, which should be enough to draw, or play 6...♘fd7 leading to great complications which provide equal chances with correct play. The most important line is 6 ♗e3, which has often been played by Belyavsky. Black has a wide range of replies; there isn't much to choose between 6...♘bd7, 6...b6, 6...c5 and 6...♘c6.

A: 6 ♗e2
B: 6 e5
C: 6 ♗e3

6 ♗c4 is seen occasionally but 6 ...♘xe4 7 ♗xf7+ ♖xf7 8 ♘xe4 is equal, and 6...c5 7 e5 (7 d5 b5!) ♘g4 is unclear.

A

6   ♗e2

This move was once very popular, but although it is still seen occasionally there are few grandmaster examples from recent years. Allowing the immediate 6 ...c5 may appear bad, but the resulting Sicilian-style positions give White an extra tempo over promising lines from the 6 f4 Najdorf, so it is surprising that it has not been played more often.

6   ...   c5

Moves such as 6...♘c6 and 6 ...♗g4 make less sense with the

bishop on e2 but the lack of defence for the White e-pawn enables Black to play ... c5. However Black will need to explore other ideas if the main line turns out badly.

7 dc

7 d5 may be met by 7 ... e6 (after 7 ... b5 8 ♗xb5 ♘xe4 9 ♘xe4 ♛a5+ 10 ♘c3 ♗xc3+ 11 bc ♛xb5 Black is at least equal, so White should play 8 e5 de 9 fe ♘g4 10 ♗xb5 ♘xe5 11 ♘xe5 ♗xe5 12 ♗h6 e6!? with complications) 8 de ♗xe6 9 0-0 (9 ♘g5 d5 10 e5 ♘e8 11 ♗f3 ♘c7 12 ♘e2 ♘c6 with equality, Prokopovic-Berus, USSR 1980) ♘c6 10 f5!? gf 11 ♗g5 fe 12 ♘xe4 d5 with a double-edged position. 7 ♗e3 cd and 7 0-0 cd lead to Sicilian Dragon positions in which White is committed to an early f4.

7 ... ♛a5
8 0-0

8 cd ♘xe4 9 de ♖e8 is bad for White.

8 ... ♛xc5+
9 ♔h1 *(20)*

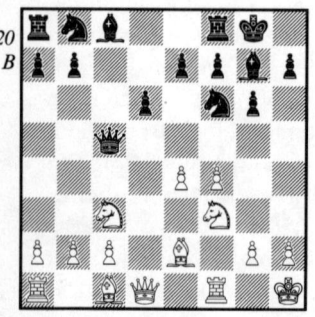

9 ... ♘bd7

This has superseded the older move **9 ... ♘c6**, when White may be able to gain a small plus with 10 ♗d3 (10 ♛e1 d5 11 e5 ♘e4 was unclear in Vatter-Pfleger, Bundesliga 1985). Then Ligterink-Gulko, Netherlands-USSR telex match 1978, went on 10 ... ♗g4 11 ♛e1 ♛h5 (11 ... ♗xf3 12 ♖xf3 ♘b4 13 ♗e3 ♘xd3 14 cd ♛b4!? 15 ♖b1 a5 16 f5 ♖ac8 was played in Short-Speelman, match 1988, and now 17 ♛d1 d5 18 e5 ♘g4 19 ♘xd5 ♘xe3 20 ♖xe3 ♛c5 21 ♛f3 ♖fd8 22 ♘xe7+! would have been good for White) 12 ♗d2 e5 (12 ... ♗xf3 was still possible, although the White rook might like to go to h3 now) 13 fe ♘xe5 14 ♘xe5 ♛xe5 15 ♗f4 ♛c5 16 ♛g3 (already Black is in terrible trouble) ♖fd8 17 e5! de 18 ♗g5 e4 19 ♗xf6 ed 20 ♛xg4 ♗xf6 21 ♘e4 ♛xc2 22 ♘xf6+ ♔g7 23 ♛h4 h6 24 ♘g4 1-0. **9 ... b5** is bad after 10 e5 de 11 fe ♘g4 12 ♛d5! ♘f2+ (12 ... ♛b6 13 ♗g5!) 13 ♖xf2 ♛xf2 14 ♛xa8 b4 15 ♘d5 ♛xe2 16 ♗g5 as given by Keene and Botterill. With 9 ... ♘bd7 Black prepares to attack e4 by the fianchetto of the c8 bishop coupled with ... ♘c5. This forces White to play ♗d3, so it appears that White has lost time moving his bishop twice, but it turns out that Black's queen excursion has cost two tempi, so White has a move more than in the Sicilian.

10 ♗d3

10 ♕e1 may well transpose into the main line, but it is slightly more flexible to play 10 ♗d3, since this move is bound to be necessary to defend e4. **10 ♕d3** a6 11 ♗e3 ♕c7 12 a4 ♘c5 13 ♕c4 led to a spectacular miscombination in Mende–Precerutti, corr. 1982 after **13 ... ♘fxe4?** 14 ♘d5! ♕d8 15 b4 b5 16 ab ab 17 ♖xa8! bc 18 ♖xc8 ♕d7 19 ♖c7 ♕d8 20 bc ♘c3 21 ♖c8 1–0. **13 ... ♗e6** 14 ♘d5 ♕d8 (14 ... ♘xd5 15 ed b5 16 ♕a2! is bad, but 14 ... ♗xd5 15 ed ♖ac8 is possible) was best, with at least equality for Black.

10 ... a6

The most common move, but there is a strong argument in favour of 10 ... b6 11 ♕e1 ♗b7 12 ♗e3 ♕c6, which makes use of the position of the queen to exert immediate pressure on e4. After 13 ♕h4 (13 f5 ♘c5 14 fg fg 15 ♗c4+ ♔h8 16 ♗d5 ♕d7 17 ♘g5 ♗a6! 18 ♖f3 ♘xd5 19 ed ♕g4 was at least equal for Black, Mortensen–D. Gurevich, Helsinki 1983) ♘c5 14 ♖f2 h6 15 ♘d4 ♕d7 16 f5 g5 17 ♕g3 ♗xe4 White could not justify his sacrifice in R. Kuijf–D. Gurevich, Beersheva 1987. This is the only line in which Black attempts to make use of the position of his queen and thereby avoid a transposition to a 6 f4 Najdorf. Nevertheless I am doubtful that Black can equalize.

11 ♕e1

11 a4 b6 may lead to positions similar to those in the last note, although in practice Black has retreated his queen to c7, e.g. 12 ♕e1 ♗b7 13 ♗e3 ♕c7 14 ♕h4 and now:

(1) **14 ...** ♘c5 15 f5 b5 16 ab ♘xd3 17 b6 ♕c4 18 ♖a4 ♘b4 19 ♘d2 ♕c6 20 ♖xb4 d5 and Black has some play for the pawn, Rusakov–Koshili, USSR 1985. Although Black drew the game this position looks somewhat better for White.

(2) **14 ... e6** (more flexible than ... e5) 15 ♖ae1 (15 f5!? is the critical move) ♖ae8 16 e5 (White releases the tension and allows Black to equalize) ♘d5 17 ♘xd5 ♗xd5 18 ♗d4 ♘c5 ½–½, Ligterink–Taulbut, IBM 'B' 1978.

(3) **14 ... e5** transposes to a 6 f4 Najdorf line with the difference that White has gained the extra move ♗c1–e3. Since the position is thought good for White even when the bishop is on c1 Black should deviate earlier. Play might continue 15 f5 (15 ♖ae1 ♖ac8 16 ♗d2 ♘c5 17 f5! gf 18 ♗h6 ♗xh6 19 ♕xh6 ♘fxe4 20 ♘xe4 ♘xe4 21 ♘h4 was good for White in Rusakov–Volchok, corr. 1981/3, but 15 ... ♖ae8 16 ♗d2 ♘c5 was much better, transposing to Ljubojevic–Miles, Skara 1980) ♖ae8 16 ♗g5! (this is the most

dangerous plan; 16 ♗h6? ♞h5 17 g4 ♗xh6 18 gh gf gave Black the advantage in Christiansen–Rogoff, USA Ch. 1978) ♕c5 17 ♞d2 ♕b4 18 ♖ab1 ♖c8 19 ♖f3 d5 20 ♖bf1 with a very strong attack, Cramling–Arnason, Reykjavik 1984.

11 ...   b5 *(21)*

11 ... e5 12 ♗e3 ♕c7 13 fe de 14 ♕h4 b5 again transposes to a 6 f4 Najdorf with the extra move ♗e3. After 15 ♗h6 ♗b7 (15 ... b4 should be met by 16 ♞d5 rather than the miserable 16 ♞d1 ♞h5 17 ♗xg7 ♔xg7 18 ♞e3 ♗b7 and Black escapes, B. Stein–Hoi, Plovdiv 1983) 16 ♞g5 ♕d6 (16 ... ♞h5 loses to 17 ♗xg7 ♔xg7 18 ♖xf7+, while 16 ... ♖ae8 17 g4 ♖e7 18 ♖f3 ♖fe8 19 ♖af1 puts Black under heavy pressure) 17 ♖ad1! White has a dangerous attack since 17 ... ♞h5 fails to 18 ♗xg7 ♔xg7 19 ♗e2.

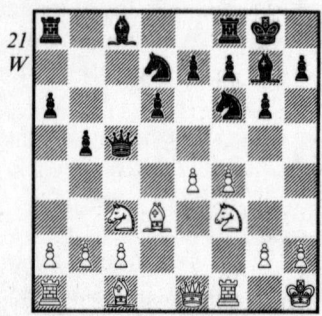

12   ♗e3

12 e5 (premature) de 13 fe ♞g4 14 ♗e4 (14 ♕e4 ♗b6! is dubious, but 14 e6 ♞de5 15 ♞e4 ♕c7 is double-edged) ♖b8 15 h3 ♞gxe5 16 ♗e3 ♞xf3 17 ♖xf3 ♕b4! (not 17 ... ♗d4?! 18 ♗xd4 ♕xd4 19 ♖d1 ♕e5 20 ♖e3 ♕c5 21 ♞d5 and now Sikora–Ftacnik, Czechoslovakia Ch. 1978 continued 21 ... ♞f6? 22 ♖c3 ♕d6 23 ♗xg6! ♞xd5 24 ♗xh7+! and White won, but even 21 ... b4 22 ♖b3 a5 23 a3 regaining the pawn leaves White a little better with his queenside passed pawns) 18 ♗a7 ♖b7 19 ♗xb7 ♗xb7 20 ♖e3 ♕xb2 and Black has fantastic compensation for the exchange, Hervir–Mailler, corr. 1983.

12 ...   ♕c7

Once again we have a 6 f4 Najdorf with White having an extra move. Although the bonus ♗e3 is not enormously useful, it is certainly better than nothing and since the Najdorf position is thought slightly better for White, we must give him a definite advantage here. Here are a couple of examples which arose from the Pirc move-order:

13 ♕h4 (13 a3 ♗b7 14 ♕h4 ♖ae8 15 f5 e6 16 ♗g5 ♕c6 17 ♖ad1 is good for White, R. Kuijf–J. Piket, Wijk aan Zee II 1987) ♗b7 14 f5 ♖fe8 15 ♞g5! and now 15 ... h6 is met by 16 ♞xf7 ♔xf7 17 fg+ ♔g8 18 ♗xh6, so Mortensen–K. Schmidt, Aarhus 1983 continued 15 ... ♞e5 16 fg hg 17 ♗d4 with a strong attack for White.

For a more detailed coverage of

the 6 f4 Najdorf positions, see the author's book *The Najdorf for the Tournament Player*.

Based on these lines it is hard to see why 6 ♗d3 is so much more popular than 6 ♗e2. In both cases White has excellent chances to gain an advantage. This makes 5 ... 0-0 a depressing prospect for Black, and helps to explain the popularity of 5 ... c5.

B

6 e5

This cannot be recommended because Black appears to have little difficulty holding the balance. If he wants to draw then 6 ... de gives him every chance to achieve his aim, while the sharp lines with 6 ... ♘fd7 are also not worse for Black.

B1: 6 ... de
B2: 6 ... ♘fd7

B1

**6 ... de
7 de**

This looks more natural than 7 fe ♘d5 8 ♗c4, when Black has a choice:

(a) 8 ... ♗e6 (8 ... c6 is untested) 9 ♘xd5 (9 ♕e2 ♘xc3 10 bc ♗xc4 11 ♕xc4 ♘c6 12 0-0 ♘a5 13 ♕b4 b6 14 ♗a3 e6 15 c4 ♕d7 is unclear, Guseinov-Zaichik, Sevastopol 1986) ♗xd5 10 ♗xd5 ♕xd5 11 ♕e2 b5 12 0-0 ♘d7 13 c3 ♘b6 14 b3 a5 15 ♗a3 ♕d7 16 ♗c5 ♘d5 17 ♕d2 ♖fb8 18 ♖ac1 b4? 19 c4 ♘c3 20 ♖fe1 was good for White in Unzicker-Chandler, Buenos Aires Ol. 1978, but a number of improvements are possible, for example 11 ... c5 or 17 ... c6.

(b) 8 ... ♘b6 9 ♗b3 ♘c6 (9 ... ♗g4 10 0-0 ♘c6 11 ♗e3 ♘a5 12 h3 ♘xb3 13 ab ♗e6 followed by ... f6 is also level, Polasek-Spilker, match Prague-Moscow 1979) 10 ♗e3 ♘a5 11 ♕e2 ♘xb3 12 ab f6 (Black has comfortable equality) 13 0-0 ♗e6 14 ♖ad1 c6 ½-½ Perecz-Schussler, Dortmund 1979.

**7 ... ♕xd1+
8 ♔xd1**

After 8 ♘xd1 Black can centralize his knight by 8 ... ♘d5 with easy equality.

8 ... ♘h5 *(22)*

This has emerged as Black's best move. The older lines 8 ... ♖d8+ and 8 ... ♘g4 have not been refuted, but White tends to maintain a slight advantage, for example 8 ... ♖d8+ (8 ... ♘g4 9 ♔e1 ♘c6 10 h3 ♘h6 11 ♗e3 f6 12 ♗c4+ ♔h8 13 ef ef is the best of the older lines restricting White to a very slight advantage) 9 ♗d2 (the usual moves are 9 ♗d3 and 9 ♔e1 but 9 ♗d2 is quite logical – the f1 bishop belongs on c4 while it is useful to have the c-pawn defended) ♘d5 (9 ... ♘e8 may be better) 10 ♘xd5 ♖xd5 11 ♗c4 ♖d8 12 ♘g5 e6 13 h4 ♘c6 14 ♘e4 h5 15 g4! hg 16 h5 gh 17 ♖xh5 ♘e7 18 ♔e2 b6 19 ♖g5

♗b7 20 ♗d3 ♔f8 21 ♖xg4 with a very strong attack, Letzelter–Sepp, Strasbourg 1972.

22
W

9 ♗c4

9 ♖g1 ♗g4 10 ♗e2 ♘c6 11 h3 ♗xf3 12 ♗xf3 ♘g3 was unclear in Velimirovic–Rukavina, Yugoslavia Ch. 1981.

9 ... ♘c6

9 ... ♗g4 is also satisfactory, e.g. 10 ♘e2 (10 ♔e2 ♘c6 11 ♗e3 transposes to 11 ♔e2?! below) ♗xf3 11 gf ♘c6 12 c3 ♖ad8+ 13 ♔c2 ♗h6 14 b4 e6 15 ♖g1 ♔h8 16 ♖g4 ♘e7 with an equal position, Ljubojevic–Timman, Bugojno 1980.

10 ♗e3

10 ♖f1 is a slight improvement. Zhuravlev–Adorjan, Sochi 1977, continued 10 ... ♗h6 (10 ... ♗g4 11 ♔e1 ♘a5 12 ♗d3 f6 13 ef ♗xf6 is suggested by Zhuravlev as being better) 11 ♘e2 ♖d8+ 12 ♔e1 ♘b4 13 ♗b3 ♗e6 14 a3 ♗xb3 15 ab ♗c4 16 g3 and White had a small plus.

10 ... ♗g4
11 ♖f1

11 ♔e2?! g5 12 fg ♗xe5 13 ♔f2 ♗xf3 14 gf ♖ad8 was slightly better for Black in Martin–Dzindzihashvili, Haifa Ol. 1976, and another good line is 11 ... ♗xf3+ 12 gf (12 ♔xf3 ♗xe5) e6 threatening 13 ... ♗h6.

11 ... ♘a5
12 ♗e2

Black gained the advantage in Panchenko–Adorjan, Sochi 1977 after 12 ♗d3 f6 13 ef ♗xf6 14 h3 ♗e6 15 ♘d2 ♘g3 16 ♖e1 ♗f5 in view of the unfortunate location of the White king.

12 ... f6
13 ef ♗xf6

Black's pieces are once again very active and he had no problems in Unzicker–Pfleger, Munich 1979, which ended 14 ♘d2 ♗xc3 15 ♗xg4 ♗xb2 16 ♖b1 ♗c3 17 ♘e4 ♗g7 18 ♖b5 b6 19 ♗xh5 gh 20 ♖xh5 ♘c4 ½–½.

B2

6 ... ♘fd7

This leads to great tactical complications. Although at one time White players adopted this variation frequently, it is rarely seen today. Therefore instead of giving a detailed survey, I shall give a quick outline of the important lines.

7 h4 *(23)*

Or:

(a) 7 ♗c4 ♘b6 8 ♗b3 (8 ♗e2 de 9 fe ♘c6 10 0-0 ♗g4 and 8 ♗d3 ♘c6 9 0-0 de 10 de ♗f5 are both level) ♘c6 9 0-0 ♘a5 10 ♘e4 ♘xb3 11 ab f6 and with the disruption of the White centre Black has attained equality.

(b) 7 ♗g5 (7 e6 fe 8 h4 ♘f6 9 ♗d3 ♘c6 10 h5 gh is not dangerous) ♘b6 8 ♗d3 ♘c6 9 d5 ♘b4 10 e6 ♘xd3+ 11 ♕xd3 fe 12 de ♕e8 with at least equality since Black is quite happy to give up the exchange if the knight comes in to f7.

(c) 7 ♗e2 c5 8 ed ed 9 d5 ♘a6 10 0-0 ♘c7 11 a4 ♘f6 12 h3 b6 13 ♗c4 a6 14 ♖b1 ♗d7 15 b4 b5 was better for Black in V. Raicevic–Nunn, Hastings 1979/80.

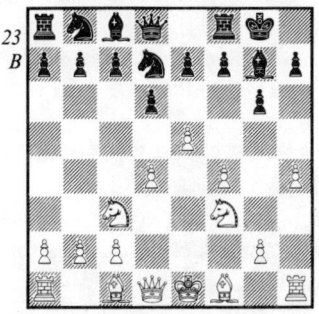

7 ... c5

Black follows the old rule that an attack on the flank is best met by a counter in the centre. Despite the artificial appearance of h4–h5 it comes perilously close to delivering mate.

8 h5

8 e6 fe 9 h5 is the alternative, with the continuation 9 ... gh 10 ♖xh5 (10 dc ♘f6 11 ♗d3 ♘c6 is fine for Black) ♘f6 11 ♖h4 cd (11 ... ♘c6 12 ♗e3 ♕a5 13 ♗d3 cd 14 ♘xd4 ♘xd4 15 ♗xd4 e5 16 fe de 17 ♗e3 e4 was fine for Black in Anand-Wolff, World Junior Ch. 1984) 12 ♘xd4 ♘c6 13 ♗e3 (13 ♘xc6 bc 14 g4 ♘d5! is unclear) ♕b6 14 ♕d3 (14 ♕d2? ♕xb2 15 ♖b1 ♘e4! ∓ while 14 g4 e5! 15 fe ♘xe5 16 ♘f5 ♕xb2 17 ♘xe7+ ♔f7! was very good for Black in the consultation game Webb + Yeo v Nunn + Goldschmidt, London 1975) ♘b4 15 ♕d2 e5 16 fe de 17 0-0-0!? (17 ♘f5 ♘xc2+! 18 ♕xc2 ♗xf5 19 ♗c4+ e6 ∓ or 17 ♗c4+ ♔h8 18 ♘f5 ♗xf5! 19 ♗xb6 ♘xc2+ 20 ♔f1 ♘xa1 21 ♗f2 ♗c2 ∓) ed 18 ♗xd4 ♕a5 19 ♗c4+ ♔h8 20 ♖dh1 ♗f5 (20 ... e5 21 ♗g5! threatens 22 ♕xf6 and 22 ♕g6) 21 ♕g5 ♘c6 (21 ... b6?! 22 ♘d5 ♗xc2 23 ♗c3!) 22 ♘d5! ♘xd4 23 ♘xe7! (23 ♘xf6 ♖xf6 24 ♖xh7+ ♗xh7 25 ♕xa5 ♖h6! ∓) ♕b6! (the only move to defend against 24 ♘g6+ since if now 24 ♕xf5 ♗h6+ wins or 24 ♘g6+ ♗xg6 25 ♕xg6 ♘h5! 26 ♕xh5 h6 with a safe extra piece) 24 ♘xf5 ♗xf5 25 ♕xf5, Estrin–Nunn, Lublin 1978, and now 25 ... ♕xb2+ 26 ♔xb2 ♘h5+ with a draw would have been a reasonable finish.

Although tricky, 8 e6 gives White no advantage.

8 ... cd
9 hg(?)

Although this is the critical test, it is a mistake regarded purely objectively. After 9 hg White has no clear route to equality, so White should choose 9 ♕xd4 which is roughly equal.

After 9 ♕xd4 de *(24)* there are two lines:

24
W

(1) **10 ♕f2** (10 fe ♘xe5 11 ♕h4 ♗f5 is good for Black) e4 11 ♘xe4 (11 ♘g5 ♘f6 12 hg hg 13 cxe4 ♘xe4 14 ♘xe4 ♕d4 is equal) ♘f6 12 ♘xf6+ ef 13 hg ♖e8+ 14 ♗e3 hg (14 ... fg is also playable, but capturing with the h-pawn should be sounder) 15 ♗d3 ♕a5+ 16 c3 ♗g4?! 17 0-0 ♘c6 18 ♘d4 f5 19 ♘xc6 bc 20 ♖fe1 and the poorly placed bishop on g4 gives White an edge, Banas–Kindermann, Trnava 1987. 16 ... ♘c6 17 0-0 ♗f5 looks a better way to steer the game towards equality.

(2) **10 ♕g1** e4 11 ♘xe4 (11 ♘g5 ♘f6 12 hg hg 13 ♕h2 ♕d4 14 ♘cxe4 ♖d8 is unclear) ♘f6 12 ♘xf6+ ef 13 hg ♖e8+ 14 ♔f2 (this is the point of playing ♕g1; White intends to deliver mate by ♕h2, but Black can defend) hg 15 ♕h2 ♘d7 16 ♕h7+ ♔f8 and Black is at least level, Gasic–Keene, Bognor 1967.

9 ...   dc
10 gf+

In Bussek–Spettel, Saarlouis 1986, White came up with the remarkable innovation 10 ♖xh7!? and after 10 ... fg 11 ♗c4+ ♔xh7 12 ♘g5+ ♔h8 13 ♔f2 ♕b6+ 14 ♔g3 he was rewarded with an enormous attack. The refutation isn't that hard: **11 ... e6!** 12 ♗xe6+ ♔xh7 13 ♘g5+ ♕xg5 14 fg ♘xe5 and Black has too much for the queen.

10 ...   ♖xf7
11 ♗c4

Or 11 e6 (11 ♘g5? cb 12 ♗c4 ♘xe5 13 ♕h5 ♕a5+ 14 ♔f1 d5! and 12 ♗xb2 ♕a5+ lose for White) and now:

(1) **11 ... ♖f6** 12 ed ♗xd7 13 ♗d3 h6 15 bc ♘c6 is the safe way to play; little is left of White's attack and Black has a positional advantage. I doubt if White can equalize.

(2) **11 ... cb** (this might win by force, but Black has to be very careful) 12 ef+ ♔f8 13 ♗xb2 ♗xb2 14 ♗c4 (14 ♖b1 ♕a5+ 16 ♔f2 ♕c5+ 16 ♔g3 ♘f6! gives Black a raging attack since 17 ♖xb2? loses to 17 ... ♘e4+ 18 ♔h2 ♕h5+ 19 ♔g1 ♕xh1+) ♕a5+ 15 ♔f1 ♘f6 16 ♖b1 (16 ♘g5 ♗f5 17 g4 ♕b4!) ♕c3 17 ♗b3!? (upon 17 ♘e5 ♗f5 or 17 ♗d3 ♗g4 White's attack comes

to a complete halt) and now Botterill and Keene gave 17 ... ♗g4 'with great advantage'. Unfortunately for this view, the correspondence game Hessmer–Hafner continued 18 ♘g5! ♗xd1? (18 ... ♕xb3 was better, but still winning for White) 19 ♖xh7! ♘bd7 (saving a few stamps) 20 ♘e6 mate. Black should play 17 ... ♗f5! 18 ♘g5 ♘c6 covering the sensitive h7 and f8 squares as soon as possible. Maybe I too have overlooked a tactical possibility, but I suspect that Black is doing very well here.

11 ...   e6
12 ♘g5 (25)

12 f5 ♘xe5 13 fe ♖e7 is very good for Black as 14 ♘xe5 ♕a5 threatens the knight on e5 and 15 ... cb+.

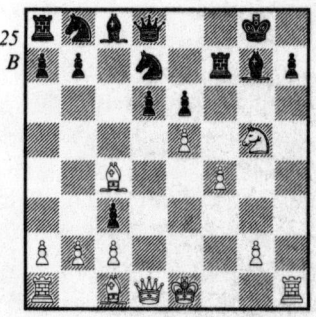

12 ...   ♘f8

This seems to be the only way to play for a win. The other move, 12 ... ♘xe5, leads to an ending after 13 ♕h5 (13 fe? cb 14 ♕h5 ♕xg5 ∓) 13 ... h6 14 fe hg 15 ♕h7+ ♔f8 16 ♕h8+ ♗xh8 17 ♖xh8+ ♔g7 18 ♖xd8 ♘c6 (18 ... ♖c7 19 ♗d3 cb? 20 ♗xb2 d5 21 ♗a3 ♗d7 22 ♗f8+ ♔f7 23 ♔d2 ♖c8 24 ♗h7! 1–0 Perecz–Hever, Hungary 1974) 19 ♖xd6 ♘xe5 20 ♗e2 (20 ♗xe6? ♖e7 21 ♗xc8 ♖xc8 and White's king is in trouble) in which Black can equalize but no more. Perecz–Nunn, Dortmund 1979 continued 20 ... ♖d7 (20 ... ♗d7 21 bc ♖c8 22 ♗e3 is not so clear) 21 ♖xe6 ♖d1+ 22 ♔xd1 ♗xe6 23 ♗xg5?? (23 bc ♖h8 24 c4 is level) ♖h8 0–1 as White has unexpectedly lost a piece!

13 ♘xf7

13 ♕h5 ♖c7! and 13 f5? cb are very pleasant for Black.

13 ...   ♔xf7
14 ♕h5+

14 f5 cb 15 fe+ ♗xe6 16 ♕h5+ (16 ♖f1+ ♔g8 17 ♖xf8+ ♔xf8 18 ♕f3+ ♕f6!! 19 ef ba(♕) 20 fg+ ♔xg7 21 ♕xb7+ ♘d7 0–1 Demichev–Seredenko, Alma–Ata 1966) ♕e7 17 ♗g5+ (17 ♕g5+ ♔e8 18 ♕h5+ ♔d7) ♔d7 18 ♗xe6+ ♘xe6 19 ♕f7+ ♔c8 20 ♕xe6+ ♘d7 21 ♕c4+ ♘c5 22 ♕g4+ ♕d7 23 ♕xd7+ ♔xd7 24 ♖b1 ♗xe5 25 ♖xh7+ ♔c6 ∓ (analysis by Botterill and Keene).

14 ...   ♔g8
15 f5

15 ♗d3 h6 16 g4 ♗d7 17 g5 ♗e8 18 ♕h3 h5 19 g6 de 20 ♕xh5 ef ∓ (analysis by Friedstein).

15 ...   ♕a5

Black stands very well. The game A. Schneider–Forgacs, Hungary 1975, continued 16 fe cb+ 17 ♕e2 (17 ♕d1 ♗xe6 18 ♗xe6+ ♘xe6 19 ♕xh7+ ♔f8 20 ♕f5+ ♔e7 21 ed+ ♔xd6 22 ♕xa5 ba=(♕) with two extra pieces for Black) ♕c7! 18 ♗b3 d5 19 ♗xb2 (19 ♗xd5 ♕xc2+) ♗xe6 20 ♖af1 ♘bd7 (White's attack has vanished completely) 21 ♖f3 ♘c5 22 ♔d1 ♖c8 23 ♖c3 ♕xe5 24 ♕xe5 ♗xe5 25 ♖xc5 ♗g4+ 0–1.

The conclusion is that 6 e5 offers White very few prospects of an advantage.

C

6   ♗e3 *(26)*

Although not as popular as 6 ♗d3, this move has become one of White's main options in the Austrian Attack. Black has several reasonable replies, with 6 ... ♘bd7 and 6 ... b6 being the most common. If Black doesn't mind transposing to other varia-tions, then 6 ... c5 and 6 ... ♘c6 are also feasible.

C1: 6 ... ♘bd7
C2: 6 ... b6

Other moves:
(a) **6 ... c5** (White can transpose into a standard line after this move, but by deviating with 8 ♕d2 he might keep a small advantage) 7 dc ♕a5 and now:
(a1) **8 ♕d2** dc 9 ♘b5 (9 e5? ♖d8) ♕xd2+ (9 ... ♕a4 10 e5 ♘e4 11 ♕d3 ♕b4+ 12 ♘d2 ♗f5 13 ♘c7 ♘c6 14 ♘xa8 ♖d8 15 ♕a3 ♘xd2 16 0-0-0 reached a critical position in Belyavsky–Timman, Tilburg 1986; Timman recommends 16 ... ♕xa3 17 ba ♘xf1 18 ♖xd8+ ♘xd8, but Belyavsky continues 19 ♖xf1 ♘e6 20 ♔d2 b6 21 ♖b1 ♗e4 22 ♘xb6 ab 23 ♖xb6 with advantage; Belyavsky appears to be correct) 10 ♘xd2 ♘a6 11 0-0-0, Belyavsky–Mednis, Vienna 1986, and now Mednis recommends 11 ... b6 12 ♗e2 ♗g4 as equal. In fact White is still slightly better, but Black is not seriously worse.
(a2) **8 ♗d3** dc (after 8 ... ♘g4 9 ♗d2 ♕xc5 10 ♕e2 ♘f6 White may transpose to Chapter 4 by 11 ♗e3, so 11 0-0-0 is the only move with independent significance; Tal–Mednis, Riga 1979 went on 11 ... ♘a6 12 e5 de 13 fe ♘g4 14 ♖de1 and now 14 ... ♘b4 15 ♗c4 ♘c6 16 ♗f4 ♘gxe5! would

have been unclear – one must add that moves such as 11 ... ♘c6 and 11 ... ♗g4 are very plausible) 9 e5 (9 ♗d2 may be stronger so that Black cannot meet e5 by ... ♘d5, e.g. 9 ♗d2 ♘c6 10 e5 ♘g4 11 h3 ♘h6 12 g4 f6 13 ef ef 14 ♕e2 f5 15 ♗c4+ ♔h8 16 g5 ♘f7 17 0-0-0 and the advance of the h-pawn was crushing, Chandler–Hazai, Keszthely 1981) ♘d5 10 ♗d2 ♘xc3 11 ♗xc3 ♕b6 (11 ... ♕c7 12 ♕e2 ♘c6 13 h4! h5 14 ♗e4 ♗g4 15 ♕c4 b6 16 0-0-0 ♖ad8 17 ♕a4 was very good for White in Kurajica–Eising, Wijk aan Zee 1974) 12 a4 (perhaps White should play more aggressively as in Kurajica–Eising) ♘c6 13 a5 ♕c7 14 0-0 ♘b4 15 ♗xb4 cb 16 ♕e1 ♕c5+ 17 ♕f2 and White still has a small advantage, Belyavsky–Speelman, Brussels 1988.

(b) 6 ... c6 7 ♗d3 ♘bd7 (the provocative 7 ... ♕b6 was played in Belyavsky–Kuzmin, USSR Ch. 1981 and after 8 ♕c1 ♘a6 9 h3 ♘b4 10 0-0 ♘xd3 11 cd ♘e8 12 g4 f5 13 gf gf 14 ♔h2 fe 15 de d5 the position was unclear, but probably better for White) 8 h3 (8 ♕d2 e5 9 0-0-0 ♘g4 10 de ♘xe3 11 ♕xe3 de 12 f5 ♕e7 13 g4 was horribly murky, Hansen–Hoi, Gausdal 1987) e5 9 de de 10 fe ♘e8 11 ♗c4! (11 ♗g5 ♕b6 12 ♗e7 ♘xe5 13 ♗xf8 ♔xf8 is a promising exchange sacrifice, trapping the White king in the centre) ♕e7 12 e6 fe 13 0-0 b5 14 ♗b3 with advantage to White, Belyavsky–Christiansen, Moscow 1982.

(c) 6 ... ♘c6 transposes to Chapter 6, line B.

(d) 6 ... ♘a6 (27) and now:

(d1) 7 h3 c5 8 e5 ♘h5 (8 ... ♘d7 9 ed ed 10 ♕d2 ♖e8 11 0-0-0 gives White an edge, but this may be relatively best) 9 ♗xa6 (9 ♔f2 cd 10 ♕xd4 ♘c7 11 g4 ♘e6 12 ♕d2 ♘hxf4 13 ♗xf4 ♘xf4 14 ♕xf4 de gives Black considerable compensation for the piece) ba (9 ... ♘g3?! 10 ♗f1! ♘xh1 11 g4 ♘g3 12 ♗g2 cd 13 ♕xd4 de 14 fe ♕xd4 15 ♗xd4 h5 16 ♔f2 ♖d8 17 ♖d1 hg 18 hg ♗xg4 19 ♔xg3 is good for White, Ligterink–Nunn, IBM II 1975) 10 g4 cd 11 ♕xd4 ♗b7 12 ♔f2 ♘xf4 13 ♗xf4 (13 ♕xf4 de 14 ♕b4 ♖b8 is also unclear) g5? (13 ... f5 was better, but I feel that objectively Black doesn't quite have enough for the sacrifice), Nunn–Adorjan, London 1975, and now 14 ♗xg5 f6 15 ef ♗xf6 16 ♗xf6 ♖xf6 17 ♘d5

♖xf3+ 18 ♔xf3 e6 19 ♔g3 would have won for White.
(d2) **7 e5** ♘g4 8 ♗g1 c5 9 h3 cd 10 ♕xd4 ♘h6 11 0-0-0 ♕a5 (11 ... ♘f5 12 ♕f2 followed by g4) 12 g4 ♗d7 (Hazai–Vadasz, Hungary 1978, continued 12 ... ♘b4 13 a3 ♘c6 14 ♕d5 ♕xd5 15 ♘xd5 de 16 ♘xe5 ♘xe5 17 ♘xe7+ ♔h8 18 fe ♗e6 19 ♗h2 with an awful position for Black) 13 ♘d5! ♕xa2 14 ♘xe7+ ♔h8 15 ♕xd6 ♕a1+ 16 ♔d2 ♕a5+ 17 ♔e3 ♗xg4 (17 ... ♖ad8 18 ♖d5 b5 19 ♕a3 ♕b6+ 20 ♘d4 wins as the White pieces cannot be dislodged from their active posts) 18 hg ♖ad8 19 ♖d5! ♕a4 20 ♕xd8 ♘xg4+ 21 ♔d3 (21 ♔e2? ♕e4+) ♘b4+ 22 ♔e2 ♘c6 (22 ... ♕a6+ 23 ♔e1 ♕a1+ 24 ♖d1 ♘xc2+ 25 ♔e2 wins) 23 ♘g5 h5 24 ♘xf7+ ♔h7 25 ♘g5+ ♔h6 ♘g8+ 1–0, Tsheshkovsky–Vadasz, Malgrat de Mar–Calella 1978.
(e) **6 ...** ♘g4 7 ♗g1 c5 8 h3 (8 ♕d2 cd 9 ♗xd4 e5 10 fe ♘c6 11 ♗g1 ♘cxe5 is less promising, Lanka–Azmaiparashvili, Rostov 1980) ♘h6 (8 ... cd must be better, but 9 ♘xd4 is still good for White) 9 dc ♕a5 10 g4 with a terrible position for Black, Toth–Sterle, corr. 1980.

C1

| 6 | ... | ♘bd7 |
| 7 | ♕d2 | |

Or 7 e5 ♘g4 8 ♗g1 (8 ♗d2?! c5 9 ed?! cd 10 ♘xd4 ♘f2! 11 ♕e2 e5! 12 ♕xf2 ed 13 ♘d5 ♘c5 14 ♘e7+ ♔h8 15 ♘xc8 ♖xc8 16 0-0-0 ♕b6 17 ♖e1? d3 0–1, Enklaar–Donner, Netherlands Ch. 1976) c5 9 e6 (in Cuartas–Pfleger, Tunta 1984, White fell into an excellent trap after 9 ♕e2? cd 10 ♗xd4 de 11 fe ♘dxe5! based on the idea 12 ♗xe5 ♘xe5 13 ♘xe5 ♕a5 followed by ... ♗xc3+; in the game 12 0-0-0 ♕a5 13 h3 ♘xf3 14 ♗xg7 ♕g5+ 15 ♔b1 ♔xg7 16 hg ♘e5 left White a pawn down for nothing) fe 10 ♘g5 ♘df6 11 ♕e2 cd 12 ♘xe6 ♗xe6 (the queen sacrifice 12 ... dc doesn't appear correct) 13 ♕xe6+ ♔h8 14 ♗xd4 was slightly better for White in L. Schneider–Kaiszauri, Eksjo 1980. Unfortunately, this critical line has not received any more practical tests.

| 7 | ... | c5 |
| 8 | 0-0-0 | |

8 dc ♘xc5 9 e5 ♘fe4 10 ♘xe4 ♘xe4 11 ♕b4 d5 12 ♗d3 b6 13 0-0 (13 ♗xe4 de 14 ♕xe4 ♗f5 15 ♕a4 gives Black some play for the pawn, but with ♘d4 coming I am not sure it is really enough) ♕c7 14 ♖ae1 ♗b7 15 ♖e2 with an edge for White, Khalifman–Azmaiparashvili, USSR Ch. 1986, or 8 d5 a6 9 e5 (9 a4 looks much better; the knight on d7 is badly placed as ... e6 cannot be played while d6 is hanging) de 10 fe ♘g4 11 e6 fe 12 de ♘de5 13 ♕xd8 ♖xd8 14 ♗xc5 ♗xe6 and Black's

active pieces are more important than the isolated e-pawn, Haik-Seret, Cannes 1987.

    8 ...   ♘g4 *(28)*

8 ... b6 (8 ... cd 9 ♗xd4 e5 10 fe ♘g4 11 ♔b1 ♘gxe5 12 ♗b5 ♘xf3 13 gf ♘e5 14 ♗e2 was Balashov–Gipslis, USSR 1981, and now 14 ... ♗e6? 15 f4 ♗h6 16 h4! ♘c6 17 ♗e3 ♗g7 18 f5 gave White a decisive attack, but even 14 ... ♕h4 would have been somewhat better for White) 9 e5 ♘g4 10 ♗g1 ♗b7 11 ♕e2 cd 12 ♘xd4 ♘h6 13 ed ed 14 h4 ♘f6 15 ♕d2 ♘h5 16 ♗c4 d5 17 ♗b3 ♘g3 18 ♖h3 ♘e4 was level in Hübner–Pfleger, Bundesliga 1983/4.

    9   ♗g1

9 dc ♘xe3 10 ♕xe3 ♘xc5 (it is strange to give up the black-squared bishop, but White does gain time) 11 e5 ♕a5 12 ♔b1 de (12 ... ♗e6 13 ♘d4 de 14 fe is also unclear) 13 ♖d5 b6 14 ♘xe5 ♗b7 15 ♘c4 ♕xc3! 16 bc ♗xd5 gave Black good compensation for the material sacrificed, Sideif-Zaid – Gipslis, USSR 1983.

    9 ...   cd
   10   ♘xd4

10 ♗xd4 e5 11 ♗g1 ef 12 ♕xd6, K. Schmidt–Keene, Aarhus 1983, and now 12 ... ♘e3 13 ♗xe3 fe 14 ♗b5 ♗xc3 15 bc ♕a5 16 ♗xd7 ♖d8 17 ♕e7 ♕xc3! 18 ♕xd8+ ♔g7 19 ♔b1 ♕b4+ would have led to a draw according to Keene. In the game 12 ... ♗xc3?! 13 bc ♘e3 14 ♕xf4! ♘xd1 15 ♗d4 was a dangerous sacrifice.

   10 ...   e5
   11   ♘de2

11 ♘f3 transposes to the last note.

   11 ...   ef
   12   ♘xf4   ♕a5
   13   ♗d4   ♘ge5
   14   ♔b1

This position is very slightly better for White, e.g.:

(1) **14** ... ♘f6 15 ♗e2 ♗d7 16 ♘fd5! ♘xd5 17 ♘xd5 ♕xd2 18 ♖xd2 ♖fd8, Mikhalchishin–Azmaiparashvili, Baku 1983, and now 19 ♗e3 would have given White the edge.

(2) **14** ... ♘c5 15 ♗e2 (15 ♘fd5 ♕d8 16 ♗e3 ♗g4 17 ♗e2 ♗xe2 18 ♕xe2 ♕h4 19 h3 ♖ae8 20 g4 ♘c6 21 ♗f2 ♕d8 and Black equalized in Belyavsky–Azmaiparashvili, USSR Ch. 1983) ♘e6 16 ♗e3 ♘xf4 17 ♗xf4 ♗e6 18 ♘d5 ♕a4 19 ♕b4 ♕xb4 20 ♘xb4 and again White has a tiny

endgame advantage, Sax–Ftacnik, Hastings 1983/4.

I am doubtful about the merits of 6 ... ♘bd7. Perhaps the main line isn't too bad for Black, but there are a number of untested ideas for White which appear quite promising.

| 6 | ... | b6 (29) |

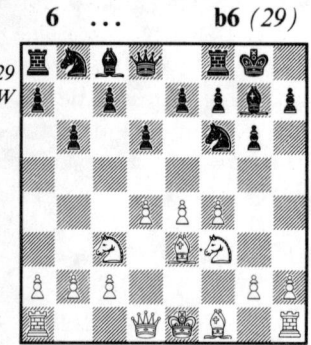

| 7 | e5 |

Almost universally played. After 7 ♗d3 ♗b7 (7 ... c5 looks good; 8 d5 e6 is fine for Black, while after 8 e5 ♘g4 9 ♗g1 cd Black is quite prepared to sacrifice the exchange should White play ♗e4) 8 f5 (8 ♕d2 c5 9 d5 e6 10 de fe 11 ♘g5 ♕e7 12 0-0-0 was double-edged in Zagorovsky–Augustin, corr. 1980) c5 9 fg hg 10 d5 ♘bd7 11 0-0 ♖e8?! 12 ♘g5 a6 13 ♕e1 ♘f8 14 ♕h4 ♕d7 15 h3 White had a strong attack in Sigurjonsson – Fries-Nielsen, Esbjerg 1978, but there are a number of possible improvements, e.g. 8 ... gf!? 9 ef c5 or 11 ... ♘g4.

| 7 | ... | ♘g4 |
| 8 | ♗g1 | c5 |

8 ... de (8 ... ♗b7 9 h3 ♘h6 10 ♕d2 c5 11 d5 looks doubtful because compared to the main line Black has spent a tempo on the not very useful move ... ♗b7; nevertheless 11 ... ♘a6 12 ♗xa6?! ♗xa6 13 g4 de 14 fe f5 15 g5 ♘f7 16 ♗h2 b5 was fine for Black in Beckemeyer–Bischoff, Bundesliga 1984) 9 de ♗b7 10 ♗d3 ♘a6 11 ♕e2?! (after 11 a3 Black has trouble justifying his play) ♘b4 12 ♗e4 ♗a6 13 ♕d2 with an unclear position, Balashov–Gufeld, USSR 1981.

| 9 | h3 |

9 ♗c4 cd 10 ♕xd4 ♗b7 (10 ... ♘c6 11 ♕e4 ♗b7 12 ♗d5 ♖c8 13 0-0-0 e6 15 ♗xc6 ♗xc6 15 ♕e2 d5 16 ♘d4 gives White an edge) 11 h3 ♘h6 12 0-0-0 ♘c6 13 ♕f2 ♖c8 14 ♗d5 b5 with a murky position, Mikhalchishin–Sznapik, Dortmund 1984.

| 9 | ... | ♘h6 |
| 10 | d5 (30) |

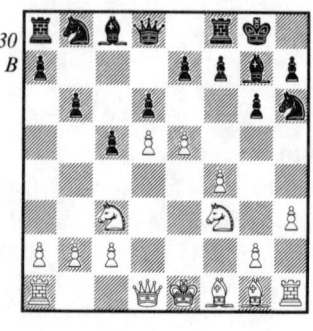

| 10 | ... | ♘d7 |

10 ... ♘f5 11 ♗f2 de **12** fe **♘d7 13 ♕e2 ♗b7 14 0-0-0 ♕b8 15 g4! ♘d4 16 ♘xd4** cd **17 ♗xd4 ♗xe5 18 ♗g2 ♗xd4 19 ♖xd4 ♕d6 20 ♖e1 ♖fe8 21 ♘b5!** was good for White in Balashov–Timman, Tilburg 1977, one of the earliest games with 6 ♗e3. Although improvements such as 13 ... ♕c7 have been suggested, it looks wrong to exchange on e5 and subsequent games have avoided giving White a mobile d-pawn. One interesting idea is **10 ... ♘a6**, trying to put pressure on d5 as opposed to e5. L. Schneider–Short, Hamburg 1981, continued **11 ♕d2 ♘c7 12 g4?** (too ambitious; 12 0-0-0 ♗b7 13 ♗e3 is sounder) **♗b7 13 ♗e3** de **14 0-0-0 ♘xd5! 15 ♘xd5 e6 16 g5 ♘f5 17 ♘f6+ ♗xf6 18 ♕f2 ♘d4 19 ♗xd4** cd **20** gf **♕xf6** with an army of pawns for the piece.

11 ♕e2

11 ♗h2 ♕c7 (or 11 ... ♘f5 12 ♗b5 de 13 fe e6 14 ♕d3 ♘d4! with equality, Cuartas–Nunn, England 1980) 12 ♕e2 transposes to the main line.

11 ... ♕c7

11 ... b5!? 12 0-0-0 (12 ♘xb5 ♗a6 and 12 ♕xb5 ♖b8 are fine for Black) b4 13 ♘e4 ♘b6 14 g4 ♗b7 15 c3? (15 c4! was better, transposing to the game) bc? (why not 15 ... ♗xd5?) 16 ♘xc3 de 17 ♘xe5 ♘xd5 18 ♘xd5 ♗xd5 19 ♗g2 e6 20 ♘c6 ♕b6 21 ♗xd5 ed 22 ♘e7+ ♔h8 23 ♘xd5 was Radulov–Sznapik, Warsaw 1979. The feeble knight on h6 is balanced by White's exposed king, so the position may be assessed as equal.

12 ♗h2 a6!

Without more ado Black starts his queenside counterplay. Since White is committed to 0-0-0 he cannot contemplate 13 a4. The move 12 ... ♘f5 is possible but risky, e.g. 13 0-0-0 a6 14 g4 ♘d4 15 ♘xd4 cd 16 ♖xd4 de 17 ♖e4 f6 18 ♖c4 ♕b8 19 ♖c6 ♗b7 20 ♗g2 b5 was very double-edged in Peters–Botterill, Hastings 1978/9. 12 ... a6 is sounder.

13 g4 b5

14 0-0-0 ♗b7 15 ♔b1, Chandler–Botterill, British Ch. 1983, and now 15 ... ♕a5 followed by ... ♘b6 would have been at least equal for Black. In the resulting position, with attacks on opposite wings, White's queenside is virtually devoid of defensive pieces and although White's build-up looks impressive it isn't easy for him to break through.

6 ... b6 leads to very sharp and unbalanced positions, but on the available evidence Black need not be afraid of White's massive pawn centre.

The best answer to 6 ♗e3 is a matter of taste, but 6 ... b6 is the front runner, with 6 ... c5, 6 ... ♘c6 and 6 ... ♘bd7 close behind.

4 Austrian Attack: 5 ♘f3 c5 6 dc

5 ... c5 must be considered Black's most reliable answer to the Austrian Attack. Black immediately breaks up White's pawn centre and heads for a Sicilian-type structure. In the next chapter we look at 6 ♗b5+, an attempt to cut across Black's strategic ambitions, but in this chapter we examine 6 dc, which forces Black to spend time with his queen regaining the pawn. Unfortunately for White the arrival of the queen on c5 prevents castling, so White has to return the time gained to bring his king into safety. This is the important difference between 5 ♘f3 c5 6 dc and 5 ♘f3 0-0 6 ♗e2 c5 7 dc, as analysed in Chapter 3. Black hopes that the bishop on g7 will become powerful on the open long diagonal, and in particular Black aims to control the square d4. The elimination of the knight on f3 by ... ♗g4xf3 is therefore part of Black's plan, while White often tries to initiate a kingside attack by ♕e1–h4, f5 etc. There have been very few new ideas in the 6 dc line since my earlier book appeared and we may evaluate the line as being very slightly better for White, but everything depends on the critical position at move 17. In any case this is a safe option for White, since he has few losing chances in the main line.

1 e4 d6 2 d4 ♘f6 3 ♘c3 g6 4 f4 ♗g7 5 ♘f3 c5

    6 dc   **♕a5**
    7 ♗d3

After 7 ♘d2 ♕xc5 8 ♘b3 ♕c7 9 ♗e2 we have reached a Sicilian Dragon position in which White has played ♘b3 voluntarily, while Black is committed to ... ♕c7. I suspect that White's concession is slightly more significant. Perhaps 9 ... ♘bd7 is the most accurate move, but Balinas–Chernin, Bangalore 1981, continued 9 ... 0-0 10 ♗e3 a6 11 g4 ♗e6, and now 12 f5 ♗c4 13 ♕d2 followed by 0-0-0 would have been unclear. **7 ♗d3** ♕xc5 8 ♗e3 ♕a5 9 ♕b5+ gives White no advantage, e.g. 9 ... ♕xb5 10 ♘xb5 (or 10 ♗xb5+ ♘c6 11 0-0-0 0-0 12 ♘d5 ♘xd5 13 ed ♘b4 14 a3 ♘a6 15 h3 ♘c7 16 ♗a4 ♗f5 17 ♗b3 ♖fc8 with good counterplay, Radulov–van der Sterren, Albena 1983) ♘a6 11 ♗d3 0-0 12 ♗xa7 (12 ♘xa7 ♗d7 13 ♘b5 ♘xe4 is no better) ♘h5 13 ♗e3 ♗xb2 14 ♖b1 ♗g7 with an equal ending, A. Sokolov–M. Gurevich, USSR Ch. 1985.

7 ... ♕xc5
8 ♕e2 0-0

Black can try other move orders such as 8 ... ♗g4 or 8 ... ♘c6, but there is no advantage in doing so.

9 ♗e3 *(31)*

9 ... ♕a5

This move is now almost universal. Formerly 9 ... ♕c7 was often played, but the queen is more actively placed on a5 and there is no reason to go back to c7. After 9 ... ♕c7 10 0-0 ♘bd7 (Black is aiming for ... e5, but the best he can hope for is a kind of 6 f4 Najdorf; 10 ... ♗g4 11 ♕e1 ♗xf3 12 ♖xf3 a6 13 ♕h4 ♘bd7 14 g4 e6 15 ♖af1 was good for White in van der Wiel–Wilder, Lone Pine 1979) 11 ♔h1 (after 11 ♕e1 a6 White should play 12 a4 or 12 ♔h1; in Byrne–Christiansen, USA Ch. 1978 the interesting idea **11 ♘b5** ♕b8 12 c4 was played and after 12 ... b6 13 ♘c3 ♗b7 14 ♖ae1 e6 15 ♗d2 a6 16 ♘g5 h6 17 ♘h3 ♕c7 18 ♘f2 ♕c6 19 ♕f3 White had a slight advantage) e5 (Stean–Sigurjonsson, Hastings 1974/5, went 11 ... e6 12 ♕e1 a6 13 ♕h4 b5 14 e5 ♘e8 15 ♘g5 h6 16 ♗xg6! fg 17 ♘xe6 ♕c6 18 ♖ad1 ♗b7 19 ♘d5 with an excellent position for White) and now we have a very similar situation to the 6 f4 Najdorf position arising from line A of Chapter 3. There would in fact be an exact transposition after 12 ♕e1 a6 13 ♕h4 b5 14 fe de, so the only question is whether Black can avoid this. In Tsheshkovsky–Peev, Moscow 1977, Black tried 12 fe (12 ♕e1 is probably more accurate) de 13 ♕e1 b6 (Yudovic gives 13 ... ♘c5 as equal, but it seems to me that 14 ♕h4 followed by ♗g5 is still a serious worry for Black) 14 ♕h4 ♗b7, but after 15 ♗g5 he played the horrible 15 ... a6? and was crushed: 16 ♘d2 b5 (16 ... ♘h5 17 ♗e7 ♖fc8 18 ♗c4 or 16 ... ♕c6 17 ♘d5!) 17 ♗xf6 ♘xf6 18 ♖xf6 ♗xf6 19 ♕xf6 ♖ad8 20 ♖f1 ♖fe8 21 ♘d1 ♖d6 22 ♕f2 f5 23 ef e4 24 fg 1–0.

It seems to me that Black has no sensible way to avoid the transposition, so we must evaluate this line as good for White.

It is also worth mentioning **9 ... ♕b4**. Although this is clearly very risky, no really convincing refutation has been put forward. After 10 0-0 (10 ♖b1? ♘xe4 and 10 0-0-0? ♘xe4 are to be avoided, while 10 a3 ♕xb2 11 ♗d2 ♘xe4+ 12 ♘xe4 d5 13 ♖hb1 de 14 ♖xb2 ef 15 ♕xf3 ♗xb2 is unclear) ♕xb2 11 ♘b5 ♘e8 we have:

(1) **12 a3** ♕xa1 13 ♖xa1 ♗xa1 14 c3 a6 15 ♘a7 and I am not sure that White has the advantage, e.g. 15 ... ♗g4 16 ♕c2 (16 ♕e1 ♗xf3 17 gf ♗b2 or 16 ♗d4 ♘d7 intending ... e5 or ... ♘c5) ♗xf3 17 gf ♘d7 18 ♕c1 ♘c5 19 ♗xc5 dc 20 ♘c6 bc 21 ♕xa1 ♘f6 and Black is better.

(2) **12 e5** ♕b4 13 ♖ab1 (13 ♘xa7 is preferred by Keene and Botterill, but even here 13 ... ♘c6 14 ♖ab1 ♕a3 15 ♘xc8 ♖xc8 16 ♖xb7 de is unclear) ♕a5 14 f5 ♗xf5 15 ♗xf5 gf 16 ed e6 17 ♕c4 ♘d7 with a murky position, Thipsay–Sturua, Frunze 1985.

10 0-0

10 ♗d2 looks artificial and in Dvoris–Chernin, USSR 1982, Black was slightly better after 10 ... ♗g4 11 h3 (11 ♘d5 ♕d8 12 ♘e3 ♗xf3 13 ♕xf3 ♘c6 is fine for Black) ♗xf3 12 ♕xf3 ♘c6 13 0-0-0 ♖fc8 14 ♔b1 ♖ab8 15 ♘d5 ♕a4 16 c3?! (White should have played for a draw by 16 ♘c3) b5.

10 ... ♗g4 *(32)*

If Black plays 10 ... ♘c6 then White should prevent ... ♗g4 with 11 h3. Black is left without a natural square for the c8 bishop, for example 10 ... ♘c6 11 h3 ♘b4 (or 11 ... ♘h5 12 ♕e1 ♗h6 13 b4! ♕d8 14 b5 ♘b4 15 f5 ♗xe3+ 16 ♕xe3 ♕b6 17 ♘d4 ♘xd3, Ljubojevic–Bujupi, Yugoslavia 1975 and now simply 18 cd is good for White) 12 ♕f2 (12 a3 also turned out well in Ljubojevic–Torre, Manila 1974 which went 12 ... ♘xd3 13 cd ♗d7 14 ♕f2 b6 15 e5 ♘e8 16 b4 ♕a6 17 ♘d5 e6 18 ♘e7+ ♔h8 19 ♘g5 h6 20 ♕h4 ♕xd3 21 ♖f3 with a very dangerous attack) ♗e6 13 ♘g5 ♘xd3 14 cd ♗d7 15 ♖ae1 ♗c6 16 ♕h4 h6 17 ♘f3 and again White has a very promising position, Klovan–Rumov, USSR 1977. The problem with 10 ... ♘c6 is that without the exchange on f3 Black is unable to get a firm grip on the central dark squares and this makes it hard for him to develop counterplay.

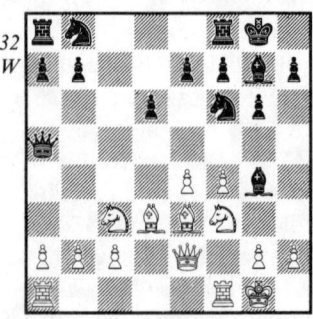

32 W

11 h3

There have been various at-

tempts to manage without this loss of tempo, but none of them has had a significant impact on Black's position:
(a) 11 ♖ad1 ♘c6 12 ♗c4 ♘h5 13 ♗b3 (13 ♖d5 ♕c7 14 ♖g5 ♗xf3 15 ♖xf3 ♘d4 16 ♗xd4 ♗xd4+ 17 ♔h1 ♘xf4! 18 ♖xf4 ♗xc3 is good for Black, Vilagos–Stipkovic, corr. 1985, since 19 bc fails to 19 ... d5; however this didn't stop Black from losing in two moves by 19 ♖h4 ♗f6?? 20 ♕h5 1–0) ♗xc3 14 bc ♕xc3 15 f5 ♘a5 16 ♗d4 ♕c7 17 h3 ♘xb3 18 cb ♗xf3 19 ♕xf3 ♘f6 (19 ... ♖ac8! is unclear) 20 ♕f4 with enough play for the pawn, Gligoric–Hort, Skopje Ol. 1972.
(b) 11 a3 ♘c6 12 ♔h1 ♘d7 13 ♕e1 ♘c5 14 b4 ♘xd3 15 cd ♕d8 16 ♖c1 ♗xf3 17 ♖xf3 e6 (Black prepares to answer 18 ♖h3 by ... f5. White's main positional threat is to activate the bishop on e3 by playing f5 and it is a useful defensive resource to play ... f5 and render this advance impossible) 18 ♘e2 a6 19 d4 ♘e7 20 ♗f2 f5 with an equal position, Ljubojevic–Timman, Niksic 1978.
(c) 11 ♕e1 ♘c6 12 ♘d2 ♗d7 (White has avoided the exchange of his knight, but at too high a cost in time) 13 a3 ♘g4 14 ♘c4 ♕h5 15 h3 ♘xe3 16 ♘xe3 ♕c5 17 f5? ♗xc3 18 bc ♘e5 with a clear positional plus for Black, Kavalek–Torre, Manila 1976.
(d) 11 ♕f2 ♗xf3 12 ♕xf3 was played in Sznapik–Pein, Manchester 1982. The only difference between this position and the main line is that White's pawn is on h2 instead of h3. Sznapik tried to make use of this by 12 ... ♘c6 13 ♔h1 ♖ac8 14 a3 ♘d7 15 ♕h3, but after 15 ... ♗xc3 (other moves are possible, but there is nothing wrong with taking) 16 bc ♘c5 17 ♗d2 ♕a4 Black had a fully satisfactory position.
(e) 11 ♘d1!? (White intends ♘f2 to make Black exchange on f3, coupled with c3 to prevent occupation of d4) ♘c6 12 c3 (12 ♘f2 ♗xf3 13 ♕xf3 ♘b4 is level) e5! 13 ♘f2 ef 14 ♗xf4 ♗xf3 15 ♕xf3 ♘e5 16 ♗xe5 ♕xe5 17 ♗c4 ♖ae8 with equality, Dolmatov–M. Gurevich, Moscow 1987.

11	...	♗xf3
12	♕xf3	♘c6
13	a3	*(33)*

A useful semi-waiting move to prevent ... ♘b4. Not, however, 13 ♘e2 ♘d7 14 c3?? ♘de5 winning, Ljubojevic–Timman, Tilburg 1978 and Zapata–Chernin,

Cienfuegos 1981 (!), nor **13 f5** ♘e5 14 ♕f2 b5 when Black has an e5 square and a queenside initiative. After **13 ♔h1** ♘d7 14 ♗d2, Thipsay–Koshy, India 1987, Black could have transposed back to the main line by 14 ... ♕b6, but 14 ... ♘c5 15 ♖ad1 ♘d4 16 ♕f2 ♘xd3 17 cd f5!= as played was also effective.

13 ... ♘d7
14 ♗d2

14 b4 ♕d8 15 ♘e2 ♗xa1 16 ♖xa1 cannot be recommended, even though White did manage to win in Ljubojevic–Torre, Manila 1975, while **14 ♘e2** ♗xb2 15 ♖ab1 ♕xa3 is just unsound.

14 ... ♕b6+

Although this has been played most frequently, 14 ... ♕d8 may be just as good, although this depends on whether White can find an answer to 15 ... e6!? below. After 14 ... ♕d8 White may play 15 ♔h1 ♖ac8 (15 ... e6!? appears better, e.g. 16 ♗c4 a6 17 ♗a2 ♕c7 18 ♖ad1 b5 19 ♗e1 ♘b6 20 ♕d3 ♖ad8 and Black is at least equal, Arnason–J. Kristiansen, Gausdal 1987) 16 ♖ab1 (16 ♕f2 was played in Ghinda–Grünberg, Romania Ch. 1974, and after 16 ... ♘c5 17 ♗e3 b6 18 ♖ad1 ♕e8 19 f5 ♘xd3 20 cd gf?! 21 ef ♔h8 22 ♘d5 ♗f6 23 ♘xf6 ef White was winning, but Black's play was very weak in this example) a6 (16 ... ♘b6 17 ♘e2 ♘d4 18 ♘xd4 ♗xd4 19 e5! de 20 f5 e6 21 fe f5 22 ♗h6, Unzicker–Timman, Nice Ol. 1974 and 16 ... ♘a5 17 ♕e2 ♘b6 18 ♘d1 ♘ac4 19 ♗c1 ♕c7 20 b3 ♘a5 21 c4 ♘c6 22 ♘e3, Wittmann–Riedner, Graz 1987, were both good for White) 17 ♕f2 (17 ♖fd1 e6 18 ♘e2 ♘c5 19 ♗e1 d5 20 c4 ♘xe4 21 ♗xe4 de 22 ♕xe4 ♕c7 was level in Arnason–Rukavina, Bor 1983) e6 18 ♘e2 ♘c5 19 f5 ♘xd3 20 cd ef 21 ef ♖e8 22 fg fg 23 ♕f7+ ♔h8 24 ♗c3 ♗xc3 25 ♘xc3 and White maintains some advantage owing to the exposed Black king, Botterill–Rukavina, Birmingham 1977.

15 ♔h1 ♘c5
16 ♖ab1

In Hort–Suttles, Zagreb 1972, White tried 16 b4, but 16 ... ♘xd3 17 ♕xd3 ♕d4 seems to equalize at once.

16 ... ♘xd3
17 cd (34)

17 ♕xd3 ♖ac8 18 ♘d5 was played in Kovacevic–Inkiov, Plovdiv 1983, and now 18 ... ♕d4! was best since 19 ♕e2 may be met by 19 ... f5 and Black extracts his queen.

We now arrive at the critical position of the 6 dc variation. Black has secured control of d4, but he faces the dangerous plan of f5 followed by a kingside attack based on ♗g5, ♘d5 and ♕g3–h4. It will be seen below that attempting to gain counterplay by 17 ... ♕b3 is too slow, so Black must employ more direct measures against the threat of 18 f5. This reduces his choice to 17 ... e6 or 17 ... f5. After 17 ... e6 White can try to play 18 f5 in any case; whether or not this succeeds depends on some long tactical variations. 17 ... f5 is sounder, but White can try Plaskett's interesting 18 g4!?

34
B

17 ... e6

This has been played frequently, but it appears tactically unsound. Of the other options 17 ... f5 is the best; the resulting positions are quite sharp, but they give White at most a very slight advantage.

(a) **17 ... ♕b3** (this is bad) 18 f5 ♕c2 (18 ... ♖fe8 19 ♗g5 ♖ac8 29 ♘d5 ♘e5 21 ♕g3 f6 22 ♗f4 ♘xd3?! 23 fg ♘c5 is Adorjan–Suttles, Hastings 1973/4, and now 24 ♕g4! e6 25 ♗h6! ♗xh6 26 ♘xf6+ ♔h8 27 ♘xe8 ♖xe8 28 ♕h5 would have won even more quickly than 24 gh+ as played) 19 ♗g5 ♘e5 20 ♕g3 f6 (White stands very well once Black has been forced to play this move) 21 ♗f4 gf 22 d4 (22 ef ♘xd3) ♘g6 23 ♖f2 ♕b3 24 ef ♘xf4 25 ♖xf4 ♖f7 26 d5 a5 27 a4 ♖c8 28 ♕e3 ♕c2 29 ♖f2! ♖xc3 30 ♕e1 ♖xh3+ 31 gh ♕d3 32 ♕f1 ♕xd5+ 33 ♕g2 ♕c5 34 ♖g1 ♔h8 35 ♖f3 ♕c6 36 ♖c3 ♕d7 37 ♕d5 ♖f8 38 ♖cg3 1–0, for if 38 ... ♖g8 39 ♕xg8+ mates, Nunn–Torre, London 1977.

(b) **17 ... f5!** In my earlier book this was recommended even though no practical tests had occurred. A few games have now been played, but they have not served to clarify the correct evaluation.

Here are the possibilities:

(b1) **18 g4** must be the critical move, when Plaskett–Carr, British Ch. 1986, continued 18 ... ♘d4 19 ♕g3 fg 20 hg e6 21 f5 gf 22 gf ♔h8 with a highly unclear position; the finish was 23 ♕h3 ef 24 ef d5 25 ♖f4 ♗e5 26 ♖h4 ♖f7 27 ♖h6 ♕c5 28 ♖e1 ♘xf5 29 ♖xe5 ♖g8 30 ♗e3 ♘xe3 31 ♕xe3 ½–½ in view of 31 ... ♕xe3 32 ♖xe3 d4. The move 18 ... ♘d4 may be wrong since the knight doesn't create any threats on d4, but the queen is driven to the superior square g3. After 18 ... fg 19 hg e6 20 f5, for example, Black may play 20 ... d5!? with great complications.

(b2) **18 ♘d5 ♕d8** 19 ef (19 ♗c3 e6 20 ♘b4) gf 20 ♗c3 e6 21 ♘b4 ♖c8 22 ♖bc1 ♕d7 with a barely perceptible edge for White, Balashov–Diesen, Karlovac 1979.

18 f5!

After this events develop by force. Balashov–Timman, Bugojno 1978, went **18 ♘e2** ♖fe8 19 ♗c3 ♖ac8 20 ♕g3 f5 21 h4 d5 22 ♗xg7 ♔xg7 23 h5 and now 23 ... de 24 de ♖cd8 would have been level. However, **18 g4** is worth considering; the reply 18 ... f5 is similar to Plaskett–Carr in the last note.

18	...	ef
19	ef	♘d4
20	♕g3	♘xf5

20 ... ♗e5 21 ♕g4 ♕b3 22 ♗f4 ♔h8 23 ♗xe5+ de 24 f6 was better for White in Arnason–Pergericht, Bela Crkva 1983.

| 21 | ♖xf5 | gf |
| 22 | ♘d5 | f4 |

The only move, e.g. 22 ... ♕d4 23 ♗c3 f4 24 ♕g4 f5 25 ♕g5 h6 26 ♕g6 or 22 ... ♕d8 23 ♗h6

23 ♘f6+

23 ♗xf4 ♕c4 is unclear, while 23 ♕g4 f5 24 ♘xb6 fg 25 ♘xa8 ♖xa8 should lead to a draw.

| 23 | ... | ♔h8 |

24 ♕h4 h6 *(35)* and now:

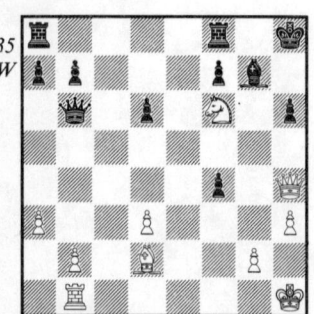

(a) **25 ♗c3?!** (threatening 26 ♘d5 and 27 ♕xh6+) ♕b5! (not 25 ... ♕e3 26 ♘g4 ♕e6 27 ♗f6! ♔h7 28 ♖e1, nor 25 ... d5 26 ♕xf4 d4 27 ♗xd4 ♕e6 28 ♗c3 ♖ad8 29 ♖e1 ♕d6 30 ♕f5 ♕xd3 31 ♖e4 ♕d1+ 32 ♔h2 ♕d6+ 33 g3 and White wins in both cases) 26 ♘d5 f6 with unclear complications, Stoica–Boudy, Varna 1980.

(b) **25 ♕xf4!** ♕b5 26 ♕h4 ♕f5 27 ♗xh6 ♗xf6 28 ♗g5+ ♕h7 29 ♗xf6+ ♔g8 30 ♕d4! (in return for a very small sacrifice White has an enormous attack; I cannot even see how Black can defend against the immediate threat of ♖f1–f4) ♖ae8 31 ♖f1 ♖e6 32 ♖f4 ♖xf6 33 ♕xf6 1–0, A. Arnason–Baumgartner, corr. 1981.

The fate of this line rests on the position after 17 ... f5. The lines with 6 ♗b5+ have run into difficulties recently, so it could be that 6 dc is due for a revival.

5 | Austrian Attack: 5 ♘f3 c5 6 ♗b5+ (and 6 e5)

In the years since *The Pirc for the Tournament Player* appeared, 6 ♗b5+ has been one of the most popular lines in the whole Pirc. New ideas for both colours have repeatedly altered the assessment of the entire variation. At the time of writing, a stunning innovation by Seirawan has revived Black's side of the argument, but I have no doubt that this is far from the last word.

1 e4 d6 2 d4 ♘f6 3 ♘c3 g6 4 f4 ♗g7 5 ♘f3 c5

6 ♗b5+

6 e5 is a significant alternative. After 6 ... ♘fd7 *(36)* White may play:

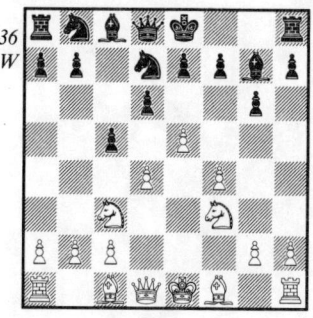

(a) **7 ed** 0-0 8 ♗e3 (8 de ♕xe7+ is far too dangerous, while after 8 dc ♘xc5 9 ♗e2 ed 10 0-0 ♘c6 11 ♗c4 ♗g4 12 h3 ♗xf3 13 ♕xf3 ♘d4 Black's active pieces are more important than the isolated pawn, Jongman–Sprenger, corr. 1981) ed 9 ♕d2 ♘c6 and Matulovic–Sigurjonsson, Vraca 1975 continued 10 ♗b5 (10 0-0-0 ♕a5 11 f5 ♘f6 12 fg hg 13 ♗h6 ♗g4 14 ♗xg7 ♔xg7 15 d5?! ♗xf3 16 gf ♘d4 17 ♕f4 ♖fe8 18 ♔b1 ♖e5 ∓ is Sax–Sigurjonsson, Vraca 1975) ♕b6 11 0-0-0 ♘f6 12 dc dc 13 ♗xc6 ♕xc6 14 ♘e5 ♕c7 15 h3 ♗e6 with equality.

(b) **7 e6** fe 8 ♘g5 ♘f6 9 dc and now:

(b1) **9 ... 0-0** 10 cd ed 11 ♗d3 (11 ♗c4 d5 12 ♗b3 should be met by 12 ... ♘c6 transposing to line b2; after 12 ... ♕b6?! 13 ♕e2 ♘c6 14 ♘a4 ♕c7 15 ♗e3 e5 16 0-0-0 White had good attacking chances in Shirazi–Matzner, Los Angeles 1981) ♘a6 12 0-0 ♘c7 13 ♗d2 ♘cd5 14 ♘xd5 ♘xd5 15 ♘xh7!? ♔xh7 16 ♕h5+ ♔g8 17 ♗xg6 ♘f6 18 ♕h4 with chances for both sides, Heidsiek–M.

Fischer, corr. 1984.
(b2) 9 ... ♘c6 (this move-order is more accurate) 10 cd (10 ♗c4 d5 11 ♗b5 d4 12 ♗xc6+ bc 13 ♘e2 ♕a5+ 14 ♕d2 ♕xc5 15 ♘xd4 ♕d5 16 c3 0-0 17 0-0 ♘h5 18 ♕e2 e5! was level in Vasiukov–Tseshkovsky, USSR Ch. 1974, while 10 ♗d3 dc 11 0-0 0-0 12 ♕e1 ♘b4 13 ♘xe6 ♘xd3 14 cd ♗xe6 15 ♕xe6+ ♚h8 was slightly better for Black, Hartston–Timman, Hastings 1973/4) ed 11 ♗c4 (11 ♗d3 0-0 is similar to b1, but Black can try 11 ... ♕b6) d5 12 ♗b3 0-0 13 0-0 ♚h8 14 ♚h1 d4 15 ♘e2 ♘d5 16 c3 dc 17 bc h6 with an equal position, Shirazi–Christiansen, Palo Alto 1981.
(c) 7 dc de 8 fe ♘xe5 (the safest, although 8 ... 0-0 9 e6 fe 10 ♗c4 ♘xc5 is also possible; Black should avoid 8 ... ♘c6 9 e6 fe 10 ♘g5 ♘d4 11 ♗e3 ♘f5 12 ♘xe6 ♗xc3+ 13 ♗d2! and White won a queen in Velimirovic–Marangunic, Yugoslavia 1982) 9 ♕xd8+ ♚xd8 10 ♘xe5 ♗xe5 11 ♘e4 f6 12 c3 ♗e6 with equality, Velimirovic–Adorjan, Skopje 1976.
(d) 7 ♗c4 cd 8 ♘g5!? (8 ♕xd4 0-0 9 ♕e4 ♘c6 10 e6 fe 11 ♗xe6+ ♚h8 12 ♕e2 ♘c5 is fine for Black, Ljubojevic–Jansa, Skopje 1976) e6? 9 ♘ce4! de 10 ♘d6+ ♚e7 11 ♘gxf7 ♕a5+ 12 ♗d2 with a crushing attack, Bauer–Ditt, Bundesliga 1982. Black has a number of better 8th moves, 8 ... 0-0! being the simplest, when I cannot see how White can justify his play (9 e6 dc).

6 ... ♗d7
7 e5

7 ♗xd7+ had a brief burst of popularity, but Black faces no special problems:
(a) 7 ... ♘fxd7 8 d5 *(37)* and now:

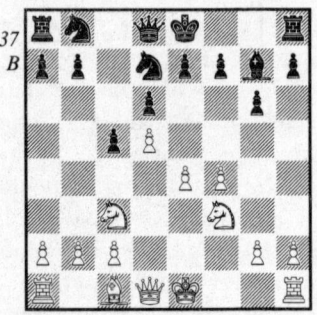

(a1) 8 ... b5?! (after this White is virtually forced to sacrifice a pawn) 9 ♘xb5 ♕a5+ 10 ♘c3 ♗xc3+ 11 bc ♕xc3+ 12 ♗d2 ♕c4 13 ♕e2 ♕xc2 and it is an open question whether White has enough compensation. Van der Wiel–van der Sterren, Baden Baden 1981 went on 14 e5 (or else ... ♘f6) 0-0 15 0-0 ♘b6 16 f5 ♘xd5 with unclear complications.
(a2) 8 ... ♘a6 9 0-0 0-0 10 ♕e2 ♘c7 11 a4! (11 ♖d1? b5! 12 ♘xb5 ♘xb5 13 ♕xb5 ♖b8 14 ♕e2 ♗xb2 15 ♗xb2 ♖xb2 ∓ Savon–Korchnoi, USSR Ch. 1973 and Black won in 44 moves) and it is

Austrian Attack: 5 ♘f3 c5 6 ♗b5+ (and 6 e5)

not easy for Black to equalize, for example 11 ... a6 (11 ... b6 12 ♖d1 a6 13 ♔h1 ♖b8 14 a5 b5 15 e5 b4 16 ♘e4 ♘b5 17 e6 fe 18 de ♘f6 19 ♘xc5 winning a pawn which was later converted into victory in van der Sterren–van Wijgerden, IBM B 1978) 12 ♖d1 ♖b8 (12 ... b6 13 e5 ♕c8 14 ♘e4! de 15 d6 ed 16 ♘xd6 ♕b8 17 ♘g5! with a clear plus for White, van der Wiel–Larsen, Amsterdam 1980) 13 a5 b5 14 ab ♘xb6 15 ♗d2 ♕c8 16 ♗e1! ♕d7 (16 ... ♘b5 17 e5 ±) 17 ♕d3 ♘c8 18 ♖a2 ♘a7 19 e5 ♘ab5 20 ♘e2 ♘a7 21 c4 ♘c8 22 ♘g3 e6?! 23 ed ♕xd6 24 ♘e4 ♕b6 25 ♗a5 ♕a7 26 d6 ♘d5 27 d7! (27 cd? c4+) ♘ce7 28 d8=(♕) ♖fxd8 29 ♗xd8 ♘c6 30 ♗h4 ♘db4 31 ♕b1 ♘xa2 32 ♕xa2 ♖xb2 33 ♕a4 ♕b6 34 ♘f6+ ♗xf6 35 ♗xf6 ♖b1 36 ♖xb1 1–0 Hort–Torre, Polanica Zdroj 1977.

(b) **7 ... ♘bxd7!** 8 e5 ♘h5 9 ♗e3 (7 ... ♘bxd7 had been rejected because 9 g4 apparently wins a piece, but Black can reply 9 ... ♘xf4! 10 ♗xf4 cd; if White recaptures on d4 then 11 ... de wins material, while if the knight moves then Black gets three central pawns for the piece) 0-0 10 ♕d2 cd 11 ♗xd4 ♗h6 12 ♗e3 ♘b6 and Black is at least equal, Hort–Suttles, Indonesia 1982.

       7 ...   ♘g4 *(38)*
Now the way parts:

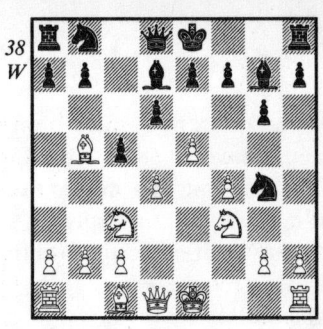

A: **8 e6**
B: **8 ♗xd7+**
C: **8 h3**
D: **8 ♘g5**

Of these, A is for aggressive, B is for boring, C is for complex and D is for dubious. The assessment of A depends crucially on Seirawan's innovation 8 ... fe. If this should be refuted then Black has to fall back on the main line, either with 12 ... ♗xd4 or with the more recent 12 ... h5!? Although both these lines are far from clear, White seems able to keep some advantage in both cases. B has been given the thumbs down by theory, but it would be more accurate to say that it is largely uncharted territory. White gets some kingside attacking chances at the cost of giving Black a powerful bishop. Chances appear equal. C leads to very sharp positions, but Black need not fear the complications. D cannot be recommended.

A

8 e6 ♗xb5

Seirawan's new idea, mentioned above, is 8 ... fe. Few books mention this move; those that do state that the reply 9 ♘g5 wins for White. However things are not so easy, e.g. 8 ... fe 9 ♘g5 ♗xb5 and now:

(1) **10 ♘xe6 ♗xd4!** 11 ♘xb5 (11 ♕xg4 ♗d7 12 f5 ♗xe6 13 fe ♗xc3+ 14 bc ♘c6 is good for Black, while 11 ♘xd8 ♗f2+ 12 ♔d2 ♗e3+ is just perpetual check, Sax–Seirawan, Brussels 1988) ♕a5+ 12 c3 (12 ♕d2 ♗f2+ 13 ♔d1 ♘e3+ 14 ♔e2 ♕xb5+ 15 ♔xf2 ♘g4+ 16 ♔g3 ♕d7 is good for Black) ♗f2+ 13 ♔d2 ♗e3+ 14 ♔c2 ♕a4+ 15 ♔b1 (15 b3? ♕e4+ 16 ♔b2 ♘f2 17 ♕f1 ♘d3+ 18 ♔a3 a6 19 ♘bc7+ ♔d7 20 ♘xa8 b5 and Black has a decisive attack) ♕e4+ 16 ♕c2 ♕xc2+ 17 ♔xc2 ♔d7 18 ♘ec7 (18 ♘bc7? ♗xc1 followed by 19 ... ♘a6) ♗xc1 19 ♔xc1 (the point of this is soon revealed) a6 20 ♘xa8 ab 21 c4 (21 a4? ba 22 ♘b6+ ♔c6 23 ♘xa4 b5 traps the knight; note that if White has taken on c1 with a rook, then 21 c4 could be met by 21 ... ♘e3+) and now Black has three possibilities according to Seirawan, namely 21 ... b4, 21 ... bc followed by occupying c6 with the knight, or 21 ... bc 22 ♘b6+ ♔c6 23 ♘xc4 b5 24 ♘d2 ♖f' 25 g3 g5 26 fg ♖f2 and according to Seirawan 'Black will score well' from this position. This may be somewhat optimistic; after 27 h4 White can make a passed pawn on the kingside, and since a4 must be met by ... b4 to prevent the rook emerging White can also have a passed a-pawn. Balanced against this are Black's active pieces and threats against the White king (by ... ♘d7–e5, ... ♘e3 and ... ♘d3+, for example). The usual cop-out 'unclear' seems well justified.

(2) **10 ♘xb5 ♕a5+** 11 c3 ♕xb5 12 ♘xe6 ♘a6 (the only move) 13 ♕xg4 ♗f6 and although the imposing knight on e6 appears strong, the position is unclear because White cannot castle and his bishop must defend the b-pawn. After 14 dc, for example, 14 ... ♔f7! creates dangerous counterplay since 15 cd ed and 15 ♘g5+ ♗xg5 16 fg ♘xc5 leave the White king exposed. Therefore Belyavsky–Timman, Belfort 1988 continued 14 d5 ♕d3 15 ♕d1 ♕xd1+ 16 ♔xd1 h5 17 g3 ♔d7 18 ♔c2 ♘c7 19 ♘xc7 ♔xc7 20 ♖e1 ♔d7 with a roughly level ending. White in fact lost after trying too hard to win.

If 8 ... fe remains unrefuted then White's main weapon against 5 ... c5 will have been defused.

9 ef+ ♔d7
10 ♘xb5

There is a tricky alternative in 10 ♘g5 h5 (39) and now:

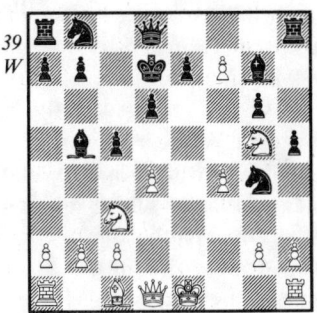

(a) **11 ♕f3** (11 ♘xb5 ♕a5+ 12 ♘c3 cd 13 ♕e2 dc 14 ♕e6+ ♔d8 is good for Black, Jensen–Keene, The Hague 1967) and in Stader–Vinke, corr. 1983, White won after 11 ... ♗c6 12 d5 ♗xc3+ 13 bc ♗b5 14 ♕e4 ♔c8 15 ♘e6 ♕a5 16 ♗d2 ♘d7 17 ♕xg6. However, 11 ... ♘c6 12 d5 ♘d4 13 ♕e4 appears more sensible; White has some compensation, but I doubt if it is really enough for a piece.
(b) **11 h3** (a useful finesse; White hits the knight at a moment when 11 ... ♘f6 is bad because of 12 ♘xb5) ♘h6 (11 ... ♘f2 12 ♔xf2 ♗xd4+ 13 ♗e3 ♗xe3+ 14 ♔xe3 gave White a large advantage in Stader–Schubert, corr. 1981) 12 ♕f3 ♘c6 (12 ... ♗c6 is similar to Stader–Vinke above) 13 ♕e4 ♗c4 (13 ... ♘xd4 14 ♘xb5 ♘xb5 15 ♘e6 picks up the g7 bishop) 14 d5 ♘d4 15 b3 with tactical chaos, Lehmann–Stempka, corr. 1986. The game

continuation 15 ... ♗a6 16 ♗b2 ♗f6 17 ♘e6 ♘xe6 18 de+ ♔c8 19 0-0-0 gave White fair play for the piece, but there were many other possibilities, e.g. 15 ... ♘xc2+ 16 ♕xc2 ♗xd5 17 ♗b2 ♕a5 18 0-0-0 ♗xf7 19 ♘xf7 ♘xf7, although in this case too 20 ♘a4 gives White reasonable attacking prospects.

10 ♘g5 is an unexplored line which may be recommended to sacrificially-inclined White players who don't mind taking a risk.

10	...	♕a5+
11	♘c3	cd
12	♘xd4	♗xd4

This move gives up the Pirc bishop but gains time by attacking White's queen. The alternative is 12 ... h5 (12 ... ♕h5 13 ♘e4 ♘c6 14 ♘g3 ♕h4 15 ♘f3 ♕f6 16 0-0 is good for White since he has completed his development without allowing the exchange of queens) 13 h3 ♘c6 14 ♘de2 (not 14 ♘xc6? ♗xc3+ 15 bc ♕xc3+ 16 ♗d2 ♕g3+ and wins, nor 14 hg ♘xd4 15 ♗e3 hg! 16 ♖xh8 ♖xh8 17 ♗xd4 ♖h1+ 18 ♔f2 ♖xd1 19 ♗xg7 ♖xa1 20 f8(♕) and White's exposed king tips the balance in Black's favour) ♘h6 15 ♗e3 ♖af8 (15 ... ♘f5 16 ♗f2 ♖af8 17 0-0 ♗xc3 18 ♘xc3 ♖xf7 was Hellers–Seirawan, Wijk aan Zee 1986, and now 19 a3 followed by b4-b5 would have been very good for White; it doesn't matter much whether Black plays ♖af8 or ♖hf8 because the rook that doesn't go to f8 usually goes to c8) 16 ♕d3 (16 0-0 ♘f5 17 ♗f2 ♖xf7 18 a3 ♘d8 19 ♕d3 ♘e6 20 ♖ad1 ♖c8 was unclear in Maus–M. Gurevich, Balatonbereny 1987; note the characteristic manoeuvre ... ♘d8–e6 opening the c-file and preventing White getting a grip on e6 by ♘e4–g5) ♘f5 17 ♗f2 ♖xf7 18 0-0-0 h4 19 ♔b1 (19 a3 ♖c8 20 ♘e4 ♘d8 21 ♔b1 ♘e6 22 c4 b6 was fine for Black in Oll–M. Gurevich, Tallinn 1987) ♖c8 20 ♕e4! (Belyavsky hits on the right plan; the queen should go to e4, leaving the knight and rook free to move to d5, while a subsequent ♖he1 will develop pressure on the e-file and inhibit the ... ♘d8–e6 idea) b6 (20 ... ♕b4 21 ♕xb4 ♘xb4 22 ♗xa7 ♖xc3 23 ♘xc3 ♘g3 24 ♖he1 ♖xf4 25 a3 ♘c6 26 ♘d5 wins material) 21 a3 ♘d8 22 ♖he1 ♕a6 23 ♘d4 ♕c4 24 ♘d5 with advantage for White, Belyavsky–Tal, Brussels 1988.

13 ♕xd4

This gives White better chances than 13 ♕xg4+ ♕f5 15 ♕f3 ♘c6 (14 ... ♗xc3+ 15 ♕xc3 ♘c6 16 ♗e3 ♖hf8 17 0-0 ♖xf7 18 ♕b3 was played in Diaz–Zaitsev, Havana 1983, and now 18 ... ♔c7 19 ♖ad1 ♖af8 would have been equal) 15 ♘e4 ♕e6 16 ♗e3 ♗xe3 (16 ... d5 17 ♗xd4 ♘xd4 18 0-0-0 ♘xf3 19 ♘c5+ ♔d6 20 ♘xe6 ♔xe6 21 gf ♖ad8 is also possible) 17 ♕xe3 ♔c7 18 ♔f2 ♖af8 19 ♘g5 ♕xe3+ 20 ♔xe3 ♔d7 followed by ... h6 and Black regains the pawn with a drawish ending.

13 ... ♘c6
14 ♕c4! *(40)*

After having tried virtually every other queen move White finally discovered that this is the best way to avoid an exchange of queens. The alternatives have virtually disappeared:

(a) **14 ♕d2** ♖hf8 (this is the safest, but 14 ... h5 15 b3 ♖hf8 16 ♗b2 was played in Zaitsev–Konopka, Moscow 1986, and now 15 ... ♕c5 would have equalized according to Zaitsev) 15 ♘d5 ♕xd2+ 16 ♗xd2 ♖xf7 17 h3 ♘f6 is equal.

(b) **14 ♕e4** ♕b6 (14 ... ♕f5 15 ♗d2 ♖hf8 16 ♕f3 ♖ab8 17 ♘e2 ♖xf7 18 0-0-0 ♘f6 is equal, Belyavsky–Carr, London 1985) 15 ♕f3 h5 16 h3 ♘h6 17 ♘d5 ♕b5 18 c3 ♘f5 19 b3 e6!? 20 ♘f6+ ♔e7 21 ♘e4 ♖ac8 22

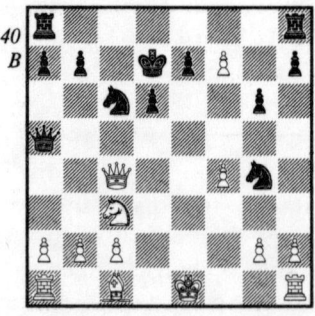

40
B

♗b2 ♘cd4! 23 cd ♖c2 with good chances for Black, Lutikov–Podgaets, USSR 1979.

(c) **14 ♕d1** ♕f5 (14 ... ♕h5 is also equal) 15 h3 ♕e6+ and White cannot sensibly avoid exchanging queens.

This position (after 14 ♕c4!) is a critical one for the assessment of 5 ... c5. Black's king is in the centre, but this is only of relevance if White can avoid the exchange of queens. Black must still regain the pawn on f7, but even achieving this does not necessarily guarantee equality. White must aim to use the time taken to win back the pawn to bring his king into safety and develop his rooks on the central files. At the moment White seems to have good chances of an advantage.

14 ... ♕b6

Black has tried almost every other legal move, but with dismal results:

(a) **14 ...** ♖hf8 15 ♗d2 and now:

(a1) **15 ...** ♕f5 16 h3 ♘f6 (in Bednarski–Peev, Lublin 1975 Black tried 16 ... ♘h6 17 0-0-0 ♖ac8 but after 18 ♖he1 ♕xf7 19 ♘d5 e6 20 ♘b4 ♕f5 21 ♘d3! his king was in grave danger) 17 0-0-0 ♕e6 18 ♕d3 (18 ♕b5 ♔c7 19 ♖he1 ♕xf7 20 g4 ♖ac8 21 ♗e3 ♔b8 22 ♕a4 led to the same general type of position, Mnatsakanian–Zaichik, Tbilisi 1983) ♕xf7 19 ♖he1 ♖ad8 20 ♔b1 ♔c8 21 g4 ♔b8 22 ♘e4 ♘xe4 23 ♖xe4 with a slight but permanent advantage for White, Timman–Spassky, Tilburg 1981. Black has no really good squares for his knight and the hanging pawns are a long-term liability.

(a2) **15 ...** ♖ac8 16 ♘d5 (this gives White a slightly better ending; 16 ♕e2 petered out to a draw after 16 ... ♕f5 17 h3 ♘f6 18 g4 ♕e6 19 ♕xe6+ ♔xe6 20 0-0-0 ♖xf7! 21 ♖he1+ ♔d7 22 ♘e4 ♘xe4 23 ♖xe4 ♖f6 in Balashov–Sigurjonsson, Cienfuegos 1975) ♕c5 17 ♕xc5 dc and Borkowski–Pribyl, Eksjo 1978, went on 18 h3 ♘f6 19 ♘xf6+ ef 20 0-0-0 ♔c7 21 f5 ♖xf7 22 ♗f4+ ♔b6 23 fg hg 24 ♖he1 ♖d8 25 ♖xd8 ♘xd8 26 ♖d1 ♘c6 27 ♖d6 and White's plus persists—Black is tied up and there are chances for White to make an outside passed pawn on the kingside. White did in fact win a long ending.

(b) 14 ... ♖af8 15 ♗d2 ♕f5 16 h3 ♘f6 17 0-0-0 ♕e6 18 ♕a4 ♔c8 19 ♖he1 ♕xf7 20 ♘b5 a6 21 ♘d4 ♘xd4 22 ♕xd4 ♕xa2 23 ♗b4 and with the threats of 24 b3 (followed by ♔d2 and ♖a1) and 24 ♖xe7 White has a distinct advantage, Sideif-Zaid–Grigorian, USSR 1977. 14 ... ♖af8 certainly leaves the queenside lacking in defence.

(c) **14 ...** ♖ac8 15 h3 ♘h6 16 0-0 ♘f5 17 ♗d2 ♕b4 18 ♕e2 ♘cd4 19 ♕f2 h5 20 ♘e4! ♕b5 21 c3

♘e2+ 22 ♔h2 ♕d3 23 ♕f3
♕xf3 24 ♖xf3 h4 25 ♖e1 ♘eg3
26 ♘g5 and having defended the
pawn on f7 White stands very
well, Szmetan–Torre, Buenos
Aires 'Clarin' 1978.

(d) **14 ... ♕f5** 15 h3 ♘f6 16 0-0
♕e6 (not 16 ... ♕xc2 17 f5! followed by ♖f2 trapping the queen)
17 ♕b5 ♖ab8?! 18 f5! ♕xf7 19
♗g5 a6 20 ♕b6 with a disastrous
position for Black, Bednarski–
Rukavina, Decin 1977.

(e) **14 ... ♕a6** 15 ♘b5! (the refutation: Black has simply misplaced his queen) ♖hf8 16 ♗d2
♖ac8 17 ♕e2 ♘f6 18 0-0 ♖xf7 19
♖fe1 ♘d8 (the only way to cover
e6) 20 c4 ♔e8 21 ♗c3 with a
massive White attack, Skrobek–
Pribyl, Decin 1978.

(f) **14 ... ♘b4** is Plaskett's idea.
After 15 ♕e4 ♘f6 16 ♕xb7+
♔e6 17 0-0 ♕xf7 18 ♖e1 ♖he8
19 ♖e2 ♖ab8 20 ♕f3 ♕f5 21
♕f2 ♘g4 22 ♕h4 ♘xc2 23
♕xh7+ ♔f8 24 ♘e4 ♘f6 25
♕h8+ ♘g8 26 ♘g5 e6 27 ♘h7+
White could find nothing better
than perpetual check in Morovic–
Plaskett, Bor 1985. Further tests
are needed, but the whole idea
appears very risky for Black.

15 ♕e2   h5 *(41)*

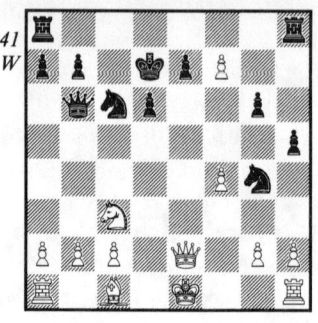

A1: 16 h3
A2: 16 ♗d2

A1

16 h3   ♘h6

16 ... ♘d4 17 ♕d3 ♘b3 18 ab
♕f2+ 19 ♔d1 ♕xg2 is refuted by
20 ♖f1 ♘f2+ 21 ♖xf2 ♕xf2 22
♕b5+ ♔d8 23 ♕xb7 ♕f1+ 24
♔d2 ♕xf4+ (24 ... ♕f2+ 25
♘e2 ♖c8 26 ♖xa7) 25 ♔e2
♕h2+ 26 ♔d3 ♕xh3+ 27 ♗e3
♕c8 28 ♗b6+.

17 ♗d2

Or 17 ♗e3 ♕xb2! (17 ... ♘d4
18 ♗xd4 ♕xd4 19 ♖d1 ♕c5?! 20
♖d5 ♕b6 21 ♖b5 ♕c6 22 0-0
was very good for White in Sax–
Pein, Manchester 1980) 18 ♔d2
♕a3 19 ♖ab1 ♕a6 (19 ... b6 20
♖b3 ♕a5 21 ♖b5 ♕a6 is also
possible; after 22 g4 hg 23 hg
♘xf7 24 ♖e1 the position was
unclear in Chandler–Kindermann, Wiesbaden 1981) 20 ♕xa6
ba 21 ♖b7+ ♔e6 22 ♖e1 ♔xf7
23 ♘e4 ♔e6! and a draw was
agreed in Kengis–M. Gurevich,
USSR 1980, since 24 ♘g5+ ♔f5

25 ♖eb1 ♖hb8 leads to an equal ending.

17 ... ♘f5
18 0-0-0

White is committed to sacrificing the exchange since 18 ♕f3 ♘b4 19 0-0-0 allows 19 ... ♘xc2.

18 ... ♘g3

Black must accept or else 19 ♖he1 gives White a clear advantage.

19 ♕d3 ♘xh1
20 ♖xh1

White has enough compensation for the exchange, but although Black faces a difficult practical task he may be able to hold the balance, e.g. 20 ... ♖af8 (20 ... ♕d4 21 ♕xg6 ♖af8 22 ♘e4 ♖xf7 23 ♕xf7 ♕xe4 24 ♖e1 ♕xg2 25 ♗c3 ♖h6 26 f5 with a positional advantage for White, Bryson–Svenningsson, corr. 1983) 21 ♕xg6 ♕a6 22 b3?! (22 ♖e1 ♕c4 23 ♕f5+ is better) ♘d8 23 ♕g7 ♕a5 and White's threats are on the wane, Aaron–Chernin, Bangalore 1981.

A2

16 ♗d2 ♘d4
17 ♕d3

Not 17 ♘d5 ♘xe2 18 ♘xb6+ ab 19 ♔xe2 ♖hf8 20 a4 ♖xf7 and White has no advantage, Vucinic–Redzepagic, Yugoslavia Ch. 1985.

17 ... ♘f5
18 ♘e4 ♖ac8

If Black allows White to complete his development unimpeded then White has an automatic advantage, for example 18 ... ♖hf8 19 0-0-0 ♖ac8 20 ♖he1 ♖xf7 21 h3 ♘f2 22 ♘xf2 ♕xf2 23 ♕d5 ♖f6 24 g4 ♘d4 25 ♕xb7+ 1–0, Diaz–Fernandez, Havana 1983. However 18 ... ♘ge3 may well be Black's best chance, e.g. 19 ♗xe3 ♕xe3 ♕xe3+ 20 ♕xe3 ♘xe3 21 ♔d2 ♘xg2 22 ♖hf1 ♖hf8 23 ♘g5 ♘h4 24 ♖ae1 ♘f5 25 ♖e4 with just a slight advantage for White, Hellers–Sundsvall 1984.

19 0-0-0!

19 ♗c3 ♖hf8 20 0-0-0 ♕e3+ 21 ♕xe3 ♘gxe3 22 ♖d2 was fine for Black in van Wijgerden–Timman, Amsterdam 1977.

19 ... ♘ge3

19 ... ♕a6 20 ♕xa6 ba 21 h3 ♘ge3 22 ♗xe3 ♘xe3 23 ♖d2 ♖c4 24 ♘g5 ♖xf4 25 ♖e1 is good for White.

20 ♗xe3 ♘xe3 *(42)*

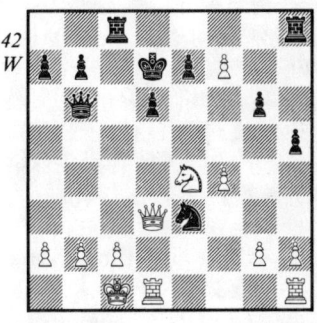

and now:
(a) **21 ♘c3 ♘xd1 22 ♖xd1 ♖hf8 23 ♕h3+ e6 24 ♖e1** (24 ♘e4 ♖c6 25 ♘g5 d5 26 ♖xd5+ is also

unclear) d5 25 ♘xd5 ♕c6 26 ♘b4 ♕c4 with roughly equal chances, Timman–van Wijgerden, Netherlands Ch. 1983.

(b) 21 c3! (White's knight is one square nearer g5 and Black's counterthreats aginst c2 are nullified) ♘xd1 22 ♖xd1 ♕a6 (this may not be best, but Black's position is difficult in any case) 23 ♕h3+ ♔c7 24 ♕e6 ♔b8, Hellers–Ivanchuk, Champigny 1984, and now 25 ♕xe7 ♕xa2 26 ♘xd6 ♕a1+ 27 ♔c2 ♕a4+ 28 ♔d2 ♕xf4+ 29 ♔e1 would have won for White.

Although matters are not totally clear, the main line of A2 appears promising for White, so Black must either try Seirawan's 8 ... fe or look for an improvement elsewhere.

B

| 8 | ♗xd7+ | ♕xd7 |
| 9 | d5 | de |

Better than 9 ... ♘a6 10 h3 ♘h6 11 g4 (11 ♗e3 may also be good for White) 0-0-0 12 ♗e3 e6 13 ♕e2 f5 (13 ... ed 14 ♘xd5 de 15 0-0-0 ♕e6 16 ♘g5 ♕e8 17 ♕c4 wins) 14 0-0-0! ♘c7 15 de ♕xe6 16 ♘g5 ♕e7 17 ♘d5 ♘xd5 18 ♖xd5 de 19 ♗xc5 ♕f6 20 ♖hd1 ♖xd5 21 ♖xd5 fg? (21 ... ♕c6 was better although still very good for White) 22 ♗xa7! ♕xf4+ 23 ♔b1 1-0, Filipowicz–Heiberg, Gausdal 1977.

| 10 | h3 | e4 |

| 11 | ♘xe4 | |

The simple 11 hg ef 12 ♕xf3 ♘a6 13 ♗d2 ♘b4 14 0-0-0 0-0-0 led to a quick White win in Hartmann–Kindermann, Bundesliga 1980 after 15 ♘e4 ♘xa2+? 16 ♔b1 ♕b5 17 ♕a3 ♘b4 18 ♘xc5 ♘xc2 19 ♔xc2 ♖xd5 20 ♗e3 and White held on to his extra piece. It is surprising that this has not been repeated, even though more circumspect play should be satisfactory for Black, e.g. 15 ... ♕b5!?.

| 11 | ... | ♘f6 |
| 12 | ♘xf6+ | |

This has been the move chosen in practice. After 12 ♘e5 Black may play:

(a) 12 ... ♕c7 (12 ... ♕a4 is an untested idea) 13 ♘g5? (13 ♘xf6+ is more reasonable, while 13 d6 ♕d8 is unclear) 0-0 14 c4 ♘bd7 15 ♘xd7 ♕xd7 16 0-0 b5 with a lead in development for Black, Bronstein–Pribyl, Tbilisi 1980.

(b) 12 ... ♕d8 13 ♘xf6+ and now Filipowicz–Drozd, Polish Ch. 1974 continued 13 ... ♗xf6 (13 ... ef! 14 ♘c4 0-0 is unclear) 14 0-0 0-0 15 c4 ♕d6 16 ♕e2 e6 17 ♘g4 and White had the initiative because Black has lost a tempo with his queen.

| 12 | ... | ♗xf6 |

The main merit of playing 12 ♘xf6+ as opposed to 12 ♘e5 is that Black cannot take with the pawn due to 12 ... ef 13 ♕e2+ ♕e7 14 ♕xe7+ ♔xe7 15 f5! with a positional advantage for White.

13 0-0 0-0 *(43)*

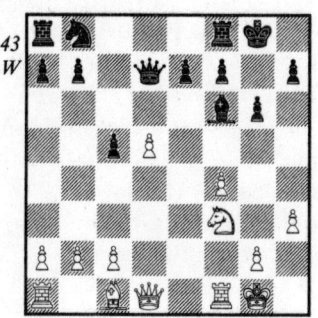

14 c4

Better than 14 ♘e5 ♛d6 (Black has gained a tempo over Filipowicz–Drozd above) 15 ♗g4 (15 c4 may transpose to the main line, but Black has the extra option of 15 ... ♘d7 16 ♘g4 ♗d4+ 17 ♗e3, Dvoretsky–Glianec, USSR 1979, and now 17 ... ♗xe3+ 18 ♘xe3 f5 would have equalized according to Dvoretsky) ♗d4+ 16 ♔h1 f5 17 ♘e3 (17 ♘e5 ♘d7 18 c3 ♘xe5 19 cd ♘d7 is also promising for Black) ♘d7 18 c3 ♗xe3 19 ♗xe3 which was slightly better for Black in Balashov–Tseshkovsky, USSR Ch. 1974, since Black has a knight outpost at e4.

After 14 c4 Black may play:
(a) **14 ... e6** 15 ♘e5 ♛d6 16 ♛b3 b6! (16 ... ♘d7?! 17 ♛xb7 ♘xe5 18 fe ♛xe5 19 ♗h6 ♖fb8 20 ♛c6 ♖c8 21 ♛a6 ♗g7 22 ♗xg7 with an edge for White, Adorjan–Pfleger, Lanzarote 1977) 17 ♘g4 ♗g7 with equality, Kuijpers–van der Sterren, Netherlands Ch. 1983.

(b) **14 ... b5** 15 ♘e5 (after 15 ♗e3 bc 16 ♘e5 ♛b5 17 ♛e2 ♘d7 18 ♗f2 ♘b6 19 ♖ad1 ♖ad8 20 ♛e4 ♖d6 Black stood better in Sokolov–Kolmakov, Moscow 1977) ♛d6 16 ♗e3 is unclear.

8 h3 cd

Although this has been the most popular move, it is probably not the best. Black should play 8 ... ♗xb5 9 ♘xb5 de (9 ... ♛a5+ 10 ♘c3 cd 11 ♛xd4 ♘c6 12 ♛e4 transposes to 9 ... ♗xb5 in the main line) 10 hg ♛a5+ *(44)* and now:

(a) **11 ♗d2** ♛xb5 12 de when 12 ... ♘c6 13 ♗c3 ♛c4 14 g3 ♖d8 15 ♛e2 ♛e6 16 g5 h5 17 gh ♖xh6 18 ♔f2 was good for White in Kristiansen–Miles, Teesside 1974. However, I can see no reason why Black should not simply take the pawn on b2. White may have enough for the pawn but he certainly has no advantage.

(b) 11 ♕d2 ♕xb5 12 de gives White the type of pawn structure he is aiming for, but only at the cost of a badly misplaced queen on d2. By 12 ... ♘c6 followed by a quick ... 0-0 and ... f6 Black should equalize.

(c) 11 c3 e4 (11 ... ♕xb5 12 de ±) 12 ♕e2 ef 13 ♘d6+ ♚d7 14 ♘xb7 ♕b6 15 ♕xf3 cd arriving at a delightfully random position. Fedorov–Tseitlin, Leningrad Ch. 1977 reeled on 16 ♕d5+ (16 ♘c5+ ♕xc5 17 ♕xa8 dc is good for Black) ♚c7 17 ♕xf7 ♕xb7 18 ♕xg7 ♕xg2 19 ♕e5+ ♝b7. Perhaps the correct result is a draw by perpetual check, but in the game 20 ♖f1 ♘c6 21 ♕b5+ ♚c7 22 ♕e2 ♕g3+ 23 ♕f2 ♕xg4 24 cd was played and now 24 ... ♘b4! was very strong according to Tseitlin.

9   ♕xd4 *(45)*

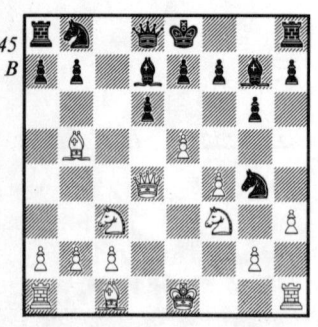

45
B

9 ...   de

There are two other important moves:

(a) 9 ... ♗xb5 10 ♘xb5 ♘c6 11 ♕e4 ♕a5+ (11 ... ♕b6!? is interesting, when 12 hg ♕xb5 13 ed 0-0-0 14 ♘g5 ed 15 ♘xf7 ♖d7 16 ♕e6 ♚c7 gave Black a dangerous initiative in Guljas–Bockinas, corr. 1983, but 12 ♕e2 ♘h6 13 ♗e3 ♕a5+ 14 ♗d2 ♕b6 15 0-0-0 is more testing) 12 ♘c3 ♘h6 13 g4 0-0-0 14 0-0 (or 14 ♗d2 de! 15 fe f5 16 ♕c4 fg 17 hg ♖hf8 with an unclear position, as in Hermlin–Chipashvili, USSR 1976) de 15 fe ♖he8? (15 ... f5 16 ef ef 17 ♗f4 ♖he8 is an improvement, but is still slightly better for White) 16 ♖e1! (White prevents ... f5 so Black has to play an artificial move) ♘g8 17 a3 f5, Timman–Sigurjonsson, Geneva 1977, and now 18 ♕c4! maintaining the pawn on e5 and threatening to throw Black back with b4 would have been very strong.

(b) 9 ... ♘h6 10 ♗d2 (10 g4 will probably transpose to 9 ... ♗xb5 since 10 g4 0-0 11 ♗xd7 ♘xd7 12 ♗e3 ♕a5 13 0-0-0 ♘b6 14 ♚b1, as in Klovan–Tseitlin, USSR 1973, is a bit better for White) ♗xb5 11 ♘xb5 ♘c6 12 ♕f2 de 13 fe a6? (as Black never castles in the game 13 ... 0-0 must be better) 14 ♘c3 ♘f5? 15 0-0-0 ♘xe5 16 ♗f4 ♘d7 17 g4 ♘d6 18 ♗xd6 ed 19 ♖xd6 (threat ♖hd1) ♕c7 20 ♖e1+ ♚f8 21 ♘g5 ♘c5 22 ♖d5 1–0 as the threat of ♖xc5 is unanswerable, Sigurjonsson–Westerinen, Geneva 1977.

10   ♕d5

White played 10 ♕c4?! in Klovan–Gofstein, USSR 1977, but after 10 ... e4! 11 hg ef 12 gf ♘c6 13 ♗d2 a6 14 ♗xc6 ♗xc6 Black was already slightly better.

10 ... e4

11 ♘g5 ♘h6 12 ♕xb7 (12 ♘gxe4 ♘c6 13 ♘c5 a6 14 ♗a4 b5 15 ♗b3 e6 16 ♕xd7+ ♕xd7 17 ♘xd7 ♔xd7 is perhaps very slightly better for White, Gaprindashvili–Keene, Tbilisi 1974) ♗xc3+ (after 12 ... 0-0 13 ♕xa8, Kurajica–Keene, Wijk aan Zee B 1974 continued 13 ... ♗xb5 14 ♘xb5 ♕a5+ 15 c3 ♕xb5 16 ♕xe4 ♘f5 17 ♕f3 and Black had no compensation for his sacrifice, but even 13 ... ♗xc3+ 14 bc ♗xb5 15 ♕xa7 ♘f5 16 ♔f2 is distinctly better for White according to Kurajica) 13 bc ♗xb5 14 ♕xa8 (14 ♕xb5+ ♕d7 15 ♕xd7+ ♘xd7 16 ♘xe4 with just an edge for White) ♗c6 (14 ... 0-0 would transpose to Kurajica's line given above) 15 ♕xa7 0-0 16 g4! ♕d5 17 ♗a3 ♖d8 18 ♕d4 ♕a5 19 ♕c5 ♕a4 20 ♖d1 and White consolidated his material advantage in Sigurjonsson–Vogt, Cienfuegos 1976.

D

8 ♘g5 ♗xb5

This is strong, so there is no need for Black to consider the unclear line 8 ... ♘h6 9 ♗xd7+ ♕xd7 10 e6 fe 11 dc ♘c6 12 0-0 0-0 13 ♗e3 ♖ad8 14 ♕e2 of Petran–Sapi, Hungary Ch. 1976.

9 ♕xg4 ♗d7
10 e6 ♗xe6
11 ♘xe6 fe
12 dc ♗xc3+

Black stands very well. Estrin–Stern, World Corr. Ch 1968/71 continued 13 bc ♕a5 14 ♗b2 ♕xc5 15 ♕xe6 ♕f5 16 ♕c4 ♘c6 17 0-0-0 0-0-0, and although White managed to draw his position at this stage was very poor.

6 | Austrian Attack: Miscellaneous

This chapter deals with the remaining lines of the Austrian Attack. Although these lines are not very frequently played, two of them have considerable importance. Most of the chapter is concerned with the Modern move-order 1 e4 g6 2 d4 ♗g7 3 ♘c3 d6 4 f4, but we also include White's unusual 5th move alternatives which may arise after 4 ... ♘f6. If Black wishes to avoid the transposition by 4 ... ♘f6 he may consider two main possibilities, 4 ... ♘c6 and 4 ... c6. Line A deals with 4 ... ♘c6, which immediately increases the pressure on d4. White should avoid the doubtful 5 ♘f3 ♗g4, when the doubling of the f-pawns by 6 ♗e3 ♗xf3 7 gf is forced, but even then an advantage is by no means guaranteed. The topic of B is 4 ... c6, a roundabout method of attacking d4 by means of ... ♕b6 and, if White plays ♘f3, by ... ♗g4. White is able to maintain his pawn centre, but at the cost of doubled f-pawns which make his position inflexible. White usually ends up with a space advantage, but has difficulty finding a constructive plan.

1 e4 g6 2 d4 ♗g7 3 ♘c3 d4 4 f4

After 4 ... ♘f6, White may try (5 ♘f3 leads to Chapters 1–5):

(a) **5 e5 de** (5 ... ♘fd7 is preferable since White has nothing better than 6 ♘f3, giving Black the choice of 6 ... 0-0 leading to Chapter 3 or 6 ... c5 reaching Chapter 5) 6 de (6 fe ♘d5 is not dangerous) ♕xd1+ 7 ♔xd1 (this ending is better for White than the similar one arising after 5 ♘f3 0-0 6 e5 de, because here White can prevent castling) ♗g4 (7 ... ♗g4+ 8 ♔e1 ♘fd7 9 ♘d5 ♔d8 10 ♘e3 is good for White) and now:

(a1) **8 ♔e1** c6 (8 ... f6 9 h3 ♘h6 10 ♘d5 ♔d8 11 ♘f3 is similar to line a2, while 8 ... ♘c6 9 h3 ♘h6 10 ♘d5 is no better) 9 h3 ♘h6 10 g4 f6 11 ef ef 12 ♗c4 f5 13 g5 ♘f7 14 ♘f3 ♘d6 15 ♗b3 ♔d7 16 h4 ♔c7 17 h5 with an edge for White, Balashov–Tseshkovsky, Moscow 1981.

(a2) **8 ♘d5** ♔d8 9 ♔e1 c6 10 ♘c3 f6 11 h3 ♘h6 12 ♘f3 ♘f7 13 ♗c4 ♖f8 (13 ... e6 14 ef ♗xf6 15 ♘e4

♗g7 16 c3 ♔e7 17 ♗e3 was also somewhat better for White in Niedermaier–Krause, Bundesliga 1985) 14 ♖f1 ♘c7 15 ♖f2 ♘a6 16 ♗e3 and Black has not equalized, Hort–Short, Amsterdam 1982.

(b) **5 ♗c4** c5 (5 ... ♘xe4 6 ♗xf7+ ♔xf7 7 ♘xe4 ♖e8 8 ♘f3 ♔g8 may also equalize but demands accurate play by Black) 6 e5 ♘fd7 7 ed (7 ♘f3 transposes to chapter 5, note to White's 6th move) 0-0 8 ♗e3 ed 9 ♕d2 ♘c6 10 dc dc 11 0-0-0 ♘d4 12 ♘f3 ♘b6 (the bishop is not well placed on c4) 13 ♗e2 ♘d5 14 ♗xd4 cd 15 ♘xd4 ♘xc3 16 ♕xc3 ♕b6 17 ♕e3 ♗f5 18 c3 ♖fe8 19 ♕f2 ♖ac8 20 g4 ♗e4 21 ♖hg1 ♖ed8 0–1 van der Wiel–Taulbut, Groningen 1977/8, as White is losing the knight on d4.

(c) **5 ♗d3** e5 (5 ... ♘c6 6 ♘f3 ♗g4 7 ♗e3 e5 8 de de 9 ♗b5 ef 10 ♕xd8+ ♖xd8 11 ♗xc6+ bc 12 ♗xf4 0–0 was at least equal for Black in Rogers–Gufeld, Canberra 1988) 6 de de 7 f5 gf 8 ef e4 9 ♘xe4 ♗xf5 10 ♘xf6+ ♕xf6 11 ♕e2+ ♗e6 12 ♘f3 ♘c6 13 0-0 0-0-0 with equality, De Firmian–Seirawan, USA Ch. 1987.

Now there is a division:

A: 4 ... ♘c6
B: 4 ... c6

4 ... a6 is sometimes used by Black players going all out for a win. Although this policy sometimes works, especially when employed against weaker opponents, 4 ... a6 is not a good move objectively. The main merit is that it is better than it looks, so White players often become overambitious. After 4 ... a6 (4 ... ♘d7 5 ♘f3 c5 6 ♗e3 ♘gf6 7 dc ♕a5 8 ♕d2 ♘xc5 9 e5 ♘fd7 10 ♘d5 ♕xd2+ 11 ♘xd2 ♘e6 12 g4! ♔d8 13 ed ed 14 ♘c4 with an advantage for White due to the weak d-pawn, Tseshkovsky–Quinteros, Manila 1976) 5 ♘f3 b5 6 ♗d3 (6 a3 is unnecessary) ♗b7 (6 ... b4 7 ♘e2 d5 8 e5 ♗g4 9 0-0 e6 10 a3 ♘c6 11 ♗d2 ♗f5 12 ♗xb4 ♗f8 13 ♗xf8 and Black had no compensation for the pawn in Inkiov–Arnaudov, Sofia 1977) 7 0-0 (7 a4 b4 8 ♘e2 ♘d7 9 c3 bc 10 bc c5 11 ♖b1 ♖b8 12 0-0 cd 13 cd ♘gf6 14 e5 ♘d5 15 ♘g5! e6 16 ♘e4! was very good for White in Ljubojevic–Sznapik, Buenos Aires Ol. 1978, but 7 ♕e2 ♘c6!? 8 e5 ♘h6 9 d5 ♘b4 10 ♗xb5+ c6 11 dc ♘xc6 12 ♗c4 0-0 13 e6 fe 14 ♗xe6+ ♔h8 was rather murky, Peters–Christiansen, USA Ch. 1984) ♘d7 8 e5 c5 9 ♗e4 (9 ♘g5 ♕b6! is unclear) ♗xe4 10 ♘xe4 cd 11 e6 (11 ed ♕b6 12 ♖e1 e6 13 c3 dc+ 14 ♗e3 ♕b7 15 ♘xc3 ♘gf6 is equal, Barbero–Bilek, Budapest 1987) fe 12 ♘eg5 ♘f8 13 ♘xd4 ♗xd4 14 ♕xd4 ♘f6 15 ♖e1 ♕c8 16 a4 with a small advantage for White, Timman–Kagan, Rio 1979. Lju-

bojevic's 7 a4 looks the soundest line for White against 4 ... a6.

A

4 ... ♘c6 *(46)*

5 ♗e3

5 ♘f3 (this is inaccurate, as is 5 d5 ♘d4) ♗g4 6 ♗e3 ♗xf3 7 gf d5 8 ♕d2 (8 ♘xd5 e6 and 8 ed ♘b4 are fine for Black) e6 9 0-0-0 ♘ge7 10 h4 h5 11 ♘a4 0-0 12 c4 dc 13 ♗xc4 is unclear, De Firmian–Kristiansen, Copenhagen 1985.

5 ... ♘f6
6 ♘f3

The alternative is 6 h3, aiming to build up a massive wall of pawns by g4, but the idea is very ambitious, e.g. 6 ... 0-0 (6 ... ♘h5 7 ♘ge2 e5 8 de de 9 ♕xd8+ ♘xd8 10 f5! gf 11 ef ♘f4 12 g4 h5 13 0-0-0, Skrobek–Seifert, Hradec Kralove 1976/7, and White stands very well as Black cannot play 13 ... hg because of 14 ♘b5) 7 g4 (7 e5 is a logical follow-up to 6 h3, but I can only find one example of it: Zude–Reeh, West Germany Ch. 1987 continued 7 ... ♘d7 8 ♘f3 e6 9 ♕d2 ♘e7 10 0-0-0 b6 11 g4 ♗b7 12 ♗g2 with a slight advantage for White) e5 (7 ... a6?! 8 ♕f3 ♖b8 9 0-0-0 b5 10 e5 ♘xd4, Kuijf–Norwood, London 1984, and now 11 ♕f2! de 12 fe would have won material in perfect safety) 8 de de 9 f5 *(47)* and now:

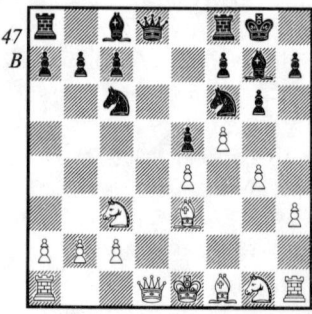

(a) **9 ... gf** 10 ef (10 gf ♘d4 11 ♘f3 c5 12 ♗g5 was slightly better for White in Fischer–Udovcic, Rovinj–Zagreb 1970, but 10 ... ♕xd1+! 11 ♖xd1 ♘d4 attacking c2 is a big improvement) ♘d4 11 ♗g2 ♕e7 (11 ... ♘e8 12 ♘ge2 ♘d6 13 ♕d3 c5 14 0-0-0 ♗d7 15 ♘g3 with advantage for White, van der Sterren–Goodman, London 1980) 12 ♕d2 (not 12 g5 ♗xf5!) ♖d8 13 ♕f2 h6 14 0-0-0 with a slight advantage for White, Arnason–Keene, London 1981.

(b) **9 ... h6** 10 ♘f3 ♕e7 11 g5 hg 12 ♗xg5 ♕b4 13 a3! ♕c5 14 ♕d2 ♘d4 15 ♕g2 ♘h5 16 0-0-0 c6 17 ♘h4 is good for White, Arnason–Goodman, Reykjavik 1982.

(c) **9 ... ♘d4** 10 ♕d2? (10 ♘f3 is

better) gf 11 gf ♘xe4! 12 ♘xe4 ♗xf5 13 ♘g3 ♘xc2+ 14 ♔e2 ♗g6! 15 ♖c1 ♘xe3 16 ♕xe3 f5 and with three pawns and an enduring attack for the piece, Black is much better, Hobell–Dorniden, West Germany 1976.

6 ... 0-0
7 ♗e2 *(48)*

There are two other reasonable moves, 7 e5 and 7 ♕d2. 7 e5 is a completely independent line, but 7 ♕d2 frequently transposes back into the main variation. Therefore we only consider in this note lines not involving a transposition.

(a) **7 e5** (Black should meet this by going into the ending with 7 ... de) and now:

(a1) **7 ... de** 8 de ♘g4 9 ♗g1 f6 10 h3 ♕xd1+ (or 10 ... ♘h6?! 11 ♗c4+ ♔h8 12 ♕e2 with an initiative for White, Anand–C. Horvath, Oakham 1986) 11 ♖xd1 ♘h6 and this ending should be slightly better for White, e.g. 12 ef ef 13 ♘d5 ♖f7 14 g4 ♗e6 15 ♖h2.

(a2) **7 ... ♘g4** 8 ♗g1 a6 (8 ... f6 9 d5 ♘b4 10 a3 ♘a6 11 h3 ♘h6 12 e6 c6 13 g4 ♘c7 14 ♘d4 c5 15 ♘f3 b5 16 ♖h2 is good for White, Kudrin–Rohde, USA Ch. 1986) 9 h3 ♘h6 10 g4 b5 11 ♗e3 (11 ♕e2 f5 12 g5 ♘f7 13 d5 ♘cxe5 14 fe de is not so easy to meet in practice, but I think White should be better objectively, Martin–Quinteros, Biel 1985) ♗b7 12 d5 ♘b4 13 ♗g2 de 14 ♘xe5 e6 15 ♘c6 ♕d6?

16 ♘e4 and wins, Kudrin–Watson, London 1987.

(b) **7 ♕d2** and now:

(b1) **7 ... ♗g4** 8 0-0-0 ♖e8 (8 ... e5 9 fe de 10 de ♕xd2+ 11 ♖xd2 ♘d7 12 ♘d5 ♘cxe5 13 ♘xc7 ♘xf3 14 gf ♗xf3 15 ♘xa8 ♗xh1 16 ♖xd7 ♖xa8 17 ♖xb7 ♗xe4 18 ♖xa7 and White is simply a pawn up, Chandler–Keene, Indonesia 1982) 9 e5 de 10 fe ♘d5 11 ♗c4 ♘b6 12 ♗b3 ♘a5 13 ♗h6 ♘xb3+ 14 ab a5 with equality, Christiansen–Hübner, Wijk aan Zee 1982.

(b2) **7 ... ♗g4** 8 ♗g1 e5 9 fe de 10 d5 ♘b8 11 h3 ♗f6 12 0-0-0 ♘bd7 13 d6 (ambitious) c6 14 ♔b1 b5 15 ♕e3 ♖e8 16 ♗h2 ♗f8 is unclear, Dvoris–Azmaiparashvili, USSR Ch. 1986.

(b3) **7 ... e5** 8 de de 9 ♕xd8 ♖xd8 10 fe ♘g4 11 ♗g5 ♖d7 12 ♗b5 transposes into the main line, but if White wishes to play Belyavsky's 12 ♘d5 then this move-order is a mistake because White's bishop is on f1 instead of e2.

There is nothing to be gained by playing 7 ♕d2 instead of 7 ♗e2; in many lines there is a transposition, while in the others ♗e2 is a more useful move than ♕d2.

Austrian Attack: Miscellaneous

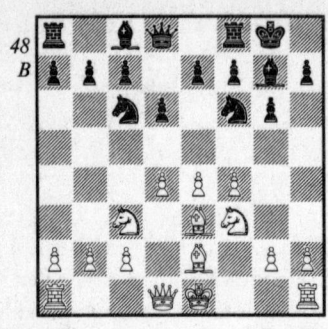
48
B

7 ... e5 *(49)*

This is the critical move, although some of the alternatives are playable:

(a) 7 ... ♗g4 (not very good, since the natural reply e5 turns out well) 8 e5 and now:

(a1) 8 ... ♘d7 9 e6 (9 h3 is a solid move which gives White some advantage) ♗xf3 (9 ... fe? 10 ♘g5 is crushing, while 9 ... ♘b6 10 ef+ ♔h8 11 ♘g5 ♗xe2 12 ♕xe2 ♕d7 13 0-0-0 ♘d8 14 h4 ♗xf7 15 ♘xf7 ♖xf7 16 h5 gh 17 ♖xh5, Smejkal–Knaak, Sandomierz 1976, is also good for White) 10 ♗xf3 ♘b6 11 d5 ♘c4 12 dc ♘xe3 13 ef+ ♔h8 14 cb (two pawns on the 7th rank by move 14 must be very unusual) ♖b8 15 ♕d3 with advantage to White, Gipslis–Olafsson, Tallinn 1975.

(a2) 8 ... de 9 de ♘d7 10 0-0 (again 10 h3 ♗xf3 11 ♗xf3 ♘b6 12 0-0 gives White some advantage) ♘b6 11 ♗c5! ♖e8 (11 ... f6 12 ef ♗xf6 13 ♕e1 is very pleasant for White) 12 h3 ♗xf3 13 ♗xf3 f6 14 ♗xc6 (14 ♕xd8 ♖axd8 15 ♘b5 was also good) bc 15 ♕f3 fe 16 fe ♗xe5? 17 ♖ad1

♘d7 18 ♕f7+ ♔h8 19 ♕e6 ♗d6 20 ♗d4+ ♘f6 21 ♖xf6 1–0, Nunn–Stojanovic, Geneva Open 1969.

(b) 7 ... ♘g4 8 ♗g1 e5 9 fe de 10 d5 ♘b8 (10 ... ♘e7 11 h3 ♘f6 12 ♗h2 awkwardly attacks the e-pawn, Bednarski–Sznapik, Poland Ch. 1975) 11 h3 ♘f6 12 ♗e3 (12 ♗h2 is simply answered by 12 ... ♘bd7, but 12 g4 c6 13 ♕d2 cd 14 ed ♘bd7 15 0-0-0 a6 16 ♗h2 ♖e8 17 g5 ♘h5 18 ♘e4 gave White a small advantage due to his passed pawn, Gipslis–Seifert, Hradec Kralove 1977/8) c6 13 0-0 cd 14 ed e4 15 ♘e5!? (intending a sacrifice which, although dangerous, may not be completely sound; 15 ♘h2 ± is the alternative) ♘h5 16 ♘xf7 ♖xf7 17 ♖xf7 ♔xf7 18 ♘xe4 (Balashov gives 18 d6! ♘f6 19 ♘xe4 ♘xe4 20 ♕d5+ ♗e6 21 ♕xe4, but after 21 ... ♘d7 it is not clear how White continues) ♕e7? (18 ... ♔g8 19 d6 ♕e8 is unclear) 19 ♗d3 ♗f5 20 ♕f3 ♘f6 21 ♘g5+ ♔e8 22 ♖e1 ♗xd3 23 cd ♘bd7 24 d6 ♘e5 25 ♕f1 ♕xd6 and now 26 ♗f4! is best, although 26 d4 was enough to win in Balashov–Tseshkovsky, USSR Ch. 1976.

(c) 7 ... e6 (this looks very slow but it is perfectly playable; White must beware of over-extension) 8 ♕d2 (8 h3 b6 9 g4 ♗b7 10 g5 ♘h5 11 ♖g1 ♘e7 12 ♘h4 c5 13 ♗xh5 gh 14 ♕d2 ♘g6 15 ♘f3 b5 16 dc b4 17 ♘e2 ♗xe4, Botterill–

Planinc, Hastings 1974/5, and 8 ♕d3 b6 9 0-0-0 ♗b7 10 a3 ♘e7 11 ♘g5 h6 12 ♘h3 ♕c8! 13 g4? c5 14 dc bc, Westerinen–Kindermann, Wiesbaden 1981, were both very good for Black and emphasize how careful White must be before making rash pawn advances) b6 9 0-0-0 (9 e5 ♘g4 10 ♗g1 de 11 fe ♗b7 12 a3 f6 13 ♘g5 ♗h6 14 ♗xg4 ♗xg5 15 ♗xe6+ ♔h8 16 ♕d3 was slightly better for White in Sznapik–Grigorov, Prague 1985) ♗b7 (9 ... ♘e7 is designed to anticipate e5; after 10 ♘g5 h6 11 ♘h3 ♗b7 12 ♗f3 ♖b8 13 g4? b5 14 ♕g2 b4 15 ♘e2 d5 Black was better in Botterill–McNab, Brighton 1984, a curious echo of Botterill–Planinc above) 10 e5 ♘g4 (10 ... de 11 fe ♘d5 12 ♗g5 is ±) 11 h3 (not 11 ♗g1? de 12 de ♕xd2+ 13 ♘xd2 ♘cxe5!) ♘xe3 12 ♕xe3 ♘e7?! (12 ... de 13 de ♕e7 offered better chances of equality) 13 g4 f6 14 ♗c4 with an edge for White, Nunn–Kindermann, Wiesbaden 1981.

(d) **7 ... a6** (this has a similar objective to 7 ... e6, but in my opinion White has much better chances of an advantage in this line) and now:

(d1) **8 e5** ♘g4 9 ♗g1 b5 10 ♘g5 (10 h3 ♘h6 11 ♗f2 ♗b7 12 0-0 ♘a5 13 b4 ♘c4 14 ♗xc4 bc 15 ♕e2 e6 16 ♖ad1 ♗xf3 17 ♕xf3 d5 is equal, Balashov–Keene, Skara 1980) f6!? 11 ♘xh7 ♔xh7 12 ♗xg4 fe 13 ♗f3 ♗d7 14 fe de

15 ♗e4 ♗h6 16 ♗e3! ♔g7 (17 ♕h5 was a threat) 17 ♗xh6+ ♔xh6 18 ♕d2+ ♔g7 19 ♕g5 ♗e8, Vera–Goodman, Mexico City 1978, and now 20 d5 e6 21 ♕xd8 ♘xd8 22 de or 22 d6 should win for White.

(d2) **8 d5** ♘a7 9 a4 c5 10 0-0 ♗d7 11 ♘d2! b5 (11 ... ♕c7 12 e5 de 13 fe ♕xe5 14 ♗xc5 is good for White) 12 e5 ♘e8 13 ♗f3 ♘c7 14 ab ♘axb5 15 ♘e4 with a clear advantage for White, Georgadze–Keene, Baguio City 1980.

(d3) **8 h3** (8 a4?! is dubious because Black can revert to the ... e6 plan, but with White having weakened his queenside pawn structure it isn't clear where his king is going; 8 ... e6 9 h3 ♘e7 10 g4?! b6 11 ♘d2 c5 12 dc bc 13 ♘c4 d5 14 ♗xc5 ♘d7! was good for Black in Marjanovic–Keene, Skara 1980) ♘h5 9 g4 ♘g3 10 ♖g1 ♘xe2 11 ♕xe2 e5 12 0-0-0 ed 13 ♘xd4 ♗d7 with a double-edged position, Pokoiowczyk–Popovic, Wroclaw 1979.

49
W

8 de

8 fe de and now:

(a) **9 de** ♘g4 10 ♕xd8 ♘xd8! (10 ... ♖xd8 11 ♗g5 transposes to the main line) 11 ♗c5 (11 ♗f4 ♘e6 12 ♗g3 ♘e3) ♖e8 12 ♘d5 ♘e6 13 ♗e7 ♘xe5 (13 ... ♚h8 is also good for Black) 14 ♘xe5 ♗xe5 15 ♗f6 ♘f4 16 ♘e7+ is Nunn–McNab, London 1979, and now 16 ... ♖xe7 17 ♗xe7 ♗xb2 is very promising for Black.
(b) **9 d5** ♘e7 10 0-0 (10 ♘xe5 ♘xe4 11 ♘xe4 ♗xe5 12 ♗h6 is doubtful as Black has the dangerous sacrifice 12 ... ♘f5! 13 ♗xf8 ♕h4+ 14 ♘f2 ♘e3) ♘g4 (the same position arises in Chapter 1 with the bishop on d3 rather than e2 and this does not change the verdict that Black has a satisfactory position) 11 ♗c5 b6 12 ♘d2 bc 13 ♗xg4 ♗xg4 14 ♕xg4 c6 15 d6 ♕xd6 16 ♖ad1 and although White won quickly in van der Wiel–McNab, Marbella 1982, at this stage Black's position is quite satisfactory.

8 ... de

8 ... ♘g4 9 ♗c1! (9 ♗g1 de 10 ♕xd8 ♖xd8 11 h3 ♘h6 is fine for Black) de 10 h3 (10 ♕xd8 ♖xd8 11 h3 ♘b4 commits White to the sacrifice 12 hg!? ♘xc2+ 13 ♚f2 ♘xa1 14 f5 followed by ♗c4 since 12 ♗d1 fails to 12 ... ♖xd1+!) ♕xd1+ (10 ... ♘f6 11 ♕xd8 ♖xd8 12 fe ♘d7 13 ♘d5 is good for White) 11 ♚xd1 ♘f6 12 fe ♘d7 13 ♘d5 ♘dxe5 14 ♘xc7 ♖b8 and Black has insufficient compensation for the lost pawn.

9		♕xd8	♖xd8
10		fe	♘g4
11		♗g5	♖d7 *(50)*

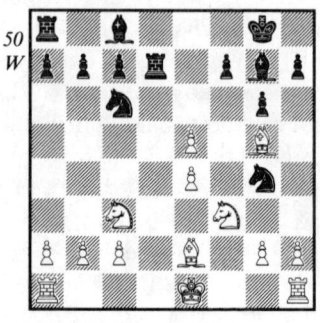

and now:
(a) **12 ♗b5** was played in Karpov–Christiansen, Linares 1981, and after 12 ... h6 White could have played 13 ♗f4 (13 ♗d2? ♖d8! was unclear in the game) g5 14 ♗g3 ♘e3 15 ♖c1! ♘xg2+ 16 ♚f2 ♘f4 17 ♗xf4 gf 18 ♖hg1 with advantage according to Timman. However I can see no reason why Black should not play 12 ... ♘xe5 13 ♘xe5 ♗xe5. All annotators give 14 ♘d5 ♗xb2 15 ♖b1 ♗e5 16 ♗f6 as good for White, but Black can reply 16 ... ♖d6! After 17 0-0 (17 ♗xc6 ♗xf6 and 17 ♗xe5 ♘xe5 are certainly fine for Black) ♗xf6 18 ♘xf6+ ♚f8 19 ♘xh7+ ♚g7 20 ♗xc6 (20 ♘g5 ♘e5) ♖xc6 21 ♘g5 f6 22 ♘f3 ♖xc2 I can see no advantage for White.
(b) **12 ♘d5** h6 13 ♗h4 ♘gxe5 14 ♘xe5 ♗xe5 15 0-0-0 ♚g7 16 ♖df1 and Black cannot easily free himself. Belyavsky–Cekro, Sara-

jevo 1982, continued 16 ... ♘d4 17 ♗d1 ♘e6 18 ♗g4 ♖d6 19 ♗e7 ♖c6 20 ♗b4 ♖c4 21 ♘d3 ♗d4 22 b3 ♗e3+ 23 ♔b1 ♖xe4 24 ♗f6+ ♔g8 25 ♗f3 and Black lost the exchange.

As so often in the Pirc, one wishes there were more examples from Grandmaster play, but on the evidence available 4 ... ♘c6 is playable for Black, although slightly less sound than the main lines. 7 ... e6 is perhaps Black's most combative option.

B

4 ... c6

It is surprising this line isn't played more often. Provided Black is careful not to castle kingside he should be able to restrict White to a very slight advantage.

5 ♘f3

5 ♗e3 (5 a4 ♘d7 6 ♘f3 e5 7 de de 8 ♗c4 ♕e7 9 ♕e2 ♘gf6 10 0-0 0-0 11 ♔h1 was a bit better for White, Belyavsky–Todorcevic, Szirak 1987) ♕b6 6 ♖b1 f5 (6 ... e5 7 ♘f3 ♗g4 8 fe de 9 ♗c4! with the idea of ♗xf7+ is very good for White) 7 e5!? de 8 fe ♗xe5 gives White some compensation for the pawn, but after 9 ♘f3 ♗g7 10 ♗c4 ♘f6 11 ♕d2 ♕b4 12 ♘e5 e6 13 0-0 ♕e7 14 ♗g5 b5 15 ♗b3 b4 16 ♗xf6 ♗xf6 17 ♘e2 a5 Black was at least equal in Hansen–Todorcevic, Rome 1988.

5 ... ♗g4

Other moves are doubtful, e.g. 5 ... ♕b6 6 h3 ♘d7 7 e5 ♘h6 8 a4 0-0 9 a5 ♕d8 10 g4! c5 11 d5 de 12 fe e6 13 ♗g5 f6 14 ef ♘xf6 15 ♗c4!, Marjanovic–Todorcevic, Belgrade 1979, or 5 ... b5 6 ♗d3 ♗g4 7 e5 ♘h6 8 h3 ♗f5 9 g4 ♗xd3 10 ♕xd3 ♕d7 11 ♗e3 ♘a6 12 0-0-0 ♘c7 13 ed ♕xd6 14 f5, Ehlvest–Granda Zuniga, Zagreb 1987, with an excellent position for White in both cases.

6 ♗e3

6 ♗c4 should not be met by 6 ... ♗xf3 7 ♕xf3 ♗xd4 8 ♘e2 ♗b6 (8 ... ♗g7 9 ♕b3 regains the pawn with some advantage for White) 9 f5 with a dangerous attack, but by either 6 ... e6 (intending ... d5) 7 d5 ed 8 ed ♘e7 9 0-0 0-0 10 h3 ♗xf3 11 ♕xf3 b5 12 ♗b3 ♕b6+ 13 ♗e3 c5, Gavela–Smejkal, Belgrade 1977, or 6 ... d5!? 7 ed ♘h6 8 h3 ♗xf3 9 ♕xf3 ♘f5 10 ♗e3 0-0! 11 g4 ♘xe3 12 ♕xe3 b5 13 ♗b3 b4, Kuijf–Todorcevic, Seville 1987, with a promising position for Black in either case.

6 ... ♕b6
7 ♕d2 *(51)*

8 ♕d3 ♘f6 8 h3 (8 0-0-0 d5! 9 e5 ♘e4 is fine for Black since if White takes the pawn his queen is trapped; the imaginative 8 ♘e5 rebounded after 8 ... d5! 9 f5 de 10 ♕c4 0-0 11 fg hg 12 ♘xg6 ♗e6 13 ♘xe7+ ♔h8 with advantage to Black, Arnason–Soltis, New York 1986) ♗xf3 9 gf is not very

logical; if this were good for White then ♕d2 followed by ♕d3 would be the right way to play in the main line!

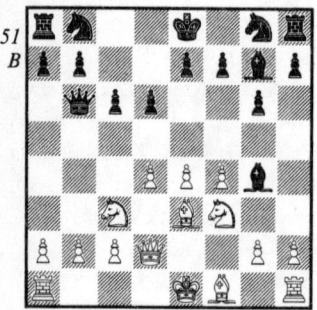

51
B

7 ... ♗xf3

7...♕xb2 8 ♖b1 ♕a3 9 ♖xb7 ♘d7 10 ♖b3 ♕a5 11 ♗e2 is good for White.

8 gf ♘d7

It is still bad to take on b2, e.g. 8... ♕xb2 9 ♖b1 ♕a3 10 ♖xb7 ♘d7 11 ♖b3 ♕a5 12 d5 ♖c8 13 dc ♖xc6 14 ♘d5 ♕xa2 15 ♘b4 ♕a1+ 16 ♔f2 ♖c8 17 e5 with an enormous White initiative, De Firmian–Soltis, USA Ch. 1983. However 8... ♘f6 9 0-0-0 ♕c7 is playable, e.g. 10 ♖g1 ♘bd7 11 f5 b5 12 ♗d3 ♘b6 with a small advantage for White, Kudrin–Hort, Lugano 1984.

9 0-0-0

Or 9 ♗h3 (9 ♘a4 ♕c7 10 c4 e6 11 ♘c3 ♘e7 12 h4 h5 13 0-0-0 a6 14 ♔b1 b5 15 c5 0-0 16 f5 was unclear in van der Wiel–Todorcevic, Budel 1987; 10 ... ♘gf6 is also possible) ♕c7 10 0-0-0 ♘b6 11 ♕d3 ♘f6 12 f5 ♘fd7! 13 ♔b1 0-0-0 14 ♖hg1 ♔b8 with a slight edge for White, Chandler–Hort, Amsterdam 1983.

9 ... ♕a5
10 ♔b1

After 10 ♖g1 b5 White adopted a strange plan in Velimirovic–Rukavina, Yugoslavia Ch. 1984; the continuation 11 a3 ♖b8 12 ♘a2 ♕c7 13 ♘b4 ♖b7 14 d5 c5 15 ♘c6 a6 16 ♕a5 ♖b6 17 ♗h3 ♘gf6 was obscure.

10 ... b5 *(52)*

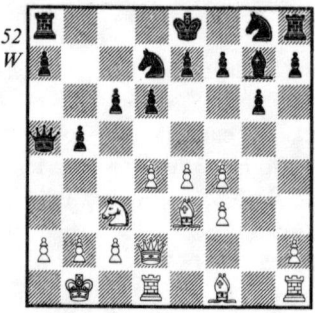

52
W

11 e5

11 f5 is also reasonable, with the possible continuation 11 ... ♘gf6 12 ♗d3 ♘b6. The dangers of castling kingside are illustrated by the line 12 ... b4 13 ♘e2 0-0 14 h4 c5 15 h5 ♖fc8 16 hg! c4 (16 ... fg 17 ♗c4+) 17 gh+ ♘xh7 (17 ... ♔h8 18 ♗h6 ♘e8 19 ♖dg1 cd 20 ♖xg7 dc+ 21 ♔c1 ♘xg7 22 ♗xg7+ ♔xg7 23 h8(♕)+ mates) 18 ♗h6 cd 19 ♖dg1 dc+ 20 ♔a1 or 19 ... ♖xc2 20 ♖xg7+ ♔h8 21 ♖xh7+ ♔xh7 22 ♗f8+ wins.

Other moves are less dangerous, for example **11 ♘e2 ♕xd2 12 ♖xd2 ♘gf6 13 ♘g3 0-0 14 f5 ♘b6 15 b3 e6** was equal in Westerinen–Hertneck, Altensteig 1987, while **11 ♗d3 ♘b6 12 ♖hg1 ♘c4 13 ♗xc4 bc 14 f5 ♖b8 15 ♘e2 ♕xd2 16 ♖xd2 ♘f6 17 c3**, Peelen–Arapovic, Lugano 1985, should have been met by 17 ... ♔d7 with rough equality.

After 11 e5, the continuation 11 ... ♘h6 (not 11 ... d5?! 12 f5 gf 13 ♕g2 ♗f8 14 e6! ♘b6 15 ♕h3 and White had a dangerous attack in Klovan–Chuit, USSR 1974) 12 ♗d3 ♘b6 13 f5 ♘xf5 14 ♗xf5 ♘c4 15 ♕d3 gf 16 ed ♕b4 17 d7+ ♔xd7 18 ♕xf5+ ♔e8 19 ♗c1 ♗h6 20 f4 ♗xf4 led to a draw in Andre–Smejkal, Dortmund 1977, in view of the perpetual 21 ♕xf4 ♘a3+ 22 ♔a1 ♘xc2+.

In summary, 4 ... c6 may be recommended for Black as leading to unbalanced positions without the usual corollary of excessive risk.

7 | Classical: Introduction and 6 0-0 ♗g4 7 ♗e3 ♘c6 8 ♕d2 e5

Together with the Austrian Attack, this is the most popular line against the Pirc in current play. The initial moves of the Classical System, 1 e4 d6 2 d4 ♘f6 3 ♘c3 g6 4 ♘f3 ♗g7 5 ♗e2 0-0, already show that the philosophy behind this line is quite different to that underlying the Austrian Attack. White contents himself with a modest centre and develops quickly behind it, putting his pieces on flexible squares to be ready for Black's counteraction in the centre, be it by ... e5 or ... c5. Despite the undoubted importance of this variation, it has suffered a gradual decline over the past decade. Although White has very few losing chances, it is also true that Black is not posed any early problems, and all too often the result is a quick draw. Therefore there has been a trend towards slightly sharper options for White, while steering clear of the full-blooded aggression of the Austrian Attack.

Black's normal response is to prepare ... e5 and White generally has the choice between exchanging, by de, or advancing with d5. The former leaves a symmetrical pawn structure with one open file down which all the major pieces are exchanged. Although endgame experts sometimes favour this line many players prefer d5, even though the position of the knight at c3, blocking the advance of White's c-pawn, makes a poor comparison with the King's Indian. On the other hand White's good development and well-centralized position sometimes enables him to start active operations on the kingside with f4.

After 6 0-0 Black has two choices, namely 6 ... ♗g4 and 6 ... c6. The former directly steps up the pressure on d4 and prepares ... ♘c6 and ... e5, while the second is more flexible and can be preparation for ... b5 or ... d5 as well as ... ♕c7 and ... e5. After 6 ... ♗g4 the sequence 7 ♗e3 ♘c6 8 ♕d2 (for ♖ad1) e5 is natural, with both sides training their pieces on the square d4. This chapter deals with the resulting position. Of course, there are alternatives after 6 ... ♗g4, such as 7 ♗e3 ♘c6 8 d5 or 8 ♘d2, and these are covered in chapter 8. The other move 6 ... c6 gives White the choice of preventing ... ♗g4 once and for all by h3 (Chapter 9), or simply to continue developing with 7 a4 or 7 ♖e1 (Chapter 10). A number of less common 6th moves are available for Black and these are sometimes employed to avoid a draw (Chapter 11). Finally in Chapter 12 we deal with lines arising from 1 e4 g6 2 d4 ♗g7 3 ♘c3 d6 4 ♘f3 which do not transpose into the main line.

1 e4 d6 2 d4 ♘f6 3 ♘c3 g6 4 ♘f3 ♗g7 5 ♗e2 0-0 6 0-0 ♗g4 7 ♗e3 ♘c6

8 ♕d2   e5 *(53)*

For 8 ... ♖e8 see Chapter 8.

After 8 ... e5 White can play 9 de or 9 d5, these two moves leading to quite different positions. White's aim with 9 de is to preserve a slight endgame advantage while avoiding any chance of defeat. 9 d5 is probably no better for White, but leads to more interesting positions.

A: 9 de
B: 9 d5

A

9 de   de
10 ♖ad1

Tal–Balashov, USSR Ch. 1976 concluded 10 ♖fd1 ♕c8 11 ♕e1 ♖d8 12 ♖xd8+ ♕xd8 13 ♖d1 ♕f8 14 h3 ♗xf3 15 ♗xf3 ♖d8 ½–½. It seems more logical to play ♖ad1 and ♕c1 as opposed to ♖fd1 and ♕e1 since the c-pawn is defended in the first line.

10 ...   ♕c8

Or:

(a) **10 ... ♕e7** (seems inferior) 11 ♗g5 (11 ♘d5 ♘xd5 12 ed ♗xf3 13 ♗xf3 ♘d4 14 ♗g4 f5 15 ♖fe1 ♕c5 16 ♗xd4 ed 17 ♗f3 is more or less equal) ♕e6 (11 ... ♗xf3 12 ♗xf3 ♘d4 13 ♘d5 ♕d6 14 c3 ♘xf3+ 15 gf ♘xd5 16 ♕xd5 ♕a6 17 ♔g2 and White's better bishop and d-file control gave him the advantage in Andersson–Mecking, Wijk aan Zee 1971) 12 ♗xf6 ♕xf6 13 ♘d5 ♕d6 14 c3 ♖ad8 15 ♕g5 ♗e6? (15 ... ♗xf3 was better, although White can still claim some advantage) 16 ♗b5 ♗xd5 17 ♖xd5 ♕e7 18 ♖xc6 ♕xg5 19 ♘xg5 bc 20 ♖a5 with a clear plus for White, Browne–Kaplan, Skopje Ol. 1972.

(b) **10 ... ♕xd2** (hardly ever

53
W

played now) 11 ♖xd2 ♖fd8 12 ♖fd1 ♖xd2 (12 ... a6 is more sensible, but this is still an inferior version of the main line) 13 ♖xd2 ♘e8 (defending the e5 pawn in preparation for ... ♖d8) 14 ♗b5! (14 ♘d5 ♗xf3 15 ♗xf3 ♘d4 16 c3 ♘xf3+ 17 gf ♗f8 18 f4 f6 19 fe fe 20 ♗g5 is also good for White) and White is clearly better e.g. 14 ... ♗xf3 15 ♗xc6 or 14 ... ♘e7 15 ♗xe8 ♖xe8 16 ♘b5.

11 ♕c1

Better than 11 ♗g5 ♗xf3 12 ♗xf3 ♘d4 when both 13 ♗e2 c6 14 f4 ♘xe2+ 15 ♕xe2 ef and 13 ♕d3 c6 14 ♘e2 ♘xf3+ 15 ♕xf3 ♕e6 16 ♘c1 ♖fd8, Enklaar–Matulovic, Wijk aan Zee 1974, are equal.

11 ...   ♖d8
12 ♖xd8+   ♕xd8

Although infrequently played, the reply 12 ... ♘xd8 may be better. Black's only problem in the main line is that White can arrange to play c3, preventing ... ♘d4, but it is not so simple for Black to play ... c6. By taking with the knight Black prepares both ... ♘e6 and ... c6. The tactical justification is that 13 ♘xe5 ♗xe2 14 ♘xe2 ♘xe4 is fine for Black, while 13 ♘d5? ♘xd5 14 ed e4 15 ♘d4 ♗xd4 16 ♗xg4 ♗xe3 even wins. Therefore Browne–Nunn, Wijk aan Zee 1983, continued 13 ♖d1 ♘e6 14 ♕d2 (14 ♘d5 ♘xd5 15 ed ♗xf3 16 ♗xf3 ♘d4 17 ♗xd4 ed 18 ♕f4 ½-½, Gheorghiu–Nunn, Lugano 1983) ♗xf3 15 ♗xf3 ½-½, as after 15 ... c6 White has absolutely nothing.

13 ♖d1   ♕f8
14 h3   ♗xf3
15 ♗xf3 (54)

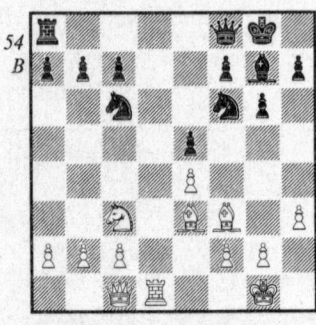

At first sight the impending exchange of rooks down the d-file renders this position a clear draw, but Black has to be careful. The g7 bishop will be out of play for a number of moves and the d5 square is more likely to be occupied than d4, which is easily defended by c3. There is some disagreement over Black's best move here; should he prevent ♘b5 or not?

15 ...   ♖d8

Or:

(a) 15 ... h5 (the idea is to exchange the troublesome bishop by ... ♔h7 and ... ♗h6) 16 ♘b5 ♖c8 17 c3 (White cannot take on a7 because the bishop will never get out again) ♔h7 18 ♘a3 ♗h6 19 ♗xh6 (19 ♘c2 is more logical

Classical: Introduction and 6 0–0 ♗g4 7 ♘e3 etc. | 71

since an exchange on e3 speeds the knight towards d5; however White's advantage is minute in any case) ♕xh6 20 ♕xh6+ ♔xh6 21 h4 ♔g7 22 ♘c4 a5 23 ♔f1 ♔f8, Cramling–Yrjola, Gausdal 1984, with a completely satisfactory position for Black (who in fact won the game).

(b) **15 ... a6** 16 ♘b1! (16 ♘e2 ♖d8 17 ♖xd8 ♕xd8 is harmless, e.g. 18 c3 h5 19 ♘g3 ♔h7 20 ♗g5 ½–½, Unzicker–Vogel, Bundesliga 1986, or 18 ♕d2 h5 19 ♕xd8+ ♘xd8 20 ♘c1 ♘e6 21 ♘d3 ♘d7 22 c3 ♗f6 23 g3 ♗g5 with equality, Abramovic–Franco, Vrnjacka Banja 1983) ♖d8 17 ♖xd8 ♕xd8 18 c3 ♕d3 19 ♘d2 ♗f8 20 ♕b1 ♕b5 21 ♕c2 ♘d8 22 ♕b3 ♕d3 (22 ... ♕xb3 23 ♘xb3 b6 was better, with just a tiny edge for White) 23 ♕c4 ♕d6 24 ♕e2 ♕e6 25 ♕d3 ♘c6 26 a3 ♕e7 27 b4 (the familiar strategy of crowding out the two knights when having the bishop pair) ♘d8 28 ♘c4 ♘d7 29 ♗g4 (Black's bad bishop never achieves a corresponding level of activity) ♘e6 30 ♘a5 (Black is in trouble by now) b5 31 ♘c6 ♕e8 32 c4 (opening the position for the bishops and acquiring a passed pawn on the a-file) ♘f6 33 cb ab 34 ♕xb5 ♘xe4 35 ♕c4 ♘d6 36 ♕d5 h5 37 ♗xe6 fe 38 ♕c5 ♘f5 39 ♕c2 ♗g7 40 b5 ♘d4 41 ♕c4 ♕d7 42 a4 ♘f5 43 ♕e2 1–0 as the a-pawn is too strong, Petrosian–Sax, Tallinn 1979.

16 ♘b5

The only move to cause Black problems, e.g. 16 ♘d5 (16 ♖xd8 ♕xd8 17 ♕d2 ♕xd2 18 ♗xd2 ♘d4 19 ♗d1 c6 20 g3 ♗f8 21 ♔g2 ♗b4 was insipid, Karpov–Timman, Amsterdam 1988) ♘xd5 17 ♖xd5 ♖xd5 18 ed ♘d4 19 ♗d1 ♘f5 is dead equal, for example 20 a3 ♕d6 21 c4 ♘xe3 22 ♕xe3 a5, Jamieson–Torre, New Zealand 1977, or 20 c3 b6 21 ♗b3 ♘xe3 22 ♕xe3 ♕d6 23 g4, Lein–Taulbut, Hastings 1978/9, with complete equality in both cases.

16 ...   ♖xd1+

After 16 ... ♖c8 White can still play for the win, for example Andersson–Chi, Buenos Aires Ol. 1978 continued 17 c3 a6 18 ♘a3 ♖d8 19 ♖xd8 ♕xd8 20 ♘c4 ♕d3 (this is similar to Petrosian–Sax above) 21 ♘d2 ♘d7 22 ♗d1 ♘f8 23 ♗c2 ♕d7 24 ♘f3 ♘e6 25 g3 ♘a5 26 ♕d2 ♕xd2 27 ♘xd2 ♔f8 28 b4 ♘c6 29 ♘c4 ♔e7 30 a4 ♔d7 31 h4 and Black was gradually pushed back.

17 ♕xd1   ♕b8 *(55)*

Better than 17 ... ♕b4 (17 ... ♕c8 18 ♘xa7 ♘xa7 19 ♗xa7 b6 20 c3! ♕a8 21 ♕a4 leaves Black trying to justify the loss of his a-pawn) 18 ♘xa7! ♕d4 (the check on d8 stops the usual bishop-trapping manoeuvre) 19 c3 ♘xf3+ 20 gf with a clear advantage for White, Kosten–van der Sterren, Balatonbereny 1983.

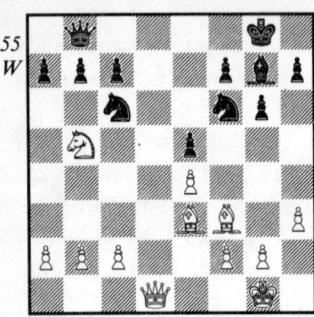

After 17 ... ♕b8 White's advantage is microscopic, e.g. 18 c3 ♗f8! (interfering with the knight's retreat to a3; 18 ... h5 19 ♘a3 ♕c8 20 ♕b3 a6 21 ♘c4 ♔h7 22 ♗g5 ♕e6 23 ♘e3 ♕xb3 24 ab left White somewhat better in Hansen–Hoi, match 1985) 19 ♗g5 ♗e7 20 ♗xf6 ♗xf6 21 ♕d7 ♕d8! 22 ♗g4 (22 ♕xc7 ♕d2 provides adequate counterplay) h5 with equality, Ivanchuk–Azmaiparashvili, Tallinn 1986.

Even the main line offers White very little, so if one also takes into account the possible improvements 12 ... ♘xd8 and 15 ... h5 the conclusion must be that White's winning chances are very remote after 9 de.

9 d5   ♘e7

This move, supporting ... f5, is better than 9 ... ♘b8, when Tal–Hort, Montreal 1979, continued 10 ♖ad1 ♘bd7 11 h3 ♗xf3 12 ♗xf3 ♔h8 13 a4 ♘g8 14 ♗e2 a6 15 a5 ♕e7 16 b4 f5 17 ef gf 18 f4

with advantage for White.

10 ♖ad1   (56)

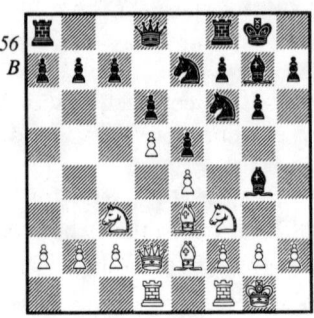

10 ...   ♗d7 (57)

There are many other possibilities, which we arrange in descending order of importance:
(a) 10 ... b5 (this move enjoyed a brief vogue as a result of Azmaiparashvili's win over Karpov, but it appears to be unsound) and now:
(a1) 11 a3 (11 b4 a6 12 h3 ♗d7 13 ♘e1 c6 14 dc ♗xc6 is fine for Black, Kuzmin–Azmaiparashvili, USSR 1985) a5 12 b4 (if White takes the pawn now then play is similar to line a2, for example 12 ♗xb5 ♗xf3 13 gf ♘h5 14 ♔h1 f5 15 ♕e1 ♘f4 16 ♖g1 h6 17 ♗xf4 ef 18 ef g5 19 ♗d3 ♔h8, Liberzon–Quinteros, Netanya 1983, and now 20 h4! ♘xf5 21 hg hg 22 ♖g2 would have been good for White) ab 13 ab ♖a3 (13 ... ♕b8 14 ♖a1 ♕b7 15 ♗g5 ♗d7 16 ♖fb1 ♖fb8 17 h3 ♘c8 was level

in Perenyi–Simic, Pernik 1980) 14 ♗g5 ♖xc3 15 ♗xf6 ♗xf3 16 ♗xf3 ♖a3, Karpov–Azmaiparashvili, USSR Ch. 1983, and now 17 ♗xe7 drawing would have been the best.

(a2) **11 ♗xb5!** ♘xe4 (11 ... ♗xf3 12 gf ♘h5 was the original idea behind 10 ... b5, but Black does not get enough for the pawn, e.g. 13 ♔h1 ♕c8 14 ♖g1 ♕h3 15 ♗e2 f5 16 ♕d3 ♘f4 17 ♗xf4 ef 18 ♘b5 with a good game for White, Rizzitano–Wolff, USA 1983; see also Liberzon–Quinteros above) 12 ♘xe4 f5 13 ♘eg5 f4 14 ♘e6 (14 ♗c5! dc 15 ♗c4 is the simplest way for White to gain an advantage) ♗xe6 15 de fe 16 ♕xe3 c6 17 ♗c4 (17 ♗a4 ♕c7 18 c4 ♖f4 19 ♗b3 ♖af8 gave Black excellent play for the pawn, N. Gonzalez–Camacho, Cuba 1985) ♕c7 18 ♗b3 d5 19 ♕c5 ♖ac8 20 ♖fe1 ♖f5 21 ♖e4! de 22 ♖d7 ♗f8 23 ♖xc7 ♖xc7 24 ♕a5 with advantage for White, Venni–Segatini, Caorle 1986.

(b) **10 ... ♘d7** (White is able to force the positionally useful exchange of white-squared bishops after this) and now:

(b1) **11 ♘g5!** ♗xe2 12 ♘xe2 h6 13 ♘h3 ♔h7 14 b3 (not 14 ♘g3 f5 15 f4, Drvota–Szymczak, Decin 1978, when 15 ... g5! would have been quite good for Black, but 14 c4 f5 15 ef is just as good as Timman's move) f5 15 ef ♘xf5 (15 ... gf 16 f4 is likewise ±) 16 f3 ♘f6 17 ♘g3 ♘xe3 18 ♕xe3 c6 19 c4 and Black's long-term problems with his dark-squared bishop give White the edge, Timman–Seirawan, Las Palmas 1981.

(b2) **11 ♘e1** ♗xe2 12 ♕xe2 f5 13 f4 ef 14 ♗xf4 ♖xc3! 15 bc fe 16 ♕xe4 ♘c5 is equal, for example 17 ♕c4 ♕d7 18 ♘d3 ♕a4! 19 ♕xa4 ♘xa4 20 c4 ♘f5 21 ♖de1 ♖ae8 22 c5 (22 ♗d2 ♘d4 23 ♖xf8+ ♔xf8 24 ♗h6+ ♔f7 was good for Black in Chernikov–Gufeld, USSR 1978) ♘c3 23 cd (23 ♖xe8 ♖xe8 24 g4? ♘d4 25 cd ♘de2+! 26 ♔h1 ♘xf4 27 ♘xf4 cd and again Black stands very well, Geller–Kuzmin, Lvov 1978) cd 24 ♖xe8 ♖xe8 25 g4 ♘d4 26 ♗xd6 ♘xd5 with equality, Yuratiev–Karasev, USSR 1977.

(c) **10 ... ♔h8** 11 h3 (favoured by Karpov; 11 ♘e1 ♗xe2 12 ♕xe2 ♘d7 gives White the choice between 13 f3 f5 14 g4 fg 15 fg ♖xf1+ 16 ♕xf1 ♘f6 17 h3 ♕d7 18 ♘f3 ♖f8 with only a very slight plus for White, as in Barle–Matulovic, Yugoslavia Ch. 1975, or 13 f4! f5 14 ♘f3 ef 15 ♗xf4 fe?! 16 ♘g5 ♘c5 17 ♘cxe4 ♘f5 18 ♘xc5 dc 19 ♘e6 with clear advantage, Bielczyk–Niklasson, Stockholm 1975) ♗xf3 (11 ... ♗d7 makes much more sense, when 12 ♘e1 ♘fg8 13 ♘d3?! f5 14 f4 fe 15 ♘xe4 ♘xd5 was promising for Black in Vogt–Plachetka, Berlin 1979; 13 f4 was the critical move) 12 ♗xf3 ♘d7 13 ♗e2 f5 14 f4! a6 (14 ... g5?! 15 fg f4 16 ♗f2 h6 17 gh ♗xh6 18 ♗g4 ♘f6 19 ♕e2 ♖g8 20 ♗e6 and Black did not have enough for the pawn in Karpov–Keene, Moscow 1977) 15 fe ♘xe5 16 ♗f2! ♕d7 17 ♖df1 fe 18 ♘xe4 ♖xf2 19 ♗xf2 and the two bishops gave White a slight advantage in Karpov–Smejkal, Leningrad 1977.

(d) **10 ... ♗xf3** (giving in without a fight) 11 ♗xf3 ♘d7 12 ♗e2 f5 13 f4 (13 g3 ♘f6 14 f3 ♕d7?! 15 ♗b5 ♕c8 16 ♖f2 a6 17 ♗f1 was also good for White in Spassky–Parma, San Juan 1969) a6 14 g4 g5?! (picturesque, but not good! 14 ... ♔h8 was better) 15 ef ef 16 ♗d4 ♗xd4+ 17 ♕xd4 ♔f7 18 ♘e4 h6 19 h4 ♖g8 20 hg hg 21 ♖d3 and the invasion down the h-file is too much for Black, Planinc–Sigurjonsson, Ljubljana–Portoroz 1977.

(e) **10 ... a6** (like 10 ... ♔h8, this is a semi-waiting move) 11 ♘e1 (11 h3 is possible) ♗xe2 12 ♕xe2 ♘h5 13 ♘d3 f5 14 ef ♘xf5 15 ♘e4 ♘xe3 16 ♕xe3 ♘f4 17 c4 ♕h4 18 f3 ♗h6 19 ♕e1 ♕e7 20 ♘xf4 ♖xf4 and Black has been left with a typical King's Indian bad bishop position, Tringov–Arnaudov, Sofia 1977.

(f) **10 ... ♘c8** (Donner's interesting idea defends the d-pawn in preparation for ... c6) 11 ♘e1 (11 h3 ♗d7 12 ♗g5 ♕e8 13 ♘h2 b5 14 ♗f3 ♔h8 15 ♘e2 ♘g8 16 ♘g3 ♘ce7 17 ♖fe1 ♕b8 18 ♗e2 ♕b7 is equal, Balashov–Hickl, Dortmund 1987) ♗d7 12 ♔h1 (12 f4 ♘g4! 13 f5 ♘xe3 14 ♕xe3 c6 15 ♔h1 ♕h4 16 ♕f3 ♗f6 17 dc bc = is Liberzon–Donner, Amsterdam 1977, while 12 f3 c6 13 dc bc 14 ♗c4 ♗e6 15 ♗b3 ♕c7? 16 ♔h1 ♘d7 17 ♗h6 ♘db6 18 ♗xg7 ♔xg7 19 f4 ef 20 ♕xf4 ♕e7 21 ♘f3 was good for White in Kaiszauri–Donner, Buenos Aires Ol. 1978, but 14 ... ♘b6 or 15 ... ♕e7 would have been unclear) ♘b6 13 ♗g5 ♘a4? 14 ♘xa4 ♗xa4 15 ♕b4 ♗d7 16 ♕xb7 winning a pawn, Larsen–Donner, England 1977. Unfortunately, Black's play in these examples did not give the idea of ... ♘c8 a fair test.

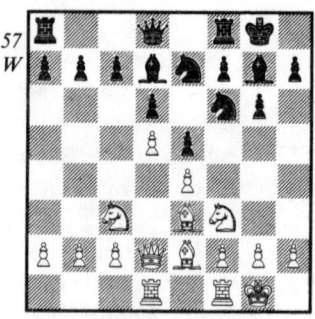

11 ♘e1

Preparing the advance of the f-pawn. Two other tries:
(a) **11 h3** ♘e8 (11 ... b5 12 b4 a5 13 a3 ♕b8 14 ♗g5 ♔h8 15 ♖b1! a4 16 ♖bd1 ♕b7 17 ♕d3 ± is Karpov–Timman, Amsterdam 1976, but 11 ... ♔h8 is reason-

able, transposing to line c in the note to Black's 10th move) 12 ♘h2 f5 13 f4 ♔h8 (13 ... ef 14 ♗xf4 ♘f6 15 ef ♗xf5 16 ♗f3 ♘d7, Vogt–Sigurjonsson, Cienfuegos 1975, and now 17 g4! ♗xc2 18 ♖de1, threatening ♗g5, wins according to Vogt) 14 ♘f3 fe 15 ♘xe4 ♘f5 16 fe de 17 ♗g5 ♕c8 18 g4 ♘fd6 19 ♘xe5!? ♖xf1+ (19 ... ♘xe4 20 ♖xf8+ ♗xf8 21 ♕d4 ♗c5 22 ♘xg6+ ♔g8 23 ♘e7+ ♗xe7 24 ♖xe7 is good for White) 20 ♖xf1 ♘xe4 21 ♘f7+ (21 ♕d4 ♘8d6 22 ♗h6 ♕g8 defends) ♔g8 22 ♘h6+ ♔h8 (22 ... ♗xh6 23 ♗xh6 ♘8f6 is unclear) 23 ♘f7+ ♔g8 24 ♘h6+ ♔h8 ½–½ Ornstein–Niklasson, Swedish Ch. 1975.

(b) 11 ♗h6 ♘c8 (11 ... ♘e8 is also possible, but 11 ... ♗xh6 12 ♕xh6 ♔h8 13 ♘e1 ♘eg8?! 14 ♕d2 ♕e7 15 f4 ef 16 ♖xf4 ♗e8 17 ♕d4 ♕e5 18 ♘f2, Planinc–Ree, Wijk aan Zee 1974, and 11 ... ♘h5 12 ♗xg7 ♔xg7 13 g3 ♗h3 14 ♖fe1 h6 15 ♘h4 ♘f6 16 f4 ♘g4 17 ♗f1 ♗xf1 18 ♖xf1 ♘g8 19 h3 ♘4f6 20 fe de, Haag–Botterill, Birmingham 1975, were both good for White) 12 ♗xg7 ♔xg7 13 ♘e1 c5 14 f4 ef 15 ♕xf4 ♕e7 16 ♘d3 ♘b6 17 ♖f2 ♗ae8 18 ♖df1 ♘g8! 19 ♕g3 a6 20 h4 ♗c8 21 h5 ♘d7 and Black's accurate play has brought a knight to e5 and equalized, Groszpeter–Mednis, Budapest 1978.

11 ...   ♘g4

11 ... b5! is more promising than at move 10 (it doesn't lose a pawn!) and in fact White has not been able to gain any advantage, for example 12 f3 ♕b8 and now:
(a) 13 ♘d3 a5 (Friedstein suggests 13 ... ♖d8 14 ♘f2 c6) 14 ♘f2 ♘h5 15 b3 ♘f4! 16 g3, Bangiev–Hait, USSR 1977, and now 16 ... ♘xe2+ 17 ♘xe2 f5 is level.
(b) 13 ♘b1 ♘h5 14 c4 bc 15 ♗xc4 f5 16 ♘d3 ♔h8 17 ♖c1 ♘f6 18 ♘c3 c6 with equality, Ostermeyer–Botterill, Teesside 1978.
(c) 13 a3 a5 14 ♘d3 c6 15 dc ♗xc6 16 ♗h6 b4 17 ♗xg7 ♔xg7 18 ab ab 19 ♘b1 ♕b6+ 20 ♔h1 ♖ab8 and Black is at least equal, Barlov–Jansa, Bor 1985.

The move 11 ... ♔h8 was played in Matulovic–Plachetka, Vinkovci 1982, and after 12 f4 ♘g4 13 ♗xg4 ♗xg4 14 ♖b1 c6 Black had 'gained' the move ... ♔h8 over the main line. Unfortunately this turned out to be a Pyrrhic victory since 15 dc bc 16 fe forced Black to take with his bishop (16 ... de 17 ♕xd8 wins a pawn as f7 is undefended) and 16 ... ♗xe5 17 h3 ♗e6 18 ♘f3 ♗g7 19 ♖bd1 ♘c8 20 e5 gave White a definite advantage.

12	♗xg4	♗xg4
13	f3	♗d7
14	f4	

14 ♗h6 ♗xh6 15 ♕xh6 c6 16 dc ♕b6+ 17 ♔h1 ♗xc6 18 f4 f6 19 ♘d3 f5! 20 fe fe 21 ♘f4 ♘f5 is

a little better for Black, Browne–Timman, Stockholm 1971/2.

14 ...   ♗g4

In Geller–Tal, Moscow 1975, White quickly gained an advantage after 14 ... ef 15 ♗xf4 f5 16 ♘f3 fe 17 ♘xe4 ♗g4 18 ♖de1 ♕d7 19 ♘eg5 ♖ae8 20 c4! due to the weakness of the square e6.

15   ♖b1

White should be able to keep a very slight advantage by 15 ♘f3, for example 15 ... f5 (15 ... ef 16 ♗xf4 f5 17 ♖de1 ♗xf3 18 ♖xf3 ♕d7 19 e5 de 20 ♗xe5 ♘c8 21 ♗xg7 ♕xg7 22 h4 ♘d6 23 ♕f4 also gives White the edge, Karpov–Nunn, Hamburg 1982) 16 fe de 17 h3 ♗xf3 18 ♖xf3 ♕d7 19 ♕d3 ♘c8 with a slight plus for White, Pfleger–Adorjan, Buenos Aires Ol. 1978.

15 ...   c6 *(58)*

16   fe

This offers better chances than 16 h3 ♗d7 17 fe (17 dc ♗xc6 18 ♖d1 ef 19 ♖xf4 f5 20 ♕d3 fe 21 ♖xf8+ ♕xf8 22 ♘xe4 ♘f5 is a little better for Black, Karpov–Adorjan, Las Palmas 1977) de 18 ♗c5 (Karpov–Timman, Tilburg 1977, continued 18 d6?! ♘c8 19 ♖d1 ♘b6 20 b3 ♗e6 21 ♘e2 ♘d7 22 ♘f3 f6 23 c4 ♔h8 24 ♔h1 ♗g8 25 ♘g3 c5! and once again Black had slightly more than equalized) cd (not 18 ... b6 19 dc nor 18 ... ♖e8 19 ♕f2) 19 ♘xd5 ♘xd5! 20 ♗xf8 ♕b6+ 21 ♔h1 ♖xf8 22 ed (after 22 ♕xd5 ♗c6 23 ♕d3 ♕d4 the e-pawn drops off) and Black's active pieces give him sufficient compensation for the exchange. Torre–Chandler, Penang 1978, went on 22 ... ♗b5 23 ♖f3 e4 24 ♖b3 ♕f6! 25 ♘d3! ♗c4 26 ♘c5 (26 ♖b4? ♗xa2 27 ♖d1 ♗xd5 was very good for Black in Berry–Chandler, London 1978) ♗xb3 27 ab ♕f5 28 ♘xb7 e3! 29 ♕xe3 ♕xd5 30 ♕f3 (30 ♕xa7 ♖e8 leaves White with problems over the stranded knight) ♕xf3 31 gf ♖e8 32 c3 ♖e3 33 ♔g2 ♖e2+ 34 ♔g1 ♗h6 35 ♘d6 ½–½ as after 35 ... ♗e3+ 36 ♔h1 ♗f4 and 37 ... ♖h2+ Black regains the pawn.

16 ...   de
17   ♗c5

White has a slight advantage. In Liberzon–Chandler, Hastings 1980/1, Black blundered by 17 ... cd? allowing 18 ♕g5 winning a piece. Perhaps Black should try 17 ... b6 (this is impossible when h3 and ... ♗d7 have been interposed because the reply dc wins material) 18 ♗a3 c5, but 19 b4 is promising for White.

The move 11...b5! is an effective antidote to White's system, so the current view is that the main line of the Classical gives White no real advantage.

8 | Classical: 6 0-0 ♗g4 7 Others

In this chapter we consider deviations from the line of Chapter 7. The most important of these are 8 ♘d2 and 8 d5. The former is an attempt to exchange off the 'bad' bishop before Black plays ... e5. Although positionally well motivated, the resulting King's Indian type positions are not especially favourable for White. The reason is that he needs to spend at last one tempo to free the c-pawn and this gives Black the chance to organize counterplay. 8 d5 forces Black to concede the two bishops; although the bishops have little scope to start with, they can become powerful later. White may be slightly better in this line.
1 e4 d6 2 d4 ♘f6 3 ♘c3 g6 4 ♘f3 ♗g7 5 ♗e2 0-0 6 0-0 ♗g4 7 ♗e3

The most common alternatives are:

(a) **7 ♗g5** ♘c6 8 ♕d2 (8 h3 is line b) ♘d7 9 ♘d5 ♘f6 (9 ... ♖e8 10 c3 ♘b6 11 ♘e3 ♗xf3 12 ♗xf3 f6 13 ♗h4 e5 14 d5 ♘e7 15 ♗g4!, Lerner–Tseshkovsky, Odessa 1974, or 9 ... h6 10 ♗xh6 ♗xh6 11 ♕xh6 ♗xf3 12 ♗xf3 ♘xd4 13 ♗d1 e6 14 ♘e3 ♕f6 15 c3 ♘c6 16 f4, Ciric–Peelen Amsterdam II 1984, and White is a little better in both cases) 10 ♘xf6+ ef 11 ♗e3 f5 12 h3 ♗xf3 13 ♗xf3 14 ♗xf4 ♘xd4 15 ♗d1 ♘e6 with equality, Byrne–Sigurjonsson, Geneva 1977.

(b) **7 h3** (White aims for a very slight advantage, but as in so many lines of this type the usual result is a draw) ♗xf3 8 ♗xf3 ♘c6 *(59)* and now:

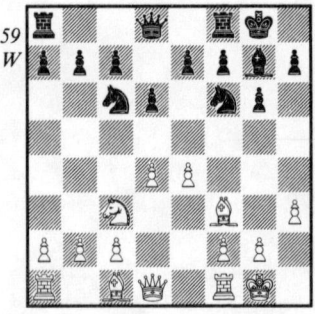

(b1) **9 ♘b5** a6 10 ♘a3 e5 11 c3 ed 12 cd d5 13 ed ♘xd5 14 ♕b3 ♘b6 15 ♘c2 ♗xd4 16 ♗f4 ♗e5 17 ♗xe5 ♘xe5 18 ♗xb7 ♖b8 19 ♗xa6 and White has a very small

advantage, Alexandria–Chiburdanidze, match 1977.
(b2) **9 ♗g5** h6 (9 ... ♘d7 10 ♘e2 f6 11 ♗e3 e5 12 g3 ed 13 ♘xd4 ♘xd4 14 ♗xd4 ♘c5 15 ♗g2 with an edge for White, Fleck–Rostalski, Bundesliga 1986) 10 ♗e3 e5 (this should be compared with line b3, since the only difference is in the position of Black's h-pawn) 11 de (11 d5 ♘e7 12 ♕d2 ♔h7 13 ♖ad1 ♘d7 14 ♗e2 f5 15 f3 f4 16 ♗f2 ♘f6 = Fabisovich–Karasev, USSR 1978) de 12 ♘e2 (12 ♘b5 a6! 13 ♕xd8 ♖fxd8 14 ♘xc7 ♖ac8 15 ♘d5 ♘xd5 16 ed ♘d4 17 ♗xd4 ed 18 ♖ac1 h5 =, Polugaevsky–Matulovic, Lugano Ol. 1968) ♕xd1 (12 ... ♕e7 as in line b3 looks better) 13 ♖axd1 ♖fd8 14 c3 ♘e8 15 g3 ♘d6 16 b3 a5 17 a4 with a small advantage for White, Vasiukov–Tseshkovsky, USSR 1982.
(b3) **9 ♗e3** e5 (9 ... ♘d7 10 d5 ♘a5 11 ♗e2 c6 12 ♖b1 ♖c8 13 ♖e1 cd, Short–Botterill, Brighton 1984, and now 14 ed might have given White an edge) 10 de de 11 ♘e2 (11 ♘b5 a6! is even better than in line b2 because h6 is free for Black's bishop) ♕e7 (11 ... ♕xd1 12 ♖fxd1 ♖fd8 13 c3 a5 14 ♘g3 was depressing for Black, Razuvaev–Azmaiparashvili, USSR Ch. 1983) 12 c3 ♖fd8 (12 ... ♖fb8?! 13 b4 a5 was played in Plachetka–Azmaiparashvili, Stary Smokovec 1983, and now 14 a3 would have given White the edge, but 12 ... a5 is a sensible move, staking out a claim to space on the queenside) 13 ♕b3 ♘a5 14 ♕b5 b6 15 ♖fd1 ♘b7 16 ♘g3 ♘d6 and White's advantage is microscopic, Speelman–McNab, Brighton 1984.

7 ... ♘c6 *(60)*

Or 7 ... ♘bd7 (7 ... e5 loses material after 8 de de 9 ♘xe5 ♕xd1 10 ♗xd1 ♗xd1 11 ♖axd1 ♘xe4 12 ♘xg6 ♘xc3 13 ♘e7+ ♔h8 14 bc ♗xc3 15 ♘d5 ♗e5 16 f4, Kaufmann–Bartos, Prague 1986) and now:
(a) **8 ♘d2** ♗xe2 9 ♕xe2 e5 10 d5 c6 (10 ... ♘e8 followed by ... f5 is a sensible alternative) 11 a4 cd 12 ed ♘e8 (12 ... ♘b6 13 ♕b5 ♘g4 14 ♗xb6 ab 15 ♘c4 ♖c8 16 ♘e4 was good for White in Kavalek–Christiansen, Los Angeles 1987) 13 a5 a6 14 ♘a4 f5 ½-½, Milos–Kavalek, Dubai 1986.
(b) **8 ♖e1** e5 9 de de 10 ♕d3 c6 11 h3 ♗xf3 12 ♗xf3 ♕e7 13 ♕c4 ♖fd8 14 ♖ed1 ♗f8 15 ♘e2 with a small edge for White, Browne–Christiansen, San Francisco 1987.
(c) **8 h3** (the simplest; with the knight on d7 White is not forced to commit his d-pawn after ... e5) ♗xf3 9 ♗xf3 e5 10 g3 c6 11 ♗g2 ♕a5 (it is harder for Black to create counterplay when White's pawn centre is intact) 12 ♕d2! ♖fe8 13 ♖ad1 b5 14 a3 and White is better, Karpov–Nunn, Tilburg 1982.

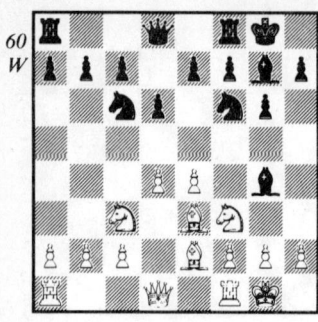

8 ♕d2

Or:
(a) **8 d5** (8 h3 ♗xf3 9 ♗xf3 transposes to line b3 in the note to White's 7th move) ♗xf3 9 ♗xf3 ♘e5 10 ♗e2 c6 and now:
(a1) **11 f4** ♘ed7 12 dc (12 ♗f3 cd and now both 13 ♘xd5 ♘xd5 14 ♕xd5 ♗xb2 15 ♖ab1 ♘b6! 16 ♕xb7 ♘c4 17 ♖xb2 ♘xe3 ∓ Tringov–Donner, Nice Ol. 1974, and 13 ed ♖c8 14 ♖e1 ♘b6 15 ♗d4 ♖c4! 16 ♘e2 ♕c7 17 c3 ♘fxd5! ∓ Grigorov–Pribyl, Varna 1976 were very pleasant for Black) bc 13 ♕d2 a5 (13 ... ♖b8 14 b3 ♕a5 15 ♖ad1 ♖fe8 16 ♗f3 ♖bd8 17 ♘d5!? ♕a3 18 ♘xf6+ ♗xf6 19 c4 ± Ubilava–Kaiszauri, USSR 1977) 14 ♗f3 ♘b6 15 b3 ♘fd7 16 a4 e6 17 ♖ad1 d5 18 ed ed with equality in Urzica–Tseshkovsky, Moscow 1977.
(a2) **11 a4** (this offers White chances for a small advantage) ♕a5 12 ♖a3 ♖fc8 (12 ... ♘ed7 13 ♕d2 ♖fc8 14 ♖b1 a6 15 f3 h5 16 ♔h1 ♔h7 17 ♖b3 cd 18 ed ♘c5 19 ♖a3 is slightly better for White, Gavrikov–Maki, Leningrad 1984) 13 ♖b3 ♕c7 (13 ... ♖ab8 14 ♕d4 c5 15 ♕d1 a6 16 f4 ♘ed7 17 g4 ♘e8 18 g5 ♘c7 19 ♗g4 ♖d8 20 ♗xd7 ♖xd7 21 f5!? with a slight plus for White, Panchenko–Ehlvest, Leningrad 1984) 14 h3 ♘ed7 15 f4 cd 16 ed ♘c5 17 ♖b4 ♘fd7 18 ♗d4 a5 19 ♖b5, again with an edge for White, A. Sokolov–Timman, Brussels 1988.
(b) **8 ♘d2** ♗xe2 9 ♕xe2 e5 10 d5 ♘d4! (10 ... ♘e7 is worse, e.g. 11 ♘c4 ♕d7 12 f3 ♖ae8 13 ♘a5 b6 14 ♘b3 ♘h5 15 a4 a5 16 ♕b5 ♕d8 17 ♕c4 ♘c8 18 ♘b5 ♖e7 19 ♘c1, Taulbut–Hartoch, IBM B 1978, or 11 a4 c6 12 dc bc 13 ♘c4 ♕c7 14 f4 ♘h5 15 fe de 16 ♖ad1 ♘c8 17 ♕f3 ♘b6 18 ♘d2 ♘d7 19 ♘b3, Rohde–Goodman, London–New York match 1976, with a small plus for White in both cases) 11 ♕d3 c6 12 ♗g5 (12 dc bc 13 ♗xd4 ed 14 ♕xd4 ♘d5 15 ♕c4 ♘xc3 16 bc ♕a5 gives Black enough play for the pawn) ♕c7 13 ♗xf6 ♗xf6 14 ♘d1 cd 15 c3 ♘e6 16 ♕xd5 ♗g5, Pachman–Adorjan, Munich 1979. Black has a favourable type of Sicilian position and is at least equal.
(c) **8 ♕d3** and now:
(c1) **8 ... e5** (very infrequently played, although it is quite logical) 9 d5 ♘e7 (9 ... ♘b4 10 ♕d2 a5 11 h3 ♗d7 12 ♗g5 ♕e8 13 ♘h2 ♔h8 14 a3 ♘a6 15 ♗h6 ♗xh6 16 ♕xh6 ♘g8 17 ♕e3 with a very small plus for White, Kar-

pov–Korchnoi, match 1978) 10 h3 (10 ♘d2 is the critical move) ♗c8! 11 ♘d2 ♘d7 12 ♘c4 f5 13 f4 ef 14 ♖xf4 (14 ♗xf4 ♘c5) g5 15 ♖ff1 f4 16 ♗d4 ♘g6 with an edge for Black, Gligoric–Nunn, Baden 1980.

(c2) **8 ... ♘d7** 9 ♖ad1 (or 9 ♘d2 ♘b4 10 ♕c4 ♗xe2 11 ♘xe2 c5 12 dc dc 13 ♖ad1 ♕c7 14 ♘f3 b6 15 c3 ♘c6 16 ♗f4 ♘de5 17 ♗xe5 ♗xe5!, Polugaevsky–Sax, Buenos Aires Ol. 1978, or 9 ♘e1 ♗xe2 10 ♘xe2 e5 11 c3 ♘e7 12 ♘f3 ed 13 ♗xd4 ♘e5 14 ♗xe5 de 15 ♕c4 c6 16 ♖ad1 ♕c7, Karpov–Timman, Amsterdam 1980, with equality in both cases) a6 (9 ... ♘b6 10 a3 d5 11 h3 ♗xf3 12 ♗xf3 e5 13 ed ♘xd4 14 ♗xd4 ed 15 ♘b5 ♘xd5 16 ♗xd5 c6 17 ♖d2 cd 18 ♘xd4 ♕b6 was level in Belyavsky–Nunn, Baden 1980) 10 ♘d2 ♗xe2 11 ♘xe2, Ivanchuk–M. Gurevich, Lvov 1987, and now 11 ... e5!? 12 c3 (12 d5 ♘e7 13 c4 f5 14 f3 f4 15 ♗f2 g5 is unclear) ed 13 cd d5 is unclear according to Chernin.

(d) **8 ♘e1** has been played once or twice, but it isn't very fearsome, e.g. 8 ... ♗xe2 9 ♕xe2 e5 (or 9 ... ♘d7 followed by ... e5) 10 de ♘xe5 11 ♖d1 ♖e8 12 ♘d3 ♘c4 13 ♗g5 h6 14 ♗h4 ♕c8 15 a3 c6 with equality, Geller–Balashov, Moscow 1981.

8 ...   ♖e8 (61)

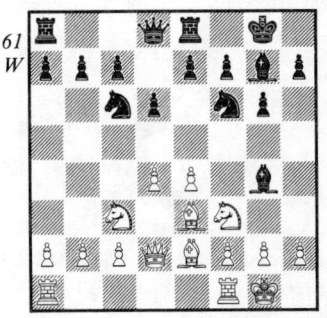

This move is the only significant alternative to 8 ... e5. The main problem is that Black will have to play ... e5 sooner or later and in the resulting position Black's ... ♖e8 is not an effective use of a tempo.

9 ♖ad1

Or 9 ♖fe1 (Andersson–Keene, Hastings 1971/2, continued 9 d5 ♗xf3 10 ♗xf3 ♘e5 11 ♗e2 c6 12 ♗d4 ♕a5 13 ♖ad1 ♘ed7 14 ♖fe1 a6 15 a3 c5 16 ♗e3 b5 17 f3 ♖ab8 =) a6 (9 ... ♗xf3 10 ♗xf3 e5 11 d5 ♘d4 12 ♗xd4 ed 13 ♘b5 is good for White) 10 ♖ad1 (10 a4 e5 11 d5 ♗xf3 12 ♗xf3 ♘d4 was fine for Black in Lengyel–M. Gurevich, Budapest 1987) ♗xf3 (10 ... e5 11 de de 12 ♕c1 ♕e7 13 ♘d5 ♘xd5 14 ed ♘d8 15 c4 f5 16 c5 ♘f7 17 d6 was good for White in Geller–Pribyl, Sochi 1984; 12 ... ♕c8 was better, but even so White's ♖fe1 is more likely to prove useful than Black's ... ♖e8) 11 ♗xf3 e5 12 de de 13 ♘a4 ♕e7 14 c3 b6 15 ♕e2 ♘d8 16 b3

♘e6 17 g3 h5 18 ♘b2 with a slight plus for White, Karpov–Spassky, Hamburg 1982.

9 ...   e5

Zhidkov–Verner, USSR 1974 continued 9 ... ♗xf3 10 ♗xf3 e5 11 de ♘xe5? 12 ♗e2 (the two bishops are a real force – White has only to consolidate his position and the central advance f4 will prove strong) a6 13 f3 ♕d7 14 a4! ♕c6?! 15 b3 ♕d7 16 ♔h1 ♘c6 17 ♗g5 and Black is in trouble.

10 de   de
11 h3   ♗xf3
12 ♗xf3

White has effectively gained a move over Chapter 7, variation A. The game Miles–Schussler, Dortmund 1979, is an excellent example of the difficulties faced by Black in this type of position: 12 ... a6 (12 ... ♕c8 13 ♕c1 ♘d8 14 ♘d5 ♘e6 15 ♘xf6+ ♗xf6 16 ♗g4 was slightly better for White in Formanek–Spassky, Reggio Emilia 1984) 13 ♘a4 ♕e7 14 c3 ♖ed8 15 ♕c2 ♘d7 16 b4 ♗f6 17 ♗g4 ♘f8 18 ♘c5 h5 19 ♗e2 ♖ab8 20 ♗c4 ♖xd1 21 ♖xd1 ♘d8 22 ♖d3 ♗g5 (Black succeeds in exchanging his bad bishop, but curiously White's own bad bishop has become very powerful at c4) 23 ♗xg5 ♕xg5 24 ♘d7 ♖c8 25 ♘xf8 ♔xf8 26 ♕d1 ♔e8 27 a4 ♕e7? (Black has defended well, but now he errs in allowing the White queen to penetrate. 27 ... h4, setting up a potential perpetual check on c1 and f4, was better) 28 ♕d2 ♘e6 29 ♕h6 ♕g5 (29 ... ♕f8 30 ♕xf8+ ♘xf8 31 ♖f3 ♘e6 32 ♗xe6 fe 33 ♖f6 wins) 30 ♕h8+ ♘f8 31 ♖f3 1–0.

9 | Classical: 6 0-0 c6 with h3

In this chapter we consider all those lines of the 6 0-0 c6 Classical in which White plays h3. There is a natural division of the material according to whether or not Black plays ... a5 (after White's a4, of course). This material is not only important for the Classical, but also for the h3, ♘f3 and ♗e3 system to be examined in Chapter 13. The reason is that after 1 e4 d6 2 d4 ♘f6 3 ♘c3 g6 4 ♘f3 ♗g7 5 h3 0-0 6 ♗e3 c6 7 a4 White quite often plays ♗e2, leading to a kind of Classical. For the sake of convenience all such variations have been moved into this chapter. You will still find lines of the h3, ♘f3 and ♗e3 system without ♗e2 in Chapter 13. There is such a close connection between the two variations that readers are strongly urged to consider the two chapters together. This chapter boasts the most confusing transpositions in the whole book, but I hope that when I have accidentally arrived at the same position twice the assessments are similar.
1 e4 d6 2 d4 ♘f6 3 ♘c3 g6 4 ♘f3 ♗g7 5 ♗e2 0-0 6 0-0 c6

A: 7 h3
B: 7 a4 a5 8 h3

In general, all the variations with an early ... a5 are in B and everything else is in A.

A

7 h3 *(62)*

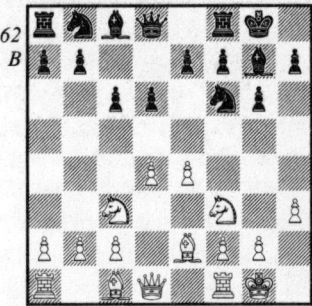

Now there are two important lines:

A1: 7 ... ♘bd7
A2: 7 ... ♕c7

A2 is the main line, but variations in which an early ... ♕c7 is not played fall into A1. Less common moves:
(a) 7 ... b5 (dubious because of White's reply) 8 e5 ♘e8 9 ♗f4 (9

♘e4 ♗f5 10 ♘g3 ♗e6 11 a4 b4 12 c4 bc 13 bc ♗d5 was only a bit better for White in Karpov–Hort, Nice Ol. 1974; 9 a4 is also possible) ♗b7 (9 ... ♘d7 10 ♕d2 ♘b6 11 ♖fe1 ♗f5 12 g4 ♗c8 13 a4 b4 14 ♘e4 is good for White, Semkov–Pribyl, Varna 1978) 10 ♕d2 ♘d7 11 ♖fd1 ♘b6 12 ♗h6 ♕c7 13 ♗xg7 (13 h4 or 13 ♕f4 are alternatives) ♘xg7? (13 ... ♔xg7 ±) 14 ♗d3 f6 15 ♕h6 ♕d7 16 ♖e1 ♗f7 17 ♘h4 ♘e6 18 ♖e3! with a very dangerous attack for White, Diesen–Rohde, USA 1976.

(b) 7 ... ♘a6 (a rather passive move) 8 ♖e1 (8 a4 ♘c7 ♗e3 d5 10 e5 ♘fe8 11 ♕d2 f5 12 ♗d3 ♘e6 13 ♘e2 ♘8c7 14 ♘h2 ♖f7 15 f4 ♗f8 16 g4 followed by ♘g3, with advantage to White, Brinck-Claussen – Kristiansen, Denmark Ch. 1988) ♘c7 9 a4 (9 ♗f1 d5 10 e5 ♘fe8 11 ♘e2 ♘e6 12 ♘f4 ♘8c7 13 ♘d3! f5 14 ef ef 15 a4 a5 16 b3 was slightly better for White in Geller–Ciocaltea, Malta 1980) b6 10 ♗f4 ♗b7 11 ♕d2 ♖e8 12 ♖ad1 ♕d7 13 ♗h6 a6 14 e5! ♘fd5 15 ♗xg7 ♔xg7 16 ♘g5 with a strong attack in Geller–Panno, Bogota 1978.

A1

7 ... ♘bd7
8 a4

Or **8 e5** (other moves are not dangerous, for example **8 ♗f4** ♕a5 9 ♕d2 e5 10 ♗e3 ♖e8 11 ♖fe1 ♕c7 12 de de 13 a4 ♗f8, Chiburdanidze–Gaprindashvili, match 1978 or **8 ♖e1** e5 9 de de 10 ♗e3 ♕e7 11 ♕c1 ♘c5 12 ♘d2 a5 13 a4 ♗e6 14 b3 ♘fd7, Janosevic–van Wijgerden, IBM II 1978, with equality in both cases) and now:

(a) **8 ... de** 9 de ♘d5 10 ♘xd5 cd 11 ♗f4 and now both 11 ... ♕c7 12 ♕xd5 ♕xc2 13 ♗b5! ♕c5 (13 ... a6 was better) 14 ♕xc5 ♘xc5 15 ♖ac1 ♘e6 16 ♗e3 b6 17 ♗c6 ♖b8 18 ♖fd1 Ermolinski–Azmaiparashvili, Kuibyshev 1986 and 11 ... ♘c5 12 ♕d2 ♘e6 13 ♗h6 b6 14 ♗xg7 ♔xg7 15 ♖ad1 ♗b7 16 ♕e3 ♕c7 17 c3 f5 18 ♘d4, Gligoric–Tringov, Skara 1980 are good for White.

(b) **8 ... ♘e8** 9 ♗f4 (9 ♖e1 de 10 de ♘c7 11 ♗f1 ♘e6 12 b3 ♕a5 13 ♗d2 ♕c7 14 ♕e2 b5 15 ♖ad1 a6 16 g3 ♗b7 17 ♗g2 with equality, Hjartarson–Todorcevic, Szirak 1987) de 10 de ♘c7 11 ♕c1 (11 ♖e1 ♘e6 12 ♗g3 and now 12 ... ♕a5 13 ♗f1 ♘b6 14 a3 ♘a4 15 ♘xa4 ♕xa4 16 b3 ♕a5 17 b4 ♕b6 18 c3 a5, Liberzon–Torre, Geneva 1977, or 12 ... b5 13 a4 b4 14 ♘b1 ♕c7 15 ♗f1 ♖d8 16 ♕c1 a5 17 ♕e3 ♘b6, Abramovic–Sznapik, Paris 1987, with roughly equal chances in both lines) ♘e6 12 ♗h6 ♕c7 (12 ... ♕b6 13 ♗xg7 ♔xg7 14 ♖d1 ♕b4?! 15 g3 ♕c5 16 ♘e4 ♕a5 17 ♕d2 ± is Matulovic–Planinc, Yugoslav Ch. 1978) 13 ♗xg7

♔xg7 14 ♕e3 b5 15 a3 ♗b7 16 ♖fe1 ♖ad8 17 ♖ad1 a6 18 ♗f1 ♘b6 and White has only a minute advantage, Ostojic–Planinc, Yugoslav Ch. 1978.

8 ... e5
9 de

I am not sure whether it is necessary to exchange on e5 immediately. In Nunn–Mohrlok, Hamburg 1987, White played 9 ♗e3 ♕e7 (9 ... ♕c7 leads to line A2) 10 ♖e1 b6 11 ♕d2 ♗b7 12 ♖ad1 a6 (12 ... ♖ad8 13 ♗g5 and 12 ... ♖fe8 13 ♗c4 are also ±) 13 de de 14 ♕d6 ♖fe8 15 ♕xe7 ♖xe7 16 ♘d2 b5 17 ♘b3 with an edge for White.

9 ... de
10 ♗e3

10 b3 ♖e8 11 ♗a3 ♗f8 gives White nothing.

10 ... ♕e7

10 ... ♕c7 transposes to line A2.

11 ♕d3

Only this move interferes with Black's plan of ... ♘c5 followed by ... ♗e6, because now 11 ... ♘c5 is met by 12 ♕c4 and the knight cannot retreat to e6 because the e5 pawn is hanging.

11 ... ♘h5 *(63)*

11 ... ♘b6 12 a5! ♗e6 (12 ... ♖d8 13 ♗c5 is very good for White) 13 ab! ♖fd8 14 ♖xa7 ♖xd3 15 ♖xa8+ ♖d8 16 ♖xd8+ ♕xd8 17 ♘xe5 with a distinct plus for White in Browne–Eising, Mannheim 1975.

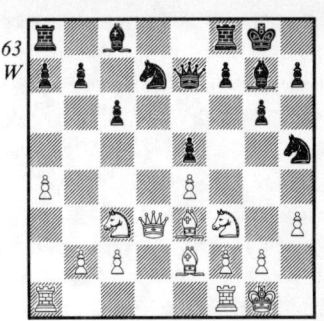

12 ♖fd1 ♘f4

13 ♕d6 ♘xe2+ 14 ♘xe2 ♗f6! (14 ... ♕xd6 15 ♖xd6 f5 16 ♖ad1 ♘f6 17 ♘c3 f4 18 ♗c5 b6 19 ♗a3 c5 20 a5 ♘e8 21 ♖6d2 ♗b7 22 ♘g5 with good chances for White, Nun–Ftacnik, CSSR Ch. 1986) 15 ♕xe7 ♗xe7 16 ♘d2 ♘c5 (or 16 ... f5 17 f3 ♘c5 18 ♘c4 fe 19 fe ♘xe4 20 ♘xe5 with an edge for White) 17 ♘c4, Browne–Rohde, USA Ch. 1987, and now 17 ... ♘xe4 18 ♘xe5 ♖e8 gives Black excellent equalizing prospects.

A2

7 ... ♕c7 *(64)*

8 a4

The move is logical as it continues White's policy of restraint. Other moves seem less promising:
(a) 8 ♗f4 ♘h5 9 ♗h2 (or 9 ♗e3 e5 10 ♕d2 ♘d7 11 a4 ♖e8 12 ♖ad1 ed 13 ♘xd4 ♘hf6 14 f3 and now not 14 ... ♘c5 15 ♗c4 a6 16 b4 ♘e6 17 a5! and White retained some advantage in Tukmakov–Uhlmann, Decin 1977, but 14 ... a6! 15 ♘b3 d5 16 ♗f4 ♘e5 17 ed ♘xd5 18 ♘xd5 cd ½–½, Tal–Gipslis, Saint John Open 1988) ♘d7 (9 ... e5 10 a4 ♘d7 11 ♕d2 h6?! 12 ♖fd1! ♖e8 13 a5 ♘f8 14 ♗c4 ♕e7 15 de de 16 ♕d6 ± is Razuvaev–Vogt, Cienfuegos 1976) 10 ♕d2 e5 11 ♖ad1 (11 a4, transposing to the above game, may be better) ♘hf6 12 ♖fe1 ♖e8 13 ♗f1 h6 14 a4 a6 15 ♔h1 and now instead of 15 ... b6 (Christiansen–Taulbut, Hastings 1978/9) simply 15 ... b5 is quite satisfactory for Black.
(b) 8 ♗e3 ♘bd7 9 a4 transposes to the main line.
(c) 8 e5 de 9 de (9 ♘xe5 ♘d5 10 ♘xd5 cd 11 ♗f4 ♕b6 12 ♕d2 ♘c6 13 c3 f6 14 ♘g4?! g5! 15 ♗h2 f5 16 ♘e3 f4 17 ♘xd5 ♕d8 was good for Black in Dorfman–Zaichik, USSR 1983, but even the superior 14 ♘f3 gives White no advantage) ♖d8 10 ♕e1 ♘d5 11 ♗c4 ♗e6 (11 ... ♘xc3 12 ♕xc3) 12 ♘g5! ♕xe5 13 ♕xe5 ♗xe5 14 ♘xe6 fe 15 ♘e4 and White is slightly better, Shamkovich–D. Bernstein, Israel 1974.

After 8 a4 there are two main possibilities, according to whether Black plays ... e5 at once, or prepares it by ... ♘bd7. We take the second of these as the main line.

8 ...   ♘bd7 *(65)*

Or 8 ... e5 (8 ... a5 9 ♗e3 e5 10 ♕d2 is just a transposition to B, note to Black's 8th move) 9 de de and now:
(a) 10 ♗e3 ♘h5 (10 ... ♘bd7 11 a5 leads into the main line, while 10 ... a5 and 10 ... ♘bd7 11 ♗c4 a5 transpose to B) 11 ♖e1 ♘f4 12 ♗f1 ♖d8 (12 ... ♘a6 13 ♘d2 ♖d8 14 ♕c1 ♘e6 15 a5 ♗f8 16 ♘a4 ♗d7 17 c3 with an edge for White, Szmetan–Schweber, Argentina Ch. 1985) 13 ♕c1 ♘e6 (the immediate transfer to d4 is best, since White has no time to organize c3) 14 ♖d1 ♘d4 15 ♘xd4 ed 16 ♗g5 ♖e8 17 ♘e2 ♖xe4 18 f3 ♖e8 19 ♘xd4 ♗d7 with equality, Rittner–Bouwmeester, corr. 1985.
(b) 10 ♗c4 (this is slightly more accurate, since White may sometimes manage without ♗e3) ♘h5 (10 ... a5 transposes to B) 11 ♖e1 ♗d7 (11 ... ♘f4? 12 ♗xf4 ef 13 e5 followed by ♘e4 is good for White) 12 ♗e3 ♘f4 13 a5 h6? (13 ... ♖d8 14 ♕c1 ± is better) 14 ♕c1 b5 15 ab ♘xb6 16 ♗b3 ♗e6 17 ♗xe6 fe 18 ♘d2 and White had a substantial advantage in

Browne–Taulbut, Lone Pine 1978.

The point about these lines is that White has a slight problem resulting from his move-order. There are three useful moves White would like to play, namely a5, ♗e3 and ♗c4. The first prevents Black from playing the positionally useful ... a5 and gains space on the queenside. The second and third are important after the exchange of pawns on e5, since ♗e3 prevents ... ♘c5 while ♗c4, by attacking f7, makes it hard for the f8 rook to move. If White can prevent both ... ♘c5 and ... ♘f8 Black will have a hard job developing his queenside pieces. Unfortunately with the move-order of this chapter White only has time for two of the three moves, so he has to decide which is the least evil. In my view, allowing ... a5 is the best choice since, as we shall see in line B, the resulting positions are still tricky for Black.

This dilemma is one of the main points behind the ♘f3, h3 and ♗e3 system of Chapter 13. Not only does White sometimes play ♗f1–c4 and gain a tempo, there is even an advantage in those lines where he plays ♗e2. The reason is that he saves the relatively useless move 0-0, which can be safely delayed, and often succeeds in playing all three 'useful' moves.

65
W

9 ♗e3

By playing ... ♘bd7 first, Black has given White the chance to play a5. As suggested above, this is probably not a good idea, and White should prefer to allow the transposition to B. The only problem with this view is the possibility of 9 ... b6 mentioned in the next note.

After 9 a5 e5 10 de we have:
(a) **10 ... de** 11 ♗e3 (as explained above, White would really like to play ♗e3 and ♗c4 here, preventing both ... ♘c5 and ... ♖d8; unfortunately White has spent a tempo on 0-0, so he cannot keep Black tied up) ♖d8 12 ♕b1 ♘f8 13 ♕a2 ♗e6 14 ♕a4 ♘h5 15 ♖fd1 ♘f4 16 ♗f1 ♖xd1 17 ♖xd1 ♕e7 and Black equalized in Spassky–Van der Wiel, Reykjavik 1985.
(b) **10 ... ♘xe5** 11 ♗e3 (although this sequence of moves is a little odd, we have to consider the resulting position because it can arise via Chapter 13) ♖e8 (11 ... ♖d8 12 ♕c1 ♘xf3+ 13 ♗xf3

♗e6 14 ♗g5 ♖e8 15 ♖d1 ♘d7 16 ♕d2 ♘e5 with an edge for White, Larsen–Kavalek, Linares 1981) 12 ♘d2 ♘ed7 13 ♘c4 ♘xe4 14 ♘xe4 ♖xe4 15 ♕xd6 ♕xd6 16 ♘xd6 ♖e7 17 ♖fd1 ♘f8 18 ♘xc8 ♖xc8 19 c3 with a small, but permanent, advantage for White, Short–van der Wiel, Biel play-off 1985.

9 ... e5

9 ... b6 10 ♕d2 ♗b7 11 ♖ad1 (if White wants an advantage he should try 11 ♖fe1, so as to meet 11 ... a6 by 12 e5, although even this isn't very clear) a6 (11 ... ♖fe8?! 12 ♗c4! points at the newly created weakness at f7, and after 12 ... e5 13 ♗b3 ed? 14 ♗xd4 White had a very good game in L.D. Evans–Winston, USA 1977) 12 ♗f4 e5 13 de de 14 ♗h2 ♖ad8 15 ♕d6 ♕c8 16 ♕b4 ♘h5 with a comfortable position for Black, O'Donnell–Gipslis, Saint John Open 1988.

10 ♖e1

10 de de is more natural, but then White has only a choice of transpositions. 11 a5 is the note to White's 9th move above, while 11 ♗c4 (probably the best) a5 is line B.

10 ... ed

10 ... b6 11 ♕d2 a6 12 ♖ad1 b5 13 ab ab 14 b4 may be a little better for White. After 14 ... ♖a3? 15 ♗xb5! ♘xe4 16 ♘xe4 cb 17 de ♘xe5 18 ♘xe5 ♗xe5, Ciric–Werner, Marseilles 1981,

White should have played 19 ♗h6 ♖d8 20 ♗g5 ♖f8 21 ♘f6+ ♔h8 22 ♗h6 ♖d8 23 ♖xe5 winning.

11 ♗xd4 ♖e8

12 ♘d2 b6 13 ♘c4 ♖e6 14 f3 (14 f4 ♗b7 is fine for Black) ♗b7 15 ♕d2 a6 16 ♗f1 ♖ae8 17 ♘e3, Short–van Wijgerden, Amsterdam 1982, and now 17 ... d5! would have been roughly equal.

B

7 a4 a5
8 h3 *(66)*

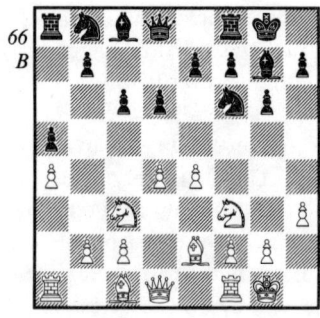

8 ... ♘a6

This is the most natural move, given that b4 is now available for occupation. However the move 8 ... ♕c7 is also important because such positions can arise by transposition from line A2. After **8 ... ♕c7 9 ♗e3 e5 10 de** (after 10 ♕d2 ♘a6 11 ♖ad1 ed 12 ♘xd4 ♖e8 13 f3 ♘b4 14 ♗c4 ♗d7 15 ♗b3 d5 16 ♕f2 ♖ac8 17 ♘de2 Black should play 17 ... c5! 18 ♗xd5 ♘xc2! 19 ♗f4 ♕b6 20 e5 ♘xd5 21 ♘xd5 ♕e6 = Polugaevsky–Uhlmann, Manila 1976, rather than 17 ... ♗e6?! 18 ♗b6 ♕e7 19

♘f4 de 20 ♗c5! ♕c7 21 ♘xe6 e3 22 ♕xe3 with advantage to White, Polugaevsky–Szabo, Montilla 1975) de 11 ♗c4 ♘a6 (Black also ran into problems with 11 ... ♘bd7 in Ciocaltea–Quinteros, Bor 1977, since 12 ♕d2 b6 13 ♖fd1 ♗b7 14 ♕d6 ♖ac8 15 g4! ♕xd6 16 ♖xd6 ♖c7 17 ♖ad1 ♗c8 18 ♔g2 ♘c5 19 ♗xc5 bc 20 ♖d8 was very promising for White) 12 ♕e2 ♕e7 13 ♖ad1 and it is not easy for Black to free himself. Bonsch–Uhlmann, East German Ch. 1976, continued 13 ... ♘c5 14 ♘g5 ♘h5?! 15 ♕d2! h6 16 ♕d6 ♕xd6 17 ♖xd6 ♘d7 18 ♘f3 ♘hf6 19 ♘h4 ♔h7 20 ♖fd1 h5 21 ♘f3 ♗h6 22 ♘g5+ ♗xg5 23 ♗xg5 ♔g7 24 f3 ♖e8 and Black is completely tied up – in fact Black played ♖b8–a8–b8 for the next 25 moves! White eventually found the plan of h4, g3, ♗f1–h3 and won.

Finally it is worth noting the experimental possibility **8 ... ♘bd7**. White may reply 9 e5, which is the same as after 8 e5 in line A1 except that the moves a4 and ... a5 have been added. This difference probably favours White, because Black cannot expand on the queenside by ... a6 and ... b5. Other ideas, such as 9 ♗e3 e5 10 de, are also playable.

9 ♗e3

Others are not dangerous:
(a) **9 ♗f4** ♘c7 (9 ... ♘b4 10 ♕c1 ♘d7 11 ♖d1 ♕c7 12 ♗c4 e5 13 ♗h6 ♘b6 14 ♗b3 was very slightly better for White in Simic–Planinc, Yugoslavia Ch. 1979) 10 ♖e1 ♘e6 11 ♗e3 ♕c7 12 ♗f1 ♖d8 13 ♕d2 ♗d7 14 ♗h6 ♗e8 15 ♗xg7 ♔xg7 16 ♗c4 d5 17 ♗b3 de 18 ♘xe4 ♘d5 with only a minute advantage for White, Spassky–Hort, match 1977.
(b) **9 ♖e1** ♕c7 10 ♗g5 h6 11 ♗e3 ♔h7 12 ♕d2 ♘b4 13 ♖ad1 ♗d7 14 ♘h2 b5 15 ♗f3 ba 16 ♘g4 h5?! (Black could have avoided creating a weakness with 16 ... ♘g8, intending ... f5) 17 ♘xf6+ ef 18 ♗f4 with advantage for White, Chiburdanidze–Gaprindashvili, match 1978.
(c) **9 ♗g5**. The aim is to gain a tempo with ♕d2 later, much as in line b. It is hard to say whether or not the time gained is worth giving up the possibility of ♗h6.

9 ... ♘b4 (67)

9 ... d5 10 ed ♘xd5 11 ♘xd5 ♕xd5 12 ♗g5 ♕d6 13 ♖e1 ♗e6 14 ♕c1 c5 was level in Ivanovic–D. Gurevich, Reykjavik 1982, but 10 e5 is the only real test.

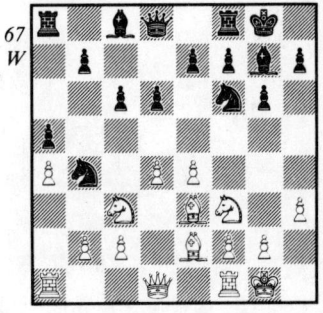

Now there is a wide choice for White:

B1: 10 ♕c1
B2: 10 ♕d2
B3: 10 ♘d2

B1
10 ♕c1

Both this and 10 ♕d2 prepare ♗h6, but with ♕c1 White keeps the d-file free for ♖d1.

10 ... ♖e8

10 ... d5 (10 ... ♕c7 11 ♖d1 d5 12 e5 ♘e8 13 ♘b1 f6 14 c3 ♘a6 15 ♗f4 ♕d8 16 ♘bd2 ♘ac7 17 ♘f1 ♘e6 with a minute advantage for White, Przewoznik-Sznapik, Poland Ch. 1987) 11 e5 ♘e8 12 ♗h6 (after 12 ♘b1 ♗f5 13 ♘e1 c5 14 c3 cd 15 cd f6 16 f4 ♖c8 17 ♘c3 White retained a small advantage in Miles-Matera, Birmingham 1975) ♗f5 13 ♗xg7 ♘xg7 14 ♖d1 ♕b6 15 ♖e1 f6 16 ♕d2 ♖ad8 17 ♖a3 ♘a6 18 ♖b3 ♕c7 19 ♘e2 with an edge for White, Gutman-Ivkov, New York 1987.

11 e5

Or 11 ♖d1 ♕c7 12 ♘d2 ♘d7 13 ♘c4 ♘b6 14 ♘xb6 ♕xb6 15 ♘b1 f5 16 c3 ♘a6 17 ♘d2 ♕d8 18 ef ♗xf5 19 ♘f3 and White is better, Gligoric-Bulat, Yugoslavia Ch. 1984.

11 ... ♘d7

12 ♗h6 f6 13 ♗xg7 ♔xg7 14 ♘e4 de 15 de ♕c7 16 c3 ♘d5 17 c4! ♘b4 18 ♖a3 ♘xe5 19 ♘xe5 ♕xe5 20 ♖e3 with a complex position in which White probably has slightly the better chances, Gutman-Rukavina, Oberwart 1986.

B2
10 ♕d2 ♕c7

In many variations Black plays the move ... d5, whereupon the reply e5 gives White a space advantage. Black should aim to free himself with ... f6, but White can usually defend e5 well enough not to have to exchange on f6 (which usually gives White nothing). Although this type of pawn structure gives White a slight plus, Black's position is solid enough to make finding a good plan hard for White. 10 ... d5 11 e5 ♘e8 12 ♗h6 f6 13 ♗xg7 ♘xg7 14 ♖d1 ♘e6 15 ♖e1 b6 16 c3 ♘a6 17 ♘e3 ±, Pfleger-Ciocaltea, Moscow 1977, is yet another example.

11 ♖ad1

Or:

(a) 11 ♗h6 e5 12 ♗xg7 ♔xg7 13 ♖ac1 ♘h5 14 ♖fe1 ♕e7 15 ♗f1 ♕f6 16 ♖e3 ♘f4 17 ♘e2 ♖e8 18 c3 ♘a6 19 ♘xf4 ♕xf4 20 ♖d1 ♕f6 21 de de 22 ♗xa6 ♖xa6 23 ♖d3 left White clearly better in Chi-Torre, China-Philippines match 1975. Black's play was rather ambitious in this example and I suspect that 11 ♗h6 isn't the right plan; White should avoid exchanges for the moment since he controls more space.

(b) 11 ♖ac1 e5 12 de de 13 ♖fd1

♖e8 (the threat was ♗c5 and ♗d6) 14 ♗c5 ♘d7? (14 ... ♗f8 was much better, but White still has an edge) 15 ♗d6 ♕b6 16 ♕g5 ♘a6 17 ♖b1 with a clear advantage for White, Braga–Piket, Wijk aan Zee II 1986.

11 ... ♖e8

11 ... ♖d8 12 ♕c1 ♗d7 13 ♖fe1 ♗e8 14 ♗g5 b5 15 e5 ♘fd5 16 ed ♖xd6 17 ♘e4 ♖dd8 18 ♗f1 ♘b6 19 ♘e5 gave White a distinct plus, Russek–Arencibia, Granma 1987.

After 11 ... ♖e8 Black has reasonable chances for equality, e.g. 12 ♖fe1 ♗d7 (12 ... e5 13 ♗f1 ♕e7 14 de de 15 ♗b6 ♘d7 16 ♗c7 ♗f8 17 ♘b1 b6 with just a faint edge for White, Unzicker–Pfleger, Bundesliga 1985) 13 e5 ♘fd5 14 ♘xd5 cd! 15 c3 ♘c6 16 ed ed 17 ♗h6 ♘d8 18 ♗xg7 ♔xg7 and the weakness of the a4 pawn makes it hard for White to mount any sort of attack on Black's doubled pawns, Spassky–Hort, match 1977.

B3

10 ♘d2 *(68)*

This may be regarded as the main line. White frees his f-pawn, which is useful for supporting e5 in case of 10 ... d5 11 e5, while the knight is pointing towards b6 and d6 if Black plays ... e5.

10 ... e5

Or 10 ... d5 11 e5 ♘e8 12 f4 (12 ♘a2 ♘xa2 13 ♖xa2 f6 14 f4 fe 15

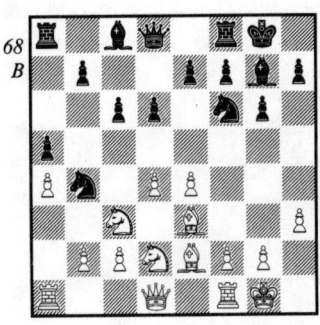

fe ♖xf1+ 16 ♗xf1 and the poor position of the rook on a2 enables Black to equalize, Speelman–Mokry, Dubai 1986) f5 (this looks odd, but 12 ... ♗f5 13 ♖c1 achieves nothing, while otherwise White can expand by g4) 13 ♘cb1 ♘c7 14 ♘f3 ♘e6 15 c3 ♘a6 16 ♕b3 with an edge for White, Beckemeyer–Rostalski, Bundesliga 1987, although as usual Black's solid position is hard to dent.

11 ♘c4

11 de de 12 ♘c4!? (12 ♘a2 ♘xa2 13 ♖xa2 ♗e6 = is a limp continuation, Estevez–Zaichik, Camaguey II 1987) ♗e6 12 ♘b6 ♕xd1 14 ♖axd1 ♖ad8 15 ♗c4 ♘xc2 16 ♗c5 ♖fe8 17 ♗xe6 fe 18 ♘c4 ♘d7 19 ♗d6 ♖c8 with a murky position, Sznapik–Nunn, Helsinki 1981.

After 11 ♘c4 d5 (11 ... ed 12 ♗xd4 d5 13 ♘b6 looks good for White) 12 de ♘xe4 (12 ... dc 13 ♕xd8 ♖xd8 14 ♗g5 ♘xc2 15 ♖ac1 ♘d4 16 ♗xc4 is also good) 13 ♘xe4 de 14 ♗c5 ♕g5 15 ♕c1

♕h4 16 ♗xf8 ♚xf8, Kuczynski–Sznapik, Poland Ch. 1987, and although the game ended in a draw Sznapik's own suggestion of 17 ♘b6 looks very good for White. Note that the third rank can be defended by ♖a3 so White need not fear sacrifices on h3.

If the main line of B3 turns out well for White then Black will either have to play ... d5 at some stage or avoid ... a5 altogether and continue as in A. Whether or not Black can avoid ... a5 permanently depends on some very subtle questions of move-order which require further practical tests.

10 | Classical: 6 0-0 c6 without h3

This chapter deals with a range of White alternatives which aim to avoid wasting a tempo with h3. Naturally White may transpose into the previous chapter at many points by playing h3 and we do not specifically mention each such instance. It is curious that these lines are far less popular than those of the last chapter. One could understand this if White's omission of h3 were immediately punished by ... ♗g4, but Black usually plays ... ♘bd7 or ... ♕c7 leading to positions similar to those in chapter 9. Of course h3 is a useful move, but it seems to me that unless there is some immediate problem with missing it out, White has more important moves to play first. Black's best reply to 7 a4 is probably 7 ... a5; White may then have nothing better than 8 h3, since 8 ♗e3 can be met by 8 ... ♘g4. Nevertheless this move-order has something to recommend it, because Black is restricted to those lines involving ... a5. The other important variation in this chapter is 7 ♖e1, which leads to completely independent positions. At the moment Black has few problems equalizing after 7 ♖e1.

1 e4 d6 2 d4 ♘f6 3 ♘c3 g6 4 ♘f3 ♗g7 5 ♗e2 0-0 6 0-0 c6 *(69)*

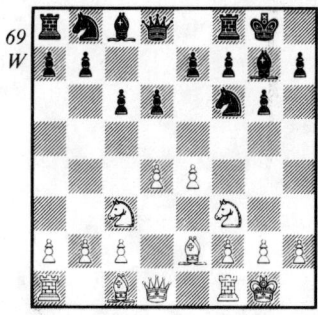

and now:

A: 7 ♖e1
B: 7 a4

Other moves:
(a) **7 ♗f4 ♗g4** (7 ... ♘bd7 8 ♕d2 ♕c7 9 e5 ♘e8 and now 10 ed ed 11 a4 ♘df6 12 h3 ♗e6 13 a5 ♕d7 14 ♘g5 ♘c7 15 ♘ce4 ♘fe8 16 c3 f5 was roughly level in Vaganian–Quinteros, Buenos Aires 'Clarin' 1978, but 10 ♕e3 maintaining the e5 pawn was better) 8 h3 (or 8

♕d2 ♘bd7 9 ♖ad1 ♗xf3 10 ♗xf3 e5 11 ♗e3 ♕a5 12 ♖fe1 ♖fe8 13 a3 ♕c7 14 h3 with an edge for White, King–Dresen, Wuppertal 1986) ♗xf3 9 ♗xf3 d5 10 e5 ♘fd7 11 ♗g5 f6 12 ef ef 13 ♗f4 ♘b6 14 h4 ♘8d7 is very slightly better for White, Vasiukov–Dzindzihashvili, USSR 1975.

(b) **7 e5** (it is hard to believe that this can be good for White, but the practical results indicate that Black's task is not trivial) de (7 ... ♘e8 8 ♖e1 ♘a6 9 ♗g5 f6 10 ef ef 11 ♗e3, Hulak–Ciocaltea, Val Thorens 1981, and now Black should have played 11 ... ♘c7 12 d5 c5 13 ♘d2 a6 14 a4 b6 15 ♘c4 with a slight plus for White, but perhaps 7 ... ♘d5!? is the most reasonable move) 8 ♘xe5 ♗e6 9 ♗f4 ♘bd7 (Black plays natural moves, but fails to equalize) 10 ♕d2 ♘xe5 11 ♗xe5 ♕a5 12 ♕e3 ♖fd8 13 a3 ♖d7 14 b4 ♕d8 15 ♘a4 b6 16 c4 ♘g4 17 ♗xg4 ♗xg4? (17 ... ♗xe5 18 ♗xe6 ♗xd4 19 ♕h3 ± was better) 18 ♗xg7 ♔xg7 19 d5! winning the pawn on c6 as a consequence of the threat of 20 ♕d4+, Smyslov–Bilek, Venice 1974. Despite these results, I suspect that a Caro-Kann player would feel happy with Black's position from the opening.

A

7 ♖e1 ♘bd7

Or:

(a) **7 ... b5** 8 e5 ♘e8 9 ed (9 ♗f4 ♘a6 10 ♕d2 ♘ac7 11 ♖ad1 ♗f5 12 a3 a5 13 h3, Andersson–Hort, Amsterdam 1979, and now 13 ... b4 would have been equal) ♘xd6 10 ♘e5 ♘f5 11 ♘xb5! ♗b7 12 ♘a3 ♘xd4 13 ♗c4 c5 14 ♗g5! ♘bc6 15 ♘xc6 ♘xc6 16 ♕xd8 ± left Black with a poor pawn structure in Tompa–Schoneberg, Leipzig 1977.

(b) **7 ... ♗g4** 8 ♗g5 (or 8 a4 ♗xf3 9 ♗xf3 e5 10 ♗e3 a5 11 ♕d2 ♘bd7 12 ♖ad1 ♖fe8 13 h3 ♕c7 14 g3 ♖ad8 15 b3 with an edge for White, Hulak–Rukavina, Yugoslavia Ch. 1984) ♕a5 9 ♕d2 ♘bd7 10 ♖ad1 e5 11 d5 c5 12 a4 a6 13 h3 ♗xf3 14 ♗xf3 b5 15 ab ab 16 ♖b1 ± is Andersson–Uhlmann, Niksic 1978.

(c) **7 ... ♘a6** 8 e5 de (8 ... ♘d5 9 ed ♕xd6 10 ♘e4 followed by ♗xa6 is also good for White, while 8 ... ♘e8 transposes to the analysis of 7 e5 above) 9 de ♘d5 10 ♘xd5 cd 11 ♗xa6 ba 12 ♘d4 and Black's two bishops do not compensate for his bad pawn structure, Speelman–Ghinda, Salonika 1984.

(d) **7 ... ♕c7** *(70)* and now:

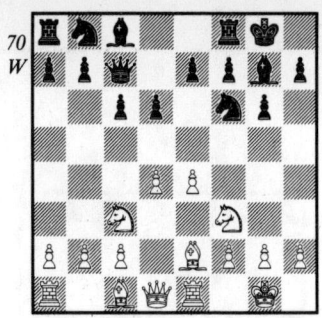

(d1) **8 ♗f4** ♘bd7 9 e5 ♘h5 10 ♗g5! (10 ed ed 11 ♗e3 should be met by 11 ... ♘b6 12 h3 ♖e8 13 ♕d2 ♘f6! 14 ♗d3 ♗e6 with equality, Geller–Adorjan, Budapest 1973, rather than 11 ... f5 12 d5! f4 13 ♗d4 c5 14 ♗xg7 ♘xg7 15 ♕d2 a6 16 a4 ♖b8 17 ♗d3 ♕d8 18 ♘e4 with advantage for White, Andersson–van der Wiel, Tilburg 1984) de 11 ♗xe7 ♖e8 12 d5 ♘f4 13 d6 ♕b6 14 ♗c4 h6 15 ♘e4 ♕xb2, Balashov–Pribyl, Helsinki 1984, and now 16 ♘fg5! would have been very good for White.

(d2) **8 e5** de 9 ♘xe5 ♘fd7 (after 9 ... ♖d8?! 10 ♗c4 ♘d5 11 ♕f3 e6 12 ♘e4 Black had a dreadful position in Diesen–Shamkovich, New York 1976, while 9 ... ♗e6 10 ♗f4 ♕a5 11 ♕d2 ♖d8 12 a3 ♕b6 13 ♖ad1 a5 14 d5! gave White a very strong initiative in Duric–Sznapik, Smederevo 1981) 10 ♘g4!? (10 ♘f3 ♘b6?! 11 h3 ♘8d7 12 ♗f1 e5 13 de ♘xe5 14 ♗f4 f6 15 ♘xe5 fe 16 ♗g3 was clearly better for White, Duric–Karner, Tallinn 1981, but 10 ... ♖d8 11 ♗g5 ♘f6 12 ♗c4 ♗g4 13 ♗b3 ♘a6 ∓ putting White's d-pawn under pressure was much better, W. Schmidt–Ermenkov, Prague 1985) ♖d8? (an awful move depriving 10 ♘g4!? of a proper test) 11 ♘h6+ ♔f8 12 ♗c4 ♘e5 13 ♗f4 ♕b6 14 ♗xe5 ♗xh6 15 ♕f3 f5 16 ♕h3 1–0, Duric–Benoit, Luxembourg 1981.

(d3) **8 a4** e5 9 de de 10 ♗c4 ♘bd7 11 b4 ♘h5 12 ♗e3 ♘df6 13 ♗c5 ♖d8 14 ♕b1 b6 15 ♗e3 ♘g4 16 ♗g5 ♖e8 17 h3 ♘gf6 18 ♕b3 and White still has slight pressure, Vukcevic–Smyslov, Hastings 1976/7.

8   ♗f4   ♕a5

The best move. 8 ... ♘h5 9 ♗g5 h6 10 ♗e3 e5 11 ♕d2 ♔h7 12 ♖ad1 ♕e7 13 a4 ♖e8 14 a5! was good for White in Karpov–Pfleger, Hannover 1983, while 8 ... b5 9 e5 ♘h5 10 ♗g5 ♘b6 11 ed ♕xd6 12 ♘e4 ♕c7 13 c3 ♘f6 14 ♘xf6+ ef 15 ♗h4 left White with the superior pawn structure in S. Gonzalez–Knezevic, Camaguey II 1987.

9   ♘d2

9 ♕d2 e5 10 ♗g5 (this turns out badly after lengthy complications, but 10 de is only equal) ed 11 ♘xd4 ♘xe4! 12 ♘xe4 ♕xd2 13 ♗xd2 d5! 14 ♗b4 ♖d8 15 ♘b5 de 16 ♘c7 ♖b8 17 ♗e7 ♖f8! 18 ♖ad1 ♗e5 19 ♗xf8 ♔xf8 20 ♗g4 f5 21 ♘e6+ ♔e7 22 ♘g5 ♘f6! with a clear plus for

Black, A. Sokolov–van der Wiel, Biel 1985.

9 ... ♕c7 *(71)*

White has forced Black to make a second queen move, but he gains no advantage from this because his knight is badly placed on d2.

71
W

10 d5

10 a4 e5 11 de de 12 ♗e3 ♖d8 13 ♕c1 ♗f8 14 ♖d1 ♘c5 is very satisfactory for Black, Pigusov–Azmaiparashvili, USSR 1986.

10 ... ♘b6!

Not 10 ... ♘c5 11 ♗f1 ♘g4 12 h3 e5 13 ♗g5 ♗f6 14 ♗xf6 ♘xf6 15 b4 ♘a6 16 a3 cd 17 ♘xd5 ♘xd5 18 ed with a positional advantage for White, Kengis–Azmaiparashvili, Moscow II 1986.

After 10 ... ♘b6 Black's pieces become very active and in Nunn–Pfleger, Bundesliga 1987, White went quickly downhill: 11 ♗f3 (11 ♘f1 was better) ♘fd7 12 a4 a5 13 ♗e3 ♘e5 14 ♗e2 f5 15 ef ♗xf5 16 f4 ♘f7 17 dc bc 18 ♘f3 e5 with a clear advantage for Black.

B

7 a4 *(72)*

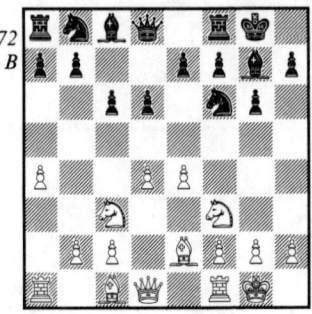

72
B

7 ... ♘bd7 *(73)*

Or:

(a) **7 ... ♕c7** and now:

(a1) **8 ♖e1** transposes to line A, variation d3 in the note to Black's 7th move.

(a2) **8 ♗e3** e5 9 de de 10 ♕c1 ♘h5? (now White can reach positions similar to those in Chapter 9, line A but with an extra move; 10 ... ♘bd7 was better) 11 ♗c4 ♘d7 12 a5 ♖e8 13 ♘g5 ♖e7 14 ♖d1 h6 15 ♘f3 with a very unpleasant position for Black in Damjanovic–Miles, Birmingham 1975.

(a3) **8 a5** e5 (8 ... ♘bd7 9 ♗e3 is untested) 9 de de 10 ♗e3 (a familiar type of position in which the pawn on a5 seriously constricts Black's queenside; by missing out h3 White has gained enough time to prevent the free development of Black's queenside pieces) ♖d8 (Tringov–Keene, Rovinj–Zagreb

1975 continued 10 ... ♘g4 11 ♗d2 ♖d8?! 12 ♕c1 ♕e7 13 ♗g5 f6 14 ♗d2 ♕f8 15 ♗c4+ ♔h8 16 h3 ♘h6 17 ♗e3 with advantage for White) 11 ♕c1 ♘bd7 12 ♗c4 ♘f8 13 ♘g5 ♘e6 14 ♘xe6 ♗xe6 15 ♗xe6 fe 16 ♕b1 with a distinct advantage for White, Nunn–McNab, Marbella 1982.

(b) **7 ... a5** (after this the main question is whether White has to transpose to chapter 9 by 8 h3 or not) and now:

(b1) **8 ♗e3 ♘g4** (8 ... ♗g4 9 ♘d2 ♗xe2 10 ♕xe2 d5 11 e5 ♘e8 12 f4 f5! 13 ef ♖xf6! 14 ♘d1 ♘d6 15 ♘f2 ♘d7 =, Rajkovic–Uhlmann, Vrbas 1977, since White's bad bishop compensates for the backward e-pawn, but not 8 ... ♘a6 9 ♘d2 d5 10 e5 ♘e8 11 f4 b6 12 ♘f3 f6 13 ♕d2 ♘ec7 14 ♘d1 ♗f5 15 ♘f2 with a good position for White, Stean–Petrosian, Skara 1980; the main difference between these two lines is that Uhlmann exchanged his bad bishop, but Petrosian did not!) 9 ♗g5 h6 (9 ... f6 10 ♗d2 ♘h6 11 ♕c1 ♘f7 12 ♗e3 e6 13 d5! cd 14 ed e5 15 ♘d2 ♘d7 16 ♘c4 and White had maintained an advantage in Szabo–Hübner, IBM 1975) 10 ♗h4 ♘a6 11 ♖e1 ♘b4 12 ♗c4 g5 13 ♗g3 ♘f6 14 ♘d2 d5 with a very satisfactory position for Black, Browne–Hort, Wijk aan Zee 1975.

(b2) **8 ♖e1 ♘a6** (8 ... ♗g4 9 ♗e3 ♘bd7 is possible) 9 ♗f1 ♘b4?! 10 ♘b1! ♗g4 11 ♘bd2 e5 12 c3 ♘a6 13 de de 14 h3 ♗xf3 15 ♕xf3 ♘c5 16 ♗c4 with an enduring advantage for White, Miles–Panno, IBM 1977. Black should have tried 9 ... ♗g4, but White is still slightly better.

(b3) **8 e5 ♘d5 9 ♘xd5 cd** gives White very little.

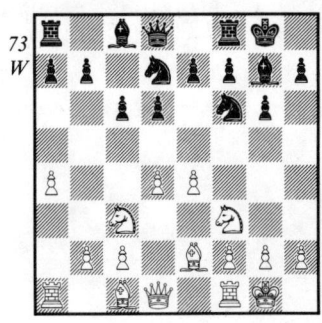

73 W

8 a5

After 8 e5 (8 b3?! c5 9 ♗b2 cd 10 ♘xd4 a6 11 a5 e6 12 ♕d2 b5 13 ab ♕xb6 14 ♖fe1 ♗b7 was equal in Panno–Sznapik, Amsterdam II 1980) Black may play:

(a) **8 ... de** 9 de ♘d5 10 ♘xd5 cd 11 ♗f4 ♕c7 (11 ... ♘c5 12 h3 b6 13 ♖e1 ♘e6 14 ♗g3 ♗b7 15 c3 ± Pribyl–Sapi, Hradec Kralove 1977–8) 12 ♖a3 (12 ♕xd5 ♕xc2 13 ♗b5 looks more promising to me) ♘xe5 13 ♔h1 ♖d8! 14 ♖e3 f6 15 b3 ♗f5 16 ♕a1 ♗e4 17 ♘d2 ♗f5 18 ♘f3 ♗e4 ½–½, Vogt–Gipslis, Tallinn 1981.

(b) **8 ... ♘e8** 9 ♗f4 (Black is rather cramped, but this position is quite playable) de (or 9 ... ♕a5

10 ed ♘xd6 11 ♖b1 ♘f5 12 b4 ♕d8 13 ♘e4 ♘b6 14 c3 ♘d5 15 ♗d2 ♘d6 16 ♘xd6 ♕xd6 with equality, Ciric–Sznapik, Warsaw 1979) 10 ♘xe5 ♘c7 11 ♗c4 ♘xe5 12 ♗xe5 ♗xe5 13 de ♗e6 with complete equality in Goodman–Matulovic, Dortmund 1977.

8 ... e5

As mentioned above, 8 ... ♕c7 9 ♗e3 is untested.

9 de de

10 ♕d6 (this move is pointless if Black can drive the queen away with gain of time, but here Black cannot expel the invader without a concession) ♘e8 (or 10 ... ♖e8 11 ♗c4 ♗f8 12 ♕d3 and f7 is weak) 11 ♕b4 h6 12 ♗e3 ♘c7 13 ♖fd1 ♘e6 14 ♕d6 and in Haik–Todorcevic, Marseilles 1987 White had a clear advantage (14 ... ♖e8 15 a6!).

Even after many years of experience it remains unclear whether or not h3 is a good idea and although the lines in this chapter are not very popular at the moment they seem to offer chances of an advantage for White.

11 | Classical: 6 0-0 Others

After **1 e4 d6 2 d4 ♘f6 3 ♘c3 g6 4 ♘f3 ♗g7 5 ♗e2 0-0 6 0-0** *(74)* we consider the following moves, arranged in decreasing order of importance.

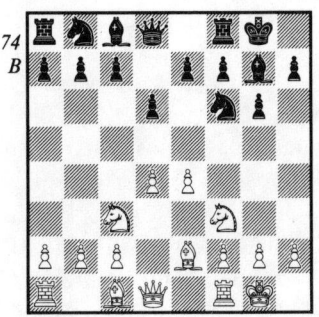

A: 6 ... ♘c6
B: 6 ... ♘bd7
C: 6 ... a6
D: 6 ... c5
E: 6 ... b6
F: 6 ... ♘a6

A

6 ... ♘c6

Black aims to step up the pressure on d4 but the move is not totally satisfactory as the knight lacks a natural retreat square after 7 d5.

7 d5 *(75)*

Or:

(a) 7 ♗e3 is most simply met by 7 ... ♗g4 transposing to the main line of the Classical. 7 ... e5 is also quite playable, since 8 d5 ♘e7 leads to positions similar to those in Chapter 7 except that Black may avoid the loss of tempo involved in ... ♗g4–d7. White may also reply 8 de, with play similar to c below except that h3 is probably more useful than ♗e3 (since the bishop belongs on g5). However, 7 ... ♘g4?! should be avoided as it loses time, e.g. 8 ♗g5 h6 9 ♗h4 ♘f6 10 d5 ♘b8 11 ♘d4 c6 12 a4 ♛b6 13 ♘b3 a5 14 ♔h1 ♘a6 15 f4 with a clear plus for White, Andersson–Kavalek, Buenos Aires 1980.

(b) 7 ♗g5 h6 8 ♗f4 ♘g4! (this move renders 7 ♗g5 harmless) 9 h3 e5 10 de ♘gxe5 11 ♘xe5 de 12 ♗e3 ♘d4 with a fine position for Black, Sakharov–Adorjan, Sochi 1976.

(c) 7 h3 e5 8 de ♘xe5 (8 ... de 9 ♗g5 also gives White an edge) 9 ♘xe5 (or 9 ♗g5 h6 10 ♗e3 ♛e7? 11 ♘d4 ♗d7 12 ♛d2 ♔h7 13 f4 with advantage for White in Pribyl–Kupka, Prague 1987; 10 ... ♘xf3+ 11 ♗xf3 ♗d7 was more sensible, but still a little better for White) de 10 ♗g5 ♗e6 (10 ... c6 11 ♕xd8 ♖xd8 12 f4 ♖e8 13 fe ♘d7 14 e6 gives White an edge) 11 ♕xd8 ♖fxd8 12 f4 ♖e8 13 f5 gf 14 ef ♗d7, Blatny–Ftacnik, CSSR 1987, and now 15 ♖ad1 is good for White.

After 7 d5 there are two moves:

A1: 7 ... ♘b8
A2: 7 ... ♘b4

Black had a dismal position after 7 ... ♘e5 8 ♘xe5 de 9 ♗e3 a6 10 ♕d2 ♕d6 11 ♖fd1 ♖d8 12 h3 ♗d7 13 a4, Vogt–Ftacnik, East Germany-Czechoslovakia match 1978.

A1

7 ...   ♘b8
8   ♖e1

Or:

(a) **8 h3** (not really necessary) c6 (after 8 ... e6 9 de ♗xe6 the continuation 10 ♘d4 ♗d7 11 ♖e1 ♖e8 12 ♗f1 ♘c6 13 ♘b3 a5 14 a3 a4 15 ♘d2 ♘a5 16 ♘f3 ±, Hulak–Marangunic, Yugoslavia 1977, is more promising than 10 ♗g5 h6 11 ♗e3 ♘c6 12 ♕c1 ♔h7 13 ♖d1 ♕c8 14 ♘d4 ♗d7 15 f4 ♖e8 with equality, Polovodin–Razuvaev, USSR 1979) 9 a4 a5 10 ♖e1 ♘a6 11 ♗g5 (11 ♗f1 ♘b4 and now both 12 ♗g5 h6 13 ♗f4 ♗d7 14 ♕d2 ♔h7 15 ♗c4 ♖c8, Ligterink–Lutikov, Jurmala 1978, and 12 ♗e3 e5 13 ♗c4 ♗d7 14 ♖e2 cd 15 ed ♘e8, Miles–Quinteros, Dortmund 1986, led to roughly level positions) ♘c5 12 ♗f1 e5 13 de ♘xe6 14 ♗e3 ♖e8 15 ♕d2 ♕c7 16 ♖ad1 ♗f8 17 ♗h6 with an edge for White, Schüssler–Quinteros, Vienna 1986.

(b) **8 ♗e3** e6 (8 ... c6 is possible) 9 de ♗xe6 10 ♘d4 ♗d7 11 ♕d2 ♘c6 12 ♘b3 a5 13 a4 ♗e6 14 ♖ad1 ♗xb3 15 cb ♘d7 16 f4 with advantage for White, Planinc–Marangunic, Yugoslavia 1977.

(c) **8 a4** a5 (8 ... e5 9 de ♗xe6 10 ♘d4 ♗d7 11 ♖e1 ♘c6 12 ♘xc6 ♗xc6 13 ♗b5 ♖e8 14 ♕d3 d5?! 15 ♗g5 de 16 ♕xd8 ♖axd8 17 ♗xc6 bc 18 ♘xe4 with a decisive advantage for White, Georgadze–Razuvayev, USSR Ch. 1978) 9 ♗c4 (9 h3 c6 transposes to line a above) ♗g4 10 h3 ♗xf3 11 ♕xf3 ♘fd7 12 ♕e2 ♘a6 13 ♖a3 ♘ac5 14 ♗a2 ♖a6 was unclear in Gurgenidze–Gulko, USSR 1979.

The lesson to be learnt from these examples is that the pawn structure e4 v d6 arising after ... e6 or ... e5 gives White some advantage unless Black can free himself quickly by means of exchanges.

8 ... e5

In Timoshchenko–Lerner, USSR 1st league 1977, 8 ... ♗g4 9 h3 ♗xf3 10 ♗xf3 c6 11 g3 ♘bd7 12 ♗g2 ♖c8 13 a4 ♘e5 14 ♘e2 cd 15 ed ♕a5 16 ♗d2 ♕c5 17 ♗c3 a position reminiscent of a g3 anti-Dragon was reached. White's pressure on the backward e-pawn gave him a slight advantage.

9 de ♗xe6 *(76)*

And now there are three possibilities for White:

(a) 10 ♘d4 ♗d7 11 ♗g5 h6 12 ♗h4 ♘c6 13 ♘b3 ♖e8 14 f3 a5 15 a4 ♘b4 16 ♘b5! with a slight advantage for White, Vasiukov–Lerner, USSR 1981.

(b) 10 ♗g5 h6 11 ♗f4 ♘c6 12 h3 makes little sense as White is just a tempo down over line c. In Azmaiparashvili–Kantsler, Tbilisi 1986, the continuation 12 ... ♔h7 13 ♕d2 d5 14 ed ♘xd5 15 ♘xd5 ♕xd5 16 ♕xd5 ♗xd5 17 ♖ed1 should have been met by 17 ... ♗e6.

(c) 10 ♗f4 ♘c6 (the miniature Tal–Petrosian, USSR 1974, concluded 10 ... h6 11 ♘d4 ♗d7 12 ♕d2 ♔h7 13 e5! de 14 ♗xe5 ♘e4? 15 ♘xe4 ♗xe5 16 ♘f3 ♗g7 17 ♖ad1 ♕c8 18 ♗c4 ♗e8 19 ♘eg5+! hg 20 ♘xg5+ ♔g8 21 ♕f4 ♘d7 22 ♖xd7 ♗xd7 23 ♗xf7+ 1–0; 14 ... ♘c6 was an improvement, but 10 ... h6 is just too slow) 11 h3 (11 ♕d2, preventing ... h6, appears to be better) h6 12 ♕d2 g5 and now 13 ♗h2 is ± according to Gufeld, but in Geller–Kuzmin, USSR 1974, 13 ♗g3 d5 14 ed ♘xd5 15 ♘xd5 ♕xd5 16 ♕xd5 ♗xd5 17 c3 ♖ac8 was dull and equal.

The conclusion is that White has a slight advantage after 7 ... ♘b8.

7 ... ♘b4

Black has slightly better chances after this more active move, but it is still not an easy job to equalize. It is hard to understand how 6 ... ♘c6 came to be popular, since in most cases Black has a drab position with only an uphill struggle towards equality in prospect. The time wasted in moving the knight evidently does not compensate for the target at d5.

8 ♖e1

Or:

(a) **8 h3** e6 (8 ... c6? 9 a3 ♘a6 10 ♗xa6 ba 11 dc e6 12 ♗f4 ♘e8 13 e5 ♕c7 14 ed led to a complete disaster for Black in Hazai–Peev, Varna 1978) 9 ♗g5 h6 10 ♗e3 (the idea of maintaining the pawn on d5 rather than exchanging on e6 is a natural reply to 7 ... ♘b4 as there are real chances of shutting the knight out with a3 and b4) ed 11 ed ♔h7 12 a3 ♘a6 13 b4 ♘b8 14 ♖b1 ♘bd7 15 ♖e1 a5 (15 ... ♘b6 $\pm$ was an improvement) 16 ♘b5! ab 17 ab ♘b6 18 c4 ♗d7 19 ♘fd4 ♖e8 20 ♗d3 with a large spatial plus for White, Gipslis–Vadasz, Budapest 1977.

(b) **8 ♗g5** h6 9 ♗e3 e6 10 a3 ♘a6 11 de ♗xe6 12 ♕d2 (12 b4 ♔h7 13 ♖b1 ♘b8 14 ♘d4 ♗d7 15 f4 ♘c6 16 ♗f3 ♖e8 with an unclear position, Timman–Adorjan, IBM 1977) ♘c5 13 ♗xh6 ♘cxe4 14 ♘xe4 ♘xe4 15 ♕e3 ♗xh6 16 ♕xh6 ♕f6 17 ♗d3 ♘c5 18 ♘g5 ♕g7 19 ♕xg7+ ♔xg7 20 ♘xe6+ fe and Black was a little better in Vogt–Vadasz, Budapest 1976.

(c) **8 a3** ♘a6 9 ♗e3 e6 10 ♗xa6 ba 11 ♘d4 ed 12 ♘c6 (note the resemblance to Tseshkovsky–Parma below) ♕e8 13 ed ♗d7 14 ♖e1 ♗xc6 15 ♗d4 ♕d7 16 ♗xf6 ♗xf6 17 ♕f3! ♕f5 18 ♕xf5 gf 19 dc ♗xc3 20 bc reaching a curious position with a whole horde of doubled pawns. White is slightly better although Black held the draw in Stean–Jansa, Italy 1976.

8 ... e6

Or 8 ... a5 (to prevent the typical a3 and b4 plan) 9 ♗f4 (9 h3 c6 10 a3 ♘a6 11 dc bc 12 e5 ♘e8 13 ed ♘xd6 14 ♗e3 ♕c7 15 ♘a4 with just a faint edge for White, Jansa–Ftacnik, CSSR 1980) c6 10 a3 ♘a6 11 dc bc 12 e5 ♘h5 (if Black plays 12 ... ♘e8 13 ed ♘xd6 then White continues with 14 ♘e5 and 15 ♗f3) 13 ed! ♘xf4 14 de ♕xe7 15 ♗xa6 and Black does not have enough for the pawn, Mikhalchishin–Hoi, Copenhagen 1979.

9 a3 ♘a6 (77)

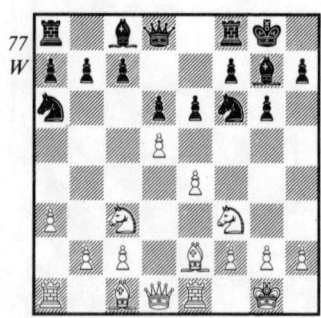

10 de

10 ♗xa6 ba 11 ♘d4 ed 12 ♘c6 ♕d7 13 ed ♖e8 14 ♗e3 ♘g4 15 ♗d4 ♖xe1+ 16 ♕xe1 ♗xd4 17 ♘xd4 ♗b7 18 ♕d2 ♘f6 ½–½ Tseshkovsky–Parma, Ljubljana–

Portoroz 1977. The weakness of the d-pawn compensates for the doubled a-pawns.

10 ... ♗xe6

11 ♘d4 ♗d7 12 ♗g5 h6 13 ♗h4 ♘c5 14 ♗c4 ♖e8 15 f3 ♘a4 (the bishop on a4 is a tactical weakness, so 15 ... ♘e6 ± was better) 16 ♘xa4 ♗xa4 17 ♕d3 (threat ♗xf7+) ♕d7 18 ♗xf6 ♗xf6 19 e5! with advantage to White, Groszpeter–Nogueiras, Cienfuegos 1980.

■

6 ... ♘bd7

Since in the three main lines 6 ... ♗g4, 6 ... c6 and 6 ... ♘c6 White has little difficulty in forcing a position in which Black has no winning chances, various moves have been devised to enable Black players to try for the win at the cost of some risk to themselves. These moves are frequently employed when a strong player is Black against a weaker opponent. After 6 ... ♘bd7 Black may play ... e5 without permitting the exchange of queens, or he may play ... c5. Unfortunately White can cross these plans with 7 e5 and leave Black wth the usual type of position without winning prospects.

7 e5

7 ♗f4 ♘h5 (7 ... c5 8 d5 a6 9 a4 ♕c7 10 ♕d2 b6 11 h3 ♗b7 12 ♖fe1 is ± as the knight on d7 would be better placed on c7, Bouaziz–Nunn, Dortmund 1979) 8 ♗g5 h6 9 ♗e3 e5 10 ♕d2 ♔h7 11 ♖fd1 ♕e7 (11 ... c6 12 de de 13 g4 ♘hf6 14 ♘xe5 ♘xe4 15 ♘xe4 ♗xe5 16 ♗xh6 ♕h4 17 ♗f4 is very good for White) 12 de de 13 ♘d5 ♕d8 14 ♕a5! b6 15 ♕a4 with a fine game for White, Diesen–Schussler, Groningen 1976/7.

7 ... ♘e8
8 ♗f4 *(78)*

Solid and sensible. 8 ♗g5 may also be good, e.g. 8 ... f6 9 ef ♘dxf6!? (9 ... ef 10 ♗f4 c6 11 d5 ±) 10 ♕d2 ♗e6 11 ♖fe1 c6 12 a4 ♘c7 13 h3 ♕d7 14 ♗h6 ± Botterill–Nunn, England 1975, but **8 e6** is far too rash and after 8 ... fe 9 ♘g5 ♘df6 10 ♗c4 d5 11 ♗d3 c5 12 dc e5 13 ♖e1 ♕c7 14 ♘b5 ♕xc5 15 ♖xe5 ♘g4 16 ♗e3 ♕c6 17 ♖xe7 ♗f6 Black had a very good position in Matulovic–Sigurjonsson, Novi Sad 1976.

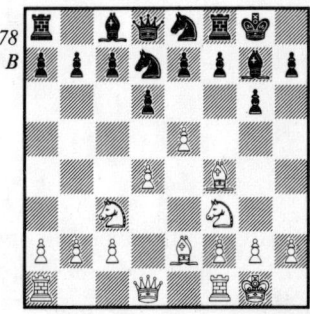

8 ... c6

8 ... c5 is risky in view of White's lead in development. Sosonko–Botterill, Ostend 1975

continued 9 ♖e1 cd 10 ♕xd4 de 11 ♘xe5 ♕b6 12 ♕xb6 ♘xb6 13 a4 f6?! 14 ♘c4 ♘d7 15 ♖ed1 e5 16 ♗e3 f5 17 ♘b5 a6 18 ♘bd6 ♘ef6 19 ♘a5 and White was already winning.

8 ... ♘b6 is an alternative which may transpose into the text, but Gheorghiu–Bohm, Le Havre 1977 deviated with 9 h3 c6 10 ♕d2 ♗e6 11 ♖ad1 f6 12 ef ef 13 ♖fe1 d5 14 ♗d3 ± and Black held the draw.

9   ♖e1

9 ♕d2 seems more accurate, for if then 9 ... f6 10 ef ef 11 d5 or 9 ... ♘b6 10 ♖ad1 with a slight advantage in both cases. The rook is not well placed on e1 and this move is just a loss of time.

9 ...   ♘b6

10 h3 ♘c7 11 ♗d3 ♘e6 12 ♗e3 de 13 de ♘d7 14 ♗d2 ♕c7 15 ♕e2 ♘dc5 16 ♖ad1 ♘xd3 (16 ... b5 was more interesting) 17 ♕xd3 b6 18 ♕e4 ½–½, Weinstein–Nunn, IBM II 1975.

Summing up, 6 ... ♘bd7 is not a bad line if you only want to draw, but like many lines against the Classical it is hard to play for a win.

C

6 ...   a6

Asking for trouble. This move offends against the normal principles of chess, and in general it has received the treatment it deserves.

White may try:

(a) **7 e5** ♘fd7 8 ♗g5 (direct and dangerous) f6?! (8 ... ♘c6 would have given White some problems over the e5 square) 9 ♗e3! fe 10 ♘g5 ♘b6 11 de ♗xe5 12 a4! e6 13 a5 ♗xc3 14 ab ♗xb2 15 ♖a4! with a very strong attack, Speelman–Nunn, Birmingham 1976.

(b) **7 ♖e1** ♘c6 8 d5 ♘e5 9 ♘xe5 de 10 ♗e3 ♕d6 11 ♕d3 ♖d8 12 ♘a4 e6 13 ♗c5 ♕d7 14 de fe (Miles–Kavalek, IBM 1977) and now 15 ♕b3!? is good for White according to Miles.

(c) **7 ♗g5** b5 8 e5 ♘e8 9 a4 f6 10 ef (10 ♗e3 is not possible with the bishop on c8 guarding e6) ef 11 ♗h4 b4 12 ♘d5 a5 13 ♖e1 with a distinct advantage for White, Holek–Ftacnik, Czechoslovakia 1978.

(d) **7 a4** transposes to a position considered in Chapter 12 under 4 ... a6.

D

6 ...   c5

This move came into prominence as a result of the final game of the 1978 Karpov–Korchnoi match. Korchnoi lost after playing 6 ... c5 and there was some surprise that Karpov replied almost immediately with 7 d5, not even contemplating the theoretical 'refutation' 7 dc. Whether this was preparation or over-the-board judgement I cannot say, but Karpov's decision has been vindicated by more recent games. White has achieved no advantage with 7 dc, so it must be right to transpose to the Schmidt Benoni by 7 d5.

7 d5

After 7 dc (7 ♗g5 cd 8 ♘xd4 transposes to the Karpov anti-Dragon system) dc 8 ♗e3 b6 9 ♕xd8 (9 ♖e1 ♘c6 10 h3 ♕c7 11 ♕c1 ♗b7 12 ♗h6 ♖ad8 is completely harmless, Hunerkopf–Davies, Bundesliga 1986, while 9 e5 ♘g4 10 ♕d5 ♕xd5 11 ♘xd5 ♘c6 12 ♗g5, Gligoric–Quinteros, Bled–Portoroz 1979, should have been met by 12 ... ♘gxe5 with an unclear position) ♖xd8 10 ♖fd1 ♘c6 11 ♖xd8+ ♘xd8 12 ♖d1 ♗b7 13 ♘d2 ♘c6 (13 ... ♘e6 14 f3 ♘d4 15 ♗d3 ♖d8 16 ♔f2 ♘d7 was also equal in Barbulescu–Xu, Timisoara 1987) 14 ♘c4 ♖d8 15 ♖xd8+ ♘xd8 16 f3 ♘d7 =, Andersson–Torre, Leningrad 1987.

7 ... ♘a6

I will make no attempt to give a full coverage of the Schmidt Benoni, but here are a few examples which demonstrate some of the typical ideas.

8 ♗f4 ♘c7
9 a4 b6

10 ♖e1 (there is some flexibility regarding White's move-order; 10 h3 is often played here) ♗b7 *(79)* and now:

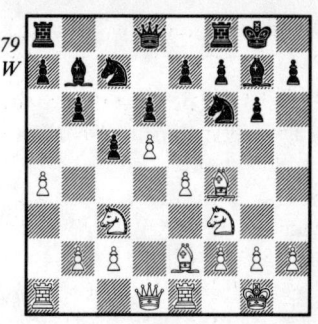

(a) **11 h3** (the combination of h3 and ♖e1 looks slightly strange because now White cannot prevent ... b5; normally White arranges to play ♗c4 and ♕d3 to stop this, but as we shall see playing ... b5 does not solve all Black's problems) a6 12 ♕d2 ♕d7 13 ♖ab1 b5 14 b4 (this idea of Psakhis is very interesting because White normally has to play unnatural moves to stop ... b5; if he can allow it and still get a good position then the Schmidt Benoni looks doubtful) a5!? 15 bc b4 16 ♕e3 dc 17 ♘e5 with advantage to White, Psakhis–Davies, Hastings 1987/8.

(b) **11 ♗c4** (the orthodox move) a6 (11 ... ♘h5?! 12 ♗g5 ♘f6 13 ♕d3 a6 14 ♖ad1 ♖b8 15 h3 ♘d7 16 ♕e3 ♗a8 17 ♗h6 ± Karpov–Korchnoi, match 1978) 12 h3 ♘h5 (12 ... ♕d7 should be met by 13 ♕d3 rather than 13 e5 ♘h5 14 ♗g5 f6! 15 ed ed 16 ♗e3 f5 17 ♕d3 ♗xc3 18 ♕xc3 f4 19 ♗d2 b5 with a fantastic position for Black, Belyavsky–Torre, Moscow

1981) 13 ♗h2 b5 (turns out badly, but a slower plan as in Karpov–Korchnoi would also leave White with the advantage) 14 ab ab 15 ♘xb5 ♘xb5 16 ♗xb5 ♗xb2 17 ♖b1 ♗g7 18 e5! de 19 ♗c4 ♖a4 20 ♖xb7 ♖xc4 21 ♗xe5 ♗xe5 22 ♖xe5 with clear advantage, Panno–Quinteros, Buenos Aires 'Clarin' 1978.

E

| 6 | ... | b6 |
| 7 | ♖e1 | |

The strongest. After 7 e5 ♘fd7 8 ♗f4 ♘c6 9 ♖e1 ♗b7 a neat trap is 10 ♗f1?! ♘xd4! 11 ♘xd4 de 12 ♗g5 ed 13 ♗xe7 dc 14 ♗xd8 cb 15 ♖b1 ♖axd8 and Black should not lose this position. Zuidema–Timman, Wijk aan Zee 1971, continued 16 ♖e3 (16 ♕g4? ♘c5 18 ♗c4 ♖d4 18 ♕e2 ♘e4 was good for Black, Burton–Nunn, Oxford 1975) ♘c5 17 ♕e1 ♗d4 18 ♖e7 ♗f6 19 ♖e3 and Black could and should have repeated moves.

| ... | ♗b7 |

7 ... ♘c6 8 d5 ♘b8 9 a4 a6 10 h3 is also dismal for Black, with Haag–Nunn, Birmingham 1975, carrying on 10 ... ♗b7 11 ♗c4 c6 12 ♗g5 ♘bd7 13 ♕d2 b5 14 dc ♗xc6 15 ♘d4 ♗b7 16 ♗d5.

8 e5

This thrust is very strong now the bishop is not covering e6. The alternative 8 ♗f1 c5 9 d5 is good only for a small plus.

| 8 | ... | ♘d5 |

8 ... de 9 ♘xe5 ♘bd7 10 ♗f3 ♗xf3 11 ♕xf3 and 8 ... ♘e8 9 e6 are both unpleasant.

| 9 | ♘xd5 | ♗xd5 |

10 c4 ♗b7 11 e6 f5 (11 ... fe 12 ♘g5) 12 d5 c6 (Maric–Quinteros, Bor 1977) and now 13 ♘g5! ♘a6 14 ♗f3 cd 15 cd ♘c7 16 ♕b3 would have maintained the d-pawn and, by covering b2, enabled White to develop his remaining pieces.

F

| 6 | ... | ♘a6 |
| 7 | ♖e1 | c5 |

Now White may transpose to D with 8 d5, but a more vigorous move is 8 e5, suggested by Geller. The game Geller–Sax, Budapest 1973, went on 8 ... ♘g4 9 ed ♕xd6 10 ♘e4 ♕c7 11 ♗xa6 ba 12 ♘xc5 e5! 13 h3 ed 14 ♘b3 ♘f6 15 ♘bxd4 and White has won a pawn, for which Black has insufficient compensation.

12 Classical: 4 ♘f3 Others

With this chapter we finish our coverage of the Classical System by examining Black 4th move deviations. All the lines here arise from the Modern move-order 1 e4 g6 2 d4 ♝g7 3 ♘c3 d6 4 ♘f3. If Black wishes to play ... a6 this seems the most sensible moment to do it, for e5 is no threat unless the knight is on f6. The lack of a central break for White gives Black more time to organize his queenside counterplay. Another move to prepare ... b5 is 4 ... c6, but this may also be played with the idea of transposing into Chapters 9 and 10. In fact many of the games quoted there started with this move-order. The final move, 4 ... ♝g4, intends increasing the pressure on d4 with ... ♘c6, but in the main line 4 ... ♝g4 5 ♝e3 ♘c6 6 ♝b5! White can maintain some advantage.

1 e4 g6 2 d4 ♝g7 3 ♘c3 d6 4 ♘f3

A: 4 ... a6
B: 4 ... c6
C: 4 ... ♝g4

A

4 ... a6

Black aims to expand on the queenside with ... b5, ... ♝b7 ... ♘d7 and ... c5. When Black has eliminated White's d-pawn, he need no longer fear the e5 thrust in reply to ... ♘gf6, so Black will be able to complete his development and castle. That, at any rate, is the plan. The most obvious point is that Black's king will be in the centre for a long time, so he will have to be on the lookout for tactical shots by White to exploit this factor. If Black's plan succeeds he could end up with a favourable type of Sicilian Dragon. It can fail in one of two ways; either White attacks the centralized king, or White plays a4 to break up Black's queenside pawn structure and obtain a positional advantage.

5 ♝e2

Or:

(a) **5 a4** and now:

(a1) 5 ... ♝g4 (logical; without ... a6 and a4 White usually replies 5 ♝e3 ♘c6 6 ♝b5, but now he has to choose another plan) 6 ♝e2 ♘c6 7 d5 (7 ♝e3 e5) ♝xf3 8 ♝xf3 ♘e5 (8 ... ♘d4 is equal according to Mednis) 9 ♗e2 c6 10 0-0 (10 a5! was better) a5! 11 ♗e3 ♘f6 12 ♖a3 ♘ed7 13 f4 0-0 14 ♔h1 ♕c7 15 ♕e1 ♖fe8 with equality, Mednis–Soltis, New York 1977.

(a2) **5 ... ♘f6** 6 ♗e2 0-0 7 0-0 b6 (slightly better than line E of Chapter 11 because 8 ♖e1 ♘c6 9 d5 may be answered by 9 ... ♘b4) 8 e5 ♘fd7 (8 ... de?! 9 ♘xe5 ♗b7 10 ♗f3, Gheorghiu–Espig, Rumania–DDR match 1984, and the weak c6 square gives Black serious problems) 9 ed?! (9 e6 is critical) cd 10 ♗g5 h6 11 ♗e3 ♘f6 12 d5 ♘bd7 13 ♕d2 ♔h7 14 ♖a3 ♗b7 15 ♖b3 ♖c8 16 h3 ♖xc3! 17 ♕xc3 ♗xd5 with at least equality for Black, Matanovic–Nunn, London–Belgrade telex match 1976.

(b) **5 ♗c4** (a dangerous move which interferes with Black's plan because ... ♘d7 will allow ♗xf7+, ♘g5+ and ♘e6) b5 6 ♗b3 ♘c6 7 0-0 ♘a5 8 h3 ♘xb3 (Black should have played ... c6 at some point and left the bishop on c8 to stop e5–e6 by White; as played he finds it hard to develop the knight on g8 without allowing this thrust) 9 ab ♗b7?! 10 ♕e2 ♕c8 11 ♖e1 e6 12 e5 ♘e7 13 ♗g5?! (13 ♘e4! would have been good for White) ♘f5 14 ♖ad1 h6 15 ♗f6 ♗xf6 16 ef ♕d8! with an unclear position, Mednis–Soltis, USA Ch. 1978.

(c) **5 ♗e3** b5 6 a4 b4 7 ♘a2 a5 8 c3 ♗b7 (8 ... ♘f6 may be better) 9 ♘d2 ♘f6 10 f3 bc 11 bc 0-0 12 ♖b1 ♗c8 with an edge for White, Werner–Nunn, Hamburg 1984.

5 ... **b5**
6 0-0

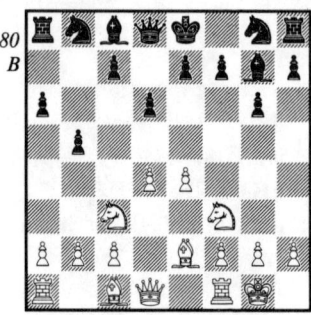

6 ... **♘d7**

Black's move-order may appear flexible, but there are significant differences between this move and 6 ... ♗b7. After **6 ... ♗b7** 7 ♖e1 ♘d7 White may play:

(1) **8 ♗g5** c5 (8 ... h6 9 ♗h4 ♘b6 10 a3 c5 11 e5! cd 12 ♕xd4 de 13 ♕e3 ♕c7 14 ♗g3 f6 15 ♘h4 gave White a decisive attack in Grünfeld–Soltis, Lone Pine 1979) 9 ♗f1 (9 d5 ♘gf6 10 ♗f1 0-0 11 ♕d2 ♕c7 12 ♖ad1 ♖fe8 13 ♗h6 ♖ad8 14 ♕f4 ♘e5! equalized for Black in Doncevic–Nunn, Bundesliga 1984; note the similarity to Britton–Nunn in the main line) cd 10 ♘xd4 ♘gf6 11 ♕d2 h6 12 ♗h4 0-0 and White might still have a very slight advantage, Bennett–Nunn, Islington Open 1975.

(2) **8 ♗f1** c5 9 a4 b4 10 ♘d5 ♘gf6! (10 ... e6? 11 ♗f4! and

now 11 ... ed 12 ed+ ♘e7 13 ♗xd6 ♗f6 14 ♗xe7 ♗xe7 15 d6 wins, so in Honfi–Vadasz, Kecskemet 1975, Black played 11 ... e5 12 de de 13 ♗g5 f6, but lost because of his queenside pawn weaknesses) 11 ♘xf6+ ♘xf6 12 d5 0-0 13 ♗c4 a5 14 ♕d3 ♘d7 15 c3 ♕b6 with equality, Geller–Hort, Linares 1983.

There is a further intriguing line after 6 ... ♗b7 7 ♖e1, namely **7 ... b4**. It seems that White cannot afford to give up a pawn by 8 ♘a4 ♗xe4 9 ♗c4 (or 9 ♗g5 ♗c6! gaining a vital tempo by attacking the knight at a4) d5! (not 9 ... ♗c6? 10 ♗xf7+ ♔xf7 11 ♘g5+ ♔e8 12 ♘e6 ♕d7 13 ♘xg7+ ♔f7 14 ♘e6 and Black cannot take at a4 because of ♕f3+) and White has little or no compensation for the lost pawn. Thus he must play 8 ♘d5. Then 8 ... e6 9 ♘xb4 ♗xe4 10 d5! is good for White, but 8 ... a5 is quite unclear; White is virtually committed to some sort of sacrifice, e.g. 9 ♗c4 e6 10 ♗g5 f6 11 ♘f4!?, or else his knight is driven back and Black can complete his development. If this line turns out to be satisfactory for Black, then 6 ... ♗b7 is the better move, for White would not be able to continue with the natural 7 ♖e1.

Another move is **6 ... ♘f6**, played by Suttles with success, e.g. 7 e5 ♘fd7 8 ♖e1 (8 ♕d3 ♘b6 9 ♗f4 ♘c6 10 ♕e4 ♘a5 11 ♗d3

b4 12 ♘d1 ♗b7 13 ♕e2 0-0 14 ♘g5 ♘c6 was quite reasonable for Black in S. Garcia–Suttles, Nice Ol. 1974) ♘c6 9 ♗f4?! (9 e6! fe 10 d5 is very dangerous) de 10 ♘xe5 ♘7xe5 11 de ♗xe5 12 ♗xe5 (12 ♗xb5+ ab 13 ♗xe5 is very good for White according to Hort, but after 13 ... ♕xd1 14 ♖axd1 ♗xe5 15 ♖xe5 c6 White is only slightly better) ♗xe5 13 ♗f3 ♗xc3 14 ♕xd8+ ♔xd8 15 ♖ed1+ ♔e8 16 ♗xa8 ♗xb2 is unclear, Weinstein–Suttles, Chicago 1973. Of course what is good for Suttles may not be good for normal chess-players.

7	♖e1	c5
8	d5	

My own view is that White should not be able to gain any advantage after d5. In positions with this type of Benoni pawn structure White is normally able to meet ... a6 by a4, halting Black's queenside expansion. Here Black has already played this move, which alleviates his cramp and gives him room to develop (e.g. ... ♗b7 is possible). 8 ♗f1 or 8 ♗g5, as in the above lines, offers a more serious test of Black's unusual opening.

8	...	♘gf6

9 ♗f1 0-0 10 h3 (Black's ambition is to play ... e6 to challenge White's advanced pawn, but for the moment the d-pawn is too weak, so he must play ... ♕c7, ... ♗b7 and ... ♖ad8 to support

d6 first) ♕c7 11 a3 (11 ♗f4 was better since 11 ... b4 may be met by 12 ♘a4 ♕a5 13 c3 defending the stray knight, followed by ♘d2–c4) ♗b7 with at least equality for Black. Britton–Nunn, London 1978, concluded 12 ♗f4 ♖ad8 13 ♕d2?! ♘e5! 14 ♕e3 e6 15 ♗xe5 de 16 de fe 17 ♘d2 ♖d4! 18 f3 ♘h5 19 ♘e2 ♘f4 20 ♘xd4 ed 21 ♕f2 ♗e5 22 a4 ♘h5 23 g4 ♗g3 24 ♕e2 ♘f4 25 ♕d1 c4 26 ab ab 27 ♗g2 ♗xe1 28 ♕xe1 e5 29 ♘f1 ♕c5 30 ♔h2 d3 31 cd ♘xd3 32 ♕d2 ♕d4 33 ♖b1 ♗xe4! 34 fe ♖f2 35 ♕g5 (35 ♕e3 ♘f4) ♖xg2+ 36 ♔xg2 ♘f4+ 0–1.

B

| 4 | ... | c6 *(81)* |

81 W

In many cases this leads back into normal lines after a subsequent ... ♘f6, but here are a few independent examples:

(a) **5** ♗e2 b5 6 0-0 ♘d7 7 a3 ♗b7 (7 ... a6 8 ♗e3 e5 9 ♕d2 ♗b7 10 ♖ad1 ♘gf6 11 ♗h6 0-0 12 ♗xg7 ♔xg7 13 h3 ♖e8 was level in G. Garcia–Nogueiras, Granma 1987) 8 ♖e1 (this is a better plan since White's bishop does nothing on e3) a6 9 ♗f1 e5 10 d5 c5 11 a4 b4 12 ♘b1 ♘gf6 13 a5 0-0 14 c3 bc 15 ♘xc3 ♘e8 16 ♘d2 f5 17 ♘c4 and White has some advantage, Botterill–Kagan, Hastings 1977/8.

(b) **5 a4** a5 (5 ... ♘f6 will transpose to standard lines, while 5 ... ♗g4 6 ♗e2 ♘d7 7 0-0 e5 8 d5 c5 9 ♘d2 ♗xe2 10 ♕xe2 a6 11 a5 was better for White, Unzicker–Ott, Bundesliga 1984/5) 6 ♗c4 ♘f6 7 e5 de 8 ♘xe5 0-0 9 0-0 ♘bd7 10 ♗g5 ♕c7 (or 10 ... ♘b6 11 ♗b3 ♘bd5 12 ♕f3 ♗e6 13 ♖ad1 ♘c7 14 ♗xe6 ♘xe6 15 ♗e3 ♕c7 16 ♖fe1 with a very slight plus for White, Browne–Rohde, New York 1984) 11 f4?! (rather too ambitious; a modest move such as 11 ♕e2 would be better) ♘b6 12 ♗b3 (Browne–Kagan, Buenos Aires Ol. 1978) and now 12 ... ♘fd5 threatening ... f6 would equalize without difficulty.

(c) **5** ♗e3 ♗g4 6 a4 ♗xf3 7 gf d5 8 a5 e6 9 ♕d2 ♕h4 10 ♘e2 h6 11 ♘f4 ♘d7 12 e5 ♘e7 is a strange plan by White which leaves him no safe place for his king, Zapata–Chernin, Saint John Open 1988.

(d) **5** ♗c4 transposes to Chapter 15, line B, note to Black's 4th move.

C

| 4 | ... | ♗g4 |
| 5 | ♗e3 | |

Or:

(a) 5 ♗e2 ♘c6 6 ♗e3 e5 7 d5 ♘ce7 8 ♘d2 ♘d7 9 g4!? (9 0-0 f5 10 f4 fe 11 ♘dxe4 ♘f5 12 ♗c1 should be enough to maintain some advantage for White) c5 10 ♖g1 ♘c8 11 g5 h6 12 h4 hg 13 hg a6 14 a4 and White was a little better in Psakhis–Belov, USSR 1977, since Black will eventually play ... f5 and after the exchange on f6 the g-pawn will be a permanent weakness.

(b) 5 ♗c4 e6 (5 ... ♘f6 is better since 6 e5 may be met by 6 ... de 7 ♗xf7+ ♚f8!) 6 ♗e3 ♘c6 7 ♕d2 ♗xf3 8 gf ♘ge7 9 0-0-0 d5 10 ♗e2 ♕d7 11 ♚b1 0-0-0 12 ♕e1 ♕e8 13 ♗b5! with a slight plus in Ivanovic–Jansa, Vrnjacka Banja 1977. Black suffers from permanent cramp and has no active plan.

5 ... ♘c6

5 ... ♘f6 6 ♗e2 (6 h3 is simple and good) 0-0 7 ♕d2 ♘c6 8 h3 ♗xf3 9 ♗xf3 e5 10 de ♘xe5 (after 10 ... de 11 0-0-0 White gains time by bringing a rook to d1 with gain of tempo) 11 ♗e2 ♖e8 12 0-0 a6 13 ♖ad1 b5 14 f3 ♘h5 15 ♚h2 ♘d7?! 16 g4! and Black's knights were driven back, Miles–Seirawan, Linares 1983.

6 ♗b5

White can transpose to note a above with 6 ♗e2, but he should avoid 6 d5 ♘e5 7 ♗e2 ♘xf3+ 8 gf ♗h5!? (8 ... ♗d7 is perfectly playable) 9 ♗b5+ ♚f8 10 0-0 e6 11 de fe 12 ♗e2 ♕h4 13 ♚h1?? (13 f4 was compulsory, although Black has a good game anyway) ♗xf3+! 0–1, Dorfman–Romanishin, Cienfuegos 1977.

6 ... a6
7 ♗xc6+ bc
8 h3 ♗xf3

8 ... ♗d7 9 ♕d2 ♕b8 10 ♖b1 ♘f6 11 ♗h6 0-0 12 0-0 ♕b7 13 ♖fe1 ♖ae8 14 e5 ♘d5 15 ♘e2 f6 16 ♗xg7 ♚xg7 17 c4 ♘b6 18 b3 left Black with a terrible position in Stean–Kotov, London 1977.

9 ♕xf3 ♕d7 *(82)*

Or 9 ... e6 (9 ... ♕b8 10 e5 ♕b7 11 0-0 ♘h6 12 ♖ad1 0-0 13 ♗c1 was also good for White in Kindermann–Hickl, Munich 1987, but after 13 ... ♕b6 14 ♕e4 ♘f5 15 b3? de White discovered that recapturing on e5 would allow ... ♘g3) 10 e5! ♘e7 11 ♘e4 ♘d5 12 ♗g5 ♕b8, Smyslov–Timman, Wijk aan Zee 1972, and now Hort suggests 13 c4! ♕b4+ 14 ♘d2 ♘e7 15 0-0 de 16 a3! ♕xb2 17 ♘e4! and White has a very dangerous attack.

82
W

10 e5! ♘h6

10 ... de 11 de ♗xe5 12 0-0 and if 12 ... ♘f6 13 ♗h6 is too dangerous.

11 0-0-0 0-0

12 ♖he1 ♚h8 13 ♗f4 ♖ab8 14 g4 ♖b4 15 ♚b1 a5 16 ♗g5 ♘g8 17 a3 and White has a permanent advantage since Black has no active play while White has chances of achieving something on the kingside, Tal–Hort, Moscow 1975.

Finally it is worth mentioning an interesting attempt by White to reach a Classical System without allowing any of the lines in this chapter. This idea runs 1 e4 g6 2 d4 ♗g7 3 ♘f3 d6 4 ♗e2. Now if 4 ... a6 5 0-0 (5 c4 ♗g4 6 ♘c3 ♘c6 7 ♗e3 e5 looks reasonable for Black) b5 6 a4 b4 7 c3 with advantage for White. The advance ... b5–b4 is not very constructive unless there is a knight on c3. Similar comments apply to 4 ... c6 5 0-0 while 4 ... ♗g4 5 ♘bd2 ♘c6 6 h3 ♗xf3 7 ♘xf3 is also a little better for White. Therefore Black players need to look at the main lines of the Classical, even if they intend adopting one of the variations in this chapter.

13 | The system with ♘c3, ♘f3, h3 and ♗e3

The fundamental position of this line is reached after the moves 1 e4 d6 2 d4 ♘f6 3 ♘c3 g6 4 ♘f3 ♗g7 5 h3 0-0 6 ♗e3. By delaying the development of his king's bishop, White retains the option of bringing it to c4 in one move. This has the effect of restraining e5 by Black, because after an exchange on e5 White's ♗c4 effectively gives him an extra tempo over the corresponding variations in Chapter 9. This system has been successfully employed by Spassky, Short and myself and in practice White has achieved excellent results. The only defect is that White's king has to stay in the centre for some moves, suggesting that Black should try violent methods to open the position up. This is the justification for recent lines based on ... d5!? Too few games have been played to judge whether this system's long summer is coming to an end, but Korchnoi–Speelman is an ominous sign that the autumn gales are approaching.

1 e4 d6 2 d4 ♘f6 3 ♘c3 g6 4 ♘f3 ♗g7

5	h3	0-0

Black has no better move:
(a) **5 ... c5** 6 dc (White can also play 6 e5 ♘fd7 7 ed cd 8 ♘xd4 0-0 9 de ♕xe7+ 10 ♗e3 ♘c6 11 ♗e2 ♘b6 12 ♘xc6 bc 13 0-0 with some advantage, Ermenkov–Bohosian, Bulgaria Ch. 1977) ♕a5 7 ♗b5+ (7 ♗d3 ♕xc5 8 0-0 0-0 9 ♗f4 ♘bd7 10 ♕d2 a6 11 ♖fe1 ♖e8 12 e5 de 13 ♘xe5 ♘xe5 14 ♗xe5 ♗e6 leads to equality, Milev–Ermenkov, Bulgaria 1977) ♗d7 8 ♗xd7+ ♘bxd7 9 cd ♘xe4 10 0-0 is untested, but looks good for White, e.g. 10 ... ♘xd6 11 ♖e1 or 10 ... ♘xc3 11 bc ♗xc3 12 ♖b1.
(b) **5 ... a6** 6 ♗d3 (6 a4 might well transpose to line A below, but Spassky's move makes good sense) ♘fd7 (6 ... b5 is strongly met by 7 e5, but 6 ... 0-0 is more solid) 7 ♘e2 c5 8 c3 ♘c6 9 0-0 b5 10 ♗e3 0-0 11 ♕d2 ♗b7 12 ♗h6 cd 13 cd ♕a5 14 ♕e3 with a slight

advantage for White, Spassky–van der Wiel, Baden 1980.

(c) **5 ... ♘c6** should be met by 6 d5 or 6 ♗e3 (see line d of the next note) instead of 6 ♗g5 0–0 7 ♕d2 d5!? 8 ♗xf6 ef 9 ed ♖e8+ 10 ♗e2 ♘b4=, McKay–Wüllenweber, Edinburgh 1986.

6 ♗e3 *(83)*

There are now two main lines, but other moves are playable.

A: **6 ... a6**
B: **6 ... c6**

Or:

(a) **6 ... b6** (see also 6 ... a6 7 a4 b6) 7 ♗c4 (7 ♗d3 ♗b7 8 0-0 c5 9 d5 ♘a6 10 ♕d2 ♘c7 11 ♗h6 b5 12 ♗xg7 ♔xg7 13 a3 a6 14 ♖fe1 e6 15 de ♘xe6 16 ♗f1 was a little better for White in Larsen–Timman, Linares 1983, but 7 ♗e2 ♗b7 8 e5 de 9 de ♘d5 10 ♘xd5 ♕xd5 11 ♕xd5 ♗xd5 12 0-0-0 e6 13 ♖he1 ♘d7 14 c4 ♗c6 was only equal, Radulov–Timman, Buenos Aires Ol. 1978) e6 (for 7 ... ♗b7 8 e5 see 6 ... a6, since the omission of ... a6 and a4 makes little difference) 8 ♗g5 (White should play 8 0-0 as in line A below) h6 9 ♗h4 ♗b7 10 ♕e2 g5 11 ♗g3 d5 12 ♗d3 c5!? with a distinctly unclear situation, Velikov–Ftacnik, Kiev 1978.

(b) **6 ... ♘a6** (there is nothing wrong with this move) 7 ♗e2 (7 ♕d2 c5 8 d5?! ♘c7 9 a4 a6 10 ♗d3 ♗d7 11 a5 ♘b5 12 ♘a4 c4 13 ♗xc4 ♘xe4 was good for Black in Kristiansen–Hartston, Esbjerg 1977, and 7 g3 b6 8 ♗g2 ♗b7 9 d5 c5 10 0-0 ♘c7 11 a4 e6 12 de fe 13 ♗g5 h6 14 ♗xf6 ♗xf6 was equal in Short–Davies, London 1985) c5 *(84)* and now:

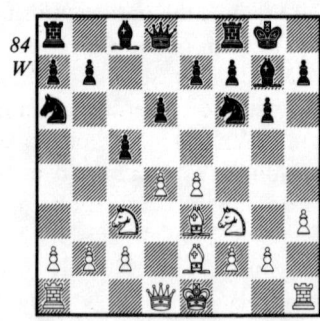

(b1) **8 dc** ♘xc5 (8 ... ♕a5 9 cd ♘xe4 10 de ♖e8 11 0-0 ♘xc3 12 bc and now 12 ... ♗xc3? 13 ♖b1 ♖xe7? 14 ♗b6! ♕a4 15 ♗b5 ♕e4 16 ♕d8+ ♔g7 17 ♖fe1! ♕f4 18 ♖xe7 ♗g4 19 ♗d4+ 1–0 was Sigurjonsson–Botterill, Hastings 1974/5, but even the improvement 12 ... ♖xe7 would have been ±) 9 e5 ♘fe4 10 ♘xe4 ♘xe4 11 ♕d5 ♘c5 reaches a position in which it is hard for White to show any advantage. Accepting the pawn by 12 ♗xc5 ♗e6 13 ♕xb7 dc gives Black enough compensation, so Nunn–Davies, London 1985, continued 12 ed ed 13 c3 ♗e6 14 ♕d2 ♘e4 15 ♕c2 d5 16 0-0 with advantage to White. Unfortunately, I discovered after the game that 12 ... ♗xb2! is good for Black since the intended 13 ♗xc5 ♗xa1 14 de ♕a5+ ♔f1 ♖e8 16 ♘g5 fails to 16 ... ♖xe7.

(b2) **8 e5** de 9 de ♘d7 10 ♗f4 (this promises little; the critical move is 10 e6) ♘b6 11 ♕c1 ♘b4 12 a3 ♘4d5 13 ♘xd5 ♘xd5 14 ♗h6 ♕a5 15 ♗d2 ♕a4 16 0-0 ♖d8 with equality, Timman–Seirawan, Niksic 1983.

(b3) **8 0-0** cd 9 ♘xd4 ♘c5 10 ♗f3 ♘e6 11 ♘b3 ♘d7 (a rather convoluted manoeuvre; 11 ... ♗d7 is more natural) 12 ♕d2 ♘b6 13 ♗e2 ♗d7 14 f4 ♘a4 15 f5 ♘xc3 16 bc ♘c7 with a double-edged position, Ivanovic–Torre, Bugojno 1984.

(c) **6 ... ♘bd7** 7 e5 ♘e8 8 ♗c4 ♘b6 9 ♗b3 c6 10 0-0 ♘c7 11 ♕e2 (11 ♖e1 ♗e6 12 ♗g5 ♕d7 13 ♘e4 f5 14 ef ef 15 ♗f4 was also good for White in Wedberg–D. Gurevich, Reykjavik 1982) ♗e6 12 ♖fe1 ♗xb3 13 ab de 14 de ♘e6 15 ♘g5 ♘xg5 16 ♗xg5 with a slight plus for White, Short–Norwood, England 1986.

(d) **6 ... ♘c6** (it seems to me that this should be played with ... a6 and a4 interposed, so that after d5 Black can reply ... ♘b4) 7 ♗c4 (7 ♕d2 e5 8 0-0-0 ed 9 ♘xd4 ♘xd4 10 ♗xd4 ♗e6 was already equal in Knoppert–Nijboer, Dieren 1986, and after 11 f4? c5 12 ♗e3 ♕a5 13 a3 b5! Black took over the initiative) ♘xe4 8 ♘xe4 d5 9 ♗d3 de 10 ♗xe4 f5!? 11 ♗xc6 bc 12 ♕d2 c5 13 0-0-0 is unclear, although in Bischoff–Marangunic, Dortmund 1987, Black was unable to justify his play and lost. Perhaps 7 ♗c4 should be met by 7 ... d5 8 ed ♘b4 followed by ... ♘bxd5 with a Caro-Kann type of position. It is strange that White did not play the obvious 7 d5 in these examples, since after 7 ... ♘b8 or 7 ... ♘b4 the position is similar to Chapter 11, line A. The main differences are that White is committed to h3 and ♗e3, but to counterbalance this he may be able to gain a tempo by playing ♗c4 in one move.

(e) **6 ... c5** 7 dc ♕a5 8 ♘d2 dc 9 ♘b3 (9 ♘c4 ♕c7 10 e5 ♘fd7 11 f4 ♘c6 was less clear in Nunn–Hertzog, Krefeld 1986) ♕c7 10 ♘xc5 b6 11 ♘b3 ♗b7 12 ♗d3 and although Black has some compensation for the pawn, there is no doubt that White is better.

A

6 ... **a6**
7 **a4** *(85)*

If White allows Black to

expand on the queenside then he cannot hope for an advantage, for example 7 ♗d3 b5 8 a4 (**8 ♕e2** b4 9 ♘b1 ♘bd7 10 ♘bd2 c5 11 dc ♘xc5 12 0-0 ♕c7 13 a3 ba 14 ♖xa3 ♘xd3 15 ♕xd3 ♗b7, Benjamin–Davies, Hastings 1987/8, and **8 ♘e2** ♘bd7 9 ♘g3 c5 10 c3 e5 11 de de 12 0-0 c4 13 ♗c2 ♗b7 14 ♕d2 ♖e8, Lobron–Seirawan, Lucerne 1982, were both level) b4 9 ♘e2 ♗b7 10 ♘g3 d5?! (10 ... ♘bd7 11 ♕d2 c5 is equal) 11 e5 ♘e4 12 0-0 c5 13 c3 and White has a slight advantage, McKay–Hort, Lucerne 1982.

85
B

7 ... b6

Or 7 ... ♘c6 (a solid move preparing ... e5) and now:
(a) **8 d5** ♘b4 (8 ... ♘a7 9 ♗e2 c5 10 dc ♘xc6 11 0-0 ♗d7 12 ♕d2 ♕a5 13 ♖a3 ♖fc8 was level in Juares Flores–Nogueiras, Granma 1987, but simply 10 0-0 is good for White) 9 a5 (9 ♗e2 c6 10 0-0 cd 11 ed ♗d7 12 a5 ♖c8 13 ♖a3 ♖xc3 14 bc ♘bxd5 was unclear, Tukmakov–Keene, Reykjavik 1976) e6 10 ♗e2 (10 ♖a4 c5 11 dc ♘xc6 12 ♗b6 ♕e7 is double-edged, but should be satisfactory for Black) ed 11 ed b5 12 ab cb 13 0-0 ♗b7 with equality, Wirthensohn–Nicevski, Chianciano Terme 1988.
(b) **8 a5** e5 9 de de 10 ♗c4 ♕e7 11 0-0 ♖d8 12 ♕b1 ♗e6 13 ♗xe6 ♕xe6 14 ♖a4 h6 15 ♕a2 ♕xa2 16 ♘xa2 ♖d7 17 ♘c1 ♖e8 18 ♘d3 with just an edge for White, Short–Davies, Hastings 1987/8.
(c) **8 ♕d2** e5 9 d5 ♘e7 10 g4 ♗d7 11 a5 c6 (this works out badly, so Black should have played 11 ... ♘e8 and waited to see what White intended to do with his king) 12 g5 ♘h5 13 ♗b6 ♕b8 14 dc bc 15 0-0-0 with advantage to White, Knaak–Pahtz, Halle 1987.

We now come to Black's most important 7th move alternative, namely **7 ... d5**. The move ... d5 can be played in a variety of positions, e.g. 6 ... a6 7 a4 d5, 6 ... c6 7 a4 d5 (or even 6 ... d5!?, although I can find no practical examples of this possibility). If White adopts the critical line then the two lines come to more or less the same thing since 6 ... a6 7 a4 d5 8 e5 ♘e4 9 ♘xe4 de 10 ♘g5 c5 and 6 ... c6 7 a4 d5 8 e5 ♘e4 9 ♘xe4 de 10 ♘g5 c5 differ only in the position of Black's a-pawn. It isn't clear whether Black would prefer the pawn to be on a6 or a7. If White adopts another plan against ... d5, then the choice of ... a6 or ... c6 introduces significant differences. In general Black is better off having played ... c6 (for example after 6 ... c6 7 a4 d5 the move ed does not come into consideration). On the other hand only the lines with e5 test Black's idea, so these differences may be unimportant for the assessment of ... d5.

For the sake of simplicity we take 6 ... a6 7 a4 d5 to be the main line. After 7 ... d5 8 e5 (8 ♗d3 de 9 ♘xe4 ♘xe4 10 ♗xe4 c5 and 8 ed ♘xd5 9 ♘xd5 ♕xd5 do not appear dangerous) ♘e4 9 ♘xe4 de 10 ♗g5 (with ... c6 instead of ... a6 the game Poulsson–Davies, Oslo 1988, continued 10 ♘d2 f5 11 f4 ef 12 ♗c4+ e6 13 ♘xf3 ♕e7 14 ♕d2 with a small advantage for White, so Black should play 10 ... c5 in any case) c5 11 dc ♕c7 12 ♕d5!? (with the pawn on a7 Ligterink–Timman, Netherlands Ch. 1987 continued 12 ♗c4 ♘c6 13 ♘xe4 ♕xe5 14 ♘c3 ♗e6 15 ♗xe6 ♕xe6 16 0-0 ♖ad8 17 ♕c1 ♗xc3 18 bc ♖d7 and Black is at least equal, but 13 e6 is the critical test when 13 ... f5 14 0-0 f4 15 ♗c1 ♕e5 16 h4 h6 17 ♘h3 ♘d4 18 c3 was unclear in Hodgson–McNab, British Ch. 1988) h6 (it seems to me that it is better to play 12 ... ♘c6!, since 13 e6 f5 appears fine for Black while otherwise Black gains time by missing out ... h6) 13 ♘xe4 ♖d8 14 ♕a2 ♗f5?! (14 ... ♘c6 is better, but 15 ♗c4 ♘xe5 16 ♗b3

is ±) 15 ♘g3 ♗xc2, Korchnoi–Speelman, Brussels 1988. Now 16 ♕c4! would have given White a winning position, but Korchnoi played 16 ♗c4? and lost after 16 ... ♕a5+ 17 ♔e2 ♘c6 18 ♗xf7+ ♔h7 19 f4 ♘b4 20 ♕e6 ♘d5 21 ♗d2 ♕d3+ 22 ♔e1 ♕xc5 23 f5 ♘e3 24 ♕xg6+ ♔h8 25 ♘h5 ♗xf5 26 ♘xg7 ♕xe5+ 27 ♔f2 ♕d4+ 28 ♔e1 ♕h4+ 29 g3 ♕e4+ 30 ♔f2 ♕e2+ 31 ♔g1 ♗e4 0–1.

8   ♗c4

Or 8 ♗d3 (8 e5 is best met by 8 ... ♘fd7 9 e6 fe 10 ♘g5 ♘f6 11 h4 c5 12 h5 cd 13 ♗xd4 gh 14 ♕f3 d5 15 ♕e3 ♘c6 16 ♗xb6 d4! with advantage for Black, Chandler–Gufeld, Wellington 1988, rather than 8 ... ♘e8 9 ♗c4 e6 10 ♕e2 ♗b7 11 ♖d1 ♕c8 12 ♗g5 d5 13 ♗a2 and Black has no antidote to the imminent h4–h5, Ermenkov–Radulov, Bulgaria Ch. 1976) ♗b7 9 0-0 ♘bd7 (9 ... ♘c6 10 ♕d2 e5 11 de de 12 ♖fd1 ♖e8 13 ♗c4 ♕xd2 14 ♖xd2 ♘a5 15 ♗a2 with an edge for White, Barlov–Davies, Bad Worishofen 1987) 10 ♖e1 e5 11 d5 (11 de de 12 ♕d2 offers better chances, but White's advantage is minute) c6 12 dc ♗xc6 13 ♗c4 ♕c7 14 ♗g5 ♗xe4 15 ♘xe4 ♕xc4 16 ♗xf6 ♘xf6 17 ♘xf6+ ♗xf6 18 ♕xd6 with equality, Eingorn–Guseinov, Kiev 1984.

8   ...   e6

The natural move is 8 ... ♗b7,

but it appears that the advance of White's e-pawn is too dangerous. Therefore Black takes time out to stop e5–e6, while at the same time preparing ... d5. After 8 ... ♗b7 (8 ... ♘c6 9 e5 ♘e8 10 ♗f4 ♘a5 11 ♗a2 c5 12 dc bc 13 0-0 was good for White in Short–Speelman, British Ch. 1987) 9 e5 ♘e4 (9 ... ♘e8 10 e6 f5 11 0-0 is good for White) 10 ♘xe4 ♗xe4 11 ♘g5 ♗xg2 12 ♖g1 ♗c6 (12 ... ♗b7 was played in Espig–Tringov, East Germany–Bulgaria 1983, but this makes no difference) 13 ♕g4! e6, Spassky–Seirawan, Zürich 1984, and now 14 h4! (instead of 14 0-0-0) gives White a decisive attack according to Spassky.

9 0-0 *(86)*

9 e5 (9 ♗g5 h6 10 ♗h4 ♗b7 11 ♕e2 ♕e8 12 0-0 ♘bd7 13 ♖fe1 ♘h5 14 ♖ad1 c6 15 ♕e3 b5 was unclear in Haugli–Karlsson, Oslo 1988) de 10 ♘xe5 ♗b7 11 0-0 ♘c6 12 ♘xc6 ♗xc6 13 ♕e2 ♕c8 14 ♖ad1 ♕b7 15 f3 ♖fe8 was fine for Black in Gochev–M. Gurevich, Eger 1987.

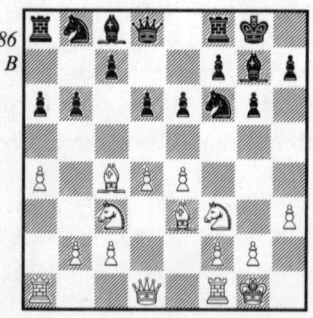

9 ... ♗b7

Or 9 ... d5 (9 ... ♘c6 10 d5 ed 11 ed ♘e7 12 ♕d2 ♖b8 13 ♗g5 ♗b7 14 ♕f4 ♘d7 15 ♕h4 f6 16 ♗d2 ♘f5 17 ♕g4 ♔h8 18 ♖fe1 ♘e5 19 ♘xe5 de 20 f4 gave White a slight advantage, Ligterink–van der Wiel, Amsterdam 1984) 10 ♗d3 (10 ed ed 11 ♗b3 is more interesting, since although the bishop appears out of play on b3, it exerts annoying pressure on d5; White may continue with moves such as ♘e5, ♕f3 and ♗g5) de 11 ♘xe4 ♗b7 12 ♘xf6+ (12 ♗g5 ½-½, van der Wiel–Ftacnik, Lyons 1988 doesn't tell us much) ♗xf6 13 c3 ♘d7 14 ♘d2 ♗g5 15 ♗e4 with just a faint edge for White, Smagin–Ftacnik, Belgrade Open 1987.

10 d5 e5

10 ... ed 11 ed ♘bd7 12 ♘d4 ♖e8 13 ♗a2 ♘c5 14 ♘c6 ♕d7 15 ♕f3 gave White a clear advantage in Short–Torre, Biel play-off 1985.

11 ♘d2 ♘bd7

12 ♗e2 ♔h8 13 a5 b5 14 ♘a2 ♘g8 15 c4 bc 16 ♗xc4 f5 17 f3 reaching a King's Indian type of position with the traditional battle of a White queenside attack against a Black kingside one. I suspect that White has a slight advantage objectively, but as usual such theoretical distinctions have little importance in a highly double-edged position. In L. Schneider–M. Gurevich, Rilton

Cup 1987, White won after a long and complex struggle.

B

6	...	c6
7	a4	(87)

It is a good idea to prevent Black's ... b5. After 7 ♕d2 (7 ♗d3 may also be met by 7 ... b5, but Lobron–De Boer, Amsterdam 1984 continued 7 ... ♘bd7 8 e5 ♘e8 9 e6 fe 10 ♘g5 ♘df6 11 h4 e5 12 de ♘g4 13 ♗c4+ d5 14 ♘xd5 cd 15 ♗xd5+ ♔h8 16 ♘f7+ ♖xf7 17 ♗xf7 ♕xd1+ 18 ♖xd1 ♗f5 and Black is at least equal) b5 8 ♗d3 ♘bd7 9 ♗h6 (9 e5 b4! 10 ef bc 11 ♕xc3 ♘xf6 12 ♕xc6 ♖b8 13 ♕a4 ♖xb2 14 ♕xa7 e5! 15 de de 16 ♕a3 e4! with advantage for Black, Arnason–Fries-Nielsen, Vejle 1984) e5 10 ♗xg7 ♔xg7 11 de de with a very comfortable position for Black, Short–Torre, Biel play-off 1985.

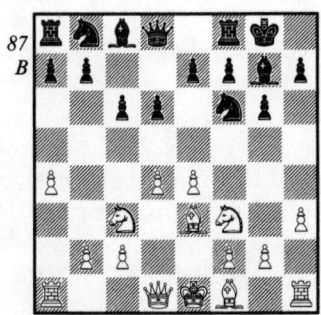

7	...	♘bd7

Not 7 ... e5 8 de de 9 ♕xd8 ♖xd8 10 ♗c4 ♘bd7 11 0-0 h6 (11 ... a5 12 ♘g5 ♖f8 13 f4 is unpleasant) 12 a5 ♗f8 13 ♖fb1 ♔g7 14 b4 ♖e8 15 ♗d3 ♗e7 16 ♘d2 with a clear advantage for White, Larsen–Schussler, Copenhagen 1979. This bears a striking similarity to Nunn–Todorcevic given below. **7 ... b6** is designed to prepare ... ♕c7 and ... e5 without allowing White to play a5. After 8 ♗e2 ♕c7 9 e5 de 10 ♘xe5 ♗e6 11 ♗f4 ♕c8 12 ♗f3 ♘d5 13 ♘xd5 ♗xd5 14 ♗xd5 cd 15 0-0 the position was equal in Benjamin–Wolff, Saint John Open 1988, but 9 0-0 e5 10 ♖e1 looks better. For **7 ... d5** see line A. Finally, **7 ... a5** 8 ♗e2 ♘a6 9 0-0 transposes to Chapter 9, line B.

8 a5

8 ♗e2 e5 9 de de 10 0-0 transposes to Chapter 9, line A1, but 8 a5 is stronger.

8	...	e5

This gives White an advantage, but the alternative 8 ... ♕c7 is also not very tempting: 8 ... ♕c7 9 ♗e2 (since Black is more or less committed to ... e5 White could consider 9 ♕d2 with the idea of 9 ... e5 10 de de 11 ♗c4, gaining the moderately useful move ♕d2; Black would probably reply in similar vein by 9 ... ♖e8 or 9 ... ♖d8, waiting for ♗e2 before playing ... e5) e5 10 de de 11 ♗c4 (11 0-0 transposes to chapter 9, line A2, note to White's 9th move) ♖e8 12 ♘g5 ♗e7 13 0-0 h6 14 ♘f3 ♘f8 15 ♕c1 ♔h7 16 ♗c5 ♖e8 17 ♖d1 with some advantage for White, Kosten–Gipslis, Jurmala 1987. Even though 8 ... ♕c7 probably fails to equalize it is certainly better than 8 ... e5.

**9 de de
10 ♕d6!** *(88)*

This is the move that puts the whole line out of business. 10 ♗c4 ♕e7 11 0-0 ♘c5 12 ♘d2 (after 12 ♘g5 ♘e6 13 ♘xe6 ♗xe6 14 ♕e2 ♘h5 15 ♗xe6 ♕xe6 16 ♗c5 ♖fd8 Black was well on the way to equality in Rohde–Leski, San Francisco 1987) ♘h5 13 ♘b3, De Firmian–Gurevich, USA 1982, and now 13 ... ♘xb3 14 ♗xb3 ♗e6 is only marginally better for White.

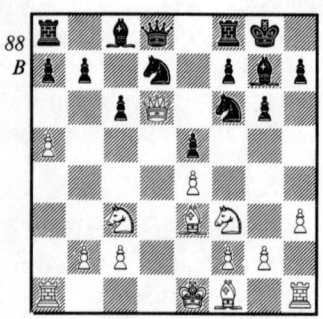

88
B

10 ... ♘e8

Playing ♕d6 in such positions is usually a waste of time because Black can expel the queen by playing moves which he would like to play in any case, such as ... ♖e8 and ... ♗f8. This position is a special case because White's pieces are well placed to exploit the weakness of f7 created by ...

♖e8, and in fact Black must make some concession to get rid of White's queen. After 10 ... ♖e8 11 ♗c4 ♕e7 (or 11 ... ♗f8 12 ♕d3 and all the natural moves fail tactically, 12 ... ♗c5 and 12 ... ♗b4 to 13 ♗xf7+ and 12 ... ♘c5 to 13 ♕xd8 ♖xd8 14 ♘xe5) 12 ♕xe7 ♖xe7 13 0-0 h6 14 ♖fd1 ♖e8 15 b4 ♗f8 16 ♖db1 a6 17 ♘d2 with a clear advantage for White, Nunn–Todorcevic, Szirak 1987.

11 ♕b4

Better than 11 ♕d2 ♕e7 12 ♗c4 ♘c7 (12 ... ♘c5 13 b4 ♘e6 14 ♗xe6 ♗xe6 15 ♗c5 ♕c7 16 0-0! ♖d8 17 ♕e3 ♘d6 18 ♗xa7 netting a clear pawn, Tal–Quinteros, Termas de Rio Hondo 1987) 13 0-0 ♘c5 14 ♖fd1 (Tal's manoeuvre is no longer effective because Black can recapture on e6 with a knight) ♘5e6 15 ♕d6 ♕xd6 16 ♖xd6 ♖e8 17 ♖dd1 f6 18 b4 ♗f8 19 ♖db1 ♔g7, Bouaziz–Todorcevic, Szirak 1987, and Black has gained a number of tempi over Nunn–Todorcevic above, which should allow him to equalize.

11 ... ♗f6

Or 11 ... ♘c7 12 ♗c4 and again Black's normal development is obstructed because the natural 12 ... ♖e8 allows 13 ♗xf7+! ♔xf7 14 ♘g5+ with a very dangerous attack.

12 ♗c4 ♕e7

13 ♕xe7 ♗xe7 14 ♗h6 ♘g7 15

0-0 ♖e8 16 ♖fd1 ♗f6 17 ♘g5 ♗xg5 18 ♗xg5 ♘c5 19 ♗e3 ♗e6 20 ♗f1 ♘d7 21 ♖d6 with a very pleasant ending for White, Nunn–Davies, Swansea 1987.

In summary, 6 ... c6 7 a4 ♘bd7 appears good for White and should be avoided, while 6 ... c6 7 a4 a5 transposing to Chapter 9 is also a little better for White. Of the older lines 6 ... a6 7 a4 b6 and 6 ... ♘a6 are the most reliable, but I would recommend one of the variations based on ... d5!? as being the best of all.

14 White plays ♗e3 and ♕d2

There are three sections to this chapter:

A: 1 e4 d6 2 d4 ♘f6 3 ♘c3 g6 4 ♗e3 ♗g7
B: 1 e4 d6 2 d4 ♘f6 3 ♘c3 g6 4 ♗e3 c6
C: 1 e4 g6 2 d4 ♗g7 3 ♘c3 d6 4 ♗e3

The move ♗e3 may introduce a variety of White plans. Firstly there is the direct ♕d2 and ♗h6 to exchange the useful bishop on g7. This plan may be very effective if Black has castled kingside too early, but assuming Black takes reasonable precautions then the immediate ♗h6 usually doesn't give White an advantage. A second idea which occurs in many positions is the kingside pawn-storm, starting with either g4 or h4. The reason for playing g4 first is that h4 may often be met by ... h5, preventing any further pawn advances on the kingside and, assuming Black has not castled, stopping ♗h6. White will normally castle queenside if he intends one of these direct plans, but this is by no means compulsory. Often White switches to positional play and kingside castling, especially if Black has committed himself by an early advance of the queenside pawns. Not only does such an advance make the queenside less comfortable for White's king, but after 0-0 White may prove that an early ... b5 is a weakness by playing a4. The strategically complex positions resulting from this system have made it very popular over the past few years; there are few lines which peter out to early equality and most lead to a sharp struggle.

We take variation A as being the main line of ♗e3 against the Pirc move-order. However this is a matter of convenience and readers should not assume that the move-order given is necessarily the most accurate. The first reason is that an early ... ♗g7 increases the force of ♗h6 by White. If Black plays ... c6 and ... b5 first (as in B) then White will be reluctant to play ♗h6 because the reply ... ♗xh6 saves

Black a clear tempo. Only after Black has developed some queenside counterplay will he contemplate ... ♗g7. The second reason is that White can try to save a tempo by missing out f3; this is the basis of variation A1, which is promising for White. It is harder for White to miss out f3 after 4 ... c6, so many players delay ... ♗g7 until White's f3, then they transpose into line A. Although these are good reasons for postponing ... ♗g7, it is an essential move and therefore most games with 4 ... c6 sooner or later transpose into 4 ... ♗g7 positions. In order to avoid a large number of transpositions from line B into line A, I have put all these games in A, whether they started with 4 ... ♗g7 or 4 ... c6. Only those lines which are particular to 4 ... c6 are left in B.

In line C, with the Modern move-order, Black may prevent ♗h6 completely by leaving the knight on g8. This too can transpose into line A if Black plays ... ♘f6, so again we only consider independent lines in section C. Black's objective is to reach a type of Sicilian by playing ... ♘d7 and ... c5 exchanging White's d-pawn, and only then complete his development by ... ♘gf6 and ... 0-0. Leaving the king in the centre for a long time carries an inevitable risk, and it seems that White's most dangerous lines are those in which he plays for a direct attack by 0-0-0 and h4.

A

1 e4 d6 2 d4 ♘f6 3 ♘c3 g6 4 ♗e3 ♗g7

At one time the move 5 f3 was played automatically on the assumption that 5 ♕d2 may be met by 5 ... ♘g4. However it is not at all clear that this knight move equalizes, in which case White gains some flexibility by playing ♕d2 first. Depending on Black's reply he may be able to dispense with f3 entirely, or he may play f3 after all, having coaxed Black into committing himself to an inferior line. Thus there are two major variations:

A1: 5 ♕d2
A2: 5 f3

Readers should note that some lines with f3 are given in A1 if they invariably arise via the 5 ♕d2 move-order.

A1

5 ♕d2 *(89)*

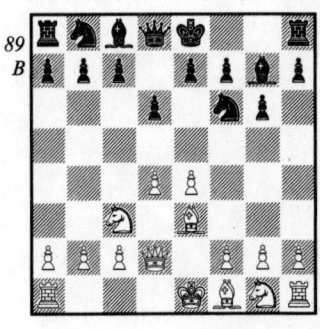

5 ... 0-0

White plays ♗e3 and ♕d2

There are two main alternatives, 5 ... ♘g4 and 5 ... c6. The former must be a critical test of White's plan, but it has not been played very frequently. The latter is an attempt to persuade White to play f3 after all; White can either transpose or pursue an independent path by 6 ♗h6. In the latter case White often plays 0-0 and seeks to exploit Black's inability to castle by positional means.

(1) **5 ... ♘g4** 6 ♗g5 (6 ♗f4 e5 7 de ♘xe5 is fine for Black) h6 (6 ... f6 7 ♗h4 e5 8 de de 9 ♕xd8+ ♔xd8 10 0-0-0+ ♘d7 11 ♘f3 ♖e8 12 ♘d5 c6 13 h3 cd 14 hg de 15 ♘d2 gave White the better ending, Lau–Ingenerf, Bundesliga 1985) 7 ♗h4 g5 (7 ... c6 8 0-0-0 b5 9 f3 ♘f6 10 ♕e1 ♕c7 11 e5 de 12 de ♘h5 13 g4 ♘f4 14 ♗f6! ♘e6 15 ♗xg7 ♘xg7 16 ♕e4 was slightly better for White in Belyavsky–Hort, Hastings 1974/5) 8 ♗g3 e5 (**8 ... f5** 9 f3 f4 10 ♗xf4 gf 11 fg ♗xg4 12 ♗e2 e5 13 ♗xg4 ♕h4+ 14 ♕f2 ♕xg4 was unclear in Hort–Timman, Tilburg 1980, but 9 ef ♗xf5 followed by 10 ♗d3 or 10 ♗c4 is good for White according to Chernin; **8 ... h5** 9 h3 h4 10 hg hg 11 ♖xh8+ ♗xh8 12 f3 followed by ♘ge2 is also good for White) and now:

(1a) **9 de** is slightly better for White according to Chernin. The only example I can find is Borgstadt–Goldschmidt, Dortmund Open 1987. This game continued 9 ... ♘xe5 10 ♘f3 ♘bc6 11 ♗b5 ♘g6 12 h4 g4 13 ♘d4 ♗d7 14 ♗xc6 ½–½, which doesn't tell us much. I suspect that Chernin is correct because the weak d5 and f5 squares should outweigh the strong point at e5.

(1b) **9 d5** h5 10 h3 ♘f6 11 ♘f3 (this leads to a draw, but 11 ♕xg5 ♗h6 12 ♕h4 is risky after 12 ... ♘bd7 intending ... ♘f8–g6, even though White may wriggle out by f3, ♗h2 and ♕f2; note that 12 ... ♖g8 must be met by 13 f4 because after 13 ♘f3 ♘bd7 White cannot now play f3) h4 12 ♕xg5 (12 ♗h2 ♗h6 is good for Black) ♗h6 13 ♕xh4 ♗g7 (13 ... ♗d2+ gives White more than enough for the queen) 14 ♕g5 ♗h6 15 ♕h4 ½–½, Kuzmin–Chikovani, USSR 1976.

(2) **5 ... c6** 6 ♗h6 (6 g3 is dubious because of 6 ... ♘g4 7 ♗f4 ♕b6 and now 8 0-0-0 ♕xd4! 9 ♕xd4 ♗xd4 10 ♖xd4 ♘xf2 is good for Black, so Salov–Mark Tseitlin, USSR 1980, continued 8 h3 e5 9 de de 10 ♗g5 h6 11 hg hg with an edge for Black) ♗xh6 (or 6 ... 0-0 7 ♗xg7 ♔xg7 8 ♘f3 ♗g4 9 0-0-0 ♘bd7 10 h3 ♗xf3 11 gf e5, Stoica–Negulescu, Romania Ch. 1986, and now 12 f4 ef 13 ♕xf4 ♕e7 would have been a little better for White; 7 0-0-0 with the idea of a direct kingside attack by h4 was also promising) 7 ♕xh6 ♕a5 8 ♗d3 and now:

(2a) **8 ... b5** 9 ♘f3 b4 10 ♘e2

♘bd7 11 0-0 (this is an example of how the advance of the b-pawn can rebound on Black) e5 12 a3 ba 13 ♖xa3 ♕c7 14 de de 15 ♘g5 with an advantage for White on both sides of the board, Kuprechik–Sznapik, Zenica 1985.

(2b) **8 ... ♘bd7** 9 ♘f3 b6 10 0-0 ♗b7 11 ♖fe1 (11 ♘g5 is also promising; White threatens ♕g7 and prevents ... ♕h5) ♕h5 12 ♕d2 c5 13 d5 0-0 14 ♘e2 ♘e5 15 ♘xe5 de 16 c4 with a slight advantage for White, Le Blancq–McNab, Bath 1987.

(2c) **8 ... ♘a6** 9 ♘f3 ♗g4 10 ♘g5 ♕c7 11 h3 ♗e6 12 0-0 ♘g8 13 ♕h4 h6 14 d5 ♗d7 15 ♖ae1 ♕b4! with murky complications, van der Wiel–van Wijgerden, Netherlands Ch. 1984.

(3) **5 ... ♘c6** 6 f3 a6 7 0-0-0 e6 8 g4 b5 9 h4 h5 10 gh ♘xh5 11 ♘ge2 ♗d7 12 ♗h3 b4 13 ♘b1 a5 14 ♗g5 ♕c8 15 c4 ♕a6 16 ♕d3 a4 17 ♘d2 ♘a5 18 ♔b1, Short–Kavalek, Dubai 1986, and White had the advantage as Black has no safe refuge for his king.

6   0-0-0

Whereas 5 ... ♘g4 was playable, 6 ... ♘g4 is definitely bad for Black so White again takes the opportunity to avoid wasting a tempo on f3. 6 f3 is less accurate and transposes to the note to Black's 5th move in line A2.

6   ...   ♘c6

After 5 ... ♘g4 7 ♗g5 c5 (7 ... h6 8 ♗h4 ♘c6 9 h3 ♘f6 10 f4 a6 11 g4 b5 12 e5 de 13 de ♕xd2+ 14 ♖xd2 was very unpleasant for Black in Yudasin–Zaichik, Lvov 1987) 8 dc ♕a5 9 ♘h3 (9 f3! ♗xc3 10 ♕xc3 ♕xc3 11 bc ♘f2 12 ♗xe7 ♖e8 13 cd ♘xh1 14 ♗b5 ♗d7 15 ♗xd7 ♘xd7 16 ♘h3 ♖ac8 17 ♔b2 is good for White according to Chernin) dc 10 ♗xe7 ♖e8 11 ♕d8 ♖xd8 12 ♖xd8+ ♕xd8 13 ♗xd8 White had a slight endgame advantage in Yudasin–Azmaiparashvili, Kuibyshev 1986.

7   f3

Now ... ♘g4 is a genuine threat, so White finally plays f3, but only after Black is committed to the unnatural ... ♘c6.

7   ...   e5
8   ♘ge2

8 d5 ♘e7 (8 ... ♘d4 9 ♘ge2 c5 10 dc bc 11 ♘xd4 ed 12 ♗xd4 ♗e6 was played in Sveshnikov–Hoi, Copenhagen 1984, and now 13 ♘a4! followed by b3 would have been good for White) 9 g4 ♘e8 10 ♘ge2 f5 11 ♖g1 f4 12 ♗f2 g5 13 h4 gh 14 ♗xh4 ♗f6 15 g5 ♗g7 16 ♔b1 ♘g6 was unclear in Sveshnikov–Quinteros, Rio 1985.

8   ...   ed
9   ♘xd4   *(90)*

White holds the advantage, e.g. 9 ... ♘xd4 (9 ... d5 10 ed ♘xd5 11 ♗g5 ♕d7 was tried in M. Gurevich–Zaichik, Lvov 1987, and now either 12 ♘xc6 bc 13 ♘xd5 cd 14 ♕xd5 ♖b8 15 b3

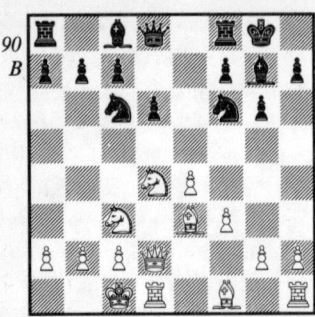

would have left Black with inadequate compensation for the pawn or 12 ♘db5 a6 13 ♘xd5 ab 14 ♘e7+ ♘xe7 15 ♕xd7 ♗xd7 16 ♖xd7 ♘c6 17 ♔b1 as in the game gave White a promising ending) 10 ♗xd4 ♗e6 11 ♗e3! ♖e8 12 ♗g5 (this prevents the reply 12 ... c6 because of 13 e5 de 14 ♕xd8 ♖axd8 15 ♖xd8 ♖xd8 16 ♘e4) ♕e7 13 g4 ♕f8 14 ♔b1 a6 15 h4 with a strong kingside attack, Chernin–Zaichik, Lvov 1987.

A2

5 f3

This is less incisive than 5 ♕d2 and sets Black fewer problems.

5 ... c6

Or **5 ... 0-0** 6 ♕d2 e5 (other moves will generally transpose into the note to Black's 6th move) 7 d5 (7 ♘ge2 ed 8 ♘xd4 d5 9 0-0-0 c5 10 ♘b3 d4 11 ♗g5 ♘c6 12 ♘d5 was ± in Sveshnikov–Zaichik, Volgodonsk 1983, but Black could have played 9 ... de 10 ♗h6 ♘c6 11 ♗xg7 ♔xg7 12 ♘xc6 ♕xd2+ 13 ♖xd2 bc 14 ♘xe4 ♘xe4 15 fe when White has only a minute advantage) c6 8 0-0-0 cd 9 ♘xd5 ♘xd5 10 ♕xd5 ♘c6 (10 ... ♗e6 11 ♕xb7 ♘d7 12 ♘e2 ♖c8 13 ♘c3 ♖xc3 14 bc ♕a5 15 ♕b4 ♕xa2 16 ♖xd6 is good for White, Chandler–Carr, London 1984) 11 ♕xd6 ♕a5 12 ♗c4 ♖d8 13 ♕c5 ♖xd1+ 14 ♔xd1 ♕d8+ 15 ♔c1 ♗f8 16 ♕d5 ♕c7 with good play for the pawn, Yudasin–Zaichik, Kostroma 1985.

6 ♕d2 *(91)*

6 a4 is inconsistent, because White usually needs the queenside for his king; J. Szabo–Trois, Satu Mare 1980, went on 6 ... ♘bd7 7 ♕d2 0-0 8 g4 (White should have contented himself with kingside castling) e5 9 h4 d5! 10 ed ed 11 ♗xd4 ♖e8+ 12 ♗e2 ♘e5 and Black held the initiative.

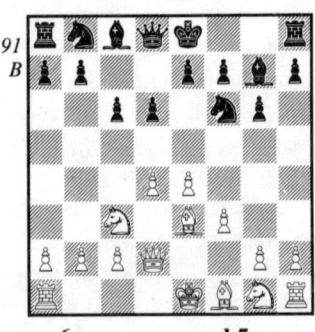

6 ... b5

Or:

(1) **6 ... 0-0** (the mixture of ... 0-0 and ... c6 is doubtful; if Black wants to expand with ... c6 and ... b5 he should not present White with a fixed target) 7 ♗h6

b5 (7 ... ♕a5 8 h4 b5 9 ♗xg7 ♔xg7 10 h5 b4 11 hg fg 12 ♘ce2 ♖f7 13 ♘h3 ♗xh3 14 ♖xh3 ♘bd7 15 ♘f4 with a dangerous attack, Gliksman–Angelov, Varna 'B' 1976) 8 ♗xg7 ♔xg7 9 ♗d3 ♗d7? (a very odd move; 9 ... b4 ± is better) 10 e5 ♘g8 11 ♘ge2 ♕b6 12 h4! de 13 de ♖d8 14 h5 and again Black's king is in trouble, Levicki–Volko, USSR 1977.

(2) **6 ... ♘bd7** (there is a good argument in favour of this move, namely that it keeps White in the dark about whether Black intends ... b5 or ... e5, but it does allow White to play ♘h3 more easily) and now:

(2a) **7 ♘h3** (this is the critical move since it immediately exploits the defect of ... ♘bd7) b5 (7 ... ♕a5 8 ♗e2 b5 9 0-0 ♘b6 10 e5 ♘fd5 11 ♘xd5 ♕xd2 12 ♘c7+ ♔d7 13 ♗xd2 ♔xc7 was equal in Liew–Weemaes, Dubai 1986, but 8 ♘f2 is more to the point) 8 ♘f2 0-0 (8 ... a5 9 ♗d3 ♗b7 10 ♘e2 e5 11 c3 0-0 12 0-0 d5 is possible, with an unclear position, I. Ivanov–Goodman, Student Olympiad, Mexico City 1978) 9 a4 b4 10 ♘cd1 a5 11 ♗e2 e5 12 c3 bc 13 bc (13 ♘xc3 ♖b8 14 ♖d1 ed 15 ♗xd4 ♕e7 16 0-0 ♘c5 17 ♗e3 d5 with a complex and roughly level position, Kr. Georgiev–Torre, Saint John Open 1988) ♖e8 14 0-0 d5 15 de, Kir. Georgiev–Torre, Leningrad 1987, and now 15 ... ♖xe5 16 ♗d4 ♖e8 17 ed cd was best, with just an edge for White. Note that the Krum Georgiev game from Saint John was played after the Leningrad game, so Torre must have been convinced that this line is not dangerous for Black.

(2b) **7 h4** h5 8 ♘h3 b5 9 ♘g5 ♗b7 (9 ... 0-0 10 0-0-0 ♘b6 11 ♗d3, Kr. Georgiev–Grigorov, Bulgaria 1984, and now 11 ... ♘c4 12 ♗xc4 bc 13 ♕e2 ♗a6! 14 g4 would have been double-edged according to Krum Georgiev) 10 ♗e2 0-0 11 0-0 a5 12 f4 (combining h4 and f4 is risky because of the weakness at g4) b4 13 ♘d1 c5 14 d5 ♘g4! 15 ♗xg4 hg with at least equality for Black, Ciocaltea–Razuvaev, Ljubljana–Portoroz, 1973.

(2c) **7 0-0-0** ♕a5 8 ♔b1 b5 9 ♗h6 ♗xh6 10 ♕xh6 ♗a6 11 ♘h3 0-0-0 12 ♘g5 ♖df8 13 a3 ♔b8 14 ♗e2 ♘e8 15 f4 ♘c7 16 e5 f6 with just an edge for White, Lau–Hort, Germany Ch. play-off 1987.

After 6 ... b5 *(92)* White has a wide range of possible moves:

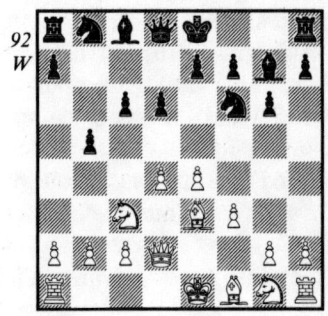

(a) 7 h4 h5 (7 ... ♕c7 8 0-0-0 ♘bd7 9 g4 h5 10 g5 ♘h7 11 f4 ♘b6 12 ♗d3 ♗g4 13 ♖f1 0-0 14 f5 b4 15 ♘d1 c5 16 ♗e2 ♗xe2 17 ♘xe2 ♖fc8 and Black has a satisfactory position, Tseshkovsky–Kuzmin, Tallinn 1979) 8 ♘h3 ♗xh3 (7 ... ♘bd7 transposes to line 2b above) 9 ♖xh3 ♘bd7 10 a4 b4 11 ♘e2 a5 12 b3 0-0 13 0-0-0 ♕c7 is unclear, Arapovic–Ciocaltea, Timisoara 1979.

(b) 7 ♗h6 ♗xh6 8 ♕xh6 ♕a5 9 ♗d3 ♘bd7 10 ♘h3 b4 11 ♘e2 c5 12 dc ♘xc5 13 0-0 ♗xh3! 14 ♕xh3 0-0 15 ♕h6 ♖fc8 with an equal position in Belyavsky–Hort, Moscow 1975.

(c) 7 g4 h5 (7 ... ♘bd7 8 a4 b4 9 ♘ce2 a5 10 g5 ♘h5 11 ♘g3 ♘xg3 12 hg c5 13 ♖d1 ♕c7 14 ♗b5 ♗a6 was murky in Mokry–Jansa, Warsaw 1987) 8 g5 ♘fd7 9 f4 ♘b6 10 ♘f3 d5 (10 ... b4 11 ♘d1 ♗g4 12 ♘h4 d5 13 e5 a5 14 b3 e6 15 ♘f2 with advantage for White since Black is cramped and the knight on f2 is heading for c5, Sveshnikov–Gulko, USSR 1975) 11 ♘e5 b4 12 ♘e2 de 13 ♘g3 h4 14 ♘xe4 ♗f5 15 ♘c5! (better than 15 ♗g2 f6 16 gf ef 17 ♕xb4 ♗f8 18 ♕b3 fe 19 0-0-0 ♘8d7 20 de ♘d5 with tremendous complications, Yudasin–Gipslis, USSR 1983) f6 (15 ... 0-0 was better, but 16 ♖g1 gives White the edge) 16 gf ef 17 ♘xg6! ♖h6 18 ♗d3 ♕d5 19 ♖g1 with a clear advantage for White, Yudasin–Azmaiparashvili, Minsk 1985.

(d) 7 ♗d3 ♘bd7 8 a4 b4 9 ♘d1 a5 10 ♘h3 e5 11 c3 0-0 12 ♘hf2 ♖e8 13 0-0 d5 14 ed (the position is similar to Kir. Georgiev–Torre in line 2a above, but the important difference is that White's bishop is on d3 instead of e2, so that 14 de ♘xe5 attacks it) ♘xd5 15 ♗g5 ♕c7 with a fine position for Black, Small–Spassky, Wellington 1988.

The conclusion is that 4 ... ♗g7 5 ♕d2 is dangerous for Black, but the older 5 f3 poses fewer problems. One of the main ideas behind 5 ... c6 is to transpose to line A2 above without allowing 5 ♕d2.

B

1 e4 d6 2 d4 ♘f6 3 ♘c3 g6 4 ♗e3 c6

5   ♕d2

As before White tries to avoid f3 for as long as possible. The alternative is 5 h3 (after 5 f3 Black may transpose to line A2 by 5 ... b5, but there is an interesting alternative in 5 ... ♕b6!? 6 b3 ♗g7 7 ♕d2 ♕a5 8 ♘ge2 0-0 9 0-0-0 b5 10 ♔b1 ♘bd7 with equality, Yudasin–Gufeld, USSR 1985) ♕a5 (5 ... ♗g7 6 g3 0-0 7 ♗g2 ♘bd7 8 ♘ge2 e5 9 a4 transposes to Chapter 17) 6 ♕d2 b5 7 ♗d3 (7 e5 b4) b4 8 ♘ce2 ♗g7 9 ♘f3 0-0 10 c4?! (10 a3 is better, when White has chances of an advantage) d5 11 ♘g3 de 12 ♘xe4 ♘xe4 13 ♗xe4 f5 14 ♗d3 c5 with an edge for Black, Belyavsky–Gufeld, Baku 1980.

5 ... b5 *(93)*

Or 5 ... ♘bd7 (5 ... ♕a5 6 ♘f3 b5 7 ♗d3 b4 8 ♘e2 ♗a6 9 0-0 ♗xd3 10 cd ♕b5 11 a3 ♘a6 12 ♖fc1 ♗g7 13 ab 0-0 14 ♖a5 ♕b7 15 b5! cb 16 ♖ca1 ♘c7 17 d5 with a large advantage for White, Zapata–van der Wiel, Brussels 1986) and now:

(a) **6 f3** e5!? (6 ... b5 transposes to the main line) 7 g4 ♗g7 8 0-0-0 h5 9 g5 ♘h7 10 f4 ef 11 ♗xf4 ♘b6 12 h4 0-0 13 ♕h2 ♗g4 14 ♗e2 ♗xe2 15 ♘gxe2 d5 with equality, Lau–Marangunic, Dortmund 1987.

(b) **6 f4** ♘g4 7 e5 ♗h6 8 ♘f3 ♘xe3 9 ♕xe3 0-0 10 0-0-0 de 11 ♘xe5 ♘xe5 12 de ♕b6 13 ♕f3 ♗e6 14 ♔b1 ♕b4 15 g3 ♕a5 16 h4 ♖fd8 with a level position, van der Wiel–Torre, Brussels 1987.

(c) **6 ♘f3** (just as in Zapata–van der Wiel above, White switches plan, replacing f3 by ♘f3 and aiming for quick development; see line 2 in the next note for a further example of this idea) ♕a5 (it would be more solid to play 6 ... e5 or 6 ... b5, the latter move having the idea 7 e5 b4) 7 ♗d3 e5 8 0-0-0 b5 9 ♔b1 ♕c7 (Black's development cannot proceed normally because 9 ... ♗g7 allows 10 ♘xb5!) 10 ♗g5 ♗e7 11 h4 a6 12 de de 13 h5!? ♘xh5 14 ♗xe7 ♔xe7 15 ♖xh5! gh 16 ♕g5+ ♘f6 17 ♘xe5 with a very strong attack for White, Kupreichik–Short, USSR–England telex match 1982.

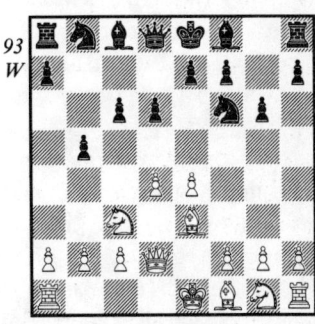

93
W

6 f3

Since this allows Black to achieve his aim of reaching line A2, the alternatives deserve close attention, particularly 6 ♗d3.

(1) **6 e5** ♘g4 (6 ... de 7 de ♕xd2+ 8 ♗xd2 ♘g4 9 f4 h5 10 ♗d3 ♗f5 11 ♘e4 is slightly better for White) 7 ed ♘xe3 8 ♕xe3 ♕xd6 9 ♘f3 ♗g7 10 a4 (or 10 ♗e2 0-0 11 0-0 ♗f5 12 ♗d3 ♗xd3 13 ♕xd3 ♘d7 14 ♖fe1 e6 15 ♘e4 ♕c7 with equality, Levitt–Akhsharumova, Saint John Open 1988) ba 11 ♖xa4 0-0 12 ♘e4 ♕c7 13 ♕a3 ♗f5 14 ♗d3 ♘d7 15 0-0 ♘b6 16 ♖a6 ♖fd8 and the position is balanced, van der Wiel–Piket, match 1986.

(2) **6 ♗d3** ♘bd7 (6 ... ♘g4 7 ♗g5 h6 8 ♗h4 ♗g7 9 h3 ♘f6 10 f4 b4 11 ♘ce2 ♕b6 12 ♘f3 ♗a6

13 0-0 ♗xd3 14 ♕xd3 with a clear plus for White, Kupreichik–Hartoch, Wijk aan Zee II 1977) 7 ♘f3 e5 (7 ... ♘b6 8 0-0 ♗g7 9 ♗h6 0-0 10 h3 ♘fd7 11 a4 b4 12 ♘e2 a5 13 ♗xg7 ♔xg7 14 c3 c5 15 cb cb 16 ♘g3 was good for White, Chandler–Nunn, London 1984) 8 0-0 ♗b7 9 ♖fe1 (9 ♖ad1 a6 10 a4 ♗g7 11 ab cb 12 de de 13 ♘xb5! ab 14 ♗xb5 ♗a6 15 ♗xa6 ♖xa6 16 ♘xe5 with advantage for White, Kupreichik–Karasev, Minsk 1976) ♘g4 10 ♗g5 f6 11 ♗h4 a6 12 h3 ♘h6 13 a4 b4 14 ♘d1 a5 15 c3 bc 16 bc and White has a clear space advantage, Barczay–Petran, Zalaegerszeg 1977.

6 ...   **♘bd7** *(94)*

6 ... ♗g7 transposes to line A2.

94
W

7   **♘h3**

Or:

(a) **7 0-0-0** ♕a5 (7 ... ♕c7 8 d5 a6 9 dc ♕xc6 10 ♘ge2?! ♗b7 11 ♘d4 ♕c7 12 g4 ♖c8? 13 g5 b4? 14 ♘cb5! ab 15 gf ♘xf6 16 ♗xb5+ ♘d7 17 e5! 1–0 Belyavsky–Kuzmin, USSR Ch.

1974 but 12 ... b4 13 ♘ce2 e5 was good for Black, so White should have played 10 g4 with an unclear position) 8 ♔b1 ♗a6 9 g4 b4 10 ♘ce2 ♘b6 11 b3 h5 12 gh? (12 g5 ♘fd7 13 f4 unclear was correct) ♘xh5 13 ♗g2 ♗g7 14 f4 ♘f6 15 c3 bc 16 ♘xc3 ♘g4 with a fine game for Black, Enklaar–Timman, Dutch Ch. 1976.

(b) **7 g4** ♘b6 8 g5 (8 h4 h5 9 g5 ♘fd7 10 a4?! ♘c4 11 ♗xc4 bc 12 ♕e2 ♗a6 13 b4 ♗g7 14 ♕d2 0-0 15 ♘ge2 ♗b7 and Black has an entirely satisfactory position, Kurajica–Ligterink, Wijk aan Zee 1977, but 10 f4 is much more dangerous) ♘h5 9 b3 ♗g7 10 ♘ge2 e5 11 a4 ba 12 ♘xa4 ♘xa4 13 ♖xa4 ♕e7 14 de de 15 ♖a5! and Black's king was permanently trapped in the centre, Schmittdiel–Marangunic, Dortmund 1987.

7 ...   **a6**

Round about here Black should admit that he has no better move than ... ♗g7. By persisting in his attempts to avoid this move he can run into trouble. If Black plays 7 ... ♗g7 then we reach line A2, note to Black's 6th move, variation 2a. Another example in support of this point is Ciocaltea–Hazai, Albena 1978, which carried on 7 ... e5 8 ♘f2 ♗b7 9 ♗e2 b4 (to play ... b4 unprovoked by a4 is a mistake) 10 ♘cd1 ed 11 ♗xd4 c5 12 ♗e3 ♕e7 13 a3 a5 14 ab ab 15 ♖xa8+ ♗xa8 16 0-0

♗g7 17 ♗f4! and White had the advantage.

8 ♘f2   e5

This is given a ? by Andersson. 8 ... ♗b7 would be more flexible.

9 ♗e2   ♕c7

10 0-0 ♗g7 11 de de 12 a4 ♗b7 13 ♖fd1 (13 ab ab 14 ♗xb5! cb 15 ♘xb5 is very dangerous) 0-0 14 ♕d6 and White is still slightly better, Geller–Andersson, Hilversum 1973.

C

1 e4 g6 2 d4 ♗g7 3 ♘c3 d6 4 ♗e3

There are now two variations, according to the method chosen by Black to prepare ... b5:

C1: 4 ... a6
C2: 4 ... c6

C1

4 ...   a6
5 ♕d2

Or 5 a4 (5 g4?! b5 6 ♗g2 b4 7 ♘d5 a5 8 h4 c6 9 ♘f4 ♘f6 10 ♗f3 e5 11 de de 12 ♘d3 h5 13 g5 ♘fd7 ∓ Speelman–Nunn, England 1974) ♘c6 6 d5 (6 ♘f3 ♗g4 is fine for Black because White lacks the move ♗b5 – see Chapter 12 for a discussion of this point, which also lies behind the line 1 e4 g6 2 d4 ♗g7 3 ♘c3 d6 4 ♘f3 a6; **6 h3** aims to prepare ♘f3, but it is rather slow and after 6 ... e5 7 ♘f3 ed 8 ♘xd4 ♘f6 9 ♗e2 0-0 10 0-0 ♖e8 11 ♗d3 ♘b4 the position was equal, Doncevic–Hickl,

Bundesliga 1987) ♘a7 (is 6 ... ♘b4 impossible?) 7 ♗e2 c5 8 h4 (8 ♘f3 followed by 0-0 is better and should give White some advantage; there is little point to h4 if White is going to castle kingside) h5 9 ♘f3 ♗d7 10 ♕d2 ♕c7 11 ♘g5 ♖b8 12 0-0 b5 with an unclear position, Schneider–Davies, Bundesliga 1986.

5 ...   b5
6 f3

6 a4 b4 7 ♘d1 a5 8 ♗d3 ♘f6 9 f3 0-0 10 ♘e2 ♘bd7 11 c3 c5?! (11 ... e5 was better) 12 0-0 ♗b7 13 ♗b5 bc 14 bc ♕c7 15 ♘b2 e6 with a slight plus for White, Ghinda–Nunn, Buenos Aires Ol. 1978.

6 ...   ♘d7 *(95)*

7 ♘h3

Or:

(1) **7 0-0-0** (this straightforward move is White's most dangerous continuation) ♗b7 8 h4 h5 (8 ... h6 9 ♘h3 e6 10 ♘f2 ♘e7 11 h5 g5 12 g3 ♘b6 13 f4 g4 14 d5! with advantage for White, Gufeld–Kindermann, Dortmund 1983) 9

♘h3 ♘gf6 (when Black gives away the g5 square by playing ... h5, White usually replies ♘h3–g5) 10 ♔b1 ♖c8 and while this type of position must be better for White, in practice it is not so easy for him to keep things under control. Anand–Davies, Moscow 1987, continued 11 ♕e1 e5 12 d5 c6 13 dc ♖xc6 14 ♘g5 ♕c7 15 ♕d2 ♖xc3 16 ♕xc3 ♕xc3 17 bc d5 18 ed ♘xd5 19 ♗d2 ♘7f6 20 ♘e4 0-0 and Black later won, although at this stage his compensation appears inadequate.

(2) **7 a4** (this move seems out of place here) b4 8 ♘d1 ♖b8 9 c3 (9 ♘h3 c5 10 a5 cd 11 ♗d4 ♘gf6 12 ♗e2 0-0 13 0-0 ♕c7 14 ♘hf2 ♘c5 15 b3 e5 16 ♗b2 ♗e6 and Black has a very favourable type of Sicilian, Chandler–Davies, Hastings 1987/8) bc 10 bc ♘gf6 11 a5 0-0 12 ♗d3 e5 13 ♘e2 d5 14 0-0 c5 15 ♘f2 de 16 fe cd 17 cd ed 18 ♗xd4 ♕e7 and Black is better, Chandler–Speelman, Hastings 1987/8.

7 ...   ♗b7

It is probably better to play ... c5 at once, e.g. 7 ... c5 8 dc (8 d5 ♘b6 9 ♘f2 offers better chances; although Black has managed to play ... b5 White's knight on f2 enhances his prospects of a kingside attack) ♘xc5 9 ♘f2 ♗b7 10 ♗e2 ♕c7 11 a3 ♖c8 12 0-0 ♘f6 13 ♗h6 0-0 14 ♗xg7 ♔xg7 with equality, Rantanen–Keene, Gausdal 1979. The reason why ...

c5 is better than ... ♗b7 is that on b7 the bishop prevents Black from supporting his b-pawn by ... ♖b8. This applies particularly when a4 has forced the Black b-pawn on to b4.

8   ♘f2

8 ♗e2 c5 9 a4! b4 10 ♘d1 ♘gf6 11 a5! (isolating the b-pawn) ♕c7 12 c3 bc 13 bc 0-0 14 ♘b2 ♖fc8 15 d5 and White stands very well, Cardoso–Larsen, Orense 1975. This example shows how ... ♗b7 can be a liability rather than an asset.

8 ...   c5

8 ... ♘gf6 9 ♗e2 e5 10 d5 ♘b6 11 a4 b4 12 ♘d1 a5 13 ♗b5+ was good for White in Ciocaltea–Popovic, Zagreb 1979.

After 8 ... c5 the game Cardoso–Keene, Nice 1974 continued 9 a3?! cd 10 ♗xd4 ♘gf6 11 ♗e2 0-0 12 h4 ♘b6 13 h5 e5 14 ♗e3 d5 15 ed ♘bxd5 16 ♗c5 ♘f4! with unclear complications, but 9 a4! was much more dangerous as in Cardoso–Larsen above.

C2

4 ...   c6
5   ♕d2

5 h3 is a sensible move. As with f3, White prevents a later ... ♘g4, but leaves the f-pawn free for f4. After 5 ... b5 6 a3 ♗b7 7 f4 ♘d7 8 ♘f3 a5?! 9 e5 ♘h6 10 ♗d3 0-0 11 0-0 c5? 12 dc b4 13 ♘a4 Black had an awful position in Kurajica–Planinc, Yugoslavia Ch. 1978. Kurajica suggests 8 ...

a6 followed by ... c5, but I still prefer White.

5 ...   ♗d7 *(96)*

5 ... b5 generally transposes to the next note.

6 f3

Or:

(a) **6 0-0-0** b5 (or 6 ... ♕a5 7 ♔b1 b5 and now 8 ♗d3 ♖b8 9 h4 h5 10 ♘f3 b4 11 ♘e2 ♘b6 12 ♘c1 ♘a4 13 ♘b3 ♕c7 14 e5 ♗g4 15 ♗f4! was good for White in Nurmi–Wockenfuss, Mexico City 1977, while 8 h4 b4 9 ♘ce2 ♘gf6 10 f3 ♘b6 11 ♘c1 ♘a4 12 g4 h5 13 g5 ♘d7 14 ♘b3 ♕b6 15 ♗c4 a5 gave Black a dangerous queenside initiative, Hawley–Sumkin, corr. 1987) 7 f4 (7 e5?! d5 8 h4 ♘b6 9 h5 gh 10 ♘h3 f6 11 ♘f4 ♗g4 12 f3 fe 13 de ♗f5 14 ♘xh5 ♗f8 15 ♘xb5! was good for White in Kupreichik–Pedersen, Teesside Student Olympiad 1974, but 7 ... de 8 de b4 and 9 ... a5 are improvements) b4 8 ♘ce2 ♘gf6 9 ♘g3 ♘g4 10 ♘f3 ♘xe3 11 ♕xe3 a5 12 e5 ♘b6 13 f5 with complications, Geller–Terler, Leningrad Ch. 1977.

(b) **6 ♗d3** b5 and now:

(b1) **7 a4** b4 8 ♘ce2 ♖b8 9 ♘f3 ♕c7 10 0-0 ♘gf6 11 c3 (11 ♗h6 0-0 12 c4 e5 13 ♘g3 ♖e8 14 ♗xg7 ♔xg7 15 b3 ♘f8! 16 h3 ♘6d7 17 ♖fe1 ♘e6 with a double-edged position, Nicevski–Tal, Lublin 1974) bc 12 ♘xc3 ♖b3 13 ♖fc1 ♕b8 14 ♖a2 0-0 15 a5 c5 16 h3 cd 17 ♘xd4 ♘c5 18 ♗c4 ♘fxe4 19 ♘xe4 ♘xe4 20 ♕e2 ♖xe3 21 ♕xe3 ♗b7 and Black has enough for the exchange, Chandler–Chernin, Amsterdam 1987.

(b2) **7 h4** h5 (7 ... ♘gf6 8 f3 ♗b7 9 g4 h6 10 0-0-0 a6 11 ♘h3 ♕c7 appears dubious since Black's h-pawn is weak, but in Horvath–Hickl, Schmallenberg 1986 Black quickly gained the advantage after 12 g5 hg 13 ♘xg5 c5 14 e5 de 15 ♕g2 ed 16 ♗xg6 0-0-0 17 ♗xf7 ♗h6) 8 f4 ♘h6 9 e5?! (9 ♘h3 =) ♘b6! 10 ♘f3 ♗f5 11 ♘g5 b4 12 ♘e4 ♘d5 13 ♘g3 ♗xd3 14 ♕xd3 and Black's white square control gives him the edge, Vitolinsh–Dzindzihashvili, USSR 1975.

(b3) **7 f4** ♘gf6 8 ♘f3 ♘g4 9 ♗g1 ♗b7 10 h3 ♘gf6 11 0-0-0 b4 12 ♘e2 ♕a5 13 ♔b1 0-0 14 h4 c5 15 e5 ♘h5 with complications, Prasad–Chernin, Subotica 1987.

(c) **6 ♗e2** b5 7 f4 (7 d5 b4 8 dc bc 9 cd+ ♗xd7 10 bc ♕a5 11 ♗d4 ♘f6 12 ♗f3 e5 13 ♗e3 ♗b5 with advantage to Black, Budde–Bree, Dortmund Open 1987) ♘gf6 8 ♗f3 (8 e5 b4!) ♘b6 9 b3 0-0 10

♘ge2 e5?! 11 ♖d1?! (11 de de 12 0-0-0 and the weak square at c5 is annoying for Black) ef 12 ♗xf4 b4 13 ♘b1 ♖e8 and Black stands well, Sax–Adorjan, Hungary 1971. White's knight on b1 will be immobile for a long time and the e-pawn is weak.

(d) **6 f4** b5 7 ♘f3 ♘b6 8 a4 b4 9 ♘d1 a5 10 ♘f2 ♘f6 11 ♗d3 ♗a6 12 ♕e2 ♗xd3 13 cd 0-0 14 0-0 ♕d7 15 ♖fc1 ♖ac8 with advantage for Black, Kupreichik–Spassky, USSR 1981, but White's play was poor and did not provide a good test of 6 f4.

6 ... b5

6 ... a6 is a waste of time and in Durao–Palacios, Cienfuegos 1977, White gained the advantage after 7 ♘h3 b5 8 a4 ♘b6 9 ♘f2 ♗b7?! 10 a5! ♘c4 11 ♗xc4 bc 12 ♘a4 d5 13 ♘b6 ♖a7 14 ♖b1 ♘f6 15 b3 cb 16 ♖xb3. However,

6 ... e5 is interesting. Christiansen–Hartoch, IBM 'B' 1978, went on 7 d5 c5 8 ♘ge2 ♘e7 9 g4 h5 10 gh ♖xh5 11 ♘g3 ♖h7 12 ♗d3 ♘f6 13 0-0-0 ♗d7 14 ♗b5 with a slight plus for White.

7 0-0-0 ♘b6
8 h4 h5

9 ♘h3 a5 10 ♘f2 b4 11 ♘b1 ♖b8 12 g4 hg 13 fg ♘f6 14 ♗e2? (14 ♕e2 was correct, with an unclear position in which Black's chances are satisfactory) ♘xg4! 15 ♘xg4 ♗xg4 16 ♖dg1 ♗h5 ∓, Evans–Suttles, San Antonio 1972.

Both 4 ... a6 and 4 ... c6 are playable. Against 4 ... a6 White has done well with lines involving a4 to undermine Black's queenside pawns, while 6 0-0-0 may be best against 4 ... c6, although there is too little experience to give a definite verdict.

15 | White plays ♗c4

There are two different White systems which involve the move ♗c4. The first is a crude but dangerous attacking plan based on ♘c3, ♗c4, ♕e2 and e5. The second is more positionally based and is distinguished by the combination of ♗c4 with an early ♘f3. The second plan is normally only possible against the Modern move-order because in the Pirc order White's e-pawn is under attack so he has no time for ♘f3 and ♗c4. Therefore the majority of this chapter is concerned with the Modern and we take this as the main line. The Pirc system is dealt with in Section A via transposition.

After **1 e4 g6 2 d4 ♗g7** we consider the following lines:

A: 3 ♘c3 d6 4 ♗c4
B: 3 ♘f3 d6 4 ♗c4

A

1 e4 g6 2 d4 ♗g7 3 ♘c3 d6 4 ♗c4
4 ... ♘f6

After 4 ... ♘f6 we reach a position which often arises from the Pirc move-order 1 e4 d6 2 d4 ♘f6 3 ♘c3 g6 4 ♗c4 ♗g7. With the Modern move-order Black has the very important alternative 4 ... ♘c6 designed to avoid this transposition. After 4 ... ♘c6 5 ♘f3 (the other move is 5 ♗e3 ♘f6 and now **6 f3** 0-0 7 ♘ge2 b6 8 ♗b5 ♗b7 9 ♕d2 ♘a5 10 b4 a6 11 ♗d3 ♘c6 12 a3 e5 ∓ Byway–Nunn, England 1977, or **6 h3** e5 7 de ♘xe5 8 ♗b3 0-0 9 ♕d2 b5 10 f3 b4 11 ♘d5 ♘xd5 12 ♗xd5 c6 13 ♗b3 a5 14 a4 d5! 15 ed ♘c4! 16 ♗xc4 ♗xb2 and Black won in Gausel–Davies, Oslo 1988) ♘f6 *(97)* (note that this position can also arise by 1 e4 d6 2 d4 ♘f6 3 ♘c3 g6 4 ♘f3 ♗g7 5 ♗c4 ♘c6) and now:

(1) **6 h3** 0-0 7 ♕e2 ♘d7 (7 ... e5 8 de de 9 0-0? ♘d4 10 ♕d3 ♘d7 11 a4?! ♘c5 12 ♕d1 c6 13 b3 ♘ce6

14 Nb1 Qf6 15 Nh2 Nf4 16 c3 Nde6 17 Ng4 Qh4 18 Nd2 Ng5 19 f3 Ngxh3+ 0–1 Povah–Nunn, England 1977, was a success for Black, but 9 Bg5 may give White an edge) 8 Be3 Nb6 9 Bb3 Na5 10 0-0 c6 11 Rfe1 d5 12 ed cd 13 Bf4 e6 14 Nd1 Nbc4 15 c3 with equality, Short–Nunn, Hastings 1979/80.

(2) 6 Be3 Bg4 7 h3 Bxf3 8 Qxf3 e5 9 de Nxe5 10 Qe2 0-0 11 0-0 Re8 12 Rfe1 Nxe4 13 Nxe4 Nxc4 14 Bg5 Qxg5 15 Nxg5 Rxe2 16 Rxe2 h6 17 Nf3 Nxb2 with an edge for Black, Weidemann–Paulsen, Bundesliga 1986.

(3) 6 Qe2 0-0 (6 ... Bg4 appears promising since 7 e5 Bxf3 8 gf Nh5 9 e6 0-0! 10 ef+ Kh8 is good for Black, but 6 ... e5 7 de Nxe5 8 Nxe5 de 9 0-0 0-0 10 Bg5 c6 11 Rad1 gave White an edge in Grönegress–Hickl, Bundesliga 1987) 7 e5 de 8 de Ng4 9 e6 fe 10 0-0 (10 Bxe6+ Kh8 is roughly level) Qd6 11 Rd1? (11 Nb5 Qd4 12 Nbxd4 Bxd4 13 h3 Rxf3 14 hg Rh3 15 gh Qg3+ would have drawn) Nd4! 12 Rxd4 Bxd4 13 Ne4 Rxf3! 14 Nxd6 Rxf2 with a winning position for Black, Jasnikowski–Sznapik, Poland 1980.

Now White has a choice; he can either continue with direct aggression by 5 Qe2, or he can revert to quieter methods by 5 Nf3.

A1: 5 Qe2
A2: 5 Nf3

A1

5 Qe2 Nc6

All the evidence is that 5 ... c6 does not equalize after 6 e5, for example:
(1) **6 ... de** 7 de Nd5 8 Bd2 Be6 (8 ... Nd7 9 Nf3 N7b6 10 Nxd5 cd 11 Bb5+ Bd7 12 Ng5 Bxb5 13 Qxb5+ Qd7 14 Qxd7+ Nxd7 is a bit better for White, P. Littlewood–Nunn, London 1975) 9 0-0-0 (9 Nf3 Nxc3 10 Bxc3 Bxc4 11 Qxc4 Qd5 12 Qe2 c5 13 Rd1 Qc6 14 0-0 0-0 15 Rfe1 was also good for White in Grönegress–Herzog, Bundesliga 1987) Nd7 10 f4 N7b6 11 Bb3 a5 12 a3 Qc8 13 Nf3 with an unpleasant position for Black, Galloway–D. Gurevich, USA 1985.
(2) **6 ... Nd5** 7 Bd2 0-0 8 h4 (8 0-0-0 should give White a slight advantage) b5 (8 ... Be6 9 h5 Nxc3 10 Bxc3 Bxc4 11 Qxc4 de 12 hg ed 13 0-0-0 c5 14 gf+ Rxf7 15 Nf3 h6 16 Bd2 Qd6 17 Rde1 with a very dangerous attack for the sacrificed pawn, Schubert–Ditt, Bundesliga 1984/5) 9 Bb3 Nxc3 10 Bxc3 a5 11 a4? (11 a3 is much better) b4 12 Bd2 de 13 de Qd4 14 e6 Bxe6 15 Bxe6 Qxb2 16 Rd1 fe 17 Qxe6+ Kh8 with advantage for Black, Herbrechtsmeier–Smejkal, Bundesliga 1986.

6 e5 *(98)*

6 Nf3 transposes to line 3 in the analysis of 4 ... c6.

6 ... Ng4

There are two reasonable alternatives and a bad one:

White plays ♗c4 | 137

(1) **6 ...** ♘xd4 7 ef ♘xe2 8 fg ♖g8 9 ♘gxe2 ♖xg7 (allowing White to keep the g7 pawn is dubious, e.g. 9 ... c6 10 ♗h6 d5 11 0-0-0 ♕b6 12 ♗xd5 cd 13 ♘xd5 ♕a5, Peters–Faelten, USA 1979, and now 14 b4! ♕a3+ 15 ♔b1 ♗d7 16 ♖d3 ♕a4 17 ♘c7+ ♔d8 18 ♘xa8 would have been crushing for White) 10 ♗h6 ♖g8 11 0-0-0 ♗e6 (the best move; 11 ... c6 12 ♖he1 ♕a5 13 ♘f4 ♗f5 14 ♗g5!, Schubert–Kappe, Bundesliga 1976, 11 ... ♗f5 12 ♘d4 e5 13 ♘f3 ♗e6 14 ♗xe6 fe 15 ♘e4 ♖h8 16 ♗g5 ♕b8 17 ♘xe5! Kindermann–Gass, Bundesliga 1978 and 11 ... e6 12 h4 ♗d7 13 ♘e4 f6 14 ♘f4 ♔f7 15 ♖he1 ♖e8 16 g4, Short–R. Miles, England 1977, are all very good for White) 12 ♗xe6 fe and now:
(1a) **13 f4** ♕d7 14 ♖he1 0-0-0 15 ♘d4 e5 16 fe ♕g4 17 ♘d5 ♖ge8 18 g3 (18 ed ♖xd6 19 ♘b5 ♖d7 is also reasonable for Black) ♕h5 19 ♗f4 c6 20 ♘e3 de 21 g4 with a roughly level position, King–Nunn, London 1980.
(1b) **13 ♖he1** g5 14 ♘d4 e5 15 ♘f3 ♕c8 16 ♗xg5, Kindermann–Balinas, London 1978, and now instead of 16 ... h6 17 ♗xh6 c6 Black should have played 16 ... ♕g4!? with an unclear position.
(1c) **13 ♘f4** ♕d7 14 ♖he1 e5 15 ♖xe5!? de 16 ♖xd7 ♔xd7 17 ♘d3 reaching a very tricky endgame to assess. Black has the material advantage of two rooks and a pawn for three minor pieces, but the extra pawn doesn't count and there are few chances to develop active play for the rooks. Weinwürm–Stadtmüller, Merano 1988, continued 17 ... ♖ad8 18 ♘e4 ♔c8 19 f3 ♖d4 20 h4 b6 21 b3 c5 and White later won unconvincingly on time. I believe this ending is slightly better for White; at any rate Black has a depressing position with no active play.
(2) **6 ... ♘d7** (the most solid move) 7 ♘f3 ♘b6 (7 ... de? fails to 8 ♗xf7+!) 8 ♗b3 (8 ♗b5 has been suggested but I cannot see any advantage for White after 8 ... 0-0) 0-0 9 h3 ♘a5 10 ♗f4 d5 (10 ... ♘xb3 11 ab f6 should also be level) 11 0-0 h6 12 ♘d1 ♗e6 13 c3 ♘xb3 14 ab ♕d7 with equality, Soltis–Quinteros, Lone Pine 1979.
(3) **6 ... ♘h5?** 7 ♗b5! (not 7 g4 ♘xd4 8 ♕d1 ♗xg4 9 ♕xd4 ♗f5 10 ♕d5 0-0 11 ♕xb7 ♖xe5 with good compensation for Black in Regan–Shamkovich, New York 1976) 0-0 (7 ... de 8 d5 a6 9 dc ab 10 cb ♗xb7 11 ♕xb5+) 8 ♗xc6

bc 9 g4 c5 (or 9 ... de 10 de ♗xg4 11 ♕xg4 ♗xe5 12 ♘f3 and Black does not have enough for the piece, Schubert–Pedersen, Groningen 1977/8) 10 dc ♗b7 11 ♘f3 ♕d7 12 ♖g1 ♕c6 13 ♘d4 ♕xc5 14 ♘b3 and again White nets the knight, Short–Botterill, London 1978.

7 e6

After this play becomes extremely sharp. The alternative is 7 ♗b5 0-0 (not 7 ... ♗d7? 8 e6 ♗xe6 9 d5) 8 ♗xc6 (8 ♘f3? fails to 8 ... de 9 ♗xc6 ed) bc 9 h3 ♘h6 10 ♘f3 c5! 11 dc (White has little choice since 11 ♗f4 ♗b7 12 0-0-0 cd 13 ♖xd4 ♘f5 leaves him with nothing to balance the two active bishops) ♗b7 12 ♗d2 (12 g4 is very risky; 12 ... de 13 ♖g1 ♗xf3 14 ♕xf3 ♖b8 15 ♕d5 ♕e8! leaves White with a seriously exposed king, Herbrechtsmeier–Wockenfuss, Bundesliga 1982/3, while 12 ... ♕d7 intending ... ♕c6 may be even more unpleasant) ♘f5 13 0-0-0 ♗xf3 14 ♕xf3 ♗xe5 15 h4 with a balanced position, Sigurjonsson–Timman, Wijk aan Zee 1980.

7 ... ♘xd4

Or 7 ... d5 8 ♗xd5 ♘xd4 9 ♕xg4 (9 ef+ ♔f8 10 ♕d1 ♗f5 11 ♗e4 ♗xe4 12 ♘xe4 ♕d5 13 f3 was unclear in Knox–Lambert, British Ch. 1977; Black is in danger of ending up with an exposed king but in my view his active pieces offer more than enough compensation) ♘xc2+ 10 ♔e2 ♘xa1 and in this extremely complicated and confusing position two moves have been played:

(1) 11 ♘f3 c6 12 ♗c4 fe 13 ♕e4 ♕b6 14 ♖d1 ♖f8 15 ♔f1 e5 16 ♕h4 ♗f5 17 ♕xh7 ♕b4 18 ♗g8 ♗c2 19 ♕xg7 ♗xd1 20 ♕xg6+ ♔d7 21 ♗e6+ ♔c7 22 ♘xd1 ♖f6 23 ♕g4 ♕d6 24 ♗g5 ♘c2 25 ♗c4 ♕b4 26 ♘c3 ♘d4 27 ♗d3 ♖d8 28 ♕g3 ♕a5 29 ♘ge4, Timmerman–van Wijgerden, Netherlands Ch. 1983, and even in this position matters are still quite unclear. Black has two rooks against three minor pieces, but his king is still exposed and his e-pawns are weak, so I suspect that White is better. The game was drawn in 76 moves.

(2) 11 ef+ ♔f8 12 ♕h4 ♘c2 13 ♘f3 h5 14 ♖d1 ♗g4 15 ♔f1 ♗xf3 16 ♗xf3 ♘d4 17 ♗xb7 ♖b8 18 ♗d5 c5 19 ♗g5 ♘f5 20 ♕f4 ♗d4 21 ♗c4 ♕d6 22 ♗b5 ♕xf4 23 ♗xf4 ♖xb5 24 ♗xb5 ♔xf7 with a likely draw in the ending, Bezemer–Je. Piket, Amsterdam II 1986.

Not 7 ... f5? 8 d5 ♘d4 9 ♕d1 c6 10 h3 b5 11 hg bc 12 ♗h6! and Black's position collapses, Farrand–J. Littlewood, corr. 1977.

8 ♕xg4 ♘xc2+
9 ♔f1

Or 9 ♔d1 ♘xa1 10 ef+ ♔f8 11 ♕h4 d5 12 ♗d3 f5 (12 ... ♗e6?! 13 ♘f3 ♗xf7 14 ♖e1 d4 15

♗g5! gave White a very strong attack in Short–Sikkel, Jersey 1978) 13 ♗xf5 gf 14 ♘f3 (14 ♗h6!? ♕d6 is also unconvincing for White) d4 15 ♘e2 e5 16 ♘g5 ♕d6 17 ♘g3 h6! 18 ♘xf5 hg 19 ♕xh8+ ♗xh8 20 ♘xd6 cd 21 h4 gxh4 22 ♗g5 d3 23 ♔d2 ♘c2 with an extra piece for Black, Knox–Hindle, British Ch. 1977.

9	...	♘xa1
10	ef+	♔f8
11	♕h4	*(99)*

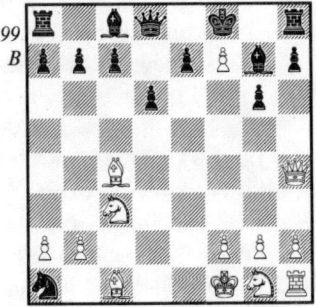

and now:

(1) **11 ... c6?** 12 ♗h6 d5 13 ♕d4 wins for White.

(2) **11 ... b5!?** is an untested suggestion.

(3) **11 ... h6?!** 12 ♘ge2 g5? (12 ... ♗f6 13 ♕g3! and 12 ... b5 13 ♘xb5 d5 14 ♗d3 are good for White, but 12 ... d5! would still have been unclear) 13 ♕h5 e6 14 h4 ♕f6 15 ♖h3! g4 16 ♖e3 ♘c2 17 ♖e4 e5 18 ♘f4! ♗f5 19 ♘cd5 ♕xf7 20 ♕xf7+ ♔xf7 21 ♘e3+ ♔f8 22 ♘xf5 ef 23 ♘xg7 ♔xg7 24 ♗d3 and Black loses his knight

(24 ... ♘a1 25 b4), whereupon the two active bishops and Black's weak pawns are far more significant than Black's theoretical material advantage, van der Plassche–M. Piket, Hilversum 1985.

(4) **11 ... d5!** 12 ♗xd5 (not 12 ♘xd5? ♗e6 with a clear advantage for Black) and now Black has the choice between forcing a draw by 12 ... ♗xc3 13 ♗h6+ ♗g7 14 ♕d4 e5 15 ♕xe5 ♗xh6 16 ♕xh8+ ♔e7 17 ♕e5+ ♔f8 or playing on by 12 ... c6 13 ♗e4 ♔xf7 14 ♘f3 with continuing complications.

Although these lines require careful defence by Black, my impression is that White's attack is not worth more than a draw and therefore 7 ... ♘g4 is probably Black's best move, with 7 ... ♘d7 a solid alternative.

A2

5	♘f3	0-0

5 ... ♘c6 transposes to the analysis of 4 ... ♘c6 above. It is worth analysing 5 ... c6 because this position can also arise if Black plays ... c6 earlier (e.g. 1 e4 g6 2 d4 ♗g7 3 ♘c3 c6 4 ♘f3 d6 5 ♗c4 ♘f6). After **5 ... c6** 6 e5 (6 ♗b3 0-0 7 0-0 ♗g4 8 h3 ♗xf3 9 ♕xf3 ♘bd7 10 ♗e3 ♕a5 11 ♖ad1 c5?! 12 e5 de 13 de ♘xe5 14 ♕xb7 with a good game for White, Jansa–Ebalard, Metz 1985; 10 ... e5 would have been more solid but White has a small advantage in any case) de 7 ♘xe5 0-0 8 0-0 ♘bd7 9 ♗g5 and now: (1) **9 ... ♘b6** 10 ♗b3 ♘fd5 11 ♘xd5 (11 ♗h4 ♗xe5 12 de ♘xc3 13 bc ♕c7 14 ♗g3 ♗e6 is fine for Black, while 11 ♘f3 a5 12 a4 ♗e6 13 ♘e4 should have been met by 13 ... ♘c7 rather than 13 ... ♘f6?! 14 ♗xf6! ef 15 ♗xe6 fe 16 ♖e1 ♖e8 17 ♘c5 as in Tseshkovsky–van der Wiel, Sochi 1980) ♘xd5 12 ♗h4 ♗e6 13 ♖e1 ♖e8 14 ♕f3 ♗f6 15 ♗g3 with an uncomfortable position for Black, Akopian–Sichinava, USSR 1987. (2) **9 ... ♕c7!** presents more problems. After **10 ♘xd7 ♗xd7** 11 ♕d2 ♖ad8 12 ♗f4 ♕a5 13 ♖fe1 ♗f5 Black had a fine position in Akopian–Movesian, USSR 1987, while the lines **10 ♗f4 ♘h5** 11 ♘xd7 ♕xd7 12 ♗e5 ♗xe5 13 de ♕f5 14 ♖e1 ♗e6 and **10 ♕e2** ♘xe5 11 ♕xc5 ♕xe5 12 de ♘g4 13 ♗xe7 ♖e8 promise nothing for White.

6 ♕e2 *(100)*

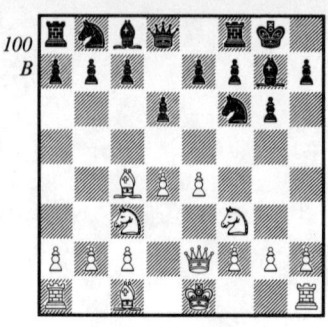

After 6 0-0 (6 ♗b3 is harmless as 6 ... ♘c6 followed by ... ♘a5 eliminates the bishop) Black equalizes easily with 6 ... ♘xe4 7 ♘xe4 (7 ♗xf7+ ♖xf7 8 ♘xe4 h6 9 ♗e3 ♗g4 10 ♘ed2 ♘c6 11 c3 g5 12 ♕b3 ♘a5 13 ♕a4 b6 is ∓, Basman–Nunn, London 1973) d5 8 ♗d3 de 9 ♗xe4 ♘d7 (the direct 9 ... c5 is also equal) 10 c3 c5 11 ♗g5 ♘f6 12 ♗c2 ♕b6 13 ♕c1 cd 14 ♘xd4 e5 15 ♘b3 ♘d5 =, Lechtynsky–Sax, Tallinn 1979.

6 ... ♗g4

A safe but slightly passive line is 6 ... c6 7 e5 (7 a4?! d5 8 ♗b3 de 9 ♘xe4 ♘xe4 10 ♕xe4 c5 11 d5 ♘d7 12 0-0 ♘f6 13 ♕h4 ♗g4 14 ♗g5 ♗f5 ∓ in view of the useless bishop on b3, Povah–Nunn, London 1976) ♘d5 8 ♗d2 (8 0-0 ♘xc3 9 bc ♗g4 10 ♗f4 and now 10 ... d5 11 ♗d3 c5 or 10 ... ♘d7!? gives adequate counterplay) ♘c7 (8 ... ♘xc3?! 9 ♗xc3 d5 10 ♗d3 a5 11 h4! with a strong attack, Pribyl–Ciocaltea, IBM 'B' 1976, or 8 ... ♗e6 9 ♘e4 ♘c7 10 ♗d3 de 11 de ♘d7 12 ♘eg5 ♗d5 13 c4 ♗xf3 14 ♘xf3 with advantage for White, Godena–Ker, World Junior Ch. 1986) 9 h3 d5 (too passive; 9 ... ♗e6 was better) 10 ♗d3 b6 11 ♗e3 ♘ba6 12 ♕d2 with an edge for White, Hort–Forintos, Moscow 1975.

7 e5 ♘h5

Other moves are bad, e.g. 7 ... ♘fd7 8 e6 ♘b6 9 ef+ ♔h8 10 ♗e6 ♗xe6 11 ♕xe6 ♕d7 12 ♘g5 ♘c6 13 ♘b5, Semenova–Gaprindashvili, Tbilisi 1976, or 7 ... ♘e8 8 ♗g5 ♘c6 9 0-0-0 ♔h8 10 ♖he1

♕c8 11 ♗d5 ♕f5 12 ♕e3 de 13 ♗xc6! bc 14 ♗xe7 ed 15 ♘xd4, Hort–Keene, Teesside 1975 with a clear plus for White in both cases.

8 h3

Black has a good position after 8 e6 ♘c6 9 ef+ ♔h8 since the f7 pawn can be easily regained by ... e6 and White may well lose the d-pawn as well.

8 ... ♗xf3

9 ♕xf3 de 10 ♕xb7 ♘d7 11 de ♘xe5 12 ♗e2 ♘f6 13 0-0 ♘e8 14 ♗e3 ♖b8 ½-½, Hort–Planinc, Ljubljana–Portoroz 1977.

B

1 e4 g6 2 d4 ♗g7 3 ♘f3 d6 4 ♗c4

4 ... ♘f6

Or:

(1) **4 ...** ♘c6 5 c3 (5 0-0 is the alternative, when 5 ... ♗g4 6 ♗xf7+ ♔xf7 7 ♘g5+ ♔e8 8 ♕xg4 ♘xd4 9 ♘a3 is good for White, so 5 ... ♘f6 is best) ♘f6 6 ♘bd2 0-0 7 0-0 e5 8 de ♘xe5 9 ♘xe5 de 10 ♖e1 c6 11 a4 ♗h6 12 a5 ♕d6 13 b4 with a slight plus for White, Tseshkovsky–Sznapik, Sochi 1974.

(2) **4 ... c5** 5 dc ♕a5+ 6 c3 ♕xc5 7 ♕b3 e6 8 ♗e3 ♕c7 9 ♘a3 a6 10 ♗b6 ♕c6 (Black's position looks very unpleasant at this stage but he equalizes surprisingly quickly) 11 0-0 ♘d7 12 ♗d4 ♘c5 13 ♕d1 (is 13 ♗xg7 ♘xb3 14 ab possible?) ♘f6 14 e5 de 15 ♘xe5 ♕c7 16 ♖e1 0-0 17 ♕f3 ♘fd7 18 ♘xd7 ♘xd7 19 ♗xg7 ♔xg7 20 ♖ad1 ½-½ Taulbut–van Wijgerden IBM 'B' 1978.

(3) **4 ... e6** (given an ! by Romanishin!) 5 ♗b3 (after 5 ♗g5 ♘e7 6 ♗b3 h6 7 ♗e3 d5 8 ♘bd2 b6 9 0-0 de 10 ♘xe4 ♗b7 11 ♘g3 0-0 Black had equalized, Kochiev–Romanishin, Leningrad 1977, while 5 0-0 ♘e7 6 c3 ♘d7 7 ♖e1 h6 8 ♗b3 b6 9 ♘bd2 ♗b7 10 ♘c4 a6 11 h3 was ± in Agzamov–Todorcevic, Belgrade 1982) ♘e7 6 0-0 0-0 (6 ... b6 7 ♗f4 ♗b7 8 ♖e1 ♘d7 9 c3 h6 10 ♘a3 0-0 11 ♕d3 ♘c6 12 ♖ad1 ♕e7 is somewhat better for White, Wittmann–Kindermann, Munich 1987, but Black doesn't play like this in order to equalize from the opening) 7 c3 b6 8 ♘bd2 ♘bc6?! (8 ... c5 is more direct) 9 ♖e1 ♘a5 10 ♗c2 c5 11 ♘f1 ♘ac6 12 ♗e3 ♕c7 13 ♖c1 ± Hübner–Petrosian, Biel 1976.

(4) **4 ... c6** (this can transpose to line B2 below, but there are some independent possibilities) 5 ♘c3 (5 0-0 d5 6 ♗b3 de 7 ♘g5 ♘h6 8 ♘xe4 0-0 9 c3 ♗g4 10 ♕d3 ♘d7 11 ♖e1 with an edge for White, G. Garcia–Chernin, Saint John Open 1988) b5 (5 ... ♘f6 transposes to the note to Black's 5th move in line A2) 6 ♗b3 (not 6 ♘xb5 d5 7 ♗b3 de 8 ♘g5 cb 9 ♘xf7 ♕xd4 10 ♕xd4 ♗xd4 11 ♘xh8 e6 with a slight advantage for Black) b4 (or 6 ... a5 7 a4 b4 8 ♘e2 ♘f6 9 e5 ♘d5 10 ♘f4 ♘xf4 11 ♗xf4 d5 12 0-0 ♗g4 13 h3 ♗xf3 14 ♕xf3 with some advantage for White, De Firmian–Alburt, USA Ch. 1984) 7 ♘d5!?

(7 ♘e2 as in De Firmian–Alburt is also possible, but this is even better) a5 8 ♘e3 e6 9 a3 ♗b7 10 ab ab 11 ♖xa8 ♗xa8 12 0-0 d5 13 e5 with a clear plus for White, Pribyl–Kosanski, Osijek 1980.

5 ♕e2 *(101)*

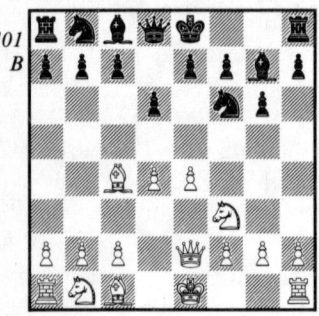

Now there are two variations:

B1: 5 ... 0-0
B2: 5 ... c6

An interesting alternative is 5 ... ♘c6 6 e5 de 7 de ♘g4 (7 ... ♘d5 8 0-0 ♗g4 9 ♖d1! ♗xf3 10 ♕xf3 e6 11 ♗b5 ♕h4 was played in Popovic–Rukavina, Zagreb 1985, and now 12 ♗xc6+ bc 13 ♖e1 leaves Black with no evident compensation for his weak pawns) 8 ♗b5 ♗d7 9 ♗f4 0-0 10 ♘c3 (10 h3? ♘gxe5! 11 ♗xe5 ♗xe5 12 ♗xc6 ♗xb2 13 ♕b5 ♗xa1 14 ♗xd7 c6 and Black wins, Vogt–Szymczak, Lublin 1974 – note that 11 ♘xe5 ♘d4 wins) a6 11 ♗c4 b5 12 ♗b3 b4 13 ♘a4 ♘a5 and Black is slightly better, Vasiukov–Ribli, Wijk aan Zee 1973. This line deserves further tests.

B1

5 ... 0-0 *(102)*

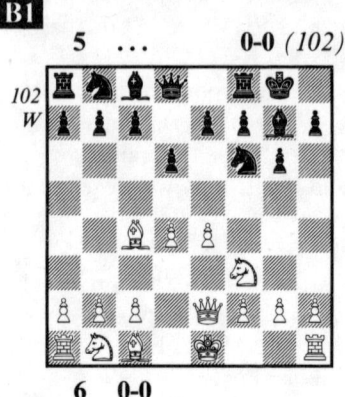

6 0-0

Others:

(a) **6 h3** c5 (6 ... ♘c6 7 0-0 e5 8 de ♘xe5 9 ♘xe5 de 10 ♗g5 h6 11 ♗h4 c6 12 ♘c3 ♕c7 13 ♖fd1 ♘h5 14 ♖d2 ♘f4 15 ♕f1 is very slightly better for White, Pytel–Dobrzynski, Poland 1977) 7 e5 ♘e8 8 c3 cd 9 cd ♘c7 (9 ... ♘c6 10 0-0 de 11 de ♘d4 12 ♘xd4 ♕xd4 13 e6! ♗xe6 14 ♗xe6 fe 15 ♕xe6+ ♖f7 16 ♘c3 ♘d6 17 ♗e3 ♕c4 18 ♘d5 with advantage for White, Kestler–Mednis, Mannheim 1975) 10 ♗f4 (10 0-0 ♘c6 11 ♖d1 d5 12 ♗b3 b6 13 ♗g5 f6 14 ef ef 15 ♗f4 gave White an edge in Quinteros–Robatsch, Nice Ol. 1974, but 10 ... de 11 de ♗e6 is equal) and now Mednis gives 10 ... de 11 ♗xe5! ♗xe5 12 de ♘c6 13 0-0 ♗e6 with an unclear position, but the immediate 10 ... ♘c6 seems better, as 11 0-0 de 12 de ♗e6 is fine for Black.

(b) **6 ♘bd2** ♘c6 (better than 6 ... c6 7 ♗b3 transposing to B2) 7 c3 e5 8 de ♘h5! 9 g3 (9 0-0 de is equal, while 9 ed?! ♘f4 gives Black splendid compensation for the pawn) ♘xe5 10 ♘xe5 ♗xe5 11 ♘f3 ♗g7 12 ♗g5 ♕e8 and Black has at least equalized in view of the weakness created by g3, Jansa–Adorjan, Sombor 1972.
(c) **6 e5** de 7 de ♘d5 8 h3 (8 ♗d2 ♗g4 9 ♘c3 ♘b6 10 0-0-0 ♘c6 11 ♗b3 e6 12 ♗f4 ♕e7 13 ♕e3 ♕b4 14 a3 ♕a5 with unpleasant pressure on White's e-pawn, Garcia–Gligoric, Saint John Open 1988, or 8 0-0 c6 9 ♖d1 ♕c7?! 10 ♗xd5 cd 11 ♘c3 e6 12 ♘b5 ♕d7 13 ♗g5 ±, Smyslov–Hamed, Subotica 1987, but 9 ... ♗g4 is better) ♘b6 9 ♗b3 (we have reached a kind of Alekhine Defence) ♘c6 10 0-0 ♘d4 (10 ... ♘a5 may be safer) 11 ♘xd4 ♕xd4 12 ♖e1 a5 13 a4 c6 with just an edge for White, Kaufman–Gligoric, Lone Pine 1980.

6 ...　　　　♗g4

6 ... ♘c6 7 e5 de 8 de ♗g4 9 ♖d1 ♕e8 10 ♗f4 ♗e6 11 ♗xe6 fe 12 ♗g3 ♖d8 13 ♘c3 ♕f7 14 h3 ♘h6 15 ♕b5! is very unpleasant for Black, Gufeld–Sigurjonsson, Tbilisi 1974 but 6 ... c6 7 e5 (7 ♗b3 transposing to B2 is better) ♘d5 8 h3 a5 9 ♖e1 de 10 de ♘a6 11 ♖d1 ♘ac7 12 a3 b5 equalized in Panno–Evans, Haifa Ol. 1976.

7　e5

7 c3 (7 ♘bd2 ♘c6 8 c3 e5 is also level) ♘c6 8 ♗b5 ♕e8!? (an unusual self-pin with the idea of playing ... a6 without allowing the reply ♗a4, which would now fail to ... ♘xd4) 9 ♘bd2 (9 d5 a6) a6 10 ♗xc6 ♕xc6 11 ♖e1 ♖ae8 12 h3 ♗c8 13 ♘f1 ♘d7 14 ♗g3 ♘b6 with equality, Torre–Hort, Amsterdam 1979.

7 ...　　　　♘e8
8　♖d1

8 ♘c3 ♘c6 9 ♖d1 ♕c8 10 ♗f4? (loses! 10 ♗d5 e6 11 ♗xc6 bc is unclear) ♕f5 11 ♗g3 ♗xf3 12 gf de 13 de ♘xe5 and Black wins, Szekely–Vogt, Budapest II 1976.

8 ...　　　　♘c6

9 ♗d5 ♕d7 10 ♗f4 e6? (10 ... ♕f5 11 ♗g3 de is unclear, but should not be worse for Black) 11 ♗b3 ♘a5 12 h3 ♗xf3 13 ♕xf3 f6 14 ed cd 15 ♘d2 ♖c8 16 c3 d5 17 ♕g4 with an advantage for White, Adorjan–Hort, Budapest 1973.

B2

5 ...　　　　c6

This is the main alternative to 5 ... 0-0, but on the evidence available White has good chances. Black tends to drift into a passive position without counterplay, while White can step up the pressure.

6　♗b3

Or 6 ♘bd2 (6 e5 de 7 de ♘d5 and now 8 0-0 0-0 9 a4 ♗g4 10 ♘bd2 ♘d7 11 h3 ♗f5 12 c3 ♘c5

13 ♘d4 ♗d3! 14 ♗xd3 ♘f4 was level in Kochiev–Chekhov, USSR 1976, while 8 h3 0-0 9 ♘bd2 ♘f4 10 ♕f1 ♗f5 11 ♘b3 ♘e6 12 ♕e2 b5 was awkward for White in Braga–Todorcevic, Rome 1988) d5 7 ♗b3 0-0 8 0-0 a5 (the start of a rather artificial plan – 8 ... ♗g4 seems a sound way to play for equality) 9 a4 b6 10 ♖e1 ♗a6 11 ♕e3 e6 12 e5 ♘g4 13 ♕f4 ♘h6 14 ♘f1 and White has an enduring advantage, Smejkal–Uhlmann, Halle 1974.

6 ... 0-0

Black equalized easily in G. Garcia–Evans, Algarve 1975, after 6 ... e5 7 de de 8 0-0 ♕e7 9 ♘bd2 ♘h5! 10 ♘c4, especially if he had now played 10 ... b5! since 11 ♘a5 ♕c7 strands the knight most uncomfortably.

7 0-0 *(103)*

After 7 ♘bd2 ♗g4 8 e5 de 9 de ♘d5 10 0-0 ♘d7 11 h3 ♗f5 12 ♖e1 Black could have equalized with 12 ... ♘c5, but in Tal–Timman, Skopje Ol. 1972, Black played 12 ... ♕c7 and the result was a Tal miniature: 13 ♘f1 ♖ad8 14 ♘g3 ♗e6 15 ♕e4! ♖fe8 16 ♕h4 f6 17 ♗h6 ♘xe5? 18 ♖xe5! fe 19 ♘g5 ♗f6 20 ♘xe6 1–0.

7 ... a5

Or:
(1) 7 ... ♗g4 8 ♘bd2 e5 9 de de 10 ♘c4 (10 h3 ♗xf3 11 ♘xf3 is solid and slightly better for White; after 11 ... ♘bd7 12 c3 ♕e7 13

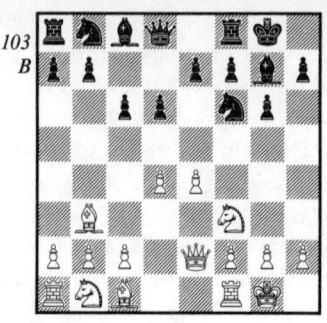
103
B

♗c2 a5 14 a4 ♘c5 15 ♖d1 ♖fe8 16 ♕c4 Black had a depressingly passive position in Kotronias–Rukavina, Pucarevo 1987) ♕e7 11 h3 ♗xf3 12 ♕xf3 b5 13 ♘e3 ♘bd7, Shamkovich–Botterill, Hastings 1977/8, and now 14 c3 would have given White an edge. I prefer 10 h3 to 10 ♘c4; they lead to similar positions, but after ♘c4–e3 it is harder for White to develop his c1 bishop.
(2) 7 ... ♘a6 8 ♖d1 ♘c7 9 ♘bd2 d5 10 e5 ♘fe8 11 ♘f1 ♘e6 12 h4! f5 13 h5 and Black has nothing to compensate for White's kingside attacking chances, Shamkovich–Bischoff, Reykjavik 1982.
(3) 7 ... ♕c7 8 e5 de 9 de ♘d5 10 ♖e1 ♘a6 (10 ... ♗g4 may be met by 11 ♘bd2 followed by h3 since 11 ... ♘f4 12 ♕e3 ♗h6 fails to 13 ♔h1) 11 c3 ♘c5 12 ♗c2 ♗g4 (12 ... b6 13 a3 a5 14 c4 ♗a6 15 ♘bd2 ♘f4 16 ♕e3 ♘fe6 17 b4 ab 18 ab ♘d7 19 h4 with a fine position for White, Tal–Gufeld, Moscow 1972) 13 ♘bd2 b6, Ner-

ney–Zlotnikov, USA 1985, and now 14 a3! would have been ± according to Alburt and Nerney.

8 a4

White was also better after 8 e5 ♘d5 9 a4 h6?! (9 ... de 10 ♘xe5 ♘d7 ±) 10 ♘bd2 de 11 ♘xe5 ♘d7 12 ♘df3 ♘7f6 13 h3 ♕b6 14 ♖a3, Tal–G. Garcia, Leningrad 1977.

8 ... ♘a6

8 ... ♗g4 9 ♘bd2 ♘a6 (9 ... e6 10 e5 de 11 de ♘d5 12 h3 ♗xf3 13 ♘xf3 ♕b6 14 h4! ♘d7 15 h5 ♖fe8 16 ♖e1 was very passive for Black, Dzindzihashvili–Speelman, Hastings 1977/8) 10 c3 ♘c7 11 h3 ♗c8 12 e5 ♘fd5 13 ♘e4 ♘e6 14 ♘eg5! with a clear advantage for White, Shamkovich–Zlotnikov, New York 1982.

9 h3 ♕b6

10 ♘c3 ♘c7 11 e5 ♘fd5 12 ♘xd5 cd 13 ♗e3 ♗f5 14 ♕d2 ♗e4 15 ♘g5 ♗f5 16 ♖fe1 ♖fc8 17 ed ed with a good position for White, Gligoric–Dimitrievic, Krk 1976.

Summing up, we can see that A is tricky, but probably not very good objectively, while B1 gives much better equalizing chances than B2. There are plenty of chances to leave established theory (e.g. 5 ... ♘c6 in B) and many lines have hardly been explored. The general feeling seems to be that these ♗c4 systems are not very dangerous for Black and over the past few years they have virtually disappeared from Grandmaster play.

16 | White plays ♗g5

In many ways this move has a similar intention to ♗e3, namely ♕d2 and ♗h6 in order to exchange the g7 bishop. However g5 is a more active square for the bishop and the pressure down the h4–d8 diagonal lends added force to a central breakthrough with f4 and e5. On the debit side White's d4 pawn is less adequately protected and the bishop on g5 can sometimes find itself in trouble if a subsequent f4 cuts off its retreat. Moreover Black can often hunt the bishop down with ... h6, and ... g5 and ... ♘h5 although this usually weakens Black's kingside so badly that he cannot play ... 0-0 later. The ♗g5 plan has been unpopular in the 1980s so we do not give a very detailed survey. As with the last two chapters, the Pirc and Modern systems must be considered separately.

A: 1 e4 d6 2 d4 ♘f6 3 ♘c3 g6 4 ♗g5 ♗g7
B: 1 e4 d6 2 d4 ♘f6 3 ♘c3 g6 4 ♗g5 others
C: 1 e4 g6 2 d4 ♗g7 3 ♘c3 d6 4 ♗g5

A

1	e4	d6
2	d4	♘f6
3	♘c3	g6
4	♗g5	♗g7 (104)

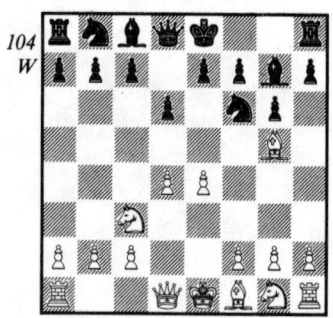

5 ♕d2

Or:

(a) **5 e5** de (or 5 ... ♘fd7 and now 6 f4 f6 is unclear, while 6 ed cd 7 ♕d2 0-0 8 0-0-0 ♘c6 9 h4!? ♗xd4? 10 h5 ♕a5 11 hg hg 12 ♗xe7! gave White a winning position in Ivanovic–Borkowski, Prisitna 1976, but 9 ... ♘xd4 was unclear) 6 de ♘g4 7 ♕xd8+ ♔xd8 8 ♘f3!? (8 ♖d1+ ♗d7 9 e6 fe 10 ♗c4 ♔e8 11 ♘f3 ♘c6 12 0-0 ♘ge5! is better for Black, Belousov–Chipashvili, USSR 1976)

♗e6 (8 ... ♘xe5 9 0-0-0+ ♗d7 10 ♘xe5 ♗xe5 11 ♗c4 gives White reasonable compensation) 9 ♗h4 ♘xe5 10 ♗g5 ♗d7 11 ♗g3 ♘bc6 12 ♗b5 ♕e8? (12 ... h6 13 ♗xc6 hg 14 ♗xb7 ♖b8 looks at least equal for Black) 13 0-0-0 f6 14 ♘ge4 with a difficult position for Black, Raaste–Parma, Nice Ol. 1974.

(b) **5 f4** and now:

(b1) **5 ... 0-0** (5 ... c6 6 ♕d2 0-0 transposes) 6 ♕d2 (6 e5?! ♘g4 7 ♘f3 ♘e3 8 ♕e2 ♘xf1 9 0-0-0 d5 10 ♖hxf1 c6 11 h3 b5 12 ♕e3 f6 13 ♗h4 a5 was slightly better for Black in Lipski–Nunn, Lublin 1978) c6 7 ♗d3 (7 ♘f3 d5 8 e5 ♘e4 9 ♘xe4 de 10 ♘g1 f6 11 ♗h4 fe 12 fe c5 is good for Black) ♕b6 (7 ... b5 8 ♘f3 ♗g4! may be better; in Santo Roman–Ftacnik, Lyons 1988, White continued 9 f5 d5 10 e5 ♘e4 11 ♘xe4 de 12 ♗xe4 gf 13 ♕f4, but 13 ... f6! won a piece) 8 e5 (8 ♘f3 ♗g4 renews the threat to the d-pawn) ♘d5 9 ♘xd5 cd 10 c3 ♘d7 11 ♘e2 ♖e8 12 a4 f6 13 ef ef 14 ♗h4 f5 with an edge for White, Romanishin–Kuzmin, Tallinn 1979.

(b2) **5 ... h6** 6 ♗h4 c5 (6 ... ♘bd7 7 e5 ♘h5 8 ♘d5? c6 9 ♘xe7 de 10 fe ♕b6 11 b3 ♘xe5 12 ♘xc8 ♖xc8 13 ♕d2 ♘g4 14 ♕e2+ ♔f8 15 ♕xg4 ♕b4+ 16 ♔d1 f5 0–1, Agnos–Plaskett, British Ch. 1986; 7 ♘f3 is more solid) 7 e5 ♘h5 8 dc ♘xf4 9 ed g5 10 ♗f2 0-0 11 ♕d2 (11 g3 ♘g6 12 ♕d2 ed 13 0-0-0 ♕f6 was unclear in Mednis–Parma, Noristoun 1973) ♘c6 12 0-0-0 ed (not 12 ... ♕a5 13 a3! ed 14 ♘b5 with a clear plus for White, Byrne–Parma, San Juan 1969) 13 cd ♕a5 14 g3 (natural, but in retrospect 14 a3 would have been better) ♘b4! 15 ♗c4 ♗e6 16 ♗d4 ♗xc4 17 ♗xg7 ♖xa2! 18 ♗xf8 ♗b3! 19 cb ♕a1+ 20 ♘b1 ♖c8+ 21 ♕c3 ♖xc3+ 0–1 Olafsson–Kaiszauri, Sweden 1974.

(c) **5 ♕e2** h6 6 ♗h4 c6 (6 ... e5?! 7 de de 8 f4! ef 9 e5 0-0 10 ♖d1 ♘bd7 11 ♘e4 g5 12 ef ♗xf6 13 ♗f2 is dubious for Black, Georgadze–Zaichik, USSR 1976) 7 0-0-0 ♘h5 (7 ... ♕a5!? is sensible) 8 ♕f3 ♕c7 9 ♔b1 ♘d7 10 g4 ♘hf6 11 g5 hg 12 ♗xg5 is equal, Polugaevsky–Parma, USSR–Yugoslavia 1969.

(d) **5 ♘f3** (this position can also arise via 1 e4 d6 2 d4 ♘f6 3 ♘c3 g6 4 ♘f3 ♗g7 5 ♗g5) c6 (5 ... 0-0 6 ♕d2 is also possible, and now not 6 ... ♗g4 7 ♕f4 ♗xf3 8 ♕xf3 ♘c6 9 0-0-0 ♕e8 10 h4 h5 11 ♗xf6 ef 12 ♘d5, which was very good for White in W. Watson–Townsend, London 1981, but 6 ... d5!? 7 ♗d3 when both 7 ... c5 8 dc ♘xe4 9 ♘xe4 de 10 ♗xe4 ♕xd2+ 11 ♘xd2 ♗xb2 12 ♖b1 ♗d4 and 7 ... de 8 ♘xe4 ♗g4 are unclear) 6 ♕d2 (6 h3 0-0 7 ♕d2 b5 8 ♗d3 ♕c7 9 a4 b4 10 ♘e2 ♘bd7 11 c3 bc 12 ♘xc3 c5 13 ♖c1 cd 14 ♘xd4 ♘c5 was at least equal for Black, Kaidanov–Azmaiparashvili, Tbilisi 1986) b5 7 ♗d3 ♗g4 (other moves are dubious, e.g. 7 ... ♘a6 8 e5 de 9 de ♗g4 10 ♗f4 b4 11 ♘e4 ♕a5 12 0-0! ♘xe5 13 ♘xe5 ♗xe5 14 a3 with excellent compensation for the pawn, W. Watson–Je. Piket, Wijk aan Zee II 1987, or 7 ... ♕c7 8 0-0-0 0-0 9 ♗h6 e5 10 h4 ♗g4 11 de de 12 ♕g5 ♘bd7 13 h5 with a dangerous attack, Veinger–Kindermann, Munich 1987) 8 ♗h6 (8 ♕f4 ♗xf3 9 ♕xf3 ♘bd7 10 0-0 0-0 11 ♖fe1 ♕c7 is equal, Zelyandinov–Vitolinsh, Chernovtsi 1967) 0-0 9 h4 ♗xf3 10 gf e5 11 de de 12 ♗xg7 ♔xg7 13 f4 ef 14 ♕xf4 ♘h5 15 ♕e3 ♕b6 with at least equality for Black, W. Watson–Nunn, Oxford 1981.

5 ... h6

5 ... c6 will tend to transpose into lines considered under B, and although 5 ... 0-0 is possible, it is generally undesirable for Black to castle too early.

6 ♗h4 (105)

Or 6 ♗f4 (6 ♗e3 ♘g4 7 ♗f4 e5 8 de ♘xe5 9 0-0-0 ♘bc6 is fine for Black) g5 (6 ... ♘c6!? 7 ♗b5 ♗d7 8 ♘ge2 a6 9 ♗xc6 bc 10 0-0 ♕b8 11 ♖ab1 a5 12 ♘g3 h5 was equal in Korzubov–Hoi, Copenhagen 1984, but 10 0-0-0 followed by ♖he1 is more dangerous) 7 ♗e3 (7 ♗g3 transposes to the main line) ♘g4 8 0-0-0 (8 ♘ge2 ♘c6 9 ♘g3 ♘xe3 10 fe h5! 11 ♗e2 g4 12 0-0-0?? allowed 12 ... ♘xd4! in Romanishin–Kuzmin, Tallinn 1979) c6 9 ♘f3 ♕a5 10 ♗b1 b5 11 b3 ♘d7 12 h4 ♘c5!? (threat ... b4) 13 ♘xb5! ♕xd2 14 ♘xd2 ♘e6 15 d5 ♘xe3 16 fe cb 17 ♗xb5+ ♗d7 18 ♗xd7+ ♔xd7 19 de+ fe and the complications have left White with a slightly better ending, Speckner–Paulsen, Bundesliga 1987.

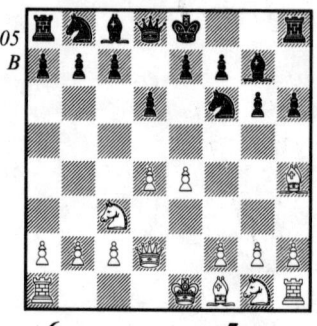

105
B

6 ... g5

6 ... c6 7 f4 gives White good chances, e.g. 7 ... 0-0 8 ♘f3 ♗g4 (8 ... ♘a6?! 9 e5 de 10 fe ♘d5 11 ♘xd5 cd 12 ♗d3 ♗e6 13 ♗f2 ♕b6 14 c3 and Black has no counterplay at all, Savon–Kuzmin, USSR 1975) 9 ♗e2 d5?! (as usual this leaves Black struggling for equality – 9 ... ♕c7 followed by ... ♘bd7 and ... e5 was more active) 10 e5 ♘e4 11 ♕e3 ♕d7 12 0-0-0 ♘a6 13 h3 ♗f5 (13 ... ♗xf3 14 ♗xf3 ♘xc3 15 ♕xc3 f5 ±) 14 ♘d2 with a persistent plus for White, Romanishin–Balashov, USSR Ch. 1977. In this line Black's ... h6 has no positive features to offset the weakening of Black's king position.

**7 ♗g3   ♘h5
8 0-0-0**

8 ♘ge2 ♘d7 followed by ... c5 gives Black good chances of exposing the weaknesses of the black squares, while **8 ♗e2?!** ♘xg3 9 hg ♘c6 10 d5 ♘d4 11 ♗d3 e6 12 ♘ge2 ♘xe2 13 ♗xe2 is slightly better for Black, Ljuca–Mednis, Sombor 1974.

8 ...   ♘c6

9 ♗b5 (9 d5 ♘d4 should be equal) ♗d7 (9 ... ♘xg3 10 hg a6 11 ♗xc6+ bc leads to a very interesting position with chances for both sides) 10 ♘ge2 e5 11 de ♘xe5 12 ♘d4 c6 13 ♗e2 ♘xg3 14 hg ♕f6 15 f4 gf 16 gf ♘g6 17 g3 and Black's inferior pawn structure gives White a small advantage, Peresipkin–Ftacnik, Kiev 1978.

B

**1 e4 d6 2 d4 ♘f6 3 ♘c3 g6 4 ♗g5
4 ...   c6**

The motivation for this move is similar to that behind 4 ♗e3 c6; Black takes the sting out of ♗h6 by avoiding the loss of time resulting from ... ♗g7 and then ... ♗xh6. The alternatives are:

(a) **4 ... h6** 5 ♗e3 (5 ♗h4 ♗g7 6 f4 c5!? 7 dc ♕a5 8 ♕d2 ♕xc5 9 ♘f3 ♘c6 10 0-0-0 ♗e6 11 h3 0-0 and Black has better attacking chances, Westerinen–Vadasz, Budapest 1976; of course 6 ♕d2 transposes to A) c6 (more sensible than 5 ... ♘g4 6 ♗c1 ♗g7 7 f3 ♘f6 8 ♗e3 and the pawn on h6 is badly placed) 6 ♗e2 ♗g7 7 ♘f3 ♕b6?! (7 ... ♗g4 is better) 8 0-0 ♕xb2 9 ♕d2 ♕a3 10 h3! with dangerous attacking chances, Pribyl–Swic, Lodz 1978.

(b) **4 ... ♘bd7** 5 f4 h6 (not 5 ... c5? 6 e5 ♘h5 7 g4! cd 8 ♕xd4 de 9 fe ♘g7 10 e6! ♘xe6 11 ♕xh8 ♘xg5 12 0-0-0 with an excellent position for White, Vasiukov–Pribyl, Zalaegerszeg 1977) 6 ♗h4 ♗g7 (6 ... ♘h5 7 ♘h3 followed by ♗e2 is good for White) transposes to line b2 in the note to White's 5th move in variation A.

5 ♕d2   b5 *(106)*

Or 5 ... ♘bd7 6 f3 (6 f4 ♗g7 7 e5 ♘d5 8 ♘xd5 cd 9 ed f6 10 de ♕xe7+ 11 ♔f2 fg 12 ♖e1 ♘e5! 13 ♗b5+ ♗d7 14 ♗xd7+ ♕xd7 15 ♘f3 0-0 16 de ♖xf4 with advantage for Black, Ree–Quinteros, Haifa Ol. 1976; 10 ♗h4 was better, but still only equal) b5 7 ♘h3 ♗g7 (7 ... h6 is always a risky move when White can retreat to e3 because it prevents Black castling; Hübner–van der Sterren, Wijk aan Zee 1984, continued 8 ♗e3 ♗g7 9 ♘f2 ♗b7 10 ♗e2 ♕c7 11 0-0 a6 12 a4 b4 13 ♘cd1 a5 14 c3 with advantage to White) 8 ♗h6 0-0 9 ♘f2 e5 10 ♗xg7 ♔xg7 11 0-0-0 ♕a5 12 ♔b1 ♖e8 13 h4 h5 14 g4 with a slight plus for White, Karpov–Gipslis, Moscow 1972.

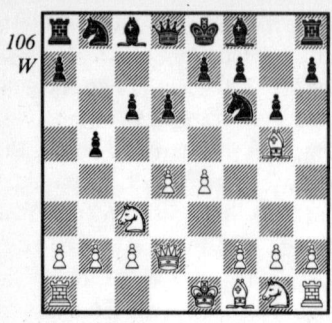
106
W

6 ♗d3 h6

A good moment for this move since in the analysis of 6 ... c6 in line A White did not play ♗d3, so White is committed to a move he might otherwise avoid. Alternatives:

(a) **6 ... ♘bd7** 7 ♘f3?! (7 ♘ge2 ♘b6 8 0-0 or 7 f4 ♘b6 8 ♘f3 ♗g7 9 0-0 as in c below is better) h6 8 ♗e3 ♘g4 9 ♗f4 e5 10 de de 11 ♗g3 ♕e7! 12 ♗h4 ♕c5 13 a3 a5 and Black is a little better, Soltis–Torre, Teesside 1975.

(b) **6 ... b4** 7 ♘ce2 a5 8 f4 ♗g7 9 e5 ♘d5 10 ♘f3 ♕b6 11 ed (a surprising move – 11 c4 looks more natural) ed 12 f5 0-0 13 ♗h6 ♗a6 14 h4 ♗xd3 15 cd ♘d7 16 h5 with a tremendous attack, Zhuravlev–Belov, USSR 1977.

(c) **6 ... ♗g7** 7 f4 0-0 (7 ... b4 8 ♘ce2 ♕b6 9 ♘f3 c5 10 e5 de 11 fe ♘fd7 12 ♗h6 0-0 13 h4 cd 14 h5 and once again the Black king is in trouble, Krnic–Slak, Krk 1976) 8 ♘f3 ♘bd7 9 0-0 ♘b6 10 f5 (10 ♖ae1 b4 11 ♘d1 c5 12 c3 bc 13 bc cd 14 cd d5! 15 e5 ♘e4 16 ♗xe4 de 17 ♖xe4 ♗a6 gives Black enough counterplay) d5 11 e5 b4 12 ef ef 13 ♗f4 bc 14 ♕xc3 with just an edge for White, Pribyl–Wagman, Eksjo 1978.

7 ♗e3

7 ♗h4 may be answered by 7 ... g5 8 ♗g3 ♘h5, e.g. 9 ♘ge2 ♗g7 10 f4 gf 11 ♗h4 ♕d7! 12 0-0-0 b4 13 ♘a4 c5 14 b3 cd with a winning position for Black, Oszvath–Webb, corr. 1987.

7 ... ♘g4

8 ♗f4 e5 9 de de 10 ♗g3 h5 (10 ... ♘d7 11 ♘f3 ♕e7 12 ♗h4 ♕e6 13 a4 b4 14 ♘d1 a5 is unclear, Tseitlin–Karasev, Leningrad Ch. 1977) 11 ♘f3 h4! 12 ♗xe5 ♘xe5 13 ♘xe5 ♕f6 14 f4 ♗h6 15 ♘e2 ♕xe5 16 fe ♗xd2+ 17 ♔xd2, Liberzon–Torre, Nice Ol. 1974, and now 17 ... ♖h5 should equalize.

C

1 e4 g6 2 d4 ♗g7 3 ♘c3 d6 4 ♗g5
4 ... c6

Or:

(a) **4 ... a6** (although this has become popular against 4 ♗e3, it has never caught on as a reply to 4 ♗g5) 5 ♕d2 b5 6 f4 (better than 6 0-0-0, which gives Black a target to aim at; Fuller–Nunn, London 1975, continued 6 ... ♘d7 7 h4 h5 8 f3 ♗b7 9 ♔b1 ♘gf6 10 ♘h3 b4 11 ♘e2 ♖b8 12 d5 c5 13 dc ♗xc6 14 ♘d4 ♗b7 15 ♘f4 ♘c5 and Black has at least equal chances) ♗b7?! (6 ... ♘d7 was better) 7 a4 b4 8 ♘d5 ♘c6 9 ♘f3 ♘f6 10

♘xf6+ ef 11 ♗h4 ♘e7 12 ♗d3 c5 13 c3 bc 14 bc 0-0 15 0-0 with a miserable position for Black in Puhm–Nunn, England–France 1975.

(b) **4 ... ♘c6** (a natural way to exploit the slight weakness of d4) and now:

(b1) **5 ♗b5** a6 6 ♗xc6+ bc 7 ♘ge2 ♖b8 8 b3 (8 ♖b1 ♘f6 9 0-0 h6 10 ♗h4 g5 11 ♗g3 ♘h5 12 f4 ♖b4! 13 ♗e1 ♗g4 14 ♕d3 ♘xf4 15 ♘xf4 gf 16 ♖xf4 h5 17 d5 ♗e5 18 ♖f1 ♕a8! 19 h3 ♗d7 was unclear in Mestel–Botterill, British Ch. play-off 1974) ♘f6 9 0-0 ♗b7 (9 ... h6!?) 10 f3 h6 11 ♗e3 0-0 12 ♕d2 ♔h7 13 ♖ad1 e6 14 ♘a4 ♘d7 15 c4, Winants–Speelman, Brussels 1988, and now 15 ... f5 would have restricted White to a slight advantage.

(b2) **5 d5** ♘e5 6 f4 ♘d7 7 ♘f3 c6 8 ♕d2 (8 ♗c4 b5 9 ♗b3 c5! 10 ♘xb5 ♕a5+ 11 ♘c3 ♗a6 is very awkward for White and in Gonzales–Salman, Saint John Open 1988, he did not get enough for the piece after 12 ♔f2 ♗xc3 13 bc c4 14 ♕d4 f6) cd 9 ♘xd5 ♘gf6 10 ♘xf6+ ♘xf6 11 ♗b5+ ♗d7 12 ♗xd7+ ♕xd7 with equality, Szalanczi–Davies, Budapest 1987.

(b3) **5 ♘ge2** h6 6 ♗e3 ♘f6 7 f3 (this is similar to some of the lines with ♗e3, except that Black has the undesirable extra move ... h6 added, which will be awkward when White plays ♕d2) ♘d7 8 ♕d2 ♘b6 9 b3 e6 10 g4 ♕f6 11 ♗g2 with a good game for White, Raaste–Chernin, Jarvenpaa 1985.

(c) **4 ... ♘d7** (4 ... c5?! 5 dc ♕a5 6 ♕d2 ♕xc5 7 ♘d5! ♗e6 8 c4 ♘d7 9 ♖c1 ♘gf6 10 f3 a5 11 ♗e3 ♕c8 12 ♘e2 ♕b8 13 ♘d4 with advantage for White, Keres–Westerinen, Tallinn 1973) 5 ♕d2 c5 6 d5 (6 ♘f3 h6 7 ♗e3 ♘gf6 8 0-0-0 ♘g4 9 ♗f4!? cd 10 ♘xd4 e5 11 ♘db5 ef 12 ♘xd6+ ♔f8, Horvath–Plachetka, R. Sobota 1975, and now 13 ♘xc8 is unclear) ♘gf6 7 f4 a6 8 a4 ♕b6! 9 ♖a2 h6 10 ♗h4 ♕b4 11 ♗d3 ♘h5 12 ♘ce2 ♕xd2+ 13 ♔xd2 ♘df6 with equal play in Krnic–Jansa, Sombor 1976.

There is little practical experience on which to base an opinion, but these alternative 4th moves may prove superior to 4 ... c6.

5   ♕d2

5 ♗c4 is a curious move which led to an advantage for White after 5 ... ♘f6 6 ♗b3 ♕a5 7 ♕d2 h6 8 ♗h4 g5 9 ♗g3 ♘h5 10 ♘ge2 ♗e6 11 0-0 ♘d7 12 ♖ad1 ♘b6?! (12 ... ♗xb3 13 ab ♕c7 ±) 13 d5! cd 14 ed ♗f5 15 ♘d4 in Vasiukov–Petran, Zalaegerszeg 1977 but 5 ... b5 6 ♗b3 b4 7 ♘e2 ♘f6 may be better.

5 ...   b5
6   f4

The most direct move. 6 ♘f3 ♘d7 7 ♗d3 h6 8 ♗e3 ♘gf6 9 h3 e5 10 0-0 a6 11 de de 12 ♖ad1 ♕e7 13 a4 h5 (a radical solution to the problem of castling) 14 ab ab 15 ♖a1 ♖xa1 16 ♖xa1 0-0 was equal in Atanasov–Todorcevic, Varna 1977.

**6 ... ♘d7
7 ♘f3** *(107)*

7 a3 (not 7 e5? f6! 8 ef ef 9 ♗h4 d5 10 0-0-0 ♘e7 11 ♗d3 ♘b6 12 ♘f3 0-0 was good for Black in Fuller–Nunn, England 1974) ♕c7 (7 ... a6 8 ♘f3 ♘b6 9 h3 ♘f6 10 ♗d3 0-0 11 0-0 ♘c4 12 ♗xc4 bc 13 ♖ae1 ♖b8 14 e5 de 15 ♘xe5 is better for White, Winants–Todorcevic, Budel 1987) 8 ♘f3 (8 d5 a6 9 e5 is unclear) ♘b6 9 h3 (9 d5 was better) ♘f6 10 ♗d3 0-0 11 g4 a5 12 0-0 b4 with a double-edged position, Lieb–Balashov, Munich 1979.

After 7 ♘f3 Black may play:

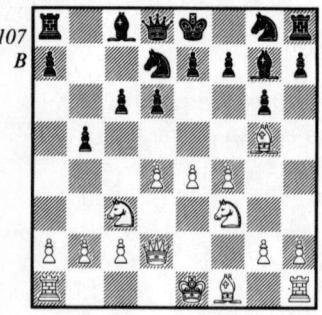

(a) **7 ... b4** 8 ♘d1 ♕b6 9 ♘e3 ♘gf6?! (9 ... h6 10 ♗h4 ♘gf6 is better, for reasons which will become apparent) 10 ♗d3 d5 11 e5 (11 ♗xf6! ♘xf6 12 e5 is strong, since 12 ... ♘e4 13 ♗xe4 de 14 ♘g5 is very good for White as in P. Littlewood–Nunn, England 1974; this explains why 9 ... h6 was better) ♘e4 12 ♗xe4 (12 ♕e2 f5 13 0-0 ♘f8 14 c3 ♘e6 15 ♗xe4 fe 16 ♘d2 ♗a6 was good for Black, Raaste–Nunn, Teesside Student Ol. 1974) de 13 ♘g1 ♗a6 14 0-0-0 ♖d8 15 ♗h4 f6 16 d5 0-0 17 dc ♘xe5! 18 ♘d5 ♘d3+! 19 ♕xd3 ed 20 ♘xb6 ab 21 ♘f3 ♗h6 22 cd ♗xd3 23 g3 ♗e4 24 ♖hf1 ♖xd1+ 25 ♔xd1 ♗xc6 0-1, Grefe–Nunn, London 1973.

(2) **7 ... ♘gf6** 8 ♗d3 ♘b6 9 0-0 0-0 10 ♖ae1 b4 11 ♘e2 c5 12 ♘g3 ♗b7 13 e5 c4 14 ♗e2 ♘fd5 with a comfortable position for Black, Tal–Kristiansen, Reykjavik 1986.

17 | White plays g3

This plan saw a surge of popularity in the early eighties, as more and more White players switched to a risk-free variation which offered the chance of lasting positional pressure. As so often happens, the new fashion was only in style for a few years before Pirc supporters began to find antidotes to White's system. Although it has never been refuted, the g3 line is now rarely seen in Grandmaster play, but on the next turn of the wheel it will probably be revived again.

White's aim is simply to maintain his pawn centre at d4 and e4, while his pieces are well posted to avoid any harassment by Black's forces. His policy is primarily restraint, sometimes coupled with a gradual expansion on the kingside by g4 and ♘e2–g3. Black has no trouble playing ... e5, but the exchange on d4 often leaves White having the slight edge associated with the resulting e4 v d6 central pawn structure. It is not so easy to suggest a typical plan for Black, because over the years he has tried almost everything!

We take the Modern move-order as the main line solely in order to discuss some possible deviations by Black, but in the vast majority of cases the Pirc and Modern move-orders quickly lead to the same position.

1 e4 g6 2 d4 ♗g7 3 ♘c3

3 g3 d6 4 ♗g2 is an interesting move-order. White wants to force Black to transpose to the Pirc move-order without allowing the ... ♘c6 system mentioned in the note to Black's 4th move (since by delaying ♘c3 White renders the sequence ... ♘c6 d5 ♘d4 impossible – he just wins the knight by c3). In Romanishin–Ivkov, Riga 1981 Black exploited White's move-order by 4 ... c5 5 dc ♕a5+ 6 c3 ♕xc5 7 ♗e3 ♕c7 8 ♘e2 ♘f6 9 h3 ♘c6?! (after 9 ... 0-0 White has almost nothing) 10 ♘a3 0-0 11 0-0 a6 12 ♘c4 b5 13 ♘b6 and by now White was slightly better.

3 ... d6
4 g3

4 ♘ge2 is another attempt to defuse the 4 ... ♘c6 system by preparing to meet ... ♘c6 with

d5. When 4 ♘ge2 has occurred in practice Black has generally transposed to the Pirc, so if White wants to play the g3 system against the Modern move-order he should probably prefer 4 ♘ge2 to 4 g3.

4 ... ♘f6

Or:

(1) 4 ... ♘d7 5 ♘ge2 e5 (or 5 ... a6 6 ♗g2 c5 7 dc! ♘xc5 8 ♗e3 and now 8 ... ♘f6 9 e5 ♘g4 10 ♗xc5 dc 11 ♕xd8+ ♔xd8 12 f4 is ± but 8 ... ♗d7 9 ♗d4 e5 10 ♗xc5 dc 11 ♕d6 ♖c8 12 0-0-0 ♖c6 13 ♕d2 is even worse, Jansa–S. Nikolic, Smederevska Palanka 1980) 6 ♗g2 ♘h6?! (6 ... ♘gf6 transposes to the main line) 7 h4 ♘g4 8 f3 ♘gf6 9 ♗e3 c6 10 ♕d2 ♘b6 11 de ♘c4 12 ef! with an excellent position for White, Bhend–Arapovic, Lugano 1986.

(2) 4 ... ♘c6 5 ♗e3 (after 5 d5 Black should play 5 ... ♘e5 because although 5 ... ♘d4 6 ♗e3 c5 7 ♘b1 ♕b6 is fine for Black, the immediate 6 ♘b1! is rather awkward) ♘f6 (5 ... e5 is playable, e.g. 6 d5 ♘ce7 7 ♗b5+? c6 8 dc bc 9 ♗a4 ♘f6 10 ♕d3 0-0 11 0-0-0 d5 with advantage to Black, Biyiasas–Nunn, Hastings 1979/80, or 6 de ♘xe5 7 f4 ♗g4 8 ♗e2, Gulko–Salman, Philadelphia 1987, and now 8 ... ♗xe2 9 ♘gxe2 ♘d7 is unclear) 6 h3 (6 d5 ♘e5 7 f4 is possible; Pytel and Ksieski gave 7 ... ♗g4 8 ♕d2 ♘f3+ as distinctly better

for Black, but readers may form their own opinion of the position after 8 fe! ♗xd1 9 ef ♗xf6 10 ♖xd1 – it follows that 7 ... ♘ed7 is better and in fact this appears satisfactory for Black) e5 (6 ... 0-0 will transpose to the main line) 7 ♘ge2 d5!? (a successful attempt to exploit the fact that White's king is temporarily stuck in the centre) 8 ♗g2 (8 de may be met by 8 ... ♘xe5 or 8 ... ♘xe4) ♘xe4 9 ♘xe4 (9 de ♘xc3 is equal) de 10 d5 ♘e7 11 ♗xe4 ♘f5 and Black is slightly better, Plaskett–McNab, Brighton 1984.

5 ♗g2 0-0 (108)

After 5 ... e5 6 de de 7 ♕xd8+ ♔xd8 8 ♘f3 ♘bd7 9 b3! ♘e8 10 ♗b2 f6 11 0-0-0 Black would have had a depressing ending even after 11 ... ♘d6, but Geller–Lerner, USSR Ch. 1979 continued 11 ... c6? 12 ♘e1! ♔c7 13 ♘d3 ♘d6 14 f4 with a clear advantage for White.

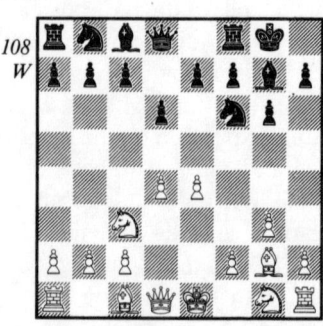

108
W

6 ♘ge2

Alternatives:

(1) **6 h3** e5 7 ♗e3 (appears strange, but this position can arise

from a 4 ♗e3 system, e.g. 4 ♗e3 ♗g7 5 h3 0-0 6 g3 e5 7 ♗g2) ed 8 ♘xd4 ♘c6 9 ♗e3 ♗e6 10 ♘ge2 ♕d7 and Black has "exploited" White's move-order, but after 11 ♕d2 ♖fe8 12 ♘f4 ♗c4 13 b3 ♗a6 14 0-0-0 b6 15 g4 White had the advantage in Dorfman–Chikovani, USSR 1979. The vigorous 11 ... b5!? must be an improvement.

(2) 6 ♘f3 (innocuous) and now:

(2a) 6 ... ♗g4 7 ♗e3 ♘c6 8 h3 ♗xf3 9 ♕xf3 e5 10 de de 11 0-0 ♘d4 12 ♕d1 ♕e7 13 ♘b1 h5! 14 ♘d2 h4 with a fine game for Black, Spassky–Timman, Tilburg 1978.

(2b) 6 ... c5 7 d5 (7 dc ♕a5 8 cd ♘xe4 9 de ♖e8 10 0-0 ♘xc3 11 bc ♗xc3 is equal, while 7 0-0 cd ♘xd4 transposes to the 6 g3 line against the Dragon, a system which is not thought dangerous for Black) ♘a6 8 0-0 ♘c7 9 ♖e1?! (9 a4) b5 10 a3 ♗b7 11 ♗g5 h6 12 ♗f4 a5 13 ♕c1 ♔h7 and Black is at least equal, Karklins–Ardaman, New York 1987.

(2c) 6 ... ♘bd7 7 0-0 e5 8 de (8 b3 ♖e8 9 ♗b2 c6 10 ♖e1 b5 11 d5 cd 12 ♘xd5 ♗b7 13 ♘xf6+ ♘xf6 14 ♕d3 ♕b6 ½–½, De Firmian–Diesen, Lone Pine 1979, 8 a4 c6 9 b3 ♖e8 10 ♗a3 ed 11 ♘xd4 ♘c5 12 ♖e1 ♗g4 13 ♕d2 ♘e6 14 ♘de2 ♕f6 with a double-edged position, Spassky–Gligoric, Montilla 1978, or finally 8 ♖e1 ♖e8 9 de ♘xe5 10 h3, Garcia Gonzalez–Smejkal, Salonika 1984, and now 10 ... ♘xf3+ 11 ♕xf3 ♗d7 followed by ... ♗c6 is more or less equal) de 9 b3 (9 ♕e2 c6 10 ♖d1 ♕c7 11 b3 ♖e8 12 ♗a3 ♕a5 13 ♗b2 ♘c5 14 ♘d2 ♘e6 15 ♘c4 ♕c7 and Black may have an edge) b6 10 a4 (10 ♗a3 ♖e8 11 ♕e2 ♗f8 12 ♗xf8 ♘xf8 13 ♖ad1 ♕e7 14 ♘d5 ♘xd5 15 ed e4 is unclear) ♗b7 11 ♘d2 ♖e8 12 ♗a3 ♗f8 13 ♗xf8 ♘xf8 14 ♘c4 ♘e6 with equality, Smyslov–Sax, Tilburg 1979.

6 ... e5

Black has also tried playing for ... c5, for example 6 ... ♘bd7 7 0-0 c5 8 h3 a6 (if Black takes on d4, we reach a g3 Dragon in which Black has played the supposedly inferior ... ♘bd7) 9 a4 (9 e5 de 10 de ♘xe5 11 ♕xd8 ♖xd8 12 ♗e3 ♘fd7 13 b3 ♘c6 14 ♖ad1 e5 was unclear in Bellon–Timman, Las Palmas 1981, while 9 ♗e3 ♕c7 10 dc ♘xc5 11 ♘f4 e6 12 ♕d2 ♗d7 13 ♖fd1 ♘e8 14 ♘d3 ♘a4 15 ♘xa4 ♗xa4 16 ♖ac1 was ± in Barlov–Smyslov, New York 1987) ♖b8 10 ♗e3 ♕c7 11 ♕d2 b5 12 ab ab 13 ♘d5 ♘xd5 14 ed with a slight advantage for White, Geller–Christiansen, Moscow 1982.

7 h3

This is the only move played these days. Although 7 0-0 was once the most popular, it has been abandoned because of line a below. After 7 0-0 *(109)* Black may play:

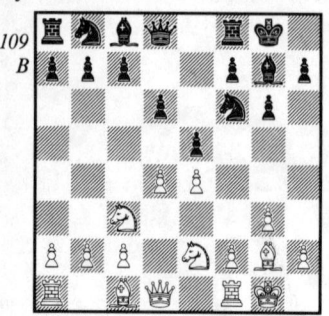

(a) **7 ... ♘c6** (this is the best way to exploit White's omission of h3, because 8 ♗e3 is met by 8 ... ♘g4) 8 de (8 d5 ♘e7 9 f4 ef 10 ♗xf4 ♘g4 11 ♕d2 c5 12 dc ♘xc6 13 h3 ♘ge5 14 b3 ♗e6 15 ♖ad1 ♖c8 16 ♔h1 ♕a5 17 ♘d5 ♕xd2 18 ♖xd2 ♗xd5 19 ed ♘b4 with equality, Gulko–van der Wiel, Amsterdam 1987) de 9 ♗g5 ♘d4 (9 ... ♗e6 10 ♕c1 ♘d4! 11 ♘xd4 ♕xd4 12 ♖d1 ♕c5 13 h3 c6 14 ♘a4 ♕a5 was equal in Speelman–Sznapik, Dortmund 1981, but 10 ♘d5 ♗xd5 11 ed ♘e7 12 c4 would have been ±; **9 ... ♕xd1!?** 10 ♖fxd1 ♘b4 11 ♖d2 c6 is an interesting idea, with the point that ♘d5 is definitely prevented and the knight on e2 is badly placed if its colleague on c3 can't get out of the way) 10 ♘xd4 ed (10 ... ♕xd4 11 ♕xd4 ed 12 ♘b5 is good for White) 11 ♘d5 ♗e6 (11 ... c6? 12 e5! cd 13 ♕xd4! wins for White as in Minic–Hulak, Yugoslavia 1974) and now:

(a1) **12 e5** ♗xd5 13 ef ♖e8! (13 ... ♗h8 14 ♕xd4 ♗xg2 15 ♕xd8 ♖fxd8 16 ♔xg2 ♖d6 17 ♗f4 ♖c6 18 c3 ♗xf6 19 ♖ad1 is slightly better for White) 14 ♕xd4 (14 ♗xd5 ♕xd5 15 fg ♕xg5 16 ♕xd4 ♕e5 and 14 fg ♕xg5 15 h4 ♕d8 are fine for Black) ♗xg2 15 ♕xd8 ♖axd8 16 ♔xg2 h6 17 ♗e3 ♗xf6 ½–½, Speelman–Nunn, Hastings 1979/80.

(a2) **12 ♕f3** ♗xd5 13 ed h6 (after 13 ... ♕d6 14 ♗f4 ♕b6 15 ♕b3 ♖ad8 16 ♖fd1 ♕xb3 17 ab ♘xd5 18 ♗xd5 ♖xd5 19 c4 ♖d7 20 ♖xa7 White has a slight edge but Black should draw) 14 ♗f4 ♖c8 15 ♕b3 (15 ♗e5! gives better chances of an advantage) c6! 16 ♗h3 ♖a8 17 dc bc 18 ♗e5 ♖e8 19 ♗xf6 ½–½, Mestel–Christiansen, Hastings 1979/80.

(b) **7 ... ed** 8 ♘xd4 ♘c6 (this is also sensible, if not quite as good as the immediate ... ♘c6; again White's 9 ♗e3 would be met by 9 ... ♘g4, so he has to retreat his knight) 9 ♘de2 ♖e8 10 h3 ♘d7 11 ♔h2 (11 ♗e3 followed by ♕d2 is more dangerous) ♘b6 (11 ... ♘c5 12 ♗e3 f5! was unclear according to Short) 12 a4 a5 13 b3 ♘b4 14 ♗e3 with a slight advantage for White, Short–Donner, Amsterdam 1982.

(c) **7 ... ♘a6** (after this the best Black can hope for is a transposition to the main line if White plays h3 soon) 8 ♖e1 c6 9 h3 ♖e8 and now:

(c1) **10 a4** ed 11 ♘xd4 ♘b4 (not 11...♘c5 12 a5 d5 13 ed ♖xe1+ 14 ♕xe1 ♘xd5 15 ♘xd5 cd 16 ♗e3 with a clear plus, Sax–Petran, Hungary Ch. 1976) 12 a5 (this allows Black to equalize, so White should permit Black to play ... a5; the resulting position is similar to line B below, but Black is already committed to the exchange on d4) d5! 13 ed (13 e5 ♘e4 14 ♘xe4 de 15 ♖xe4 ♖xe5 16 ♖xe5 ♗xe5 17 c3 ♗xd4 18 cd ♗e6 19 ♖a4 ½–½, Gulko–Hort, Biel 1987) ♖xe1+ 14 ♕xe1 c5 15 ♘ce2 ♘fxd5 16 ♗d2 ♕f8 17 c3 cd 18 cb ♗e6 19 ♘f4 ½–½, Kuypers–van Wijgerden, Wijk aan Zee 'B' 1979.

(c2) **10 ♗g5** h6 11 ♗e3 ♕c7 12 ♕d2 ♔h7 13 ♖ad1 ♗d7 14 g4 ♖ad8 15 ♘g3 ♗c8 16 f4 (Karpov's kingside pawn advance has left Black in an unpleasantly cramped position) b5 17 a3 b4?! (17... ♕b7 was better, but White still stands well) 18 ab ♘xb4 19 ♘ce2 ed 20 ♘xd4 a5 21 c3 with an excellent position for White, Karpov–Timman, Montreal 1979.

(d) **7 ... c6** (this usually transposes into the main line after a subsequent h3) 8 a4 ♕c7 9 a5 (it is tricky for Black to develop after this move since a bishop on e3 will menace the a-pawn, preventing the rook on a8 moving) ♗g4 (Black tries to exploit the lack of h3, but it is not a success) 10 ♗e3 ♖e8 11 f3 ♗e6 12 ♕d2 ♘a6 13 ♔h1 ♖ad8? 14 d5 winning a pawn, Mestel–Taulbut, Hastings 1978/9.

After 7 h3 *(110)* Black may adopt a range of plans:

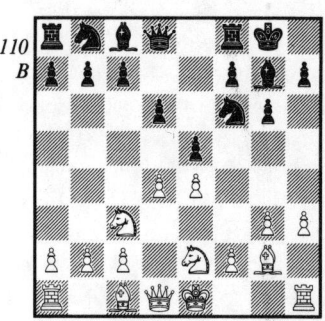

A: 7 ... ♘c6
B: 7 ... c6
C: 7 ... ♘bd7

These are in descending order of merit. The ... ♘c6 plan is the most direct way of exerting pressure on White's centre, and Black may follow up in two ways. He can either swap everything on d4, which leaves him slightly worse but with good drawing chances, or, in many lines, he may move the c6 knight (usually to b4) and play dynamically with ... c5 and ... ♗c6 aiming for active piece play and a grip on d5 to compensate for the backward d-pawn.

In line B Black intends to play ...a5 and ... ♘a6–b4; this is also not a bad plan, although White may be able to keep an edge. Line C has been most frequently played, but on current evidence Black cannot equalize and I would advise Black players to avoid it altogether.

Note that the 7 ... ♘bd7 variation usually involves ... c6 as well, so in B we consider only those lines with ... c6 which do not continue ... ♘bd7. The only other possibility worth mentioning is **7 ... a6** 8 a4 (8 0-0 b5 9 de de 10 ♗g5 c6 11 ♕c1 ♘bd7 12 ♖d1 ♕e7 13 ♕d2 ♖e8 14 ♕d6 ♗b7 =, Godena–Piket, World Junior Ch. 1986) b6 9 0-0 ♗b7 10 d5 (there seems no reason to play this so soon; 10 ♖e1 is more accurate) c6 11 dc ♘xc6 12 ♗g5 h6 13 ♗e3 ♔h7 14 ♕d2 ♘a5 15 b3 with an edge for White, Wessendorf–van der Wiel, San Bernadino 1986.

A

7 ... ♘c6

After 7 0-0 White could not play 8 ♗e3 because of the reply 8 ... ♘g4, but thanks to 7 h3 White can maintain his pawn centre.

8 ♗e3 ♖e8

Or:

(a) **8 ... ed** 9 ♘xd4 ♘xd4 10 ♗xd4 ♗e6 (by exchanging immediately Black hopes to develop his bishop to a better square, but it fails to equalize) 11 0-0 ♕d7 12 ♕f3 ♘e8 13 ♗xg7 ♘xg7 14 ♔h2 f5 15 ef ♘xf5 16 ♕xb7 ♖ab8 17 ♕xa7 ♖xb2 18 ♘d5 with advantage to White, Gufeld–Pribyl, Tbilisi 1980.

(2) **8 ... b6** (a rather dubious idea) 9 0-0 ♗b7 10 ♖e1 (10 d5 ♘e7 11 ♕d2 ♕d7 12 a4 c6 was played in Krnic–Franco, Vrnjacka Banja 1983, and now 13 a5 is good for White) ♖e8 11 ♕d2 ♕d7 12 ♖ad1 ♖ad8 13 de ♘xe5 14 b3 ♕c8 15 ♗g5 with a clear plus for White, Hort–Nunn, Wijk aan Zee 1983.

9 0-0 ed

After 9 ... a6 10 a4 the most likely result is a transposition to the main line by 10 ... ed (it is unwise to wait any longer with this exchange since 10 ... ♗d7 11 d5 ♘e7 12 a5 may be good for White) 11 ♘xd4 ♗d7. From Black's point of view 9 ... a6 is the best move-order, because White's options are more restricted.

10 ♘xd4 ♗d7 *(111)*

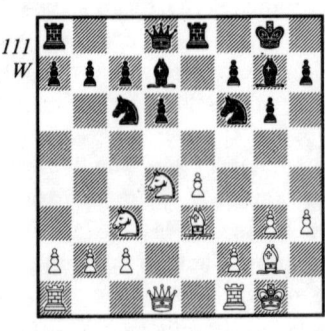

11 ♖e1

Or:

(1) **11 ♘de2!?** b5 12 a3 a5 13 ♘f4

b4 14 ab ab 15 ♖xa8 ♕xa8 16 ♘cd5 ♕c8 17 ♘xf6+ ♗xf6 18 b3, Paulsen–Zessinger, Bundesliga 1985, and although the exchanges have freed Black's position somewhat, the d5 square still gives White an edge.

(2) **11 a4** (it appears strange to play this voluntarily) ♘xd4 12 ♗xd4 a5 (Black should probably head for liquidation by ... ♗c6 and ... ♘d7) 13 ♖e1 ♗c6 14 ♕d2 ♖e6 15 ♖ad1 ♕e7 16 ♘d5 ♗xd5 17 ed ♖xe1+ 18 ♖xe1 ♕d7 19 ♕c3 ♘h5 20 ♗xg7 ♘xg7 21 ♖e4 with advantage to White, Gufeld–Gipslis, Volgograd 1985.

11 ... a6

11 ... ♘xd4 12 ♗xd4 c5 13 ♗e3 ♗c6 14 ♕d3 ♕b6 15 ♖ab1 ♖ad8 16 b4 ♕c7 17 b5 ♗d7 18 ♗g5! ♖b8 19 e5 and White has a very good position, Ivanov–D. Gurevich, Hastings 1983/4.

12 a4 *(112)*

Or 12 f4 (12 ♔h2 should be met by 12 ... ♘xd4 13 ♗xd4 ♗c6, rather than 12 ... ♘e5 13 b3 c5 14 ♘de2 ♗c6 15 ♕d2 ♕a5 16 ♖ad1 ♖ad8 17 ♗g5! ♕b6 18 ♘f4 ♖d7 19 ♗xf6 ♗xf6 20 ♘fd5 ♗xd5 21 ♘xd5 ♕d8 22 ♘xf6+ ♕xf6 23 f4 with advantage to White, Zaichik–Vogt, East Berlin 1988) ♘xd4 (12 ... ♕c8 13 ♔h2 h5 14 ♘xc6 ♗xc6 15 ♗d4 ♕d7 16 ♕d3 ♖ad8 was equal in Abramovic–Terzic, Zenica 1986) 13 ♗xd4 c5 14 ♗xf6 (accepting the pawn is very risky, but 14 ♗f2 ♗c6 15

♕d2 ♕c7 16 ♖ad1 ♖ad8 gives White nothing) ♗xf6 15 ♕xd6 ♗d4+ 16 ♔h2 ♖e6 17 ♕d5 ♖b6 and Black has good compensation for the pawn, Byrne–Christiansen, USA Ch. 1984.

After 12 a4 Black may play:

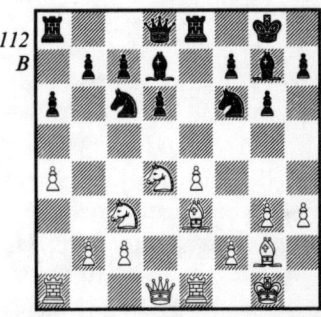

(1) **12 ... ♘a5!?** 13 g4 (13 b3 c5 14 ♘de2 ♗c6 is unclear) c5 14 ♘de2 ♗c6 15 ♘g3 ♕b6 16 ♖b1 ♘c4 17 ♗f4 ♕a5 18 ♕d3 ♕b4 and in Wockenfuss–Plaskett, Lugano 1986 White could not keep Black's piece activity under control; the game continued 19 ♘a2 ♕xa4 20 ♘c3 ♕b4 21 ♘a2 ♕b5 22 ♘c3 ♘xb2! with advantage to Black.

(2) **12 ... ♘b4** 13 ♕d2 c5 14 ♘b3 ♗c6 15 f3 (horribly passive; 15 ♗f4= was better) ♕c7 16 ♘e2 ♖ad8 17 c3 d5 18 ♗f4 ♕b6 19 e5 ♘e4! and once again Black's latent initiative has burst out, Sek–Ksieski, Poland 1981.

(3) **12 ... ♘e5?!** (this is the only bad choice) 13 a5! c5 14 ♘b3 ♗c6 15 ♘d2 ♕c7 16 f4 ♘ed7 17 ♗f2 and Black's ... c5 has just left him

with a collection of weaknesses, Pigott–Nunn, London 1980.

B

    7 ...   c6
    8 a4

If White doesn't play this, then Black can reply ... b5, for example:

(1) **8 ♗e3** b5 9 0-0 (9 de de 10 ♗c5 ♕xd1+ 11 ♖xd1 ♖e8 12 ♘c1 a5 13 ♘d3 ♘a6 14 ♗e3 ♘b4 15 ♖d2 ♘d7 16 0-0 ♘f8 17 ♘c5 ♘a6 18 ♖fd1 ♘xc5 19 ♗xc5 ♘e6 and Black equalized in Makarychev–Torre, Saint John Open 1988) ♗b7 (9 ... b4 10 de de 11 ♘a4 ♗a6 12 ♖e1 ♗b5 13 ♘c5 ♘fd7, Popovic–Chernin, Subotica 1987, and now 14 ♘xd7 ♗xd7 15 a3 ba 16 ♖xa3 ♕c7 is ±) 10 a3 ♘bd7 11 ♕d2 ♖e8 12 ♖fe1 a6 13 d5 (Black was threatening ... ed followed by ... c5) cd 14 ed ♘b6 15 b3 ♕c7 with an unclear position, Dzandzgava–M. Gurevich, Lvov 1987.

(2) **8 0-0** b5 9 b3 (9 ♗e3 is line 1 above, while 9 a3 ♘bd7 10 d5 cd 11 ♘xd5 ♗b7 12 ♘xf6+ ♘xf6 13 ♘c3 a6 14 ♗g5 ♖c8 15 ♕d2 ♖c4 16 b3 ♖c5 was roughly level in Klinger–Cuijpers, Vienna 1984) ♕c7 10 ♗g5 ♖e8 11 ♕d2 b4 12 ♘a4 ed 13 ♗xf6 ♗xf6 14 ♘xd4 ♗b7 15 c3 (15 ♖ad1 ♘a6 16 ♖fe1 is ± according to Tal, but it looks more like equality to me) bc 16 ♘xc3 ♘d7 17 ♖ac1 ♕b6 with equality, Tal–Torre, Brussels 1987.

Although these lines without a4 do not appear very promising at the moment, they are a critical test because if White can delay a4 for a move, then Black's plan of ... a5 and ... ♘a6–b4 becomes much harder to execute.

    8 ...   a5

Or 8 ... ♗e6 (8 ... ♖e8 9 0-0 ed 10 ♘xd4 ♘a6 11 ♖e1 transposes to line c1 in the note to White's 7th move) 9 0-0 d5 10 ♗g5 ♕d7 11 ed ♘xd5 12 de ♘xc3 13 ♘xc3 ♕xd1 14 ♖axd1 ♗xe5 15 ♖fe1 ♗xc3?! (15 ... ♗g7 would have kept White's advantage to a minimum) 16 bc ♔g7 17 ♗f4 ♖e8 18 ♖b1 ♖e7 19 ♖ed1 with strong pressure for White, Nunn–Carr, London 1985.

    9 0-0   ♘a6
    10 ♗e3 *(113)*

This has been universally played but 10 ♗g5!? is worth considering. If Black plays ... h6 then White replies ♗e3 followed by ♕d2, gaining time, while after 10 ... ♘b4 11 ♕d2 ♖e8 12 ♖ad1 White intends a quick f4.

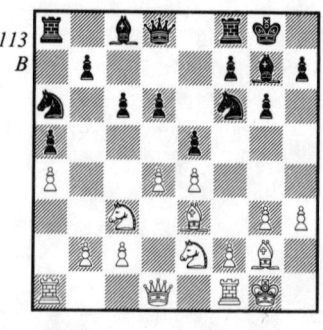

    10 ...   ♘b4

Or:

(1) 10 ... ♕c7 11 ♕d2 ♖e8 12 g4 ♘b4 (12 ... ed 13 ♗xd4 ♘c5 14 ♘g3 is also ±) 13 f4 ed 14 ♗xd4 d5 15 ed cd (15 ... ♘bxd5 16 ♘xd5 ♘xd5 17 ♗xd5 cd 18 ♗xg7 followed by ♕d4+ and ♘c3 is good for White) 16 ♘g3 with a slight plus for White, Miles–Suradiradja, Indonesia 1982.

(2) 10 ... ed!? 11 ♗xd4 (after 11 ♘xd4 Black replies 11 ... ♘c5) ♘b4 12 f4 (12 ♕d2 followed by ♖ad1 would restrain ... d5) ♖e8 13 g4 d5! (having spent too much time moving his kingside pawns, White receives the traditional counter-blow in the centre) 14 e5 ♘d7 15 ♘g3 b6 16 ♖e1 ♗a6 17 ♘a2 ♘xa2 18 ♖xa2 with an unclear position, Martinovic–Gligoric, Yugoslavia Ch. 1986.

11 ♕d2 ♗e6

Now Tal suggests 12 f4!?, but it has not been tried out.

12 ♖ad1 ♗c4

13 ♖fe1 ♖e8 (13 ... ♕e7 14 b3 ♗a6 15 de de, Lerner–Tal, Jurmala 1983, and now Tal assesses 16 ♗b6! as slightly better for White; 13 ... ♕c7 is an untested idea, but it could transpose to the main line) 14 ♔h2 ♕c7 15 f4 ♕e7 (this looks odd, but once White has played f4 the idea of de followed by ♗b6, which is the usual answer to ... ♕e7, holds much less force) and now Barlov–Parma, Yugoslavia Ch. 1982, continued 16 ♘c1 ♘h5 17 fe de 18 d5 cd 19 ♘xd5 ♗xd5! 20 ed ♕d6 21 c3 ♘a6 22 ♗f3 ♘f6 ½–½. One possible improvement is the simple 16 b3, driving the bishop back to a6 and preventing the later capture on d5. Another idea is the risky 16 g4!?, but if Black cannot exploit the fragile White position quickly he is in danger of being squashed.

C

7 ... ♘bd7

It is worth mentioning a couple of general points. Firstly the move ... ed is usually met by ♗xd4 rather than ♘xd4. The reason is that ♘xd4 does nothing to help the e-pawn, which will come under fire by ... ♘c5 and ... ♖e8. On the other hand ♗xd4 enables White to meet the attack against e4 by a timely e5 undermining the c5 knight. Secondly, the move ... ♘b6 is often tempting but is usually a mistake; it is easy for White to play b3, when the knight on b6 has little future.

8 0-0 *(114)*

8 ♗e3 ed (8 ... c6 will probably transpose to the main line, but Black decides to try something different) 9 ♗xd4 ♘b6 10 0-0 ♗d7 (after 10 ... c5 11 ♗e3 ♘c4 12 ♗c1 followed by b3 and ♗b2 Black has not justified the weakening of his pawn structure) 11 ♕d3 c5!? 12 ♗e3 ♗c6 13 ♖ad1 ♖e8 14 b3 ±, Chandler–Ftacnik, Vrsac 1981.

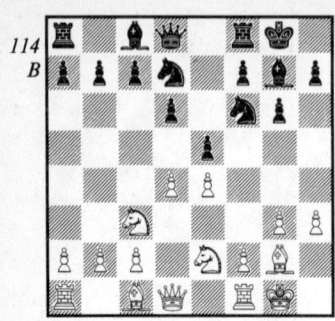
*114
B*

8 ... c6

Or 8 ... ♖e8 and now:
(1) 9 ♗e3 (I believe this is the more accurate move because it prevents the ...ed and ...♘c5 manoeuvre, e.g. 9 ...ed 10 ♗xd4 ♘c5 11 e5!) with a further division:

(1a) 9 ... a6 10 a4 ed 11 ♗xd4 ♖b8 12 g4?! (12 a5 is much better) b5 13 ab ab 14 ♘g3 b4 15 ♘b1 c5 16 ♗e3 ♘e5 17 ♘d2 h6 with at least equality for Black, Sveshnikov–Speelman, Hastings 1977/8.

(1b) 9 ... ♕e7 10 g4 ed 11 ♗xd4 ♘c5 12 ♘g3 c6 13 a4 ♘e6 14 ♗e3 ♘d7 15 ♕d2 ♘e5 16 b3 ♕f6 was fine for Black in A. Ivanov–Zaichik, USSR Young Masters 1977, but 10 ♖e1 is better.

(1c) 9 ... b6 10 g4 (10 d5 ♗b7 11 ♕d2 ♗f8 12 f4! c6 13 f5 b5 14 dc ♗xc6 15 ♘d5 ♗xd5 16 ed was also slightly better for White in Gufeld–Torre, Baku 1980) h5 (10 ... ed 11 ♗xd4 ♗b7 12 ♘g3 intending g5 is dangerous for Black) 11 g5 ♘h7 12 h4 ♗b7 13 ♕d2 f6 14 f4! and White has some

advantage, Miles–Kavalek, Bundesliga 1981.

(2) 9 ♖e1 ed 10 ♘xd4 ♘c5 (10 ... a5 11 ♗f4 a4 12 ♕d2 ♘e5 13 b3 ab 14 ab ♖xa1 15 ♖xa1 c6 16 g4 ♘fd7 17 ♖d1 and Black has not been able to free himself, Karpov–Lerner, USSR Ch. 1983) 11 ♗f4 (11 ♘b3 ♘xb3 12 ab ♗d7 13 ♗e3 ♕c8 14 ♔h2 ♗c6 15 ♗d4 ♖e6 16 ♕d3 may be more accurate, when White still held an edge in Aseev–M. Gurevich, USSR 1983) h6 (11 ... ♘h5 12 ♗e3 ♘f6 13 f3 is also reasonable, but now not 13 ... a5?! 14 ♕d2 ♘fd7?! 15 ♖ad1 a4 16 ♘db5 and Black is quite unable to free his position, Bisguier–Taulbut, Lone Pine 1978) 12 ♘b3 (12 g4 h5 13 g5 ♘h7 14 h4 f6 is unclear) g5 (although this creates a slight weakness the time gained is more important) 13 ♗c1 ♘xb3 14 ab ♗d7 15 ♗e3 a6 16 ♕d2 ♗c6 17 ♗d4 ♘h5! and Black has equalized.

9 a4 *(115)*

Preventing ...b5 is best. After 9 ♗e3 b5 (9 ... ♖e8 10 ♖e1 ♕c7 11 ♕d2 b5 12 a3 a6 13 ♖ad1 ♗b7 14 ♗h6 ♖ad8 15 g4 ♘b6 16 ♗xg7 ♔xg7 17 ♘g3 h6 18 b3 ed 19 ♕xd4 c5 20 ♕d2 d5 was level in Grünfeld–Greenfield, Munich 1987) 10 a3 ♗b7 11 g4 a5 12 ♘g3 b4 13 ♘ce2 d5 again gives Black good counterplay, Kuczynski–Jansa, Warsaw 1987. Since White's whole strategy is built on restraint, it is inconsistent to allow Black to expand on the queenside.

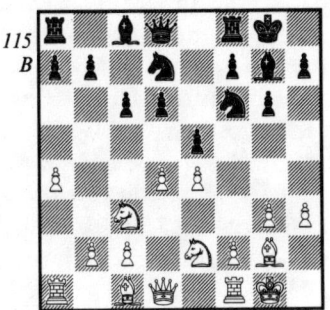
115
B

9 ... a5

It is not clear whether this precaution is necessary. White's a5 is not a very strong threat, but it does improve White's position on the queenside and even if Black delays ... a5 he usually finds it necessary sooner or later. The alternatives are:

(1) **9 ... ♖e8** and now:
(1a) **10 ♗e3** ed (10 ... d5 11 ed cd 12 de ♘xe5 13 ♗g5 ♗e6 14 ♘f4 d4 15 ♘cd5 ♗xd5 16 ♘xd5 ♘c6 17 b4 h6 18 ♗xf6 ♗xf6 19 b5 ♘a5 20 ♘xf6+ ♕xf6 21 ♕d2 picking up the h-pawn, Machulsky–Karasev, USSR 1st league 1977) 11 ♗xd4 ♕e7 (11 ... ♘f8 12 ♗e3 ♘e6 13 g4 h5?! 14 g5 ♘h7 15 h4! 16 f4 fg 17 hg ♘ef8 18 ♕d2 ♕e7 19 ♖ae1 ♗g4 20 ♘d4 with clear advantage, Sveshnikov–Tseshkovsky, Sochi 1976, or 11 ... ♘b6 12 b3 ♕e7 13 g4 ♘bd7 14 ♘g3 c5 15 ♗e3 d5 16 ed ♘xg4 17 ♗d2 ♗xc3 18 ♗xc3 ♘e3 19 ♕d2 ♘xf1 20 ♖xf1 with an enormous attack for the sacrificed material, Konieczka–Zysk, Bundesliga 1986) 12 f4 b6 13 g4 ♗b7 14 ♘g3 h6 15 ♕d2 ♖ad8 16 ♖fe1 a5 17 ♖ad1 with a good game for White, Wockenfuss–Pfleger, Bundesliga 1986.

(1b) **10 ♖e1** ♕c7 11 g4 ♘b6 12 d5 ♘bd7 (after 12 ... cd White interposes both a5 and g5 before playing ♘xd5) 13 a5 ♘f8 14 ♗e3 cd 15 ed with an advantage for White, Mandl–Seyb, Bundesliga 1985.

(2) **9 ... ♕c7** 10 ♗e3 ♖e8 11 ♖e1 ♘f8 (11 ... ed 12 ♗xd4 ♘c5 13 e5 ♘fd7 14 ed ♕xd6 15 ♗xg7 gives White a favourable ending) 12 a5 ♘e6 13 d5! ♘f8 14 ♕d2 cd 15 ed ♗d7 16 ♘a4 with some advantage for White, Nunn–Pfleger, Plovdiv 1983.

(3) **9 ... b6** 10 ♗e3 ♗b7 11 g4 (11 a5!? and 11 ♕d2 are possible improvements) h5 12 g5 ♘h7 13 h4 ed 14 ♗xd4 ♘e5 15 f4 c5 16 ♗xe5 de 17 f5 ♕xd1 18 ♖axd1 ♖fd8 19 ♘d5 ½-½, Wilder–Benjamin, USA Ch. 1986.

10 ♗e3 *(116)*

10 ♗g5 ♖e8 11 ♕d2 ♕b6 (exploiting the absence of the bishop from e3) 12 ♗e3 ed 13 ♗xd4 c5 14 ♗xf6 (14 ♗e3 ♘e5 15 b3 ♗xh3 16 f4 ♗xg2 17 fe ♘xe4 wins material for Black) ♘xf6 15 ♖fd1 ♗d7! with an unclear position which is not worse for Black, Trois–Balogh, Zalaegerszeg 1980.

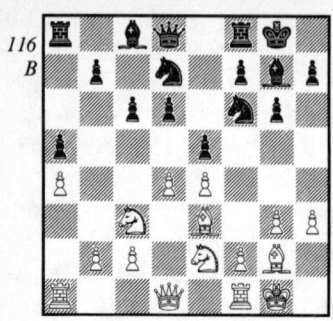

10 ... ♛e7

This is a major decision point for Black. Two other moves are possible, but since all choices fail to equalize, it is hard to recommend one rather than another:

(1) **10 ... ♖e8** 11 ♛d2 (11 ♖e1 is also good) ♘b6? (as we have noted, this move rarely turns out well; here it enables Black to play ... d5, but this fails to solve his problems; 11 ... ed 12 ♗xd4 ♘c5 was better when 13 ♗xc5 dc 14 ♛xd8 ♖xd8 15 f4 is slightly advantageous for White) 12 b3 ed 13 ♗xd4 d5 14 ed ♘bxd5 15 ♘xd5 ♘xd5 16 ♗xg7 ♔xg7 17 ♖ad1 ♗e6 18 ♘d4 ♘c7 19 ♛f4! ♛e7 20 ♖fe1 ♖ec8 (20 ... ♖ac8 21 ♛e5+ and ♛xa5) 21 ♖d3! ♛f6 22 ♛d6 ♖a6 (22 ... ♗d5 23 ♛xf6+ ♔xf6 24 ♗xd5 ♘xd5 25 c4 followed by ♖f3+ and ♖e7 wins) 23 ♖f3 ♛d8 24 ♘xe6+ ♘xe6 25 ♖xe6 fe 26 ♛e5+ ♔g8 27 ♛xe6+ ♔h8 28 ♖f7 1–0, Speelman–Nunn, British Ch. 1979.

(2) **10 ... ed** 11 ♗xd4 (11 ♘xd4 is dubious, e.g. 11 ... ♖e8 12 ♖e1 ♘c5 13 f3 ♛c7 14 ♗f2 ♗d7 15 ♛d2 ♖ad8 16 ♖ad1 ♗c8 17 ♘de2 ♛b6 and thanks to f3 White's position is much less active than usual, Barlov–Rukavina, Yugoslavia Ch. 1984) ♖e8 12 g4 (12 f4 is also possible, e.g. 12 ... ♘c5 13 ♗xc5 dc 14 e5 or 12 ... b6 13 g4 ♘c5 14 ♘g3 with a promising position in both cases) b6 13 ♘g3 ♗a6 14 ♖e1 c5 15 ♗e3 ♘e5 16 b3 with a very poor position for Black, Sveshnikov–Grigorian, USSR 1981.

11 ♖e1 ♖e8

Or 11 ... ♖d8 12 ♛d2 ed 13 ♗xd4 ♘e5 14 ♛c1! (if White plays 14 f4 as in Barlov–Hickl below then the point of Black's ... ♖d8 is revealed after 14 ... ♗xh3! 15 fe de 16 ♗xh3 ed followed by ... ♘xe4 with three pawns and an attack for the piece) ♘h5 15 f4 ♘c4 16 ♗f2 and Black is in trouble because the threat of b3 is very strong, Nunn–Hunt, Peterborough 1984.

12 ♛d2 ed

13 ♗xd4 ♘e5 14 f4 ♘c4 15 ♛c1 c5 16 ♗f2 ♗d7 17 g4 ♗c6 18 ♘g3 ♘d7 19 ♗f1 ♘cb6 20 ♛d2 ♘f8 21 ♘b5 ♘e6 22 c3 with a miserable position for Black, Barlov–Hickl, Zagreb 1987.

18 | White plays c3

In this chapter we are concerned only with the Modern move-order. It is theoretically possible to transpose into this Chapter from the Pirc by 1 e4 d6 2 d4 ♘f6 3 ♗d3 g6 4 ♘f3 etc., but in practice Black has exploited White's 3 ♗d3 with 3 ... e5!, which we cover in chapter 22. Since the same reply would meet 3 ♘d2, we can conclude that the c3 systems are only playable against the Modern. However, a transposition is certainly possible from queen's pawn openings, and this occurs quite frequently, for example 1 d4 ♘f6 2 ♘f3 g6 3 ♗g5 ♗g7 4 ♘bd2 0-0 5 c3 d6 6 e4 leads into variation B below. There are special problems of move-order associated with the 1 d4 route which we do not deal with here since they are irrelevant if the game starts 1 e4.

1 e4 g6 2 d4 ♗g7
3 c3

If White wishes to adopt line B below, which aims to play ♗g5 and delay the development of the king's bishop, then he has to play 3 c3 rather than 3 ♘f3. The reason is that 3 ♘f3 d6 4 c3 ♘f6 already forces either ♗d3 or ♘d2, both of which rule out line B. On the other hand, if White intends to play the standard line with c3, ♘f3, ♗d3 and 0-0, then 3 ♘f3 may be more accurate, because it cuts down Black's possible 3rd move deviations (for 3 ♘f3 c5, see Chapter 22).

3 ... d6 *(117)*

Or 3 ... c5 (3 ... d5 4 ♘d2 de 5 ♘xe4 is quite sensible if Black follows up by 5 ... ♘d7 and 6 ... ♘gf6, but in Torre–Barlov, Zagreb 1987 the extravagant 5 ... ♕d5 6 ♗d3 ♘c6 7 ♘e2 e5 8 0-0 f5 9 ♘d2 ♕f7 10 ♗c4 ♗e6 11 ♕b3 was very good for White; however 4 ed ♕xd5 5 ♗e2! is more dangerous for Black) and in this 2 c3 Sicilian position White may play:

(1) **4 dc** ♕c7 5 ♗e3 ♘a6 and now:
(1a) **6 ♗xa6** ba is critical, but how should White continue? 7 ♗d4 ♘f6 8 f3 ♖b8 was unclear in Stein–Lein, USSR 1960, and 7 ♘f3 ♗b7 8 ♘bd2 ♘f6 9 e5 ♘g4 10 ♗d4 ♘xe5 11 0-0 is also nothing special for White. Prob-

ably **7 ♘d2 ♘f6 8 f3 ♗b7 9 ♘e2** is best, when Black has only slight compensation for the pawn.

(1b) **6 ♘a3 ♘xc5 7 ♘b5 ♕c6 8 ♕d5 ♘e6 9 ♕xc6** (9 ♘xa7 ♗xc3+ 10 ♔d1 ♗xb2! 11 ♘xc6 bc 12 ♕b3 ♗xa1 13 ♘f3 ♗g7 14 ♗d3 ♘f6 was good for Black in Yap–Sunye, Havana 1985; 10 ♔e2 was better, when 10 ... ♕a4 11 ♘xc8 ♕c2+ 12 ♔f3 ♕xb2 is unclear according to Sunye) bc 10 ♘d4 with equality, Milos–Quinteros, Corrientes 1985.

(2) **4 ♘f3 ♕a5** (4 ... cd 5 cd d5 6 ed ♘f6 7 ♗b5+ is also slightly better for White) **5 ♘bd2 cd** and now the safest way to gain a small advantage is 6 ♘b3 and 7 cd, but 6 b4!? is also possible.

We consider four lines in this chapter:

A: **4 f4**
B: **4 ♗g5**
C: **4 ♘f3 ♘f6 5 ♘bd2**
D: **4 ♘f3 ♘f6 5 ♗d3**

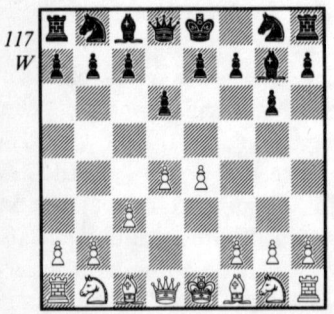
117
W

In A White intends e5 to smother the bishop on g7 with a chain of pawns on the diagonal. Although popular several years ago this line is now rarely seen, a shift due more to fashion than to the discovery of a clear-cut equalizing line for Black.

Lines B, C and D represent a quieter approach by White. He intends castling and completing his development before undertaking active operations in the centre. The point of line B is to delay the development of the king's bishop, in order that it can move to c4 or b5 without loss of time. The negative side is that White is immediately committed to playing ♘d2.

In line C we deal with the development of the bishop to e2. These ultra-solid variations promise White very little and are only really useful if you are playing for a draw or are facing an opponent who will be trying to win. D represents the current treatment. White intends ♗d3 and ♗g5, posting both bishops on reasonably active squares, and only then ♘bd2 or ♘a3. Black must defend accurately or else White gets a nagging positional edge, but in the main line Black faces few problems.

A

4 f4   ♘f6

4 ... e5 is dubious since both 5 de de 6 ♕xd8+ ♔xd8 7 fe ♘c6 8 ♗g5+ ♔e8 9 ♘a3 ♗d7 10 ♘f3 ♘xe5 11 ♗f4, Ree–Hartoch, Bad Pyrmont 1969 and 5 de ♕h4+ 6

g3 ♕e7 7 ed ♕xe4+ 8 ♕e2 ♕xe2+ 9 ♘xe2 cd 10 ♘a3 ♗e6 (10 ... ♗d7 11 ♗g2 ♗c6 12 0-0 is also good for White) 11 ♘b5 ♚d7 12 f5! gf 13 ♗f4, Portisch–Suttles, Siegen Ol. 1970 are dreadful for Black.

5 ♗d3

The other move is 5 e5 and now:

(1) **5 ... ♘d5** 6 ♘f3 0-0 7 ♗d3 (7 ♗c4 c6 8 0-0 de fe f6 10 ♘bd2 ♗d7 11 ef ef 12 ♘e4 ♚h8 13 ♗b3 ♘7b6 14 c4 ♘e7 was satisfactory for Black in Stefanov–Grunberg, Romania Ch. 1977) de (not 7 ... c5 8 0-0 ♘c6 9 ♗e4 de 10 de ♘b6 11 ♘a3 ♗e6 12 ♕e2 ♕c8 13 ♕b5 ♘b8 14 ♗e3 ♘a6 15 ♖ad1 with advantage to White, D. Gurevich–Benjamin, USA Ch. 1986) 8 de c6 9 ♘a3 ♘d7 10 ♗e4 ♘c5 11 ♗xd5 cd 12 0-0 b6 13 ♗e3 ♗a6 =, King–Davies, Bundesliga 1986.

(2) **5 ... de** (it is better to take on e5 at a moment when White must recapture with the f-pawn) 6 fe ♘d5 7 ♘f3 0-0 8 ♗c4 c5! (this active move gives Black a very comfortable game) 9 0-0 (9 dc ♗e6 10 ♘g5 ♘c6! is good for Black) cd 10 cd ♘c6 11 ♘c3 ♗e6 12 ♗b3 ♘a5 13 ♘g5 ♘xc3! 14 bc ♗d5 15 e6 (typical Tal, but 15 ♖b1 ∓ was safer) ♘xb3 16 ef+ ♖xf7! 17 ♗xf7 ♕a5! with advantage to Black, Tal–Vadasz, Tallinn 1977.

5 ... e5

Better than 5 ... 0-0 6 ♘f3 ♘bd7 (6 ... c5 7 dc dc 8 e5 ♘d5 9 ♗e4 ♘b6 10 ♕e2 ♘c6 11 0-0 f6 12 ♘bd2 ♕c7 13 a4 was good for White in Qi–Balashov, Taxco 1985) 7 e5 ♘g4 8 ♘g5! ♘b6 9 0-0 f6 10 ♘xh7 ♚xh7 11 f5 fe 12 ♕xg4 gf 13 ♕h5+ ♚g8 14 ♗h6 ♗xh6 15 ♕xh6 ♖f6 16 ♕g5+ ♚f7 17 ♘d2 ♕d7 1–0, Herzog–Wedberg, 1982.

6 ♘f3 *(118)*

6 fe de 7 de ♘g4 (7 ... ♘xe4?? 8 ♕a4+) is slightly better for Black.

After 6 ♘f3 Black has tried a range of moves, but practical experience is limited. We give a short selection:

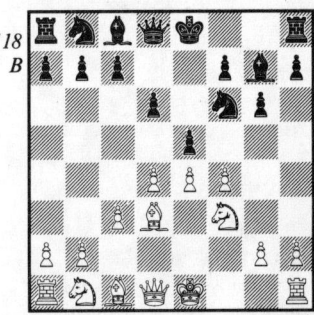
118 B

(a) **6 ... ed** 7 cd 0-0 8 ♘c3 ♘c6 9 0-0 ♗g4 (9 ... ♘h5 10 ♗e3 ♖e8 11 ♕d2 ♗g4 12 d5 ♘b4 13 ♗b1 ♗xf3 14 ♖xf3 c6 15 a3 ♘a6 16 dc bc 17 ♗a2 with a distinct plus for White, Portisch–Bilek, Hungary 1978) 10 ♗e3 ♘d7 (10 ... ♖e8 looks better) 11 ♗e2! ♘b6 12 ♖c1 ♖e8 13 h3 ♗xf3 14 ♗xf3 f5 15 e5 and White stands well,

Kapengut–Zhidkov, USSR 1974.
(b) **6...♗g4** 7 fe de 8 ♗g5 h6 (8 ...♘bd7 9 ♘bd2 h6 10 ♗h4 g5 11 ♗f2 0-0 12 h3 ♗h5 13 d5 favoured White in Spassky–Suttles, Vancouver 1971) 9 ♗h4 g5 10 ♗f2 ed 11 cd ♘c6 12 ♘bd2 ♘h5 13 ♗b5 ♘f4 14 0-0 0-0 15 ♕a4 gave White a small advantage in Spassky–Olafsson, Moscow 1971.

(c) **6...♘c6** (perhaps the soundest move, although one should note that 6...ef 7 ♗xf4 0-0 8 0-0 c5 and 6...♘h5 7 fe de 8 ♗g5 f6 are also possible for Black) 7 0-0 (7 d5 ♘b8 is not dangerous as 8 fe de 9 ♘xe5 fails to 9...♘xe4) 0-0 8 fe de 9 d5 ♘e7 10 c4 (10 ♘xe5 leads to the forced sequence 10...♘fxd5 11 ♘xf7 ♖xf7 12 ♖xf7 ♔xf7 13 ed ♕xd5 14 ♕f1+ ♔e8! when Pribyl assesses the position as equal – certainly Black's active pieces make it hard for White to exploit the position of the Black king) c6 11 ♘c3 ♘e8 (11...cd 12 cd ♘e8 = is Boleslavsky's analysis) 12 ♕b3?! (12 ♗e3) f5!? 13 ♘g5 ♔h8! 14 c5 h6 with complications favouring Black, Poloch–Pribyl, Czechoslovakia 1977.

B

4 ♗g5 ♘f6

Not 4...c5 5 dc dc 6 ♕xd8+ ♔xd8 7 ♘a3! ♔h6 8 ♗h4 ♗e6 9 f3 ♘f6 10 ♗f2 ♘bd7 11 h4 a6 12 g4 ♘e8 13 ♘h3 with a favourable ending for White, Petrosian–Bouaziz, Las Palmas 1982.

5 ♘d2 0-0

Or:

(1) **5...♘c6** 6 ♘gf3 h6 7 ♗h4 g5 8 ♗g3 ♘h5 9 ♗c4 (weakening the dark squares by 9 d5 must be wrong and after 9...♘b8 10 ♘d4 ♘xg3 11 hg c5 12 ♗b5+? ♔f8 13 ♘c2 ♕b6 14 a4 a6 White was losing a pawn or two in Westerinen–Hickl, Altensteig 1987) e6 10 ♕c2 ♕e7 11 0-0-0 ♘xg3 12 hg ♗d7 13 ♖he1 g4 14 ♘h2 h5 15 ♔b1, Barbero–Davies, Budapest 1987, and now instead of the extraordinary 15...♖b8 Black should have played 15...0-0-0 =.

(2) **5...h6** 6 ♗h4 e5 7 de (7 **f4** ♘bd7 8 ♘gf3 ♕e7 9 fe de 10 ♗d3 g5 11 ♗f2 0-0 12 ♕e2 ed 13 cd c5 14 e5 ♘g4 15 ♕e4 f5 with a very sharp position which is probably good for Black, Kavalek–Dzindzihashvili, New York 1984; after **7 ♘gf3** ♕e7 8 ♗d3 0-0 9 0-0 ♘bd7 10 ♖e1 ♖d8 11 ♗f1 ♘f8 White had an edge in Cifuentes–Ftacnik, Dubai 1986, but 7...ed 8 cd g5 9 ♗g3 0-0 10 ♗d3 ♘h5 is unclear) de 8 ♘gf3 ♘bd7 9 ♗e2 0-0 10 0-0 ♕e8 11 ♕c2 ♘h5 12 ♖fe1 ♘f4 (I can't see any advantage for White after 12...♗f6!) 13 ♗f1 ♘b6 14 a4 a5 15 ♘c4 and White has an edge, Vladimirov–Ivkov, Havana 1986.

The above two lines suggest that Black should try exploiting

White's slightly odd move-order. By delaying ♘f3 White has made it easier for Black to play ... e5 and variation 2 above is the best way to make use of this.

6 ♘gf3 *(119)*

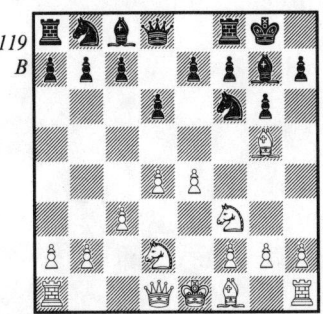

It turns out that by delaying the development of the f1 bishop, Black's defence is made more difficult. After **6 ... h6** 7 ♗h4 ♘c6 8 ♗b5! ♗d7 (8 ... a6 9 ♗xc6 bc 10 0-0 is also ±) 9 0-0 a6 10 ♗c4 White's bishop occupies a more active square than usual and in Smyslov–Nunn, Tilburg 1982 the continuation 10 ... e5 11 de de 12 ♖e1 ♕e8 13 a4 ♘h5 14 ♘b3! left Black in trouble because keeping the knight out of c5 by ... b6 leaves the a6 pawn weak. **6 ... c6** 7 a4 h6 8 ♗h4 ♕c7 9 ♕c2 e5 10 de de 11 ♗c4 ♘h5 12 0-0 a5 13 ♖fd1 ♘a6 14 ♘e1! was similarly good for White in Ermenkov–Todorcevic, Prokuplje 1987. If Black wants to return to more or less normal lines, then **6 ... ♕e8** is probably his best bet, since White has no better reply than 7 ♗d3, when Black can safely play 7 ... ♘c6 without having to worry about ♗b5. On the whole, though, Black is probably better off trying one of the lines given in the note to Black's 5th move.

C

4	♘f3	♘f6
5	♘bd2	0-0
6	♗e2 *(120)*	

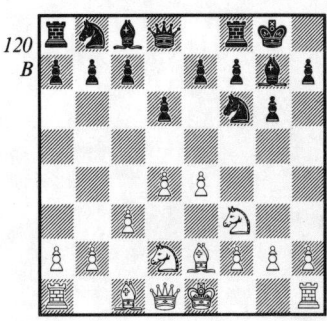

6 ...   ♘c6

Safest, but other moves are possible:

(a) **6 ... c5** 7 dc dc 8 0-0 ♘c6 9 ♕c2 b6 (9 ... ♕c7 10 ♖e1 ♖d8 11 a4 ♘g4 12 ♘f1 ♘ge5, Wockenfuss–Vogel, Bundesliga 1987, and now 13 ♘3d2 intending f4 would have been ±) 10 ♘c4 ♗b7 11 a4 ♕c7 12 ♖e1 ♘a5 (12 ... ♖ad8 13 ♗f1 transposes to Hodes–Kuznetsov, USSR 1978, which continued 13 ... ♘g4 14 a5 ♘ce5 15 ♘fxe5 ♘xe5 16 ab ab 17 ♕b3 and White was better) 13 ♗f1 ♘xc4 14 ♗xc4 ♘g4 15 a5 with an edge, Petrosian–Mecking, Palma de Mallorca 1969.

(b) **6 ... b6** 7 0-0 ♗b7 (or 7 ... e6 8 ♖e1 ♗b7 9 ♗f1 ♘bd7 10 a4 c5 11 b4 ♕c7 12 a5 ♖d8 13 ♕b3 cd 14 cd ba 15 ba with an edge for White, Wockenfuss–Nunn, Bundesliga 1986) 8 ♕c2 (8 e5!?) c5 (in Velimirovic–Nunn, Moscow 1977, Black prevented the advance e5–e6 by 8 ... e6, but 9 a4 c5 10 a5! ba? 11 dc d5 12 ed ♕xd5 13 ♘b3 ♘bd7 14 ♖d1 ♕e4 15 ♗d3 ♕g4 16 h3 ♕h5 17 ♘g5 1–0 was unpleasant) 9 a4 ♕c8 10 a5 cd 11 ♘xd4 ♘a6 12 ♖d1 ♘c5 13 f3 ba 14 ♖xa5 and White is a little better, Maric–Hulak, Bor 1977.

(c) **6 ... ♗g4** 7 0-0 ♘bd7 8 h3 ♗xf3 9 ♗xf3 c6 10 ♖e1 ♕c7 11 a4 ♖fe8 12 ♘c4 ♖ad8 13 ♗f4! e5 14 ♗g3 h5 15 a5 ♗h6 16 ♕b3 was slightly better for White in Andersson–Hort, Tilburg 1980.

7 0-0 e5

All lines lead to equality. There is a strong argument for delaying this move, first of all because White has no threat and secondly because Black would prefer to recapture with a piece, e.g. 7 ... ♖e8 (7 ... ♘d7 is also very sensible, so as to end up with a knight on e5 after a later dxe5) 8 b4 (8 ♖e1 e5 9 de ♘xe5 10 ♘xe5 ♖xe5 =) a6 (8 ... e5 is unclear after 9 b5 ed 10 cd ♘b8, but not 9 ... ♘b8 10 de de 11 ♗c4 ♗e6 12 ♗xe6 ♖xe6 13 ♘g5 ♖e7 14 ♗a3 ♖d7 15 ♕b3 with powerful threats, Dely–Hazai, Zalaegerszeg 1977) 9 ♗b2 d5!? 10 e5 ♘h5 with equality, Kostic–Nunn, Lugano 1982.

8 de ♘xe5

9 ♘xe5 de 10 ♕c2 ♗e6 (Fuchs–Matulovic, Kapfenberg 1970, continued 10 ... ♗h6 11 ♖d1 ♕e7 12 ♘c4 ♗xc1 13 ♖axc1 b6 and Black has equalized) 11 ♘f3 ♘e8 (11 ... ♘d7 12 ♘g5 ♕e7 13 ♖d1 ♖fd8 14 ♗e3 ♘f8 15 ♘xe6 ♘xe6 16 ♕b3 b6 17 ♗c4 left White with a slight plus which Larsen converted into a win in Larsen–Quinteros, Las Palmas 1974) 12 ♘g5 ♗d7 13 f4 (highly anti-positional, but White obtains some tactical chances against f7) ♕e7 14 fe ♕xe5?! (14 ... ♗xe5 =) 15 ♗f4 ♕c5+ 16 ♔h1 h6? 17 ♘xf7! ♖xf7 18 ♕b3 and Black is in trouble, Fuller–Richardson, Guernsey 1976.

D

4 ♘f3 ♘f6
5 ♗d3 0-0
6 0-0

Or 6 ♘bd2 ♘c6 7 0-0 (other moves are not dangerous, e.g. 7 b4 e5 8 de ♘xe5 9 ♘xe5 de 10 ♘c4 ♗e6 =, or 7 h3 e5 =) e5 (if Black wants to delay ... e5, then 7 ... ♘d7 is the correct approach since 7 ... ♖e8 8 ♘c4 ♘d7 9 b4! a6 10 a4 e5 11 ♗g5 ♗f6 12 ♗xf6 ♕xf6 13 d5 ♘e7 14 a5 ♕g7 15 ♘e3 gave White some advantage in Ljubojevic–Keene, Rovinj–Zagreb 1975) 8 de de 9 ♘c4 ♕e7 10 b4 ♖d8 11 b5 ♗e6 12 ♗a3

♕e8 13 ♕c2 ♗xc4 14 ♗xc4 ♘a5 15 ♗e2 b6 and White retains a slight advantage, Knezevic–Tal, Leningrad 1977. I suspect that 7 ... ♘d7 is best in this variation, when Black should equalize.

    6 ...   **♘c6** *(121)*

Once again Black prepares ... e5 in the most straightforward manner. Alternatives are:

(1) **6 ... ♘bd7** 7 ♗g5 (7 ♖e1 e5 8 h3 ♖e8 9 ♗g5 h6 10 ♗h4 a6 11 a4 b6 12 ♘bd2 ♗b7 13 b4 ♕c8 14 ♕b3 with a space advantage for White, Panno–Larsen, Buenos Aires 1983; there is a strong argument for 8 ... h6 by analogy with the 7 h3 line in the main variation) h6 8 ♗h4 e5 (8 ... g5 9 ♗g3 ♘h5 10 ♘a3 e5 11 de de 12 ♖e1 ♘f4 13 ♗f1 ♕e7 14 ♘c4 ♖d8 15 ♕c2 ♘f8 16 ♘e3 ♘8g6 17 ♘d2 c6 18 ♘dc4 ±, Seirawan–Nunn, Baden 1980) 9 ♘bd2 ♕e8 10 ♖e1 ♘h5 11 ♗f1 ♘b6 (11 ... f5 fails to 12 ef gf 13 de de 14 ♘xe5 ♘xe5 15 ♘c4) 12 a4 a5 13 ♘c4 ♘xc4 14 ♗xc4 ♘f4 15 ♗g3 with a small advantage for White, Plachetka–Ftacnik, CSSR Ch. 1986.

(2) **6 ... ♘h5** 7 ♖e1 e5 8 de de 9 ♗g5 ♕e8 (9 ... f6!? may be possible, e.g. 10 ♗c4+ ♔h8 11 ♕xd8 ♖xd8 12 ♘xe5 ♗f8!) 10 ♘a3 ♗e6 11 ♗e3 f6 12 ♗c4 ♗xc4 13 ♘xc4 ♕f7 14 ♕b3 and White, with his superior bishop, is slightly better, O. Rodriguez–Keene, Barcelona 1980.

(3) **6 ... c5** (this leads to a completely different type of position) 7 dc (7 h3 cd 8 cd ♘c6 9 ♘c3 e5 10 de de 11 ♗e3 ♕e7 12 ♖c1 ♖d8 13 ♕e2 ♗e6 should not pose any real problems for Black, Lobron–Davies, Bundesliga 1985) dc 8 h3 ♘c6 (according to Korchnoi, Black should prevent the development of the c1 bishop to the h2–b8 diagonal, so 8 ... ♕c7 is correct) 9 ♕e2 (9 ♗f4!) ♕c7 10 ♖e1 ♘d7 11 ♗c2 b6 12 a4 ♗b7 with an equal position, Korchnoi–Nunn, Brussels 1986.

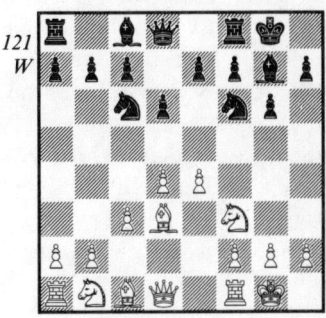

121
W

    7   **♗g5**

Or:

(1) **7 d5** ♘b8 8 c4 ♗g4 (8 ... e6 9 de ♗xe6 10 ♘c3 ♘a6 11 ♖e1 ♘c5 12 ♗f1 gave White a persistent edge in Barczay–Pribyl, Decin 1978) 9 h3 ♗xf3 10 ♕xf3 ♘a6 11 ♘c3 ♘d7 with an unclear position. Korchnoi–Sznapik, Lucerne 1982 continued 12 ♗e2?! ♘ac5 13 ♗d2 a5 14 ♖ab1 e6 15 ♗d1 f5! ∓.

(2) **7 b4** a6 (7 ... e5 loses a pawn after b5) 8 ♘bd2 e5 (8 ... ♖e8 9 a4 e5 10 d5 ♘e7 11 c4 ♘g4 12 h3

♘h6 13 c5 is very good for White, Commons–Ermenkov, Primorsko 1976, but 8 ... ♘d7!? is worth a try) 9 de ♘h5 10 ♘c4 de (10 ... ♗g4!?) 11 ♘e3 ♘f4 12 ♗c4, Augustin–Ftacnik, Stary Smokovec 1976, and now 12 ... ♗e6 is unclear.

(3) **7 h3** e5 8 ♖e1 (8 ♗e3 ed?! 9 cd ♘b4 10 ♘c3 ♘xd3 11 ♕xd3 ♖e8 12 ♖e1 c6 13 ♗f4 d5 14 ed ♖xe1+ 15 ♖xe1 ♗f5 16 ♕c4 ♘xd5 17 ♘xd5 cd gave White an edge in Yudasin–Azmaiparashvili, USSR 1983, while 8 de ♘xe5 9 ♘xe5 de 10 ♗g5 should be met by 10 ... h6 rather than 10 ... ♕e8 11 ♕f3 ♕c6 12 ♘a3 b6 13 ♗b5 ♕e6 14 ♗c4 ♕e7 15 ♗d5 with advantage to White, Zysk–Dresen, Bundesliga 1987) and now:

(3a) **8 ... ♗d7** 9 ♗e3 ed (the same dubious idea as in Yudasin–Azmaiparashvili above; 9 ... ♘h5 is better) 10 cd ♘b4 11 ♘c3 ♘xd3 12 ♕xd3 ♖e8 13 e5 ♗f5 14 ♕b5 is good for White, Dolmatov–Eingorn, USSR 1983.

(3b) **8 ... ♘h5** 9 ♗g5 ♕e8 10 ♗b5 ♗d7 11 de de 12 ♘a3 a6 13 ♗f1 ♘f4 14 ♕c1 ♘e6 15 ♗h6 f6 16 ♗xg7 ♔xg7 17 ♘c4 ♘cd8 18 ♘e3 with equality, Bastian–Ingenerf, Bundesliga 1985.

(3c) **8 ... ♖e8** 9 a3 (according to Dolmatov 9 d5 is good for White) h6 10 ♗c2 ♘h5 11 b4 ♕f6 12 d5 ♘e7 13 c4 ♘f4 14 ♘c3 a6 15 ♗xf4 ♕xf4 16 c5 h5 17 ♘a4 ♗h6

18 cd cd 19 ♘b6 ♖b8 20 ♗a4 ♖f8 21 ♖a2 with advantage to White, Karlsson–Jansa, Oslo 1988. The Swedish grandmaster's play was very original in this game; perhaps 10 ... a5, taking steps to prevent White's queenside expansion, was more appropriate.

(3d) **8 ... h6** 9 ♗e3 ♘h5 10 ♘bd2 ♘f4 11 ♗xf4 ef 12 b4 ♘e7 13 a3 ♗d7 14 ♘f1 b5 (14 ... c5 may be better, trying to bring the dark-squared bishop to life) 15 ♕d2 g5 16 ♕e2 a6 with an unclear position, Dolmatov–Kuzmin, USSR 1982.

7 ... h6

7 ... ♘d7 8 a4 ♕e8?! 9 ♘a3 a6 10 ♕d2 f6 11 ♗h6 e5 12 ♗xg7 ♔xg7 13 b4 ♘d8 14 a5! and White has a clear advantage on the queenside, Vaganian–Ermenkov, Salonika 1984.

8 ♗h4 *(122)*

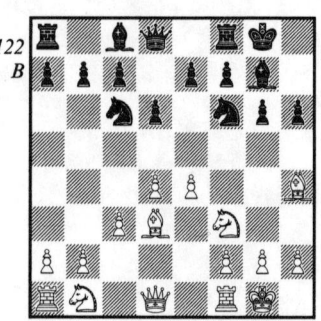

8 ... e5

Or 8 ... ♘h5 9 ♘bd2 (9 ♘a3 ♘f4 10 ♗c2 ♗g4 11 ♕d2 and now 11 ... g5 allowed a typical

Tal attack after 12 ♘xg5 hg 13 ♗xg5 ♘g6 14 f4 f6 15 f5, Tal–Hoi, Jurmala 1985, but 11 ... ♗xf3 12 ♕xf4 ♗e2 13 ♖fe1 ♗a6 14 ♕e3 g5 15 ♗g3 e5 would have been unclear according to Tal) ♘f4 (9 ... ♕e8 10 ♖e1 e5 11 de de 12 ♗f1 was equal in Thesing–Nunn, Bundesliga 1987) 10 ♗c2 ♕e8 11 ♘c4 e5 12 de ♘xe5 13 ♘fxe5 de 14 ♘e3 ♗e6 15 ♗b3 a5 16 ♘d5 ♗xd5 17 ♗xd5 g5 ½–½, Lau–Hickl, Munich 1988.

9 de

9 ♘bd2 ♕e8 10 de de 11 ♘c4 ♘h5 12 b4 ♘f4 13 b5 ♘b8 14 ♗g3 ♕xb5 15 ♘cxe5 ♘xd3 16 ♕xd3 ♕xd3 17 ♘xd3 ♘a6 18 ♗e5 ♖e8 19 ♗xg7 ♔xg7 was equal in Kalinin–McNab, Bath 1987.

After 9 de Black may recapture either way:

(1) **9 ... ♘xe5** 10 ♘xe5 de 11 ♘a3 c6 (11 ... ♕e8 12 f3 ♗e6 13 ♗f2 b6 14 ♗c4 ♗d7 15 ♗e3 ♔h7 16 ♖f2 ♗c6 17 ♖d2 a6 18 ♕f1 ♕c8 19 ♖ad1 was good for White, Bischoff–Bilek, Budapest 1985) 12 ♕f3 ♗g4 13 ♕xg4 ♘xg4 14 ♗xd8 ♖fxd8 15 ♖ad1 b6 with equality, Vaganian–Jansa, Biel 1985.

(2) **9 ... de** 10 ♘a3 ♗e6 11 ♕c2 (11 ♖e1 ♕e8 12 ♗b5 ♘d7 13 ♘c4 f6 14 ♗xc6 bc 15 ♘a5 h5 16 ♗g3 ♘b6 17 ♕e2 c5 18 b3 g5 was also fine for Black, Yusupov–Seirawan, Montpellier 1985) ♕e8 12 ♖fe1 ♘h5 13 ♘c4 ♗g4 14 ♘fd2 ♗f6 15 ♗xf6 ♘xf6 16 ♘e3 ♗e6 17 ♗c4 ♖d8 18 ♖ad1 ♕e7 with complete equality, Sharif–Ftacnik, Lyons 1988.

19 | White plays c4

After 1 e4 g6 2 d4 ♗g7 it is possible for White to play 3 c4, with the plan of setting up a King's Indian type of position by ♘c3, ♘f3, ♗e2 and 0-0. This line is of considerable theoretical importance because it can arise from a variety of move-orders starting 1 c4 or 1 d4 in addition to the Modern route. The main question is whether Black has to allow a transposition to the King's Indian or whether he can find some alternative to ... ♘f6 and preserve the individuality of the variation. Since we do not consider any of the lines of the King's Indian in this book, this chapter contains the following attempts by Black to avoid ... ♘f6.

1 e4 g6 2 d4 ♗g7 3 c4 and now:

A: 3 ... d6 4 ♘c3 ♘c6
B: 3 ... d6 4 ♘c3 e5
C: 3 ... d6 4 ♘c3 ♘d7
D: 3 ... ♘c6

A is a sharp line which exploits the omission of ... ♘f6 to create an immediate attack against d4. In the resulting complex play Black needs to play accurately, but in this case he obtains a reasonable position. In B we consider those lines with ... e5 in which Black plays ... ♘c6. The main line with de and ♕xd8+ gives White a slightly better ending, and the lack of real winning chances for Black puts many players off 4 ... e5. In line C we cover the remaining variations with ... e5, namely those in which ... ♘d7 is played. In this variation it appears that Black runs considerable risks if he persists in avoiding the transposition to the King's Indian. The problem is that White is not forced to play d5 quickly; the resulting fluid situation in the centre makes it hard for Black to cope simultaneously with two different plans by White, de and d5. Line D is a dubious and rare sideline by Black.

The variations in this chapter are often favoured by Black players aiming to avoid well-worn theoretical paths. Because there is a wide choice at each move, games tend to leave theory early on, and the resulting complex positions will suit those who like tricky middle-game situations. They are also suitable for Black players needing to avoid a draw.

There is one move-order which is not catered for in the above scheme which is well worth a mention. This is 1 e4 g6 2 d4 d6 3 c4 e5; indeed many players adopt 2 ... d6 with the aim of putting White off 3 c4. The point is that 4 de de 5 ♕xd8+ ♔xd8 is nothing to fear because the bishop on f8 is as well posted there as on g7, while compared with variation B White lacks the useful ♘c3. Therefore White's options are severely reduced. Moreover after 4 ♘c3 Black need not transpose by 4 ... ♗g7, but can continue 4 ... ♘c6 5 d5 ♘ce7 6 ♗d3 ♗g7 (6 ... h5? is too risky, e.g. 7 f4 ♗g7 8 ♘f3 ef 9 ♗xf4 ♘f6, Hübner–Seirawan, Tilburg 1983, and now 10 0-0 0-0 11 h3 would have been good for White) and White is committed to the unusual ♗d3, or even 4 ... ed 5 ♕xd4 ♘f6 6 ♗g5 ♘bd7 7 f3 ♗g7 8 ♕d2 0-0 9 ♘h3 ♘e5 10 f4 ♘eg4 with unclear play, Mestel–McNab, Bath 1987.

| 3 | ... | d6 |
| 4 | ♘c3 | ♘c6 *(123)* |

A logical attempt to step up the pressure on d4 at the first opportunity. There is an immediate divergence:

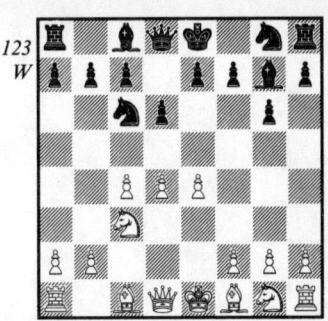

A1: 5 d5
A2: 5 ♗e3

Line A1 is a sharp attempt to refute Black's idea. Play is complex and accuracy is demanded of both players, but no clear verdict can be given since the key line leads to a highly obscure situation. A2 leads to King's Indian type positions and the main line, in which Black plays an early ... f5, appears good for White. However there are interesting deviations for Black earlier, so 4 ... ♘c6 is playable.

A1

| | 5 | d5 |

Play now becomes distinctly tactical and revolves around Black's attempts to maintain the knight on d4.

| | 5 | ... | ♘d4 |

5 ... ♘e5 has been met by 6 h3 c6 7 ♗e3 and now both 7 ... ♕a5 8 ♖c1 ♘f6 9 ♕d2 0-0 10 ♗e2 b5 11 cb cb 12 a3 b4 13 ♘a2 ♘xe4 14 ♕xb4 ♕xd5 15 ♘c3 ♘xc3 0–1, Iclicki–Jadoul, Brussels 1985, and

7 ... ♘f6 8 f4 ♘ed7 9 ♘f3? ♘h5! 10 ♔f2? ♘xf4! 11 ♗xf4 ♕b6+ 12 ♔g3 ♕xb2, Pergericht–van der Wiel, Brussels 1985, were practical successes for Black. However, the obvious 6 f4 ♘d7 7 ♘f3 is good for White.

6 ♗e3

6 ♘ge2 c5 (6 ... ♘xe2 7 ♗xe2 ♘f6 ± is playable, but it is an admission of defeat to give up the outpost at d4 without a fight) 7 ♘xd4 cd 8 ♘b5 ♕b6 9 c5! dc (not 9 ... ♕xc5 10 ♗d2 ♕b6 11 ♕a4 ♗d7 12 ♗a5 ♕a6 13 ♕b4) 10 ♗f4 ♔f8 11 ♖c1 (11 b4? d3! 12 ♗xd3 ♕f6 13 ♘c7 ♕xf4 14 ♘xa8 ♗c3+ was very good for Black in Alexandria–Chiburdanidze, USSR 1982, while 11 ♗c7 ♕f6 12 a4 ♗d7 13 ♖c1 a6 14 ♘a3 ♖c8 15 ♖xc5 d3 is unclear according to Cardon) a6 12 ♗c7 ♕f6 13 ♘a3 b5 14 ♖xc5 d3 15 ♗xd3 ♕xb2 16 ♘c2 ♘f6 with a very complicated position which eventually turned out better for White, Azmaiparashvili–Davies, Albena 1986.

6 ... c5
7 ♘ge2

7 dc ♘xc6 8 ♖c1 ♘f6 leads to a kind of Maroczy Bind position in which White's development is backward compared with the normal Sicilian positions. Black should have a satisfactory position, but in Suba–Mestel, Las Palmas 1982, White consolidated his space advantage after 9 f3 0-0 10 ♘ge2 a6 11 ♘f4 ♗d7 12 ♗e2 e5?! 13 ♘fd5 ♘xd5 14 ♘xd5 ♘d4 15 0-0 ♗e6 16 ♗d3. Black should probably try more vigorous measures, such as 10 ... ♘h5 followed by ... f5.

7 ... ♕b6 *(124)*

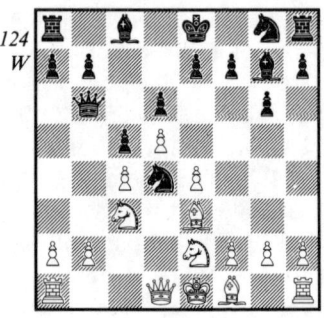

8 ♘xd4

Or:

(1) **8 ♘a4** ♕a5+ 9 ♗d2 ♕a6 (9 ... ♕c7 10 ♗c3 is good for White) 10 ♘xd4 (10 ♘ec3 ♗d7 11 ♗d3 ♘f6 12 0-0 0-0 13 a3? ♘g4 14 f4 f5! and Black stands better, Keene–Bilek, Teesside 1972) ♗xd4 and now:

(1a) **11 ♗e2** ♘f6 12 ♘c3 0-0 13 ♕c2 ♗g4 14 ♗d3 ♗d7 15 0-0 with some advantage for White as Black's only active plan, ... f5, is very risky, Uhlmann–Timman, Amsterdam 1975.

(1b) **11 ♕c2** ♗d7 12 ♘c3 ♕b6 13 ♖b1 f5 14 ♗d3 fe 15 ♘xe4 ♘f6 16 ♘g5 (16 ♘xf6+ would have been clearly better for White according to Sosonko) ♘g4 17

0-0 ♘e5 with just an edge for White, Sosonko–Chandler, Indonesia 1982.

(1c) **11 ♘c3** ♗d7 (11 ... ♕b6 12 ♘b5 ♗xb2 13 ♖b1 ♗g7 14 ♕a4 ♔f8 15 ♗a5 ♕a6 16 ♕a3! b6 17 ♘c7 ♕xa5+ 18 ♕xa5 ba, Polugaevsky–Ljubojevic, Reykjavik 1987, and now 19 ♔d2! would have been good for White) 12 ♗d3 ♘f6 13 0-0 0-0 14 h3 ♕b6 15 ♖b1 ±, Tisdall–Johansson, Malmo 1986/7.

(2) **8 ♕d2** and now:

(2a) **8 ... ♗g4?** 9 f3 ♗xf3 10 ♘a4 ♕a6 11 ♘xd4 cd 12 ♗xd4 ♗xd4 13 ♕xd4 ♘f6 14 c5 ♕a5+ 15 ♘c3 dc 16 ♕e5! ♗g4 17 d6 0-0-0 (17 ... ♔f8 18 ♗c4 1-0, Filutowski–Dilt, corr. 1975) 18 de ♖d4 19 ♕xf6 and White wins, Timman–Suttles, Hastings 1973/4.

(2b) **8 ... f5** 9 0-0-0 ♘xe2+ 10 ♗xe2 ♘f6 11 ef ♗xf5 12 ♗h6 ♗xh6 13 ♕xh6 0-0-0 14 ♖he1 ♖hf8 and now 15 ♗f1 retains a plus for White. Ivkov–Hübner, West Germany 1975, continued 15 ♗f3? ♕a6! and White's c-pawn caused problems.

(2c) **8 ... ♘f6** *(125)* with a further branch:

(2c1) **9 ♘xd4** cd 10 ♗xd4 (10 ♕xd4 ♕xb2 11 ♘b5 ♕b4+ 12 ♗d2 ♕a4 13 ♘c7+ ♔d8 14 ♘xa8 ♘h5 15 ♕d3 ♗xa1 and the stranded knight is a serious problem for White) ♘xe4 11 ♗xb6 ♘xd2 12 ♘b5 (12 ♔xd2 ab is

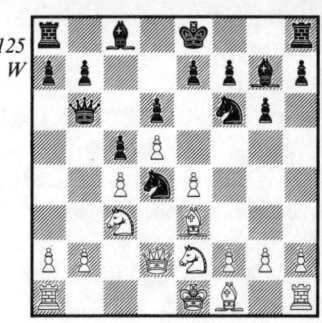

125
W

more solid, but Black's excellent bishop compensates for his doubled pawns) ab 13 ♘c7+ ♔d8 14 ♘xa8 ♗xb2 15 ♖d1 ♘e4 16 ♗d3 ♘c5 17 ♘xb6 ♗g4 18 f3 ♗xf3 19 gf ♗c3+ 20 ♔e2 ♔c7 and with one pawn and a tremendous black-squared grip for the exchange Black is not worse, Farago–Keene, Esbjerg 1981.

(2c2) **9 f3** ♗d7 10 ♘a4 ♕a6 11 ♘xd4 ♕xa4 12 ♘b5 0-0 13 ♗h6 ♗xh6 14 ♕xh6 a6 (or 14 ... ♕b4+ exchanging queens with equality) 15 ♘c3 ♕b4 16 ♕d2 f5 and Black has equalized, Donner–Timman, Wijk aan Zee 1974.

(2c3) **9 h3** 0-0 10 ♖d1 (10 0-0-0 ♘xe2+ 11 ♗xe2 ♕a5 followed by ... b5 is asking for trouble) e5 11 de ♘xe6 12 g3 ♗d7 13 ♗g2 ♗c6 gives an unclear King's Indian style battle between active pieces and a backward d-pawn, Bohm-van der Wiel, Netherlands Ch. 1982.

8 ... cd
9 ♘a4 ♕a5+

The queen sacrifice 9 ... de 10

♘xb6 ef+ 11 ♔xf2 ab is doubtful because White can happily leave his a1 rook en prise to Black's bishop: 12 ♕d2 (12 ♕c2 ♗d4+ 13 ♔e1 ♘f6 14 ♗e2 0-0 15 ♖d1 ♗e5 16 a4 h5 was unclear in Agdestein-Keene, Gausdal 1983) ♘f6 13 ♗d3 ♘g4+ 14 ♔e2 0-0 15 h3 ♘e5 16 b3! (intending a4 followed by ♖af1) f5 17 a4 ♘xd3 18 ♕xd3 fe 19 ♕e3! with a clear plus for White, Miles-Rohde, London 1984.

10 ♗d2

10 b4 ♕xb4+ 11 ♗d2 ♕a3 12 ♗c1 is a draw by repetition, Keene-Suttles, Hastings 1973/4, and Bilek-Davies, Budapest 1987.

10 ...   ♕c7

11 c5 (11 ♗d3 ♘f6 12 b4 ♘g4 13 ♖c1 0-0 14 0-0 ♘e5 15 ♘b2 a5 16 ♗b1 ab 17 ♗xb4 b6 18 a3 ♘d7 19 f4 ♘c5 was unclear in Korchnoi-Speelman, Beersheva 1987) ♘f6 (11 ... dc 12 ♗b5+ ♗d7 13 ♗xd7+ ♕xd7 14 ♘xc5 ♕b5 15 b4 ♘f6 16 a4 ♕b6 17 0-0 was good for White in Seirawan-Keene, Netherlands 1982) 12 ♗b5+ ♗d7 13 c6 bc 14 dc ♗e6 15 ♕c2 0-0 16 0-0 d5 with a very double-edged position, Danailov-Harkov, Bulgaria 1984.

A2

5   ♗e3   e5

Or 5 ... ♘f6 (5 ... f5 6 ef ♗xf5 7 ♘f3 ♘f6 8 d5 ♘e5 9 ♘xe5 de 10 ♗e2 0-0 11 0-0 is a disaster for Black, Tarjan-Cuartas, Ecuador 1976, while after 5 ... ♘h6 6 d5 ♘e5 7 h3 f5 8 ♕d2 ♘ef7 9 f4 e5 10 fe ♗xe5 11 0-0-0 ♗g7 12 ♘f3 0-0 13 ♗d4 a6 14 ♗xg7 ♔xg7 15 ef ♘xf5 16 ♖e1 ♘g3 17 ♖g1 ♕f8 18 ♘e2 White's knights are heading for e6, Cramling-Bilek, Boras 1986) 6 d5 (6 f3 is a Sämisch King's Indian and 6 ♗e2 e5 7 d5 ♘d4 8 ♗xd4 ed 9 ♕xd4 0-0 10 ♕d3 ♖e8 11 ♘f3 ♘d7 gave Black adequate play for the pawn in Ligterink-Keene, Netherlands 1981) ♘e5 7 f4 (7 h3 is a waste of time, but 7 ... c6 8 f4 ♘ed7 9 ♗d3 ♕a5 10 ♘e2 ♘c5 11 0-0 ♘xd3 12 ♕xd3 cd 13 cd 0-0 14 a3 ♗d7 was still marginally better for White in Partos-Bischoff, Mitropa Cup 1982) ♘ed7 8 ♘f3 0-0 9 ♗e2 e6 10 de fe 11 ♘g5 ♕e7 12 0-0 with some advantage for White, Tal-Christiansen, Wijk aan Zee 1982.

6   d5   ♘ce7

6 ... ♘d4 7 ♘ge2 ♘xe2 8 ♗xe2 f5 9 ef gf 10 f4 ♘e7 11 fe de 12 ♗g5 ♕d7 13 c5 0-0 14 ♕b3 ♔h8 15 0-0-0 was good for White in Korchnoi-Bohm, Netherlands Ch. 1977.

7   g4   (126)

Or 7 c5 f5 8 cd (or 8 ♗b5+ ♔f8 9 f3 ♗h6 and now both 10 ♗f2 ♘f6 11 h3 ♔g7 12 ♘ge2, Olafsson-Keene, Reykjavik 1972 and 10 ♕d2 ♔g7 11 cd cd 12 ♘ge2 a6 13 ♗d3 ♗xe3 14 ♕xe3 ♘f6 15 h3 f4 16 ♕f2 g5, Henley-Suttles, Indonesia 1982 are unclear) cd 9 ♗b5+ (9 ♕a4+ ♗d7 10 ♘b5 ♚f8 11 ♕b3 ♗xb5 12 ♗xb5 fe 13 ♘h3 a6 14 ♗c4 b5 15 ♗e2 h6 16 0-0 ♘f6 17 a4 ♘exd5 18 ab ab 19 ♖ad1 ♘xe3 20 fe ♚e7 21 ♘f2 ♖f8 22 ♘g4 ♕b6? 23 ♘xe5! de 24 ♕b4+ ♚f7 25 ♗c4+ 1–0 was Makarov-Rasin, Leningrad Ch. 1977) ♗d7 (9 ... ♚f8 10 f3 ♗h6 11 ♗xh6+ ♘xh6 12 ♕d2 ♘f7, Koraksic-Ivkov, Zemun 1980, and now 13 f4 would have been good for White) 10 ♗xd7+ ♕xd7 11 f3 ♘f6 12 ♘h3 h6 (12 ... fe 13 fe ♘g4 14 ♕f3 ♖f8 15 ♕g3 ♘xe3 16 ♕xe3 ♘g8 would have been unclear according to Petrosian) 13 ♘f2 0-0 14 ♕a4! with a clear plus for White, Petrosian-Ivkov, Bugojno 1982.

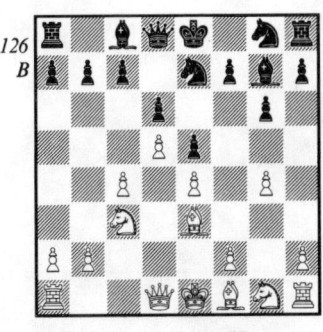

126
B

7 ... f5

White can maintain an advantage after this, so Black should explore one of the alternatives:
(1) **7 ... ♘f6** 8 f3 (8 g5 ♘d7 9 h4 h5 is also unclear) ♘d7 (8 ... h5 is an untested possibility) 9 h4 f5 10 h5 h6 11 gf gf 12 ♕d2 ♘f6 13 0-0-0 f4 14 ♗f2 b6 15 ♗h4 ♘h7 with a double-edged position, Petursson-Speelman, Hastings 1986/7.
(2) **7 ... c5** 8 ♗d3 (8 h4 f5 9 gf gf 10 ♕h5+ ♚f8 11 ♗h3 ♘f6 12 ♕d1 b5! 13 ef bc 14 ♘f3 h6 15 ♖g1 ♘xf5 16 ♗xf5 ♗xf5 was good for Black, Bagirov-Davies, Cascais 1986) f5 9 f3 ♘f6 10 h3 0-0 11 ♕d2 a6 12 a3 ♗d7 13 b4 ♕c7 14 ♘ge2 ♚h8 15 ♖b1 b6 16 ♖b2 and White has the advantage, Dlugy-Barreras, Havana 1985. Black's play was too passive in this example; 9 ... ♗h6 10 g5 f4!? is more active, or 9 ... h5 as in the next note.

8 gf

8 f3 ♘f6 9 h3 h5! (9 ... 0-0 10 ♗d3 c5 11 ♘ge2 ♗d7 12 a3! fe? 13 ♘xe4 ♘xe4 14 ♗xe4 b5 15 cb ♗xb5 16 ♘c3 gave White a clear advantage in Ghitescu-Sikora, Warsaw 1979) 10 g5 ♘d7 11 h4 a5 12 ♕d2 ♘c5 13 0-0-0 b6 14 ♗e2 0-0 15 ♘h3 ♗d7 16 ♕c2 a4 17 ♘f2 ♕b8 with an unclear position, Miles-Kohlweyer, Dortmund 1986.

8 ... gf
9 ♕h5+ ♚f8

Or 9 ... ♘g6 10 ef ♕h4 *(127)* and now:
(1) **11 ♕xh4 ♘xh4 12 ♘b5 ♚d8 13 ♘xa7 ♗xf5 14 ♘b5 ♗h6!?** (after 14 ... ♗e4 15 f3 ♘xf3+ 16 ♘xf3 ♗xf3 17 ♖g1 ♗f6 an old analysis by Boleslavsky gave 18 ♗e2! ♗xe2 19 ♚xe2 ♘e7 20

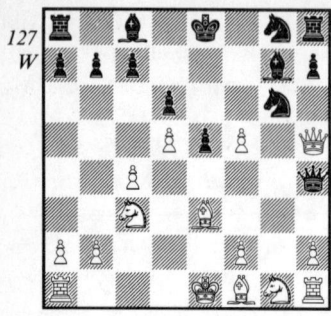

♖af1 ♗h4 21 ♖g4 ♞g6 22 ♖xh4 with good winning chances for White. In Ivkov–Notaros, Novi Sad 1976 White preferred 18 ♔d2 but after 18 ... h5 19 ♗h3 ♗g4 20 ♗xg4 hg 21 ♖g2 ♔d7 22 ♞c3 ♗e7 had only a very slight edge) and the thought-provoking game Sorosi–Arapovic, Bern 1987 continued 15 ♞c3 ♗xe3 16 fe ♞f6 17 ♗h3 ♗e4 18 ♞xe4 ♞xe4 19 ♗g4? ♖g8 20 h3 h5 0–1. At first sight this looks like nothing more than a swindle, but in fact White is quite tangled up and Black has reasonable play for a pawn.

(2) **11 ♕f3!** ♞6e7 12 ♗d3 ♞h6 (12 ... a6?! 13 ♞ge2 ♞h6 14 ♖g1 ♗f6 15 ♞e4 ♞hxf5 16 ♖g4 ♞d4 17 ♕xf6 ♕xf6 18 ♞xf6+ ♔f7 19 ♞xd4 wins for White, Riemersma–van der Werf, Dieren 1986) 13 f6 ♗xf6 14 ♞e4 ♞hf5 15 ♕h5+! ♔d8 16 ♞xf6 ♕xf6 17 ♗g5 ♕g6 18 ♕xg6 with an excellent ending for White, Benjamin–McCarthy, Somerset 1986.

10 ♗h3

Not 10 ef ♞f6 11 ♕d1 ♞xf5 12 ♗h3 ♖g8 13 ♕d3 ♞xe3 14 ♕xe3 ♗h8 15 ♞ge2 ♞g4 16 ♗xg4 ♖xg4 17 ♕h6+ ♔g8 18 b3 ♗g7 and Black's bishops became extremely powerful in Partos–Seirawan, Biel 1985.

10 ... ♞f6
11 ♕f3 f4
12 ♗d2

and White has a good position, e.g. 12 ... a6 13 ♗xc8 ♕xc8 14 ♕d3 ♖g8 15 ♞f3 ♗h6 16 0-0-0 ♕d7 17 h4 ♕e8 18 ♔b1, Liberzon–Czerniak, Netanya 1975, 12 ... c6 13 ♞ge2 ♗xh3 14 ♕xh3 ♕d7 15 ♕xd7 ♞xd7 16 ♞c1 ♖c8 17 ♞b3 cd?! 18 cd, Portisch–Minic, Ljubljana–Portoroz 1973, or 12 ... ♖g8 13 0-0-0 ♗h8 14 ♗xc8 ♕xc8 15 ♕e2 a6 16 ♞f3 ♕h3 17 c5 ♔f7 18 ♔b1 ♞d7 19 cd cd 20 ♖c1, Hübner–Dresen, Bundesliga 1985, with a clear advantage for White in all three cases.

B

1 e4 g6 2 d4 ♗g7 3 c4 d6 4 ♞c3 e5 *(128)*

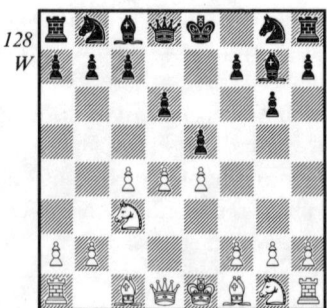

There are now two main variations:

B1: 5 ♘f3
B2: 5 de

Line B1 leads to positions in which White has to work hard to prove any advantage, but in the main-line game Larsen–Mestel he keeps a slight plus, mainly because of his 3 to 2 pawn majority on the kingside. Line B2 is a depressing prospect for Black. It appears harmless enough, but the early exchange of queens does not give Black any real relief. Although he can develop his minor pieces fairly easily, Black runs into problems because his king obstructs the development of his rooks. White keeps a slight advantage in all the main variations at little risk to himself.

Less common alternatives:
(a) **5 ♘ge2** ♘c6 (5 ... ed transposes to B1) 6 d5 (after 6 ♗e3 the reply 6 ... ed transposes to B1, while 6 ... ♘h6 7 f3 f5 8 ♕d2 ♘f7 should be met by 9 d5 ♘e7 10 0-0-0 0-0 11 ♔b1 c5 12 dc bc 13 c5 ±, Sahovic–Todorcevic, Yugoslavia 1981, rather than 9 ef gf 10 de de 11 ♕xd8+ ♘fxd8 12 f4 ♘e6 13 0-0-0 0-0 14 g3 ♘ed4 unclear, Semkov–Piasetski, Saint John Open 1988) ♘ce7 7 ♘g3 (7 ♗e3 is illogical and after 7 ... f5 8 f3 ♘f6 9 h3 0-0 10 ♕d2 c6 11 dc bc 12 0-0-0 fe 13 fe d5! 14 ed cd 15 ♘xd5 ♘exd5 16 cd ♘e4 Black had an excellent position, Cebalo–Todorcevic, Sainte Maxime 1982) c5 8 h4 h5 9 ♗e2 ♗d7 10 a3 ♘c8 11 ♗g5 f6 12 ♗d2 ♗h6! proved adequate for Black in Forintos–Lim, Vukovar 1976.
(b) **5 d5** and Black can transpose to the King's Indian by 5 ... ♘f6, but he may also try 5 ... ♘d7, 5 ... ♘e7 or 5 ... f5. We give a couple of recent examples: **5 ... ♘d7** 6 h4 (6 ♗e2 is sounder, with play similar to C except that White is prematurely committed to d5; 6 ♗e3 is a direct transposition to C, note to White's 5th move, line 1) h5 7 g3 a5 8 ♗h3 ♗h6 9 ♘f3 ♘c5 10 ♔f1 ♗xh3+ 11 ♖xh3 ♕d7 12 ♔g2 ♗xc1 13 ♕xc1 ♘f6 unclear, or 5 ... f5 6 h4 (6 ef should also be good for White after 6 ... ♗xf5 7 ♗d3 or 6 ... gf 7 ♕h5+ ♔f8 8 ♘f3 ♘f6 9 ♕h4) ♘f6 7 ♗g5! (7 ♗d3 f4 8 ♘f3 0-0 9 ♗d2 h6 10 b4 a5 11 a3 may be an edge for White, Martinovic–Todorcevic, Cuprija 1986) h6 8 ♗xf6 ♕xf6 9 h5 g5 10 ef ♗xf5 11 ♗d3 with advantage for White.
(c) **5 ♗e3** (a very odd move since after Black exchanges on d4 White will waste time with his bishop) ed 6 ♗xd4 ♘f6 7 f3 0-0 8 ♕d2 ♘c6 9 ♗e3 ♗e6 10 ♖d1 ♖e8 11 b3 ♘e5 12 ♘ge2 ♗xc4! 13 bc ♘xc4 14 ♕c1 ♘xe3 15 ♕xe3 c6 16 g3 ♕a5 17 ♔f2 d5 and Black has enough compensa-

tion for the piece, Lalic–Ivkov, Yugoslavia Ch. 1983.

B1

  5 ♘f3 ed

Or:

(1) **5 ... ♘c6** *(129)* and now:

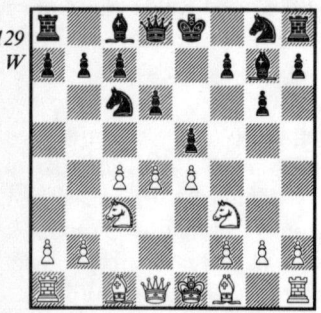

129
W

(1a) **6 ♗g5** f6 (6 ... ♕d7 7 de de 8 ♘b5! would have been good for White anyway after 8 ... f6 9 ♗e3 ♕e7 10 ♕d5 ♘b4 11 ♕d2 ♘a6, but 8 ... ♘d4? 9 ♘fxd4 was an instant disaster since 9 ... ed loses to 10 ♗f4, Miles–Quinteros, Puerto Madrya 1980) 7 ♗e3 ♘h6 8 de de 9 ♕xd8+ ♔xd8 10 0-0-0+ ♗d7 11 h3 ♘f7 12 c5 ±, Janosevic–Vadasz, Belgrade 1977.

(1b) **6 de** ♘xe5 (after 6 ... de! 7 ♕xd8+ Black cannot play 7 ... ♘xd8 because of 8 ♘b5 ♘e6 9 ♘g5, but 7 ... ♔xd8 is unclear because White cannot play f4 as in B2) 7 ♘d4 (7 ♘xe5 de 8 ♕xd8+ ♔xd8 9 ♗g5+ f6 10 0-0-0+ ♗d7 11 ♗e2 was good for White after 11 ... fg 12 ♗g4 ♘f6 13 ♖xd7+ ♘xd7 14 ♖d1 h5 15 ♖xd7+ ♔e8 16 ♗e6 in

Knaak–Vadasz, Budapest 1977, but 11 ... ♕e8 is much better) a6?! (7 ... ♘c6 transposes to the main line, but 7 ... ♘e7 looks the best to me) 8 ♗e2 c5 9 ♘c2 ♗e6, Polugaevsky–T. Petrosian, USSR Ch. 1983, and now 10 f4! ♘xc4 11 f5 gf 12 ef ♗xf5 13 0-0 wins for White according to Petrosian, but I am not sure why! 13 ... ♗e6 14 ♘d5 ♘e5 15 ♘ce3 ♗e7 is dangerous and 14 ♗xc4 ♗xc4 15 ♕g4 ♗xf1 16 ♕xg7 ♕f6 17 ♕xf6 ♘xf6 18 ♔xf1 ♖g8 may be a bit better for White, but I would not describe either of these as winning.

(1c) **6 d5** ♘ce7 7 ♗e2 f5 (7 ... ♘f6 8 0-0 0-0 transposes to a King's Indian) 8 ef (8 0-0 ♘f6 9 c5 is good for White after 9 ... fe 10 cd ef 11 de ♕xe7 12 ♗xf3 or 9 ... dc 10 ♘xe5 fe 11 ♗b5+ ♔f8 12 f3, so Skembris–Todorcevic, Paris 1983, continued 9 ... 0-0 10 cd cd 11 ♘d2 f4 12 ♘c4 g5 13 f3 ♔h8 with an unclear position) gf 9 ♘g5 ♘g6 10 ♗h5 ♘e7 11 f4 ♗f6 12 fe de 13 0-0 0-0 14 g4 ♕d6 15 gf ♕c5+ 16 ♔h1 ♗xf5 17 ♕e2 with advantage to White, Ree–Hübner, Wijk aan Zee 1984.

(2) **5 ... ♗g4** 6 d5 ♘e7 7 ♗e2 0-0 8 0-0 ♗xf3 (8 ... ♘d7 9 ♖b1 ♗xf3 10 ♗xf3 f5 11 b4 ♘f6 12 c5 ♔h8 13 ♗e3 was similarly good for White, Syre–Knaak, DDR 1973) 9 ♗xf3 ♘d7 (9 ... f5 10 c5! dc 11 ♕b3) 10 ♗e2 f5 11 f3 f4 12 ♖b1 g5 13 b4 b6 14 ♕c2 ♖f6 15

♘a4 with c5 to come, and White has a clear advantage since Black's attack is much less dangerous without his white-squared bishop, Timman–Romanishin, Indonesia 1983.

6	♘xd4	♘c6
7	♗e3	♘ge7
8	♗e2	

Or 8 h4 f5 9 h5 fe 10 ♘xe4 ♘f5 11 ♗g5 ♕d7 12 ♘f6+ ♗xf6 13 ♗xf6 0-0 14 ♘xf5 ♕xf5 15 ♗d4 ♕e4+ 16 ♗e3 ♘b4 17 ♖c1 ♗f5 with a very unclear position, Vaganian–Mestel, Hastings 1974/5.

8 ... 0-0 *(130)*

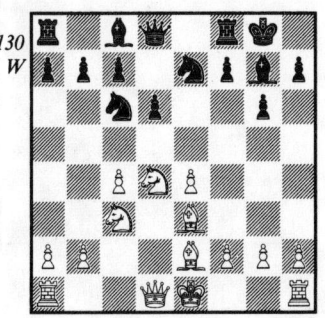

9 0-0

9 g4!? (after 9 ♕d2 f5 the only dangerous move is 10 0-0, transposing to the next note, since 10 ef may be met by either 10 ... ♗xd4 11 ♗xd4 ♘xf5 12 ♗e3 ♘xe3 13 ♕xe3 ½–½, Dlugy–Seirawan, USA Ch. 1987, or 10 ... ♘xf5 11 ♘xf5 ♗xf5 12 ♖d1 ♔h8 13 0-0 ♕e7 14 b3 ♖ae8 15 ♘d5 ♕f7 16 h3 b6 with equality, Piasetski–Larsen,

New York 1984) ♗e6 (9 ... ♘xd4 10 ♗xd4 ♗xd4 11 ♕xd4 c5 12 ♕e3 ♘c6 13 0-0-0 ♘d4 14 h4 f5 15 gf gf 16 ♘d5 was good for White in Lerner–Azmaiparashvili, USSR Ch. 1986) 10 ♖g1 (10 h4 is given as ± by Byrne and Mednis, but 10 ... ♘xd4 11 ♗xd4 ♗xd4 12 ♕xd4 ♘c6 followed by ... ♘e5 looks fine for Black) ♘xd4 11 ♗xd4 ♘c6 12 ♗xg7 ♔xg7 13 ♕d2 ♕h4 with at least equality for Black, D. Gurevich–Seirawan, USA Ch. 1987.

9 ... f5
10 ♘xc6

Or 10 ♕d2 (10 ef ♗xd4 11 ♗xd4 ♘xf5 is slightly better for Black) fe (after 10 ... ♘xd4 11 ♗xd4 f4 12 ♗xg7 ♔xg7 13 ♕d4+ ♔h6 14 ♘d5 ♘c6 15 ♕c3 followed by c5 or 10 ... ♗xd4 11 ♗xd4 f4 12 c5 ♗e6 13 cd ♘xd4 14 ♕xd4 ♘c6 15 ♕d2 cd 16 ♖fd1 White has some initiative in both cases) 11 ♘xe4 ♘f5 12 ♘xf5 ♗xf5 13 ♘c3 (13 ♘g3 ♗e6 14 ♗h6 ♕h4 15 ♗xg7 ♔xg7 16 f4 ♖ae8 was equal in Eising–Larsen, Dortmund 1961) ♕f6 14 ♖fd1 ♔h8 with equality.

10 ... bc

11 ♕d2 (11 ♗d4 ♗xd4 12 ♕xd4 c5 13 ♕d2 fe 14 ♘xe4 ♗b7 15 ♘g5 ♕d7 16 ♖fe1 ♖ae8 was level in Farago–Bischoff, Budapest 1987) fe 12 ♘xe4 ♘f5 (12 ... ♖b8 is Larsen's suggestion) 13 ♗g5 ♕e8 14 ♗d3 ♕f7 (14 ... h6 ±) 15 ♖ae1 ♗e6 16 b3 a5? 17

♘c3 with a distinct advantage for White, Larsen–Mestel, Lone Pine 1978.

B2

5	de	de
6	♕xd8+	♚xd8
7	f4	

The only move to cause Black problems, e.g. 7 ♗e3 (7 ♘f3 f6 8 ♗e3 ♗e6 9 ♘d2 ♘d7 and 7 ♗g5+ f6 8 ♖d1+ ♘d7 9 ♗e3 c6 10 g3 ♚c7 11 ♗h3 ♗h6 are equal) ♘h6 8 ♖d1+ ♘d7 9 ♘f3 f6 and in Pahtz–Smyslov, Berlin 1979, White got a bit carried away and played 10 ♘xe5 fe 11 ♗g5+ ♚e8 12 ♘d5 ♖b8 13 ♘xc7+ ♚f8, but didn't really have enough for the piece.

       7 ...   ♘c6

Or:

(a) **7 ... ♘d7** 8 ♘f3 c6 (8 ... f6?! 9 fe ♘xe5 10 ♘xe5 fe 11 ♗g5+ ♗f6 12 0-0-0+ ♗d7 13 ♗e3 c6 14 g4! h6 15 h4 left Black in a very uncomfortable position in Romanishin–Dvoretsky, USSR Ch. 1974) 9 ♗e2 (9 fe ♘xe5 10 ♗f4 f6 11 0-0-0+ ♚e8 12 ♗e2 ♗h6 13 ♗xh6 ♘xh6 14 ♘xe5 fe led to an early draw in H. Olafsson–Ljubojevic, Reykjavik 1987) f6 (after 9 ... ♘e7 10 0-0 ♚e8 11 ♖b1 h6 12 ♚h1! ef 13 ♗xf4 g5 14 ♗d6 ♘g6 15 e5 g4 16 ♘d4 ♗xe5 17 ♘f5! White had a very strong initiative in Gheorghiu–Keene, Teesside 1975) 10 0-0 (White also kept an edge after 10 ♗e3 ♚e8 11 g3 ♘h6 12 h3 ♘f7 13 f5 ♗h6 14 ♗xh6 ♘xh6 15 g3 ♚e7 16 0-0-0, Farago–Radulov, Belgrade 1982) ♚e8 11 g3 ♘h6 12 ♚g2 ♘f7 13 ♗e3 ♗f8 14 ♖ad1 b6 15 a3! ♗e7 16 ♘e1 ♗c5?! 17 ♘c2 ♗xe3 18 ♘xe3 h5 19 b4 with lasting pressure for White, Hübner–Benko, Hungary 1976.

(b) **7 ... ♗e6** 8 ♘f3 (8 fe ♘d7 9 ♗g5+ ♚c8 10 ♘f3 h6 11 ♗h4 g5 12 ♗g3 ♘e7 13 0-0-0 ♘c6 with equality, Baragar–Hergott, Canada 1986) ♘d7 *(131)* and now:

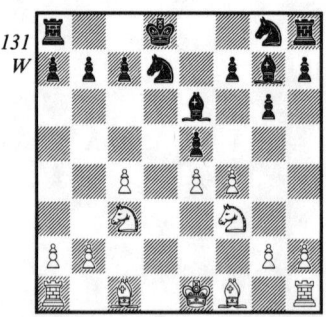

(b1) **9 g3** h6 10 ♗e3 c6 11 ♗d3 ♗h3 12 ♗f1 ♗g4 13 ♗e2 ef 14 gf ♗xc3+ 15 bc ♘gf6 is fine for Black, Klarner–Petrosian, Sochi 1977.

(b2) **9 ♗e3** (inaccurate since in many lines the bishop can move to f4 of g5 directly) ♘e7 10 ♗e2 ♘c6 11 g3 h6 12 ♖d1 ♚c8 13 0-0 ef 14 gf ♗xc3 15 bc ♖e8 with equality, Polgar–Seret, Cannes 1987.

(b3) **9 fe** ♘e7 10 ♗f4 (10 ♘d5 h6

11 ♗e3 ♘c6 12 0-0-0 ♘cxe5 13 ♗d4 ♔c8 14 ♗e2 c6 and Black frees himself, Loffler–Dresen, Bundesliga 1986) ♘c6 11 0-0-0 ♔c8 12 ♗g5 ♘cxe5 13 ♘xe6 ½–½ is Gheorghiu–Quinteros, Manila 1974.

(b4) 9 ♗e2 h6 (Black made an interesting attempt to manage without ... h6 in Cvetkovic–Todorcevic, Belgrade 1982, but after 9 ... ♘e7 10 0-0 ef 11 ♗xf4 ♘c6 12 ♖ad1 ♔c8 13 ♘b5 ♘de5 14 ♖d5! f6 15 ♗xe5 fe 16 ♗g5 ♗xd5 17 ed a6 White could have played 18 ♘xc7! with a slight advantage) 10 0-0 (after 10 fe ♘e7 11 ♘d5 ♘xe5 12 ♗f4 ♘7c6 13 0-0-0 ♔c8 14 c5 a6 15 ♖d2 ♖e8 16 ♖hd1 ♔b8 17 h3, Cebalo–Rukavina, Zagreb 1985 and 10 h3 ♘e7 11 0-0 ef 12 ♗xf4 g5 13 ♗h2 ♘g6 14 ♖ad1 c6 15 ♘d5!, Kouatly–Todorcevic, Budel 1987 White has some advantage, so there is a choice of good continuations) ♘e7 11 ♘d5 (11 ♗e3 ef 12 ♗xf4 g5 13 ♗g3 g4 14 ♘h4 ♗d4+ 15 ♔h1 ♗e5 led to a quick draw in Adorjan–Todorcevic, Szirak 1987) ♖e8 12 ♘xe5 ♘xe5 13 fe ♗xe5 14 ♗xh6 ♗xb2 15 ♖ad1 ♔c8 16 ♗f4 with advantage for White, Tarjan–Mestel, Hastings 1977/8.

8 ♘f3 *(132)*

Or 8 fe ♗e6 (8 ... ♘xe5 9 ♘f3 ♘xf3+ 10 gf ♗xc3+!? 11 bc ♗e6 12 ♗g5+ f6 13 0-0-0+ ♔e8 14 ♗h4 ♔f7 15 ♗e2 was also very slightly better for White, Cvetkovic–Todorcevic, Yugoslavia 1981) 9 ♗g5+ ♔c8 10 ♘f3 h6 11 ♗f4 g5 12 ♗e3 ♘ge7 13 0-0-0 and White has an edge, Uhlmann–Larsen, Aarhus 1971. Although Black has not completely equalized White's advantage after 8 fe is certainly very small.

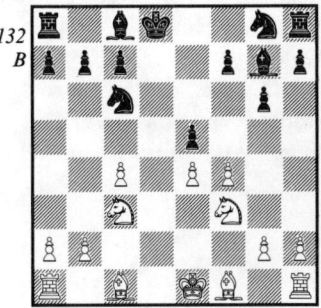

132
B

8 ... ♘d4

8 ... f6 (8 ... ♗g4 9 fe ♗xf3 10 gf ♗xe5 11 ♗g5+ ♔e8 12 0-0-0 ♘d4?! 13 f4 ♘e6 14 fe ♘xg5, Tarjan–Matulovic, Novi Sad 1975, and now 15 ♘d5! with the idea 15 ... ♘e6 16 ♗h3 ♖c8 17 ♖hf1! leaves Black badly tangled up; 12 ... h6 13 ♗e3 ± was better) 9 ♗e3 ♗e6 10 ♖d1+ ♔c8 (10 ... ♔e8 11 fe fe 12 ♘d5 ♖c8 13 c5 followed by ♗c4 is good for White) 11 ♗e2 ♘h6 12 fe ♘xe5 13 ♘xe5 fe 14 0-0 with advantage to White, Vaganian–Mestel, Skara 1980.

After 8 ... ♘d4 White can retain a slight advantage, e.g. 9 ♗d3 (9 ♔f2 ♘xf3 10 gf f6 11 ♗e3 c6 12 ♖d1+ ♔e8 13 h4 ♘h6 14 fe fe 15 h5 ♘f7 16 ♗h3 was also good for White, Suba–Ivkov, Las Palmas 1979) ♘xf3+ 10 gf ♘e7 11 fe ♗xe5 12 ♗e3 (12 ♗h6 c6 13 0-0-0 ♔c7 14 h4 ♘g8 15 ♗e3 ♘f6 =, Pribyl–Taimanov, Brno 1975) ♗d7 13 0-0-0 ♔c8 14 f4 ♗g7 15 ♖he1 ♖e8 16 ♗f1 ♗e6 17 ♔c2 and Black is still slightly worse, Tukmakov–Mestel, Hastings 1983.

On the basis of these practical examples White has good chances of keeping the initiative after 7 f4.

C

3	...	d6
4	♘c3	♘d7
5	♘f3	

This is the most common move, but White can choose between a wide range of alternatives:

(1) 5 ♗e3 e5 (5 ... c5 6 ♘ge2 a6 is most likely to transpose into a type of ... ♘bd7 system against the Sämisch) 6 d5 *(133)* (6 ♘ge2 transposes to line 3 below, while 6 de de 7 ♘f3 ♘gf6 8 ♘d2 h5 9 ♗e2 ♘h6 10 ♗xh6 ♖xh6 11 b4 a5 12 a3 ♘f8 was level in Seirawan–Nogueiras, Zagreb 1987) and now:

(1a) 6 ... a5 7 h4 (7 ♗d3 ♗h6 8 ♕d2 ♗xe3 9 ♕xe3 ♘c5 10 0-0-0 ♗d7 11 ♗c2 ♕e7 12 f4 ♘f6 13 g3 0-0 14 ♘f3 ± since White's space advantage is more important than

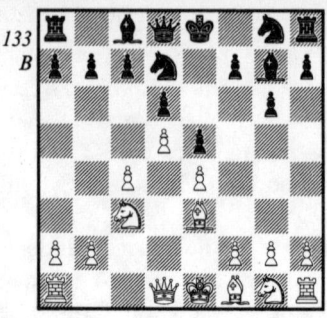

Black's theoretically better bishop) ♘gf6 8 g4 ♘c5 9 f3 h5 10 g5 ♘fd7 11 ♕d2 0-0 12 0-0-0 ♘b6 13 ♘h3 ♗d7 with a balanced position, Ernst–Speelman, Subotica 1987. When the kingside becomes blocked like this White can only make progress by f4, but this activates the g7 bishop and puts White's king in danger.

(1b) 6 ... ♘h6 7 g4 (Ernst's idea turns out better when the knight is on h6 because Black cannot block the kingside; 7 f3 f5 8 ♕d2 ♘f7 9 0-0-0 c5?! 10 ef gf 11 ♗d3 ♘f6 12 ♕c2 ♕d7 13 ♘ge2 was good for White in Pipkov–Ghinda, Sofia 1977, but 9 ... ♘f6 was better) f6 8 h4 ♘f7 9 ♕d2 h5 10 gh ♖xh5 11 ♘ge2 ♘f8 12 ♘g3 ♖h7 13 h5 and White has a clear advantage, Ernst–Akesson, Sweden Ch. 1986.

(1c) 6 ... ♘e7 7 ♗d3 0-0 8 ♘ge2 f5 9 f3 ♘f6 10 ♕d2 c5 11 a3 f4 12 ♗f2 a6 13 b4 b6 14 ♖b1 g5 with equality, Mititelu–Ghizdavu, Romania 1969.

(2) **5 f4** (an attempt to exploit Black's slow 4 ... ♘d7) e5 (5 ... c5 6 d5 ♗xc3+ 7 bc ♘gf6 8 ♗d3 ♕a5 9 ♕b3 b5 10 cb a6 11 b6! ♘xb6 12 ♕a3 ♕xa3 13 ♗xa3 with a slightly better ending for White, Hübner–Spassky, Bundesliga 1981) 6 fe de 7 d5 ♘h6 (7 ... ♘gf6 gives Black an inferior variant of the Four Pawns' Attack against the King's Indian) 8 ♘f3 0-0 9 ♗e2 (9 h3 f5 10 ♗g5 ♘f6 11 ♗d3 ♘f7 12 ♗h4 h6 13 ♕c2 g5 14 ♗f2 ♘d6 15 ♘d2 was ± in Suetin–Gipslis, USSR 1980) f6 (since Black plays ... f5 later this involves a loss of time, but at least it prevents the reply ♗g5; after 9 ... f5 10 ♗g5 ♘f6 11 0-0 ♘f7 12 ♗h4 ♕e7 13 ef gf 14 ♔h1 ♗d7 15 ♕b3 b6 16 ♖ae1 White was much better in Adorjan–Kristiansen, Esbjerg 1985) 10 0-0 ♘f7 11 ♗e3 f5 12 ef gf 13 ♕c2 ♘f6 14 ♔h1 ♘g4 15 ♗g1 e4 16 ♘d2 ±, van der Sterren–Todorcevic, Budel 1987.

(3) **5 ♘ge2** e5 6 ♗e3 ♘h6 (6 ... ♘gf6 7 f3 is a Sämisch) 7 f3 (normal, but 7 h3 f5 8 g3 0-0 9 ♕d2 ♘f7 10 ef gf 11 0-0-0 c6 12 f4 ♘b6 13 b3 e4 14 g4! fg 15 ♘g3 d5 16 f5 gave White a very dangerous kingside attack in Murey–Ciocaltea, Netanya 1983; not 7 ♘g3?!, though, because of 7 ... ♘g4! 8 ♕xg4 ed 9 ♗g5 ♘f6 10 ♕f3 dc 11 e5? de 12 ♖d1 ♗g4!, Wiedenkeller–Johansson, Sweden 1985) f5 8 ♕d2 ♘f7 (8 ... fe 9 ♘xe4 ♗f5 10 ♗g5 ♗h6 11 h4! ♗xg5 12 hg with a clear plus for White, Spassov–Ermenkov, Bulgaria Ch. 1984) 9 0-0-0 0-0 and now I would expect 10 ef gf 11 f4 to be the critical continuation, with a slight advantage to White.

(4) **5 ♗e2** e5 6 d5 (6 ♘f3 transposes to the main line) h5 (White's idea is to meet 6 ... ♘gf6 by 7 g4, but even this is far from clear after 7 ... ♘c5 8 ♗f3 h5 9 g5 ♘h7 10 h4 f6 and White may suffer because of his poor development) 7 ♘f3 ♗h6 8 ♗xh6 ♘xh6 9 h4 f6 10 b4 ♘f7 11 ♘d2 c5 12 a3 ♔f8 with a roughly equal position, Diez del Corral–Ciocaltea, Malaga 1981.

**5   ...   e5
6   ♗e2 *(134)***

A.   Petrosian–Tseshkovsky, Minsk 1976 continued 6 g3 c6 7 ♗g2 ed 8 ♘xd4 (this looks a bit risky for White but Black couldn't find a flaw in the game) ♘e5 9 ♕e2 ♕b6 10 ♘c2 ♗g4 11 f3 ♗e6 12 ♘e3 ♘f6 with a position similar to the King's Indian. 6 ♗g5!? is interesting, since in Skembris–Todorcevic, Prokuplje 1987, White was slightly better after 6 ... f6 7 ♗e3 ♘h6 8 h3 ♘f7 9 ♗d3 0-0 10 0-0 ♖e8 11 ♖e1 ♘f8 12 ♕c2 ♘e6 13 ♖ad1 ♘fg5 14 ♘xg5 fg 15 de ♗xe5 16 c5.

Now there are three possible lines:

White plays c4

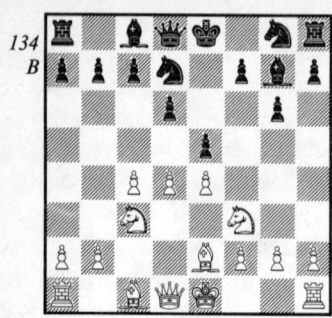

C1: 6 ... ♘h6
C2: 6 ... c6
C3: 6 ... ♘e7

Line C1 is distinctly dubious since the advance h4–h5 exposes Black's backward development. The other two lines are both playable, although I suspect that Black's chances are poorer than if he simply transposes to the King's Indian.

The eccentric 6 ... f6 left Black in a mess after 7 0-0 ♘h6 8 ♖b1 ♘f7 9 b4 c6 10 ♕b3 f5 11 de de 12 c5 ♘f8 13 ♗c4, Sahovic–Ciocaltea, Nis 1981.

C1

    6 ...   ♘h6
    7 h4   f6

7 ... ed (7 ... c6 8 d5 c5 9 h5 a6 10 a3 ♕c7 11 ♕c2 ♖b8 12 a4 ♘f6 13 ♘h2 ♘hg4 14 ♘xg4 ♘xg4 15 a5 is clearly better for White, Hort–Panno, Manila 1976) 8 ♘xd4 ♘c5 9 h5 c6 10 ♗f4! ♕e7? 11 ♗f3 g5?! 12 ♘xc6! bc 13 ♗xd6 with a winning position, A. Rodriguez–Rakic, Vrnjacka Banja 1977.

    8 h5

White can get a slight advantage in perfect safety by 8 ♗xh6 ♗xh6 9 h5 c6 10 d5 ♕e7 11 ♘h4 ♘f8 12 ♗g4 ♗xg4 13 ♕xg4 ♕d7 14 ♕f3 ♗g5 15 g3, Knaak–Peev, Leipzig 1977.

    8 ...   c6

8 ... ♘f7 9 hg hg 10 ♖xh8+ ♗xh8 11 ♗e3 f5?! (opening the position up is rather unwise; 11 ... c6 is better, but 12 ♕d2 followed by 0-0-0 is still good for White) 12 g3 c6 13 ef gf 14 de de 15 ♕c2 ♘f8 16 ♘h4 ♕f6 17 0-0-0 with an excellent position for White, Mohring–Knaak, East Germany 1978.

    9 de   de

10 ♘h4 ♘f7 (10 ... ♘f8 11 ♕xd8+ ♔xd8 12 ♗e3 g5?! 13 0-0-0+ ♔c7 14 ♗c5! and now 14 ... gh? loses to 15 ♗d6+ ♔b6 16 c5+ ♔a5 17 ♗c7+ ♔b4 18 ♔c2 a5 19 a3+ ♔xc5 20 ♘a4 mate, so Nemet–Ivanovic, Yugoslavia Ch. 1977 continued 14 ... ♘f7 15 ♘f5 ♗xf5 16 ef with some advantage to White) 11 ♗e3 ♘f8 12 ♕d2 ♗b4 13 0-0-0 ♖g8 14 hg hg, Ivkov–Ivanovic, Yugoslavia Ch. 1978, and now 15 a3 would have been awkward for Black since 15 ... ♗c5 is bad after 16 ♗xc5 ♘xc5 17 ♕xd8+ ♘xd8 18 ♘xg6.

C2

    6 ...   c6

The idea is to wait for 0-0

before playing ... ♘h6, ruling out the reply h4.
**7 0-0   ♘h6
8 ♖b1**

Although 8 c5 dc 9 de 0-0 10 h3 ♔h8 11 ♗f4 ♘g8 12 ♕d6 ♕e8 13 a4 h6 14 ♖fd1 was good for White in Uhlmann–Ciocaltea, Bucharest 1978, strangely enough it has not been repeated.

8 ...   0-0 *(135)*

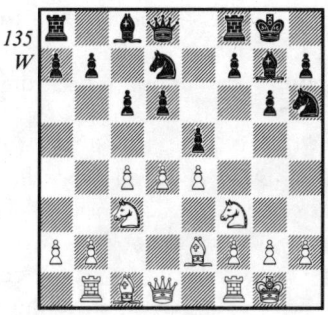

9   b4

Or 9 de de 10 b4 f5 (10 ... ♕e7 11 c5 a5 12 a3 ab 13 ab f6 14 ♘d2 ♘f7 15 ♘c4 ♖d8 16 ♕b3 ♘f8 17 ♘b6 ♗e6 18 ♗c4 ♖ab8 was unclear in Cebalo–Kovacevic, Yugoslavia Ch. 1985; various improvements have been suggested for both sides, e.g. 16 ♕c2!? or 13 ... ♖d8, but in general this type of position should be slightly better for White) 11 ♘g5 ♕e7 12 c5 ♔h8 13 ♗c4 b5 14 ♗b3 a5 15 a3 a4 (15 ... ♘f6 16 f3 f4 17 ♗b2, Plachetka–Peev, Maribor 1977, and now 17 ... ♘fg4! is equal, but 16

ef! gf 17 ♖e1 would have been ±) 16 ♗a2 ♘f6 17 ♕d6 ♕d6 18 cd ♖d8 19 ♖d1 ♗f8?! 20 f4! ♖xd6 21 ♗b2 with advantage to White, Adamski–Hawelko, Poland 1981.

9 ...   ed

9 ... f5 (9 ... a5 10 b5 ed 11 ♘xd4 ♕c7 12 ♗f4 ♘e5 13 ♕d2 ♘hg4 14 h3 ♘f6 15 ♗h6 ±, Polugaevsky–Ljubojevic, Palma de Mallorca 1972) is an interesting alternative. After **10 ef** gf 11 ♘g5 ed 12 ♘e6 ♕f6 13 ♘xf8 ♘xf8 14 ♘a4 ♘g6 15 f4 ♗e6 16 h3 ♕f7 17 ♕c2 ♖c8 Black had a clear advantage in Vadasz–Gaprindashvili, Vrnjacka Banja 1975, while **10 d5** ♘f7 11 ♕c2 ♘f6 12 ♘d2 ♘g5 was comfortable for Black in Ribli–Knaak, Camaguey 1974. Another possibility is **10 ♗g5** ♕e8 11 c5 (11 d5 ♘f7 is unclear) dc 12 dc ♘f7 13 ♗c1, which is slightly better for White according to Sokolov, but I doubt this because Black has gained at least one tempo over the last note. Probably 10 c5 dc 11 dc is best, when 11 ... ♔h8 12 ♘g5 ♕e7 transposes to the last note, but Black may have better options.

10 ♘xd4   ♘e5

And now:
(1) **11 b5** ♕h4 12 bc bc 13 ♖b3 ♗g4 14 f3 ♗e6 15 ♘xe6 (15 f4! is good for White according to Friedstein) fe 16 ♕xd6 ♘hg4! 17 fg ♖xf1+ 18 ♗xf1 ♖f8 was highly unclear in Portisch–Mele-

ghegyi, Hungary 1979; the complications eventually led to a draw.
(2) 11 h3 ♕h4 12 ♖b3 (12 f4 ♕g3! 13 fe ♗xh3 14 ♖f2 ♗xe5 15 ♔f1 ♕h2 16 ♗f3 ♘g4 gave Black sufficient compensation for the piece in Rochel–Bata, corr. 1983) g5 13 ♘f3 ♘xf3+ 14 ♗xf3 g4 (14 ... ♗e6!?) 15 hg ♘xg4 16 ♗xg4 ♗xg4 17 ♘e2 ♖fe8 18 ♖g3 ♗e5 19 f4 ♕xg3 20 ♘xg3 ♗xd1 21 fe ♗c2 22 ed with unclear complications, Donner–Ljubojevic, Nice 1974.

C3

6 ... ♘e7 *(136)*

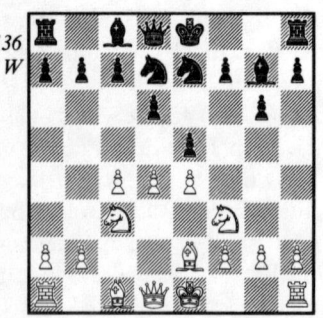

7 d5

White has tried numerous moves in this position, and it is far from clear which is the best:
(1) **7 de** (playing this so soon lets Black off lightly) de 8 b3 0-0 9 0-0 b6 10 ♗a3 ♖e8 11 h4 ♗b7 12 ♘g5 h6 (White weakens the kingside but wastes time) 13 ♘f3 ♘c6 14 h5 g5 15 ♘h2 ♘d4 and Black has a comfortable position, Portisch–Kagan, Rio 1979.

(2) **7** ♗e3 0-0 (7 ... ed 8 ♘xd4 ♘c5 9 0-0 a5 10 ♕d2 0-0 11 ♖ad1 ♗d7 12 ♖fe1 ♕c8 13 ♗f1 ♖e8 14 f3 ±, Bukic–Nikolic, Yugoslavia Ch. 1969) 8 ♕d2 (8 0-0 transposes to line 3) f5 9 cf (9 ♗h6 ♗xh6 10 ♕xh6 ed 11 ♘xd4 ♘e5 12 f4 ♘f7 13 ♕h4, Hort–Suttles, Lugano 1968, and now 13 ... fe 14 ♘xe4 ♘f5 15 ♕xd8 ♘xd8 would have equalized according to Hort) gf 10 ♗g5 e4 11 ♘h4 ♘f6 12 0-0 c5 13 dc dc 14 ♕xd8 ♖xd8 15 f3 with a slight plus for White, Ree–Panno, Amsterdam 1977.

(3) **7 0-0** 0-0 8 ♗e3 (8 ♖e1 followed by ♗f1 is also possible; Black again replies with ... h6 and ... ♔h7 and not 8 ... ♘c6 9 ♗g5 f6 10 ♗e3 ed 11 ♘xd4 ♘de5 12 c5! with clear advantage, Savon–Oszvath, Debrecen 1970) h6 (8 ... f5 9 ef gf 10 de de 11 ♗g5 h6 12 ♗h4 c6 13 ♕d6 ±) 9 ♕d2 (9 ♕c2!? is interesting because if Black continues with ... ♔h7 then ... f5 will be tactically dubious because of the diagonal line-up of queen and king; in Cebalo–Minic, Yugoslavia 1986 Black played 9 ... f5 10 de de 11 ♖ad1 f4, but 12 ♗c5 ♖f7 13 ♗a3 ♗f6 14 c5 ♖g7 15 ♘d5 ♘c6 16 b4 a6 17 ♗b2 was ±) ♔h7 10 ♖ad1 (10 de de 11 ♖ad1 is worth considering, to prevent Black recapturing on e5 with a knight) ♘c6 11 ♕c2 (11 ♘d5 ♘f6?! 12 de ♘xe5 13 ♘xe5 de 14 ♕c2 ♗d7 15

♗g4 was ± in van Scheltinga–Bednarski, Wijk aan Zee II 1973, but 11 ... f5!? appears better) b6 12 de ♘dxe5 13 ♘xe5 ♘xe5 14 h3 ♗e6 15 b3 g5 16 ♘b5 ♘g6 with equality, Gavrikov–Ermenkov, Tunis 1985.

(4) **7 h4** 0-0 (7 ... h6 is also possible, e.g. 8 d5 f5 or 8 h5 g5 9 ♗e3 f5, but this has not been tested in practice) 8 h5 ed 9 ♘xd4 ♘c6 10 ♗e3 ♖e8 11 ♕d2 ♘xd4 12 ♗xd4 ♗xd4 13 ♕xd4 ♕f6 14 ♕e3 ♘b6 15 0-0-0 ♗e6 16 b3 a5 17 a4 with an edge for White, Mikhalchishin–Norwood, Lvov 1986.

7 ...   0-0
8 h4

More dangerous than 8 g4, although even this was slightly better for White after 8 ... f5 9 ♘g5 ♘f6 10 gf gf 11 ♖g1 fe 12 ♘cxe4 ♘xe4 13 ♘xe4 ♔h8 15 ♗g5 ♗f5 16 ♘g3, Uddenfeldt–Haik, Stockholm 1974/5.

After 8 h4 there are two possibilities for Black:
(1) **8 ...** ♘**f6** 9 ♘g5 (9 ♘h2! is a good move, preparing g4, which is also the answer to 9 ... h5; otherwise White can follow up by ♗e3 and h5 with good chances on the kingside) c6 10 ♗e3 h6 11 ♘h3 b5 12 dc b4(12 ... bc may be better) 13 c7! ♕d7! 14 ♘b5, Polugaevsky–Haik, Salonika 1984, and now 14 ... ♘xe4 15 ♗f3 ♗b7 16 ♕d3 f5 is unclear according to Polugaevsky.

(2) **8 ... f5** 9 ♘g5 (9 h5 appears more logical to me) ♘c5 10 ♗e3 h6 (10 ... ♘xe4 11 ♘gxe4 fe 12 g4! with a slight plus for White, Cvetkovic–Minic, Yugoslavia 1986) 11 ♗xc5 hg 12 ♗a3 gh 13 ♖xh4 fe 14 ♘xe4 ♘f5 15 ♖h2 ♘d4 16 ♕d3! is unclear according to Cvetkovic.

D

3 ...   ♘c6

A risky variation which cannot be recommended.

4 ♘f3

After 4 d5 ♘d4 5 ♘e2 (or 5 ♘c3 e5 6 ♘ge2 c5 7 ♘xd4 ed 8 ♘b5 d6 9 b4 b6 10 bc bc 11 ♕a4 ♔f8 12 ♗f4 ♗e5 13 ♗xe5 de Black succeeded in holding the draw in Rodriguez–van Wijgerden, IBM 'B' 1978) e5 (5 ... c5 6 ♘xd4 cd 7 ♗d3 e5 8 0-0 d6 9 f4 ♘h6 10 f5 f6 11 ♘d2 a5 12 ♕f3 was good for White in Kurz–Colditz, Bundesliga 1987) 6 ♘xd4 ed 7 ♗d3 (7 ♗e2 c5 8 0-0 d6 9 f4 ♘e7 10 g4!? f5 11 ef gf 12 g5 0-0 13 a4 ♘g6 14 ♘a3 ♖e8 with equality, Ernst–Hamed, Subotica 1987) d6 8 0-0 ♘f6 9 ♘d2 0–0 10 h3 ♘d7 11 ♘f3 c5 12 ♗d2 White was a little better in Korchnoi–Tal, Moscow 1975.

4 ...   e5
5 ♗g5

5 de ♘xe5 6 ♘xe5 ♗xe5 7 f4, although untried, offers good chances of an advantage. It can be seen that White has few problems

obtaining a small plus, although it is not clear if he can do any better.

5 ...   f6

6 ♗e3 d6 7 ♘c3 (preserving the option of exchanging on e5; 7 d5 ♘ce7 8 c5 ♗h6 9 ♕c1 ♗xe3 10 ♕xe3 f5 11 cd cd 12 ♗b5+ ♔f8 13 ♘c3 fe 14 ♕xe4 ♘f6 led to a quick draw in Gligoric–Keene, Teesside 1972) ♘h6 (7 ... ♗h6 was better, although White still has some advantage) 8 de! fe (8 ... de 9 ♕xd8+ ♔xd8 10 0-0-0+ is also awkward) 9 h3 ♘f7 10 ♕d2 0-0 11 0-0-0 ♗e6 12 ♗e2 a6 13 ♘d5 b5 14 c5 ♘e7 15 g4! and White has a good position, Janosevic–Nunn, Birmingham 1975.

20 | Unusual White systems

In this chapter we look at two plans for White which crop up occasionally. The first involves the move ♗f4 and although it looks odd to allow ... e5 with gain of tempo, by the time Black has arranged this White has played ♕d2 and ♗h6. Theoretically Black should equalize, and so ♗f4 tends to be used as a surprise weapon. The second plan concerns the move h4. White can try this at various points and in some positions it is a reasonable choice. Although it has become more popular recently it is very double-edged and frequently rebounds on White with disastrous effects. For the sake of convenience we take the Modern move-order as the main line, but the Pirc move-order transposes at move 4.

A: White plays ♗f4
B: White plays h4

A

1 e4 d6 2 d4 ♘f6 3 ♘c3 g6
4 ♘f3

Or the immediate 4 ♗f4 ♗g7 5 ♕d2 (5 h3 0-0 6 ♘f3 c5 7 dc ♕a5 8 ♗d3 ♕xc5 9 0-0 ♘c6 10 ♖e1 ♗e6 11 a3 ♖ac8 12 ♕c1 ♖fd8 is equal, Shirazi–D. Gurevich, USA Ch. 1986) c6 (5 ... 0-0 6 0-0-0 c6 7 ♗h6 ♕a5 8 ♗xg7 ♔xg7 9 f4 ♗e6 10 a3 b5 11 e5 ♘d5 12 ♘ge2 ♘d7 13 ♘xd5 ♕xd2+ 14 ♖xd2 ♗xd5 15 ♘c3 gave White a slightly better ending, Kuzmin–Adorjan, Budapest 1978) 6 ♘f3 b5 7 ♗d3 0-0 (7 ... ♗g4 8 e5 ♘h5 9 ♗e2 b4 10 ♘d1 ♗xf4 11 ♕xf4 ♗c8 12 ♗c4 d5 13 ♗d3 ±, Musil–Forintos, Maribor 1977) 8 h3 ♘bd7 9 e5 b4 10 ♘e2 de 11 de ♘d5 12 ♗h2 ♘c5 13 ♗c4 a5 14 ♘ed4 ♘b6 15 ♗e2 ♘ca4!? 16 ♘xc6 ♕c7 17 ♘fd4 e6 18 a3 ♗b7 19 ♗b5 ♘xb2 with an unclear position which eventually turned out better for Black, Ornstein–Gulko, New York 1987.

4 ...   ♗g7
5   ♗f4(137) **c5**

A few examples to show what can happen if Black is not careful: (a) 5 ... ♗g4 6 h3 ♗xf3 7 ♕xf3 ♘fd7 8 e5! ♘c6 9 0-0-0 a6 10 ♗c4 0-0 11 ♗d5! ♘db8 12 h4 e6 13 ♗b3 de 14 de ♕e7 15 ♕e3! ♕b4

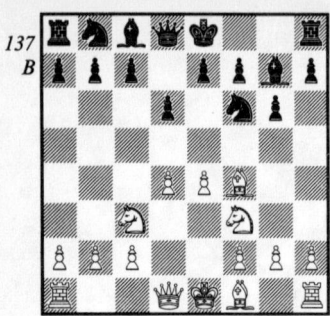
137
B

16 h5 g5 17 ♗xg5 ♘xe5 18 ♖h4! 1–0, Holmov–Petran, Zalaegerszeg 1977.
(b) **5 ...** ♘c6 6 ♕d2 0-0 7 d5 e5 8 de ♗xe6 9 0-0-0 ♖e8 10 ♘g5 ♕d7 11 f3 ♖ad8 12 ♘xe6 ♕xe6?! 13 ♘d5 ♘xd5 14 ed ♕f6 15 c3 ♘e7 16 ♗d3 ♕h4? (16 ... ♗f8 was a better way to give some air to the queen) 17 ♗b5! (covering a4 with gain of tempo) c6 18 dc bc 19 ♗g5 ♕h5 20 h4! cb 21 g4 ♕xg5 22 hg d5 23 ♕h2 b4 24 cb ♘c6 25 f4 ♖e4 26 ♕xh7+ 1–0, Holmov–Belyavsky, USSR 1977.
(c) **5 ...** a6 6 ♕d2 b5 7 ♗h6 0-0 8 ♗xg7 ♔xg7 9 ♗d3 b4 10 ♘e2 c5 11 dc dc 12 e5 ♘g8 13 h4 h5 14 ♘f4 ♗g4 15 e6! f5 16 ♘e5 ♖f6 17 f3 ♕d4 18 ♘fxg6 1–0, Vorotnikov–Rachmanevlov, Leningrad 1985.

      6   dc   **♕a5**
      7   ♘d2

7 ♗b5+ ♗d7 8 ♕d3 (8 ♕e2 is a better try since the sacrifice 8 ... ♘xe4 9 ♗xd7+ ♘xd7 10 ♕xe4 ♗xc3+ 11 bc ♕xc3+ 12 ♔e2 ♘xc5 looks unsound after 13 ♕e3 ♕xc2+ 14 ♘d2, while Black will lack ... c4 if play continues as in the game) dc 9 0-0 0-0 10 ♗xd7 ♘bxd7! 11 e5?! c4! 12 ♕xc4 ♘h5 13 ♖fe1 (13 e6? ♘b6) ♖ac8 14 ♕d4 ♖fd8 with good compensation for the pawn, Horvath–Petran, Hungary Ch. 1976.

      7   ...   **♕xc5**

8 ♘b3 ♕b6 9 ♕d2 ♘c6 10 ♗e3 ♕c7 11 0-0-0 0-0 12 h4 ♗e6 13 ♗h6 a5 with a double-edged position, Ivanovic–Marangunic, Yugoslavia Ch. 1977.

B

1 e4 g6 2 d4

Or 2 h4 h5 (2 ... d5 3 ed ♕xd5 4 ♘c3 ♕a5 5 h5 ♗g7 6 ♗c4 ♘c6, Davies–Zysk, Budapest 1987, and now 7 ♘ge2 is unclear) 3 ♗c4 (3 d4 ♗g7 transposes to the next note) ♘f6 4 ♘c3 c6 5 e5 d5 6 ef dc 7 ♕e2 ♗e6 8 ♘h3 ef 9 ♘f4, Rigo–Kristiansen, Hungary 1985, and now 9 ... ♕d7 10 d3 cd 11 ♘xd3 ♗e7 12 ♗e3 0-0 13 0-0-0 is unclear according to Cserna, but in my view the onus is very much on White to justify his pawn sacrifice.

      2   ...   **♗g7**
      3   ♘c3

3 h4 h5 (3 ... c5!? 4 dc ♕a5+ 5 c3 ♕xc5 6 ♗e3 ♕c7 7 h5 d6 8 ♗d4 ♗xd4 9 ♕xd4 ♘f6 10 hg fg 11 ♘d2 ♘c6 12 ♕e3 with an edge for White because of his superior pawn structure, Palosch–Hickl,

Graz 1987) 4 ♘c3 d6 5 ♗c4 ♘c6 6 ♗e3 ♘f6 7 f3 e5 8 d5 ♘d4 9 ♘ge2 ♘xe2 10 ♗xe2 ♕e7 11 ♕d2 a6 12 ♗g5 ♕d7 13 0-0-0 ♗h7 14 g4 ♘xg5 15 hg hg 16 ♖xh8+ ♗xh8 17 ♖h1 ♗g7 18 ♖h7 ♔f8 was unclear in Povah–Nunn, British Ch. 1979.

3 ... d6
4 ♗e2

Or 4 h4 ♘f6 (4 ... ♘c6 5 ♗e3 ♘f6 6 f3 e5 7 d5 and now either 7 ... ♘d4 or 7 ... ♘e7 8 ♕d2 c6 9 dc bc 10 0-0-0 d5 with an unclear position, Mariotti–Forintos, Rome 1977) 5 f3 and now 5 ... h5 6 ♗c4 ♘c6 7 ♗e3 e5 is fine for Black.

4 ... ♘f6

This position more often arises from the Pirc move-order 1 e4 d6 2 d4 ♘f6 3 ♘c3 g6 4 ♗e2 ♗g7.

5 h4 *(138)*

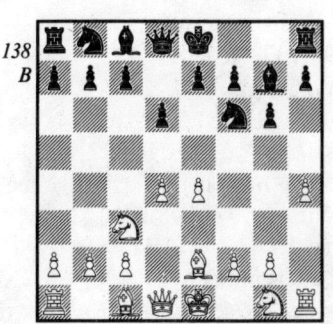

138
B

5 ... c5

Or:
(1) **5 ... h5** and now:
(1a) **6 ♘f3** 0-0 (6 ... ♘bd7 is bad as White can play e5–e6: 6 ... c6 7 ♘g5 ♕c7 8 a4 e5 9 d5 a5 10 f3 0-0 11 0-0 ♘a6 12 ♗xa6 ba 13 ♗e3 was ± in Papp–Lazco, Hungary 1981 and 6 ... ♘c6 7 d5 ♘e5 8 ♘xe5 de 9 ♗g5 a6 10 ♕d2 ♕d6 11 f3 ♗d7 12 a4 gave White an edge in Mortensen–Hoi, Denmark Ch. 1986) 7 ♘g5 ♘c6 8 ♗e3 e5 9 d5 ♘d4 10 ♕d2 (10 ♗xd4 ed 11 ♕xd4 c6 gave Black more than enough for the pawn in Wade–Smyslov, Havana 1965; this pawn offer is typical and almost always gives Black enough compensation) c6 11 dc bc 12 f3 ♖b8 was fine for Black in Mestrovic–Werner, Saarlouis 1986.
(1b) **6 ♗g5** (6 ♘h3 may be met by 6 ... ♗xh3 7 ♖xh3 ♘bd7 or 6 ... ♘c6, when 7 ♘g5 0-0 transposes to 1a above) c6 7 ♕d2 ♕c7 8 0-0-0?! (premature) ♘bd7 9 f4 b5 10 ♗f3 (10 e5 b4! is a common trick) b4 11 ♘ce2 a5 12 f5 gf 13 ef ♘b6 14 ♗g3 ♘c4 15 ♕e2 d5! 16 ♘xh5 ♖xh5! 17 ♗xh5 a4 18 ♘h3 b3 19 cb ab 20 a3 ♖xa3! 21 ba ♕a5 22 ♖d3 ♕xa3+ 23 ♔b1 ♗xf5 24 ♘f2 b2 25 ♗xf7+ (25 ♖e1 ♘e4! threatens ... ♘c3+ and if 26 ♖xa3 ♘c3 mate) ♔xf7 26 ♗xf6 ♕a1+ 27 ♔c2 b1(♕)+ 28 ♖xb1 ♕a2+ 0–1, Sax–Kestler, Nice Ol. 1974.
(2) **5 ... ♘c6** (I regard this as dubious) 6 h5 gh (6 ... e5 7 h6 ♗f8 8 ♘f3 and now 8 ... ♗g4 9 de de 10 ♕xd8+ ♖xd8 11 ♗g5 ♗e7 12 ♗xf6 ♗xf6 13 ♘d5 is good for White, so Malaniuk–

Guseinov, USSR 1984, continued 8 ... ed 9 ♘xd4 ♗e7, when 10 ♗f4 would have given White the advantage) 7 ♗b5 (7 ♗g5!? ♗g4 8 f3 ♗d7 9 ♕d2 e5 10 de de 11 0-0-0 h6 12 ♗h4 ♘e7 13 ♗c4 ♗e6 14 ♕e1 ♕c8 15 ♘d5 is good for White, Kuijf–Piket, Wijk aan Zee II 1986) ♗d7 8 ♘ge2 a6 (8 ... e6 9 ♗g5 h6 10 ♗h4 ♘e7 11 ♗xd7+ ♕xd7 12 ♕d3 ♘g6 13 ♗xf6 ♗xf6 14 ♖xh5 is also good for White, Boersma–Hartoch, Netherlands Ch. 1985) 9 ♗xc6 ♗xc6 10 ♘g3 ♖g8 11 ♗g5 (11 d5 ♗d7 12 ♘xh5 is unclear) b5 12 ♕d3 ♕d7 13 ♘ce2 ♗b7 14 ♗xf6 ♗xf6 15 ♘xh5 may be slightly better for White, but in Smejkal–Ftacnik, Novi Sad 1984, the players agreed to a draw here.

6 dc

6 d5 0-0 7 h5 b5 8 hg (8 ♗xb5 ♘xe4 9 ♘xe4 ♕a5+ 10 ♘c3 ♗xc3+ 11 bc ♕xb5 is at least level for Black) b4! 9 gh+ ♔h8 10 ♘b1 ♘xe4 11 ♗d2 ♘f6 is good for Black since the Black king is well-defended by the pawn on h7.

6 ... ♕a5
7 ♔f1

7 ♗d2 ♕xc5 8 h5 gh (8 ... 0-0 is more solid) 9 ♘h3 ♘c6 10 ♘f4 ♘g4 11 ♘d3 ♕d4 12 ♘d5 ♘ce5, Malaniuk–Azmaiparashvili, USSR Ch. 1986, and now instead of 13 0-0 ♔f8!, which was good for Black, 13 ♖f1 would have been ± according to Malaniuk.

7 ... ♕xc5

8 ♗e3

Better than 8 h5 ♘xh5 9 ♗xh5 ♗xc3 10 bc gh 11 ♕d4 ♕xd4 12 cd, Karner–Golubenko, USSR 1987, and now 12 ... f5 13 e5 de 14 de ♘c6 15 ♖xh5 ♗e6 is ∓.

8 ... ♕a5
9 h5 *(139)*

And now:

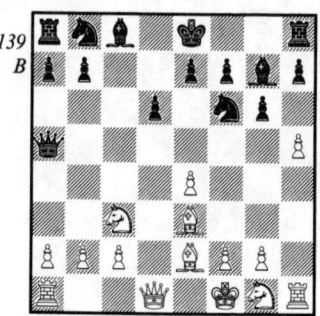

(1) **9 ... gh** 10 ♘h3 (10 ♗xh5 ♘c6 11 ♗e2 ♗e6 followed by a quick ... d5 is good for Black, but Romero recommends 10 f3 ♘c6 11 ♕d2 ♘e5 12 ♖d1 ±) ♘c6 (10 ... ♗g4 11 ♘f4 ♗xe2+ 12 ♕xe2 ♘c6 13 ♘xh5 ♘xh5 14 ♖xh5 ♕c7 15 ♘d5 ♕d7 16 c3 was good for White in Balashov–Pfleger, Munich 1979, while 10 ... ♘g4 is met by 11 ♗d2) 11 ♘f4 ♘g4 12 ♗d2 ♕b6 13 ♕e1 (13 ♖e1 ♗xc3 14 bc ♘f6 15 f3 ♗e6 16 ♗h4 ♘d7 is unclear) ♗d4 14 ♘cd5 ♕xb2 15 ♖b1 ♕xc2 16 f3 ♘ge5 17 ♖c1 ♕xa2 18 ♘c7+ ♔d8 19 ♘xa8 f5! and according to Romero Black is slightly better, Romero–Lopez, Benidorm 1985.

(2) **9 ... ♘xh5** 10 ♗xh5 ♗xc3 11 bc gh and Black is slightly better according to *Informator*, Lhagvasuren–Azmaiparashvili, Moscow II 1986. Rather flimsy evidence, but the attack on c3 is awkward since 12 ♖xh5 ♕xc3 13 ♗d4 ♕c4+ followed by ... e5 is safe for Black, while if White defends c3 with queen or knight it is not so easy to recover the pawn at h5.

21 Black plays an early ... c6

Many systems in the Pirc and Modern involve the move ... c6, but here we deal mainly with those lines in which Black omits ... d6 so that he can play ... c6 and ... d5. The only exception to this is line A below, where Black plays 1 e4 d6 2 d4 ♘f6 3 ♘c3 c6 in order to quickly develop his queen. This is a somewhat risky and artificial plan, but it does have some Czechoslovakian supporters.

All the other lines in this chapter start with the Modern move-order. The main variation begins 1 e4 g6 2 d4 ♗g7 3 ♘c3 c6 whereby Black plans to adopt a Caro–Kann-like formation if White plays 4 ♘f3 or a blockade on the white squares after 4 f4 d5 5 e5. Both these lines are important, and there is a third possibility, namely 4 ♗c4, by which White intends to delay or prevent ... d5.

Sometimes Black adopts the move-order 1 e4 g6 2 d4 c6. This is basically an anti-f4 move-order. If 3 f4 d5 4 e5 Black claims to have gained from not having played ... ♗g7, since in line B3 below he often plays ... ♗f8. On the other hand White's omission of ♘c3 is also quite useful, since it becomes easier to support the centre by c3. In practice White has usually ducked the issue of who benefits from the differences and played 3 ♘c3 d5 4 ♘f3 (or 4 h3), transposing to line B2 after the reply ... ♗g7.

A: 1 e4 d6 2 d4 ♘f6 3 ♘c3 c6
B: 1 e4 g6 2 d4 ♗g7 3 ♘c3 (and 3 c3) c6

A

1 e4 d6 2 d4 ♘f6 3 ♘c3 c6
4 f4

This is the critical move. 4 ♘f3 g6 is likely to transpose to the Classical, while 4 a4 ♕a5 5 ♗d2 e5 6 de de 7 ♘d5 ♕d8 8 ♘xf6+ ♕xf6 9 ♘f3 ♗g4 10 ♗g5 ♕xg5 11 ♘xg5 ♗xd1 12 ♖xd1 led to a quick draw in Casper–Pribyl, Jurmala 1987.

    4 ...   **♕a5** *(140)*

4 ... ♕b6 5 e5 ♘d5 6 ♘xd5 cd 7 ♗d3 ♘c6 8 c3 g6 9 ♕e2 ♗g7 10 ♗e3 0-0 11 ♘f3 f6 12 0-0 ♕c7 13

ef ♖xf6 14 ♖ae1 was good for White, Zukerman–London, New York 1987.

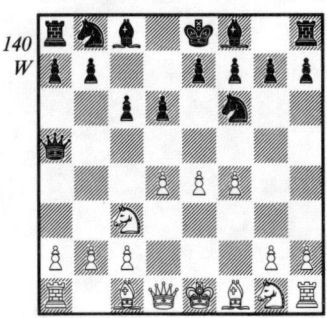

140
W

5 ♗d3

Or:

(1) **5 e5** ♘e4 6 ♕f3 (6 ♗d3 ♘xc3 7 ♕d2 g6 8 bc ♗h6 is unclear) ♘xc3 7 ♗d2 ♗f5 8 ♗d3 (8 ♗xc3 ♕d5 9 ♕xd5 cd 10 0-0-0 ♘c6 11 ♘e2 e6 12 ♘g3 ♗g6 13 ♗e2 0-0-0 14 ♖hf1 ♘e7 was level in Toshkov–Pribyl, Jurmala 1987) e6 9 ♗xc3 (9 bc d5 10 c4 ♗b4 is unclear) ♕d5 10 ♗xf5 ef 11 ♕xd5 cd 12 ♘f3 ♘c6 13 0-0-0 ♗e7 with a more or less equal position, Purgin–Tseitlin, USSR 1987.

(2) **5 ♗d2** e5 (5 ... ♕b6 6 ♘f3 d5 7 e5 ♘e4 8 ♗d3 ♘xd2 9 ♕xd2 e6 10 ♘e2 and now 10 ... ♕xb2 11 0-0 g6 12 ♖ab1 ♕a3 13 c4 ♕e7 14 ♖fc1 is very dangerous for Black, but even 10 ... c5 11 c3 ♘c6 12 0-0 ♗d7 13 ♔h1 g6 14 ♖ad1 was ± in Baras–Ufimtsev, corr. 1985) 6 ♘f3 ♗g4 7 fe de 8 ♘d5 ♕d8 9 ♘xf6+ ♕xf6 10 de ♕g6 11 ♗d3 ♘d7 12 ♗c3 with a slight plus for White, Ftacnik–Mokry, CSSR 1987.

5 ... e5
6 de

The safest continuation. 6 ♘f3 ♗g4 (6 ... ed 7 ♘xd4 ♗e7 8 ♘f3 ♕b6 9 ♕e2 0-0 10 ♗d2 ♕xb2 is unclear according to Tseitlin) 7 de de 8 0-0 (8 fe ♘fd7 9 ♗f4 ♗b4 is fine for Black) ef 9 ♗xf4 ♘bd7 10 h3 ♗xf3 11 ♕xf3 ♘e5 is equal, Suetin–Pribyl, Debrecen 1987.

6 ... de
7 f5

This simple plan causes Black the most difficulty because his c8 bishop cannot be developed to an effective square. The only practical example continued 7 ... ♘bd7 8 ♘f3 ♗c5 (an ambitious attempt to stop White castling; 8 ... ♘c5 9 0-0 was ±) 9 ♗d2 ♘g4 10 ♘g5! ♘f2? (this is going too far, but even the superior 10 ... ♘df6 11 ♘d5 ♕d8 12 ♘xf6+ ♘xf6 13 ♕f3 followed by 0-0-0 is better for White) 11 ♕h5 g6 12 ♕f3 ♘xh1 13 fg ♖f8 14 g7 ♕c7 15 g8(♕) 1-0, Arnason–Pribyl, Jurmala 1987. Weak play by Black, but White's 7 f5 plan looks promising.

B

1 e4 g6 2 d4 ♗g7
3 ♘c3

If White plays 3 c3 Black may still continue 3 ... c6, but this is playing into White's hands because after ... c6 and ... d5 the move c3 is more useful than ♘c3. After 3 c3 c6 we have:

(a) **4 f4** d5 5 e5 h5 6 ♘d2 (an interesting idea, but simply 6 ♗e3 is better for White than B3 below) ♘h6 7 ♘df3 ♗f5 8 ♗e3 ♕b6 9 ♕b3 ♘a6 10 h3 ♘c7 11 ♗e2 ♗e4 12 ♘h4 ♘f5 13 ♘xf5 gf 14 ♘f3 h4 15 0-0 (15 ♘g5 followed by ♘xe4 is also good) ♗xf3 16 ♖xf3 with advantage for White, Plachetka–Ciocaltea, Lucerne 1982.

(b) **4 ♘f3** d5 5 e5 ♘h6 6 ♗f4 (6 ♗e2 0-0 7 0-0 f6 8 c4 ♗e6 9 ♘c3 dc 10 ♕c2 ♘f7 11 ef ef 12 d5 ♗xd5 13 ♖d1 led to obscure complications in A. Sokolov–B. Schneider, Lugano 1985) f6 7 ♗d3 ♘f7 8 ♕e2 fe 9 ♘xe5 ♘xe5 10 ♗xe5 ♗xe5 11 ♕xe5 0-0 12 ♘d2 ♘d7 13 ♕e6+ ♖f7 14 0-0 ♘c5 15 ♕e3 ♘xd3 16 ♕xd3 ♗f5 17 ♕e3 ♕b6 18 b3 ♕a6 19 ♘f3 gave White a clear positional advantage in Hort–B. Schneider, Bundesliga 1986.

3 ... c6 *(141)*

Now White has a choice of three possible moves. The first is the most straightforward in that to achieve ... d5 Black has to make a concession. The second aims for rapid piece development, while the third sets up a space advantage to offset Black's grip on the White squares.

B1: 4 ♗c4
B2: 4 ♘f3
B3: 4 f4

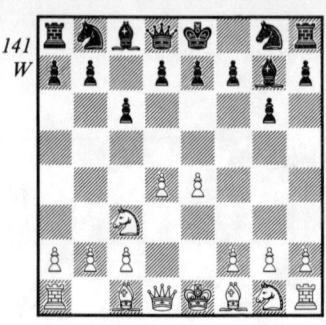
141 W

Or 4 ♗e3 d5 5 ♕d2 de 6 ♘xe4 ♘d7 (6 ... ♘f6 7 ♘xf6+ ef 8 ♘f3 0-0 9 ♗e2 f5 10 0-0 ♘d7 11 c4 ♘f6 12 ♖ad1 ♖e8 13 ♖fe1 ♗e6 14 ♗h6 was good for White in Hübner–Dzindzihashvili, Tilburg 1985) 7 0-0-0 ♘gf6 8 f3 ♘xe4 9 fe ♘f6 10 e5 ♘d5 11 ♗h6 ♗xh6 12 ♕xh6 ♗f5 13 ♘f3 ♕a5 14 ♗c4 with perhaps just an edge for White, Kupreichik–Grigorov, Lvov 1986.

B1

4 ♗c4 d6

Or:

(a) **4 ... d5** 5 ed b5 6 ♗b3 b4 7 ♘ce2 (7 dc? bc 8 c7 ♕xc7 9 ♕f3 ♘f6 10 ♕xa8 0-0 gives Black fantastic compensation for the exchange) cd and now:

(a1) **8 ♗d2!** (first played by Pritchett) a5 (not 8 ... ♘c6 9 ♗a4, while 8 ... ♘a6 9 a3 ba 10 ♖xa3 ♘c7 11 ♕a1 a6 12 ♗a5 ♘f6 13 ♗a4+ ♗d7 14 ♖c3 ♖c8 15 ♘f3 was good for White in Pritchett–Ristoja, Groningen 1969/70) 9 a3 ba 10 ♖xa3 ♘c6 (10 ... ♘f6 11

♕a1) 11 ♘f3 (11 ♕a1 e6! 12 ♗a4 ♘e7) ♘f6 12 ♘e5 ♘xe5 13 de ♘e4 14 ♗e3 e6 15 f3 ♕h4+ 16 g3 ♘xg3 17 ♗f2 ♕b4+ 18 c3 ♕xa3 19 ba ♘xh1, Ghinda–B. Schneider, Dortmund 1986, and now 20 ♗c5! would have been very good for White according to Ghinda.

(a2) **8 ♘f3** (not so good because it gives Black a breathing space) ♘f6 9 0-0 0-0 10 a3 ba 11 ♖xa3 ♗b7 (11 ... ♘c6 12 ♗f4 ♘h5 13 ♘e5 ♗b7 14 ♘xc6 ♗xc6 15 ♗a4 ♗xa4 16 ♖xa4 ♕b6 17 ♗c1 ♖fc8 and Black has strong queenside pressure, Herbrechtsmeier–B. Schneider, Bundesliga 1985) 12 ♘f4 ♘bd7 13 ♖e1 (13 ♗d2 ♕b8 14 ♘d3 ♗c6 15 ♖e1 e6 16 ♘fe5 ♗b5 17 ♕f3 ♖c8 is also ±, Neunhoffer–Dresen, Bundesliga 1986) e6 14 ♘d3 ♕b6 15 ♗d2 ♗c6 16 ♗a5 ♕b7 17 ♘fe5 ♗b5 18 ♕f3 with a very slight advantage for White, Nunn–Dresen, Bundesliga 1986.

(b) 4 ... b5 5 ♗b3 b4 (5 ... a5 6 a4 b4 7 ♘ce2 d5?! 8 e5 ♗f5 9 ♘g3 ♕d7 10 c3 ♘a6 11 ♘xf5 ♕xf5 12 ♗c2 ♕d7 13 ♘f3 with advantage for White, Nunn–Wicker, London 1978) 6 ♘ce2 (6 ♘a4 d6 7 ♘f3 ♘f6 8 e5 ♘d5 9 0-0 0-0 10 h3 ♗e6?! 11 ♖e1 ♘c7 12 ed ed 13 ♗g5 ♕d7 14 ♕d2 ♘ba6 15 c4 bc 16 bc was ± in Ljubojevic–Cardoso, Nice Ol. 1974, but supporting ... d5 by 10 ... ♘a6 followed by ... ♘ac7 would have given equal chances) ♘f6 7 e5 ♘d5 8 ♘f4 (Black is given no time to reinforce this knight) ♘b6 (or 8 ... ♘xf4 9 ♗xf4 0-0 10 h4 d6 11 ♕e2 a5 12 h5 d5 13 ♗a4 c5 14 dc ♗d7 15 ♗xd7 ♘xd7 16 c6 ♘c5 17 ♘f3 and White stands well, M. Adams–Basagic, Hastings II 1987/8) 9 ♘f3 d5 10 0-0 ♗g4 11 h3 ♗xf3 12 ♕xf3 e6 13 ♕g3 ♗f8 14 c3 bc 15 bc ♗e7, Knezevic–Kosanski, Yugoslavia 1976, and now 16 a4 followed by ♗a3 would maintain a positional plus.

(c) **4 ... e6** 5 e5 d5 6 ed ♕xd6 7 ♘f3 ♘e7 8 0-0 ♘f5 9 ♘e4 ♕b4 10 ♗b3 ♘xd4 11 c3 ♘xf3+ 12 ♕xf3 ♕e7 13 ♗g5 with a strong White initiative, Ghinda–Lepine, Val Thorens 1977.

5   ♕f3

This is the only independent move for White since 5 ♘f3 transposes to Chapter 15, line B, note to Black's 4th move, variation d. The point is that 5 ... ♘f6 fails to 6 e5, so Black is forced to make another pawn move. On the other hand the White queen obstructs the development of the king's knight.

5   ...   e6 *(142)*
6   ♗e3

White has two reasonable alternatives:

(a) **6 ♘ge2** ♘d7 (6 ... b5 7 ♗b3 a5 8 a3 ♗a6?! 9 ♗e3 ♘d7 10 h4 h5 11 ♘f4 ♘f8 12 d5 is good for White, Short–Jones, England 1977) 7 ♗f4 ♕e7 8 h4 (the start of

Black plays an early ... c6

142
W

a rash plan) ♘gf6 9 h5 ♘xh5 10 ♖xh5 gh 11 ♕g3 ♗f8 12 0-0-0 e5 13 ♗g5 f6 and White has little to show for his sacrifice, Hodgson–Gavrikov, Tallinn 1987.

(b) **6 ♗f4!?** ♕e7 (6 ... ♗xd4 7 0-0-0 is too dangerous since 7 ... e5 loses to 8 ♗xe5, and 6 ... b5 7 ♗b3 a5 8 a3 ♗xd4 9 0-0-0 ♕b6 10 ♗xd6 ♘d7 11 ♘ge2! ♗g7 12 ♘f4 ♗e5 13 ♘xe6 fe 14 ♗xe6 gave White a winning attack in Ghinda–Ciocaltea, Romania Ch. 1977) 7 e5 d5 8 ♗d3 ♘d7 9 ♕e3 (White intends ♘f3 to support e5) ♕b4 10 0-0-0?! (I prefer 10 ♖b1 ±) b5 11 ♘f3 ♕a5 12 ♘d2 ♕b6 unclear, Ochoa–Soltis, New York 1987.

It may be that 6 ♗f4 is the way to proceed, but developing the bishops on c4 and f4 in best Reinfeld style makes them perfect targets for a Black central pawn push.

After 6 ♗e3 the game Nunn–Keitlinghaus, Krefeld 1986 continued 6 ... ♘d7 (6 ... b5 7 ♗b3 ♘d7 8 ♘h3 ♘b6 9 0-0 b4 10 ♘a4

♕c7?! 11 a3 ba 12 ♖xa3 ♘xa4 13 ♖xa4 ♘e7 14 ♗g5! 0-0 15 ♗f6 ♗b7? 16 ♘g5 h6 17 ♗xg7 ♔xg7 18 ♕xf7+! 1–0 was Nunn–Swanson, Groningen 1974/5) 7 ♘ge2 ♘e7 8 ♗b3 b5 9 0-0 a5 10 a3 ♗a6 11 ♖fe1 0-0 12 ♖ad1 d5 13 ♗g5 with an edge for White.

B2

4 ♘f3 d5
5 h3

Although this is by far the most common move, White may attempt to do without it, e.g. 5 ♗f4 (or 5 ♗e2 ♗g4 6 ♗e3 ♘h6 7 h3 ♗xf3 8 ♗xf3 de 9 ♗xe4 ♘f5 10 ♗xf5 gf 11 ♕f3 ♗xd4 12 0-0-0 ♗xe3+ 13 ♕xe3 ♕c7 14 ♕g5 with advantage for White, Kurajica–Bulat, Yugoslavia Ch. 1984) ♗g4 (5 ... de is better) 6 ed cd 7 ♘b5 ♘a6 8 h3 ♗xf3 9 ♕xf3 ♘f6 10 c3 0-0 11 ♗d3 ♕d7 (11 ... ♘e8 12 ♕g3 maintains the bind by covering c7 and d6) 12 0-0 ♖fc8 13 ♖fe1 ♘b8 (by covering c7 with his rook Black has at least managed to expel the irritating knight from b5) 14 a4! a6 15 ♘a3 and White is still better, Pavlov–Tacu, Romania 1977.

5 ... ♘h6

This combative move intends ... f6, ... ♘f7 and ... e5. The resulting play is often quite sharp, so many players prefer one of the two solid alternatives:

(1) **5 ... de** 6 ♘xe4 ♘d7 (6 ... ♘f6 7 ♘xf6+ ef 8 ♗d3 0-0 9 0-0

♘d7 10 ♗f4 ♖e8 11 ♕d2 ±, Panchenko–Gofstein, USSR 1976) 7 ♗c4 (7 ♗d3 ♘gf6 8 ♘xf6+ ♘xf6 9 0-0 0-0 10 ♖e1 ♖e8 11 c3 b6 12 ♘e5 ♗b7 13 ♕f3 ♕c7 14 ♗c4 e6 15 ♗f4 c5 16 ♕e2 ♘d5 17 ♗g3 cd 18 cd ♕e7 is equal, Ueter–Borngasser, Bundesliga 1986) ♘gf6 8 ♘xf6+ (**8 ♕e2** ♘xe4 9 ♕xe4 ♘b6 10 ♗b3 a5 11 a4 ♗f5 12 ♕h4, Keres–Donner, Amsterdam 1971 and **8 ♘g3** 0-0 9 0-0 c5 10 c3 ♘b6 11 ♗b3 c4?! 12 ♗c2 ♗e6 13 ♘e5 ♘d5 14 ♗f4, Borngasser–Hamacher, Dortmund 1987, were both ±) ♘xf6 9 0-0 0-0 10 ♖e1 ♗f5 11 ♗b3 ♕d6 12 ♕e2 ♖ae8 13 c3 ±, Balashov–Petrosian, USSR Ch. 1976. This type of position is very solid for Black, but White can preserve a slight advantage.

(2) **5 ... ♘f6** *(143)* and now:

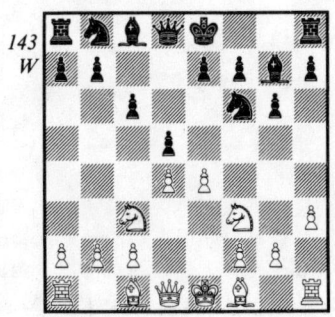

(2a) **6 e5** ♘e4 7 ♗d3 (7 ♘xe4 de 8 ♘g5 c5! 9 dc ♕a5+ 10 ♗d2 ♕xc5 11 ♗c3 ♘c6! is equal) ♘xc3 8 bc c5 9 0-0 (9 dc 0-0 10 ♗e3 ♘d7 11 ♗d4 ♕c7 12 0-0 ♘xe5 13 ♘xe5 ♗xe5 14 ♕e2 ♗h2+ 15 ♔h1 e5 16 ♗e3 e4 is also equal, Chandler–Gufeld, Hastings 1986) c4 10 ♗e2 ♕a5 11 ♗d2 f6 12 ef ef 13 ♘h4 0-0 14 f4 f5 15 g4!? fg 16 hg ♕d8 17 ♘g2 ♘c6 18 ♖b1 ♖b8 19 ♗f3 b5 with an unclear position, Popovic–Ehlvest, Vrsac 1987.

(2b) **6 ♗d3** de 7 ♘xe4 ♘xe4 8 ♗xe4 0-0 (8 ... ♗f5 9 ♗xf5 ♕a5+ 10 c3 ♕xf5 11 0-0 and now both 11 ... 0-0 12 ♖e1 ♖e8 13 ♗g5 e6 14 ♖e5! ♗xe5 15 de ♘a6 16 ♕d4 h6 17 ♗xh6, Ivanov–Zaichik, USSR 1975, and 11 ... ♘d7 12 ♖e1 e6 13 ♕b3 b6 14 ♕a3 a5 15 c4 ♗f8 16 ♕b3 ♗b4 17 ♖e2, Lobron–Grünfeld, Lucerne 1979, were clearly better for White) 9 0-0 ♘d7 and now:

(2b1) **10 ♖e1** c5 11 c3 cd 12 ♘xd4 (after 12 cd ♘f6 13 ♗c2, Mariotti–Tseshkovsky, Manila 1976 continued 13 ... ♗e6? 14 ♖xe6! fe 15 ♘g5 with advantage to White, but the correct 13 ... b6 14 ♗f4 ♗b7 equalizes) ♘c5 13 ♗c2 e5 14 ♘b3 ♕c7 (14 ... ♘xb3 15 ♕xd8 ♖xd8 16 ♗xb3 gives White a faint edge based on his queen-side majority, Beckemeyer–Dresen, Bundesliga 1986, and White did in fact win the game) 15 ♘xc5 ♕xc5 16 ♗b3, again with an edge for White, Gipslis–Zaichik, Tbilisi 1977.

(2b2) **10 c3** c5 11 ♗g5 (11 ♗c2 cd 12 ♘xd4 e5 13 ♘b5 a6 14

♘d6 ±, Bronstein–Tseshkovsky, USSR Ch. 1973) h6 12 ♗f4 cd 13 cd ♘f6 14 ♗c2 ♗e6 15 ♕d2 ♗d5 16 ♘e5 ♖c8 17 ♖fe1 ♘h5 is level, Kudrin–Dzindzihashvili, USA Ch. 1984.

(2b3) **10** ♗g5 h6 11 ♗e3 c5 (11 ... ♕c7 12 ♕c1 ♔h7 13 ♗f4 ♕a5 14 c3 ♘f6 15 ♗c2 ♗f5 16 ♖e1 ♗xc2 17 ♕xc2 e6 18 ♗e5 ♖fd8 19 a4 with a slight advantage for White, Barlov–Dzindzihashvili, New York 1987) 12 dc ♕c7 13 ♕e2 ♖b8 (a very odd move; 13 ... ♘xc5 14 ♕c4 ♘e6 ± is more sensible) 14 ♕b5 ♘f6 15 ♗d3 e5 16 ♗c4 ♗d7 17 ♕b3 and Black doesn't have enough for the pawn, Chandler–Christiansen, Salonika 1984.

We conclude that Black cannot fully equalize after 5 ... de or 5 ... ♘f6, although the solid nature of Black's position makes it hard for White to increase his advantage.

6 ♗f4

The most direct move, but it has the defect that if White fails to stop ... e5 then the move will come with gain of tempo. White may also play 6 ♗d3 (6 ♗e2 0-0 7 0-0 f6 8 ♖e1 ♘f7 9 ♗f1 comes to the same thing) 0-0 7 0-0 f6 8 ♖e1 ♘f7 9 ♗f1 (the veiled attack on d5 prevents ... e5) ♖e8 (9 ... e6 10 a4 a5 11 b3 ♘a6 12 ♗a3 ♖e8 13 ed ed was also safe for Black, Darga–Dresen, Bundesliga 1985) 10 ♗e3 b6 11 ed cd 12 ♘b5 a6 13 ♘a3 b5 14 c3 ♘c6 15 ♘c2 e5 16 de fe was equal in Mokry–Grigorov, Prague 1985. Such quiet methods are unlikely to pose much of a challenge for Black.

6 ... f6 *(144)*

Other moves leave Black in a passive position, e.g. 6 ... 0-0 7 ♕d2 de 8 ♘xe4 ♘f5 9 c3 ♗e6 10 ♗d3 ♗d5 11 0-0 ♖e8 12 ♖fe1 ♘d7 13 g4! ♗xe4 14 ♖xe4 ♘d6 15 ♖e2 ♘b6 16 ♖ae1, Gheorghiu–Bellon, Orense 1975, or 6 ... de 7 ♘xe4 ♘f5 8 c3 0-0 9 ♗d3 b6 10 0-0 ♗b7 11 ♖e1, Nicevski–Notaros, Yugoslavia 1973, with advantage for White in both cases.

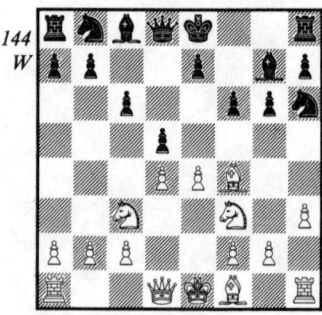

144 W

7 ed

7 ♕d2 is also critical, for example 7 ... ♘f7 8 0-0-0 (not 8 ♗e2? e5! 9 ♗g3 ♗h6 10 ♕d1 de 11 ♘xe4 f5 12 ♘c3 e4 13 ♘e5 ♗e6 with advantage for Black, Hernando–Diez del Corral, Orense 1975) e5 9 ♗e3 de? (9 ... c5! would have led to great complications) 10 ♘xe4 f5 11 ♘eg5

f4? 12 ♗xf4! ef 13 ♖e1+ ♔d7 (13 ... ♔f8 14 ♘xf7 ♔xf7 15 ♗c4+ ♔f8 16 ♕b4+) 14 ♘xf7 ♕f6 15 ♘xh8 ♗xh8 16 ♖e4 1–0, Tarjan–Bellon, Torremolinos 1975.

7	...	cd

8 ♘b5 0-0! (White gained a clear advantage after 8 ... ♘a6? 9 c4! 0-0 10 cd ♕xd5 11 ♘c3 ♕a5 12 ♗c4+ ♘f7 13 0-0 in Chesca–Vaisman, Romania Ch 1975) 9 c4 (better than the immediate 9 ♘c7) a6 10 ♘c7 e5 11 ♘xa8 ef 12 c5 (now the knight can emerge) ♗f5 13 ♘b6 ♘c6 14 ♗e2 ♗e4 15 0-0 ♘f5 16 ♕a4 g5 with a murky position, Hunerkopf–B. Schneider, Bundesliga 1986. White has preserved his extra exchange, but his d4 pawn is weak, the knight on b6 is out of play and Black had a dangerous kingside initiative. The game continued chaotically by 17 ♖ad1 h5 18 ♘d2 ♘fxd4 19 ♘xe4 de 20 ♗c4+ ♔h8 21 ♗d5 f5 22 ♖xd4 ♗xd4 23 ♗xc6 bc 24 ♖d1 e3 25 fe (25 ♖xd4 e2) ♗xe3+ 26 ♔h1 ♕e7 27 ♕xc6 ♖f6 28 ♕c8+ ♖f8 29 ♕c6 ♖f6 30 ♕c8+ ♖f8 ½–½.

5 ... ♘h6 is a dynamic line for Black, but both 7 ♕d2 and 7 ed are critical for Black's survival chances.

B3

4	f4	d5
5	e5	

This is unpopular with White players at the moment, possibly because of the game Pasman–Ciocaltea given in the note to Black's 11th move. If White can keep the position under control his space advantage will be an important factor in the long run, but Black has active pieces and White must be careful. Plans are more important than precise analysis in this position, so we content ourselves with a less detailed analysis than usual in order to concentrate on the general strategy.

5	...	h5
6	♗e3	♘h6
7	♘f3	♗g4
8	♗e2	e6

White plays natural developing moves, while Black is controlling the white squares f5 and g4 and aims for the exchange of his bad white-squared bishop.

9	♕d2	

Note that 9 h3? would be a mistake due to 9 ... ♗xf3 10 ♗xf3 h4 permanently crippling White's pawns. Therefore h3 must be prefaced by g3. In fact 9 g3 would be possible at once but the move played is more flexible since it gives White the chance to move his king instantaneously to either side of the board.

9	...	♘d7
10	g3	♘f5
11	♗f2	*(145)*

Although the black-squared bishop is White's bad bishop it has an important function in holding up ... c5 and ... h4, so it must be preserved. In fact the break ... c5 plays a minor part in this variation since White generally has the two bishops and any opening of the position increases their strength.

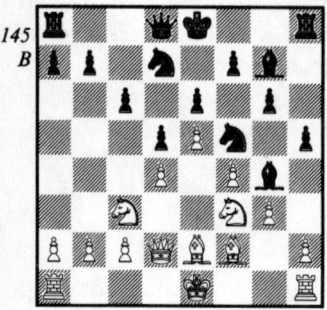
145
B

11 ... b5?!

This pawn advance doesn't achieve much since White rarely castles queenside in any case. The critical line is 11 ... ♗f8 (11 ... h4 loses a pawn to 12 ♘xh4 ♗xe2 13 ♘xf5) 12 h3 ♗xf3 13 ♗xf3 and now:

(a) 13 ... h4?! 14 g4 ♘g3 15 ♖g1 ♕b6 16 0-0-0 ♕a6 and White decided to swap queens before collecting the pawn on g3 in Arnason–Christiansen, Reykjavik 1986, but 17 ♕d3 ♕xd3 18 ♖xd3 c5 19 ♘b5 c4 20 ♖dd1 ♖c8 21 ♗xg3 hg 22 ♖xg3 a6 23 ♘c3 b5 gave Black counterplay. The immediate 17 ♗xg3 must be very good for White.

(b) 13 ... a5 14 ♔f1! a4 15 ♔g2 ♘b6 16 b3 ♗b4 17 ♕d3 ♗d7 18 ♘e2 ab 19 ab ♖xa1 20 ♖xa1 ♕c7 21 c4! with a clear advantage for White, Marjanovic–Ciocaltea, Istanbul 1980. This bears a close resemblance to the main line game Radulov–Velikov.

(c) 13 ... ♗b4! (Black's best chance) 14 a3 (or 14 ♔f1 ♕a5 15 ♔g2 ♘b6 and now 16 g4 fails to 16 ... ♘c4 17 ♕e2 ♘xb2!) ♕a5 15 g4 hg 16 hg ♖xh1+ 17 ♗xh1 ♘e7 18 ♗h4 ♘b6 and Black was at least equal in Pasman–Ciocaltea, Beersheva 1982.

12 h3

White is ill-advised to castle long since the queenside pawn advance coupled with ... ♗f8 and ... ♘b6–c4 can give Black a decisive attack with great speed.

12 ... ♗xf3

13 ♗xf3 ♘b6 14 b3 (White is careful to restrict the activity of Black's pieces; now he is ready to move his king to the safety of g2 and then play the fundamental thrust g4) ♗f8 15 ♘e2! (or else ... ♗b4 would force the weakening a3) a5 16 ♔f1 ♗e7 17 ♔g2 a4 (17 ... ♕c7 has been recommended, but Black still has a poor position) 18 g4 ♘g7 (18 ... ♘h4+ 19 ♗xh4 ♗xh4 20 g5 and 18 ... hg 19 hg ♘h4+ 20 ♗xh4 and g5 are terrible for Black) 19 ♗e3 ♕d7 20 ♖af1 ♕c7 21 ♘c1! (having driven Black into passivity on the kingside White now aims to invade the Black squares

on the other wing by playing his bishop round to b4) ♕a7 22 ♘d3 ♕a5 23 ♕f2 ♔c7 24 ♗d2 ♕a7 25 ♕e1 ♘c8 26 ♕e3 ♘b6 27 ♗b4 ♗xb4 28 ♘xb4 ♘d7? (in his haste to cover the sensitive square c5 Black allows a crushing blow, but with chances to break through on either wing, White must have won in the end) 29 c4! (exposing c6 as a surprising weak spot!) ab 30 cd ed 31 ♕c3 1–0, Radulov–Velikov, Bulgaria 1971.

22 | Odds and Ends

We finish with a few lines which do not fit into any of the earlier chapters.

A: 1 e4 g6 2 d4 ♗g7 3 ♘c3 c5
B: 1 e4 g6 2 d4 ♗g7 3 ♘f3 c5
C: 1 e4 d6 2 d4 ♘f6 3 ♗d3 e5
D: 1 e4 d6 2 d4 ♘f6 3 ♘c3 g6 4 ♗e2 ♗g7 5 g4

Lines A and B more properly belong to the Sicilian Defence but we give a quick round-up here for the sake of completeness. The same point may be made about line C, in which Black doesn't normally play ... g6, but we include it so that Pirc players are aware of it. Line D is a true Pirc, but it isn't very good and is hardly ever played.

A

1	e4	g6
2	d4	♗g7
3	♘c3	c5
4	dc	

After 4 ♘f3 cd 5 ♘xd4 we have a Sicilian Dragon while 4 d5 transposes to a Schmidt Benoni. 4 e3!? is possible, when 4 ... ♕a5 5 ♕d2 cd 6 ♗xd4 ♘f6 7 ♗xf6 ♗xf6 8 ♘d5 ♕xd2+ 9 ♔xd2 ♔d8 10 ♘xf6 ef 11 ♗c4 ♖e8 12 f3 ♖e7 13 ♘e2 gave White a big endgame advantage in Russek–Zapata, Bayamo 1987.

4 ... ♕a5 *(146)*

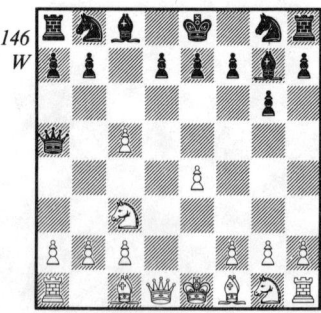

5 ♗d2

Or 5 ♘f3 ♘f6 (accepting the sacrifice by **5 ... ♗xc3+** 6 bc ♕xc3+ 7 ♗d2 ♕xc5 is very dangerous for Black, with 8 ♗d3 followed by ♕e2 or 8 ♖b1 giving good attacking prospects; the immediate **5 ... ♕xc5** is bad owing to 6 ♘d5! followed by ♗e3) 6 ♗d3 (6 ♘d2 ♕xc5 7 ♘c4 ♕c6! 8 ♘d5 ♘xd5 9 ed ♕f6 doesn't lead to any clear advantage for White) ♕xc5 7 ♗e3 ♕a5 (7 ... ♕h5 is worth considering) 8 ♕d2 ♘c6 9 0-0 0-0 10 h3 d6 11 a3 ♗e6 12 ♘g5 d5 (12 ... ♗d7 13 f4) 13 ed ♗xd5 14 b4 ♕d8 15 ♖ad1 with a slight advantage for White, Sveshnikov–Romanishin, USSR Ch. 1977.

5 ... ♕xc5
6 ♘d5 ♘a6 7 ♘f3 e6 (not 7 ... ♗xb2? 8 ♖b1 ♗g7 9 ♗xa6 ba 10 0-0 e6 11 ♗b4 with a massive attack for White, nor 7 ... ♘f6? 8 b4! as in Weidemann–Kunstowicz, Bundesliga 1986) 8 ♗c3 ♗xc3 9 ♘xc3 ♘f6 10 ♕d2 0-0 11 0-0-0 with advantage to White, Barle–Forintos, Maribor 1977.

B

1 e4 g6 2 d4 ♗g7 3 ♘f3 c5
4 dc

The alternatives are just transpositions, e.g. **4 c3** transposes to Chapter 18, note to Black's 3rd move, line 2. **4 ♘c3** is almost certain to lead to a Sicilian after 4 ... cd, since the alternative 4 ... ♕a5 5 ♗e3 ♘f6 6 ♕d2 ♘c6 7 dc ♘g4 8 ♗c4 ♕b4 9 ♗b3 is good for White. **4 c4** may lead to a Maroczy Bind after 4 ... cd, or to another line of the Sicilian after 4 ... ♕a5+.

4 ... ♕a5+
5 c3

5 ♘c3 is the note to White's 5th move in line A above.

5 ... ♕xc5
6 ♗e3 ♕c7 7 ♗d4 e5? (7 ... ♘f6 8 e5 ♘g4 9 ♘a3! is still better for White) 8 ♗e3 ♘f6 9 ♘a3! 0-0 10 ♘b5 ♕c6 11 ♘xe5 ♕xe4 12 ♘xf7! with a clear plus for White, Maric–Tringov, Bar 1977.

For more information on these lines consult a book on the Sicilian or *ECO* volume B, section B27.

C

1 e4 d6 2 d4 ♘f6 3 ♗d3

As promised in the introduction of Chapter 18, we deal with this attempt by White to counter the Pirc move-order with a c3 system. Another somewhat similar attempt is 3 f3 (trying to reach a Sämisch King's Indian after 3 ... g6 4 c4) e5 4 de de 5 ♕xd8+ ♔xd8 6 ♗c4 ♗e8 7 ♗e3 ♘bd7 8 ♘d2 ♗c5 9 ♘f1 c6 10 ♘e2 ♔e7 11 g4 ♗xe3 12 ♘xe3 g6 13 h4 h5 with comfortable equality, van der Wiel–Nunn, Marbella 1982.

3 ... e5

The most sensible answer is to change plans and reach a type of Philidor Defence where Black has very good chances for equality.

4 c3

Or 4 ♘e2 ♗e7 5 0-0 0-0 6 d5 ♘h5 7 c4 ♗g5 8 ♘bc3 g6 (8 ... ♘bd7 is better according to Gufeld) 9 ♖b1 ♘bd7 10 b4 f5 11 ef gf 12 f4 ef 13 ♘xf4 ♘xf4 14 ♗xf4 ♘e5 with at least equality for Black, Chiburdanidze–Gufeld, Havana 1985.

4 ... d5 *(147)*

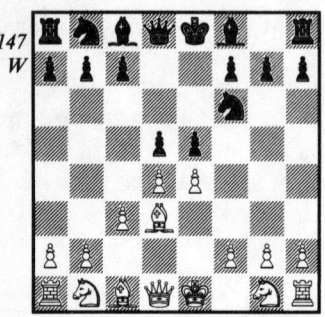

5 de ♘xe4 6 ♘f3 (not 6 ♗xe4 de 7 ♕a4+ ♗d7 8 ♕xe4 ♗c6 9 ♕g4 h5 10 ♕h3 ♕d7 with advantage for Black) ♘c6 7 0-0 (7 ♕e2 ♘c5 8 ♗c2 ♗g4 9 0-0 ♕d7 10 ♖d1 0-0-0 11 b4 ♘e6 was unclear in Psakhis–Chernin, Irkutsk 1983) ♗g4 8 ♗f4 ♗e7 9 h3 ♗h5 10 ♗e2 0-0 11 ♘bd2 and now A. Sokolov–van der Sterren, Salonika 1984, continued 11 ... ♘c5 12 ♘b3 ♘e6 13 ♗g3 ♕d7 14 ♕d2 ♖ad8 15 ♖ad1 with a slight plus for White. However, 11 ... f6 is the critical move and I very much doubt if White can gain any advantage.

D

1 e4 d6 2 d4 ♘f6 3 ♘c3 g6 4 ♗e2 ♗g7 5 g4 *(148)*

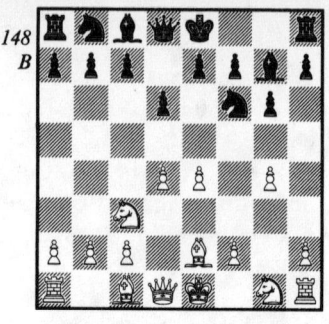

5 ... c6

Or:
(a) 5 ... ♘a6 6 g5 ♘d7 7 h4 c5 8 d5 c4!? 9 h5 (9 ♗xc4 ♕c7 is unclear) ♘ac5 10 h6 ♗xc3+ 11 bc f6 12 ♕d4 ♕a5 13 ♗d2 0-0 14 f4 b5 15 ♘f3 ♕c7 16 0-0 e5! and the breaking open of the centre gives Black the advantage, Katalimov–M. Tseitlin, USSR 1978.

(b) 5 ... h6?! 6 h3 c5 7 d5 0-0?! (perhaps Black imagined that with 6 h3 White had abandoned the idea of an attack down the h-file, but the weakening move ... h6 makes it well worth while despite the loss of a tempo) 8 h4! e6 9 g5 hg 10 hg ♘e8? (10 ... ♘h7 followed by ... ♖e8 and ... ♘f8 was better) 11 ♕d3 ed 12 ♘xd5 ♘c6 13 ♕g3 ♗e6 14 ♕h4 f5 15 ♕h7+ ♔f7 16 ♕xg6+! ♔xg6 17 ♗h5+ ♔h7 18 ♗f7+ ♗h6 19 g6+ ♔g7 20 ♗xh6+ 1–0, Liu Wen Che–Donner, Buenos Aires Ol. 1978.

6 g5 ♘fd7

7 h4 b5 8 h5 ♖g8! 9 hg (this move is a mistake because it leads to Black gaining control of the h-file; 9 a3 is unclear) hg 10 ♘f3 b4 11 ♘b1 a5 12 a4 c5! 13 d5 ♘b6 14 c4?! ♔d7! (the king will be safe on

c7 and by connecting his queen and rook Black ensures that ... ♖h8 will seize the open file) 15 ♘bd2 ♖h8 (we give the rest of this superb game) 16 ♖g1 ♔c7 17 ♖b1 ♖h3 18 b3 ♕h8 19 ♘f1 ♘8d7 20 ♗f4 ♘e5 21 ♘xe5 ♗xe5 22 ♗xe5 ♕xe5 23 f3 ♗d7 24 ♕c2 ♕d4 25 ♖g2 ♖h1 26 ♖f2 ♕h8! 27 f4 ♕h4 28 ♖d1 f6 29 gf ef 30 e5 fe 31 fe ♖f8 32 ed+ ♔b7 33 ♗d3 ♖e8+ 0–1, Kovacevic–Seirawan, Wijk aan Zee 1980. This artistic demonstration of the power of the Black squares and the long diagonal is a fitting way to end a book on the Pirc.

Index of Variations

Pirc move-order

(A) *Austrian Attack*
1 e4 d6 2 d4 ♘f6 3 ♘c3 g6 4 f4 ♗g7
5 ♘f3

    5 e5   58
    5 ♗c4   58
    5 ♗d3   58

Now we have: (I) 5 ... 0-0
                 (II) 5 ... c5

(I)
5 ... 0-0
6 ♗d3
    6 ♗c4   23
    6 ♗e2   23
    6 e5
        6 ... de   27
        6 ... ♘fd7   28
    6 ♗e3
        6 ... ♘bd7   34
        6 ... b6   36
        6 ... others   32–4
6 ... ♘c6
    6 ... ♗g4   12
    6 ... ♘bd7   13
    6 ... c5   13
    6 ... c6   13
    6 ... ♘a6   14–22
        7 e5   14
        7 0-0   17
7 0-0
    7 e5 de
        8 fe   3

        8 de   5
        7 others   2
7 ... ♗g4
    7 ... e5   7
8 e5   9

(II)
5 ... c5
6 ♗b5+   45
    6 e5   45
    6 dc ♕a5
        7 ♗d3
            7 ♘d2   38
            7 ♕d3   38
    7 ... ♕xc5
    8 ♕e2 0-0
    9 ♗e3 ♕a5
        9 ... ♕c7   39
        9 ... ♕b4   40
    10 0-0 ♗g4
        10 ... ♘c6   40
    11 h3
        11 others   41
    11 ... ♗xf3
    12 ♕xf3 ♘c6   41
6 ... ♗d7
7 e5
    7 ♗xd7+   46
7 ... ♘g4
8 e6
    8 ♗xd7+   54
    8 h3   55
    8 ♘g5   57
8 ... ♗xb5
    8 ... f3   48

9 ef+ ♔d7	
10 ♘xb5	
10 ♘g5	49
10 ... ♕a5+	
11 ♘c3 cd	
12 ♘xd4	
12 ... h5	49
12 ... ♗xd4	50

(B) *Classical*
1 e4 d6 2 d4 ♘f6 3 ♘c3 g6 4 ♘f3 ♗g7 5 ♗e2 0-0 6 0-0

6 ... ♗g4	
6 ... ♘c6	
7 d5	
7 others	99
7 ... ♘b8	100
7 ... ♘b4	101
6 ... ♘bd7	103
6 ... a6	104
6 ... c5	104
6 ... b6	106
6 ... ♘a6	106
6 ... c6	
7 ♗f4	93
7 e5	94
7 ♖e1	94–6
7 h3 ♕c7	
7 ... b5	83
7 ... ♘a6	84
7 ... ♘bd7	84
8 a4	
8 others	86
8 ... ♘bd7	
8 ... e5	86
9 a5	87
9 ♗e3	87–8
7 a4 a5	
7 ... ♘bd7	96–8
7 ♕c7	96

8 h3	
8 others	97
8 ... ♘a6	
8 ... others	88–9
9 ♗e3	
9 others	89
9 ... ♘b4	
10 ♕c1	90
10 ♕d2	90
10 ♘d2	91
7 ♗e3	
7 ♗g5	78
7 h3	78
7 ... ♘c6	
7 ... ♘bd7	79
8 ♕d2	
8 d5	80
8 ♘d2	80
8 ♕d3	80
8 ♘e1	81
8 ... e5	
8 ... ♖e8	81
9 d5	
9 de	69
9 ... ♘e7	
10 ♖ad1 ♗d7	
10 ... others	72–4
11 ♘e1	
11 h3	74
11 ♗h6	75
11 ... b5	75
11 ... ♔h8	75
11 ... ♘g4	75–7

(C) *Other White systems*
1 e4 d6 2 d4 ♘f6
3 ♘c3

3 ♗d3	209
3 f3	209

3 ... g6
    3 ... c6   198
4 ♘f3
    4 ♗e2 ♗g7
        5 h4   195
        5 g4   210
    4 ♗e3 ♗g7
        4 ... c6   128
    5 ♕d2   123
        5 f3   126
    4 ♗c4 ♗g7
        5 ♘f3
            5 ♕e2   136
        5 ... 0-0
            5 ... ♘c6   135
            5 ... c6   139
        6 ♕e2   140
            6 0-0   140
    4 ♗g5 ♗g7
        4 ... c6   149–50
        4 ... others   149
    5 ♕d2
        5 others   146–7
    5 ... h6   148
    4 g3 ♗g7
        5 ♗g2 0-0
            5 ... e5   154
        6 ♘ge2
            6 others   154
        6 ... e5
            6 ... ♘bd7   155
        7 h3
            7 0-0   156
        7 ... ♘c6   158
        7 ... c6   160
        7 ... ♘bd7   161
4 ... ♗g7
5 h3
    5 ♗g5   147
    5 ♗f4   193

5 ... 0-0
    5 ... others   113
6 ♗e3 a6
    6 ... c6   118–21
    6 ... others   114–15
7 a4
    7 ♗d3   115
7 ... b6
    7 ... ♘c6   116
    7 ... d5   116–17
8 ♗c4   117–18
8 ♗d3   117
8 e5   117

Modern move-order

1 e4 g6
2 d4
    2 h4   194
2 ... ♗g7
    2 ... c6   198
3 ♘c3
    3 h4   194
    3 c3 d6
        3 ... c5   165
        3 ... c6   199–200
    4 ♘f3
        4 f4   166
        4 ♗g5   168
    4 ... ♘f6
        5 ♘bd2   169
        5 ♗d3   170
    3 c4 d6
        3 ... ♘c6   191
    4 ♘c3 ♘d7
        4 ... ♘c6
            5 d5   175
            5 ♘e3   178
        4 ... e5
            5 ♘f3   182

5 de	184
5 others	181
5 ♘f3	
5 others	186–7
5 ... e5	
6 ♗e2	
6 ... ♘h6	188
6 ... c6	188–90
6 ... ♘e7	190
3 ♘f3 d6	
3 ... c5	209
4 ♗c4 ♘f6	
4 ... others	141
5 ♕e2	
5 ... 0-0	142
5 ... c6	143
5 ... ♘c6	142
3 ... d6	
3 ... c5	208
3 ... c6	
4 ♗e3	200
4 ♗c4	200
4 ♘f3	202
4 f4	205
4 f4	
4 h4	195
4 g3	
4 ... ♘d7	154

4 ... ♘c6	154
4 ♗g5	
4 ... a6	150
4 ... ♘c6	151
4 ... c6	150–2
4 ♗e3	
4 ... a6	131
4 ... c6	132
4 ♗c4	
4 ... ♘c6	135
4 ♘f3	
4 ... a6	107
4 ... c6	110
4 ... ♗g4	110
4 ... ♘c6	
4 ... a6	59
4 ... c6	65
5 ♗e3 ♘f6	
6 ♘f3	
6 h3	60
6 ... 0-0	
7 ♗e2	
7 e5	61
7 ♕d2	61
7 ... e5	
7 ... others	62–3
8 de	64–5
8 fe	64

15⁰⁰